Hilda McKenzie
She left school at fourteen to become an apprentice at a drapery store, left there to learn book binding at a local printers, was an assistant and a cashier for a grocery firm and later became a telephonist at a turf accountants' office. She was fifteen when her first short story was published, and her first novel, *Rosie Edwards*, was praised by *Publishing News* as 'a nostalgic and evocative family saga'. She has a grown-up son and daughter, and still lives in Cardiff with her husband.

Also by Hilda McKenzie

Bronwen
Rosie Edwards

The Sisters

Hilda McKenzie

HEADLINE

First published in 1993
by HEADLINE BOOK PUBLISHING PLC

First published in paperback in 1993
by HEADLINE BOOK PUBLISHING PLC

10 9 8 7 6 5 4 3 2 1

ISBN 0 7472 4116 3

Phototypeset by Intype, London

Printed and bound in Great Britain by
HarperCollins Manufacturing, Glasgow

HEADLINE BOOK PUBLISHING PLC
Headline House
79 Great Titchfield Street
London W1P 7FN

For Liz, my daughter-in-law and friend, with love.

Also in affectionate remembrance of my dear friend Nancy Rees Morgan who died so tragically on 27th March 1944, aged twenty-one.

ACKNOWLEDGEMENTS

My grateful thanks to the following:

Gayle Osborne, head librarian, Trowbridge and St Mellons library and her staff Gina, Sarah and Liz for all their help. Also the ever helpful staff at Cardiff Central library.

The publishers Cwmni Cyhoeddi GWYNNE Cyf. Penygroes, Caernarfon for allowing me to use part of the Welsh lullaby 'Hwiangerdd'.

Patrick Pilton, Editor, *South Wales Echo* for allowing me to use headlines of historical interest from his paper.

Prologue

Thump! Thump! Thump! The banging on the scullery ceiling brought a shower of loose plaster falling like dirty snowflakes about Gwen's shoulders.

'All right! All right!' she yelled in frustration when with hardly a pause the banging started again. Pushing the damp grey hair from her glistening forehead, she peered through the steam for the wooden tongs and prodded the washing down into the gas boiler. Then after drying her hands on the roller towel, she lifted the latch and opened the door.

A billow of steam preceded her into the kitchen-cum-living room and out into the passage leading to the stairs. What could Lucy want this time? she wondered crossly. Twice in the last half-hour she'd been called to the bedroom. First her sister had wanted a cup of tea and a welsh cake, a sure sign that she was on the mend. The second time had been for Gwen to empty the commode. It wasn't fifteen minutes since she'd washed and dried it and returned it to the seat of the heavy oak armchair that accommodated it, for even now in 1963 her sister's old-fashioned terraced home had no bathroom or indoor toilet.

Lucy lay against the embroidered pillows, the faded

prettiness of her face framed by a halo of silver curls.

'Make another pot of tea, Gwen. Bring a cup for yourself so's we can have a little talk.'

To hide her annoyance at being disturbed yet again Gwen crossed to the window and looked out over the neighbours' back yards where lines of washing billowed in a cutting east wind; all except Lucy's, which with all the interruptions wouldn't be ready to peg out for another half-hour at least.

'Influenza,' the doctor had said when almost a fortnight ago Gwen had been summoned to the house, but yesterday he'd assured them that Lucy was over the worst.

'You'd be better downstairs,' he'd told his patient. 'Potter about, rest when you're tired, eat light nourishing meals – you'll soon feel strong again.'

But Lucy had been determined to stay in bed, perhaps feeling that by doing so she would keep her sister with her all the longer. Several times since she'd felt better she had tried to get Gwen to sit down and talk about the past, but Gwen was determined not to. Until she'd been called to the house by a worried neighbour she and Lucy hadn't spoken to each other in over forty years.

For the last couple of weeks Gwen'd cooked for Lucy, coped with the washing, kept the fires going, plumped up her pillows, and during the first few days bathed her to keep the fever down, but she still felt hurt at what her sister had done, even after all these years, and the hard core of her resentment showed no sign of melting away.

'Can't we talk, Gwen? Can't we at least try to be friends?' Lucy's plaintive voice broke into her thoughts now, but Gwen knew that she couldn't entirely forgive. Although it was a very long time ago, too much had happened and, because of Lucy, her life and other lives too had been shattered.

2

Gwen turned away from the window and faced her younger sister, admiring grudgingly the neat features, the cornflower blue eyes – unhappy, troubled eyes, but still deeply blue despite her sixty-two years. Hair that was silver now curled becomingly about her small face. Feeling herself unbend a little towards the woman in the bed, she said abruptly, 'I'll fetch the tea.'

Downstairs, setting the cups on the tray, Gwen thought of the happy childhood she'd shared with her sisters living in the comfortable rooms behind and above the little parlour shop – her mother had kept a shop in the converted parlour, helping to supplement Dada's pay as a clerk with a firm of wholesalers. One side of the long counter that stretched across the width of the room had been covered with jars of boiled sweets, trays of home-made toffee, bunches of liquorice laces and other confectionery, together with glass bottles of herb and ginger beer. The other side, leaving sufficient space between to serve the customers, had displays of small necessities like needles and threads, crochet hooks, button hooks, shoe-horns, candles, moth balls, combs, hair-slides and hair-pins. The deep shelves set against the wall behind the counter were filled with such things as bath-brick, soda, matches, Hudson's washing-up powder, pumice stone and many other items very necessary at the turn of the century for day to day living.

Then, waiting for the kettle to boil Gwen sat by the fire remembering the day that Lucy was born. How excited she'd been, an eight year old with big brown eyes, her long, wavy chestnut brown hair pulled back into a wide ribbon bow, impatiently waiting to see her new baby sister.

It had been a cold February day in 1901, and in the big front bedroom a bright fire had burned in the grate. She had lain across the foot of the bed on top of the patchwork quilt, gazing adoringly down at the baby asleep in the cradle by her mother's side, feeling very proud and happy when Mama told her: 'Going to call her Lucy we are, just like you wanted, Gwen.'

The kettle coming to the boil brought Gwen's thoughts quickly back to the present, but as she poured the water into the tea-pot and remembered Lucy's determination to talk, her thoughts flew to another time, forty odd years ago, a time of bitterness and recrimination, a time that had drastically altered the whole course of her life, when she'd cried herself to sleep night after despairing night and wished with all her heart that her sister Lucy had never been born.

Chapter One

Little Gwenith Llewellyn pulled the bedclothes about her head and drew her feet up as far as they would go as she tried to find a patch of warmth.

The small back bedroom was icy cold, and with all the panic of sending for the midwife and Aunt Fan filling the big iron kettles and a saucepan and putting them on top of the range to boil, her father rushing to light the fire in the front bedroom – the room that was over the parlour shop – and the baby clothes being brought out and draped over the brass rail of the guard to air, she had been rushed off to bed early. The customary hot brick wrapped in several thicknesses of flannel, placed in her bed every winter's night, making a haven of warmth to stretch her feet down into, was sitting bare of its covering and forgotten by everyone except herself in the oven at the side of the kitchen range.

If only I could go and fetch it, she thought longingly, but at eight years old her mother had said that she was far too young to be trusted with candles or matches, and the stretch of oilcloth between her and the bedroom door might just as well have been the arctic wastes of Siberia she'd been learning about at school for she could never persuade her feet to take her over it without a light, not until the mouse that she sometimes heard scuttling across the polished floor in the middle of the night was caught, and neither Dada with the poker nor the mouse-trap baited with cheese had managed to do that.

Shivering, she lay there listening to the sounds that from time to time broke the stillness. The creaking of the stairs as Aunt Fan rushed up and down them. Mama had once been as thin as Aunt Fan, but over the last months she'd got really fat. Must have been eating lots of lossins from the shop, Gwen told herself with a smile, and after all the times she'd warned her and Mair about the consequences of eating too many sweets.

She heard the clanging of the coal-bucket as her father went to replenish the front bedroom fire, and a little later Mrs Dobbs the midwife calling down for more hot water. Why did she want all that hot water? Everyone knew that Mrs Dobbs brought the babies with her in her big brown bag. Surely she would have washed and dressed this one before popping it in to bring to Mam?

Because her mother had felt so tired lately Gwen had been allowed to help her sister in the shop. It had been lovely chatting with the customers, putting the money in the drawer and giving change, though she always had to show this to Mair before handing it over the counter. And it had been lovely too, despite her mother's warning, to pop a sweet into her mouth whenever she felt like one.

They'd managed very well, the two of them, going into the shop as soon as they came home from school, taking it in turns to have their tea, though Mair would bring hers in with her so that she could keep her eye on things. And then on the 22nd of last month Queen Victoria had died – she remembered the date because she'd kept the piece in the paper for her scrap book.

Gwen thought she'd always remember that evening in January. The family had been sitting comfortably around the kitchen fire, Dada in his wooden armchair smoking his pipe, her mother in the comfortable one with lots of cushions had been sewing something white, Mair as usual reading a book, and she'd been drinking her cocoa as slowly as she could so's to put off going to bed. Suddenly there'd been a lot of noise outside, a lot of shouting coming faintly from the street, and she'd put her mug of cocoa down on the table and rushed towards the front door with Mair right behind her. As they pulled open the door they could hear news-boys yelling '*Echo*! *Echo*!' followed by a gabble of words that they couldn't make out, the boys' hob-nailed boots sparking the flag-stones as they ran.

'Hurry, Mair!' Dada cried, fumbling in his pocket for a halfpenny and putting it into her hand.

'Put youer coat on, girl,' her mother had insisted. 'It's bitter out there.'

Dada had tutted impatiently, anxiously watching the boys, their raucous cries growing fainter as one by one they disappeared around the corner. By the time Mair was ready to chase after them even the echo had faded away.

'It will be about the Queen, pooer soul,' her mother had said, looking sad.

When Mair came back, shivering even in her warm coat, Dada took the paper, and, glancing at it first, read them a bit about Queen Victoria passing away at six-thirty that evening at Osborne House on the Isle of Wight, surrounded by her children and grandchildren.

'Prince Albert Edward will be king now at last,' Dada had told them, stroking his drooping moustache.

'They call him Bertie, don't they?' Mama asked.

7

'Yes, but he'll be given his proper name when he's crowned.'

Gwen remembered how excited she'd felt about a prince coming to the throne. In all her picture books princes were handsome young men who fell in love with beautiful princesses. She'd had quite a shock when her father had pointed to a picture in the paper which he told her was of the king to be, for he'd had a beard and a moustache and looked more like a grandfather than a prince; a jolly grandfather, Gwen thought, but an old man just the same.

Mair had dressed the little shop window all in black that night, allowing Gwen to help. It had been sad of course but exciting too, sewing the black satin ribbon rosettes to pin around the big picture of the Queen wearing a cap with a long fall of lace down her back, a picture that they'd last displayed at her Diamond Jubilee about four years ago. Mair had made a big fan of black crêpe paper as a background to the portrait.

Their mother had been very pleased with the display and the following day the shop had been closed as a mark of respect, but it had been a waste of time for when the shop was closed the customers just banged the knocker on the front door and had to be let in to wait in the passage while what they wanted was fetched from the shop.

She must have dozed off for at the sound of Mair's voice her eyes flew open to see shadowy candlelight dancing on the ceiling, and her sister coming towards her, telling her, 'We've got a baby sister, Gwen.'

Despite the bitter cold Gwen was out of bed and running towards the door when Mair caught her arm and led her gently back to bed, saying, 'We can't see her tonight, love. Doctor Powell is still with Mama, and Aunt Fan says she's very tired.'

Gwen wanted to talk but Mair fell into an exhausted sleep as soon as her head was on the pillow. There was so much Gwen had wanted to ask her. She lay awake wishing the morning would soon come, wondering who the baby was like, falling asleep at last just as a wet and windy dawn lightened the lace curtains.

The next morning, dressed in their dark school dresses covered by clean broderie anglaise pinafores, hair brushed and boots polished ready for school, the girls were greeted at the door of the front bedroom by Aunt Fan.

'There she is, the little angel,' she cried pointing to the cradle by the side of the bed. Mama, looking pale and exhausted, smiled at them from her pillows as they gazed down at the baby who was fast asleep.

When Mair knelt by the cradle, Gwen lay face downwards across the foot of the bed on top of the patchwork quilt and gazed at her tiny sister in wonder.

'We're going to call her Lucy just like you wanted, Gwen,' her mother told her, and looking up at her mam Gwen saw dark shadows almost like bruises beneath her kindly brown eyes.

Tiring at last of watching the sleeping child, she glanced around the comfortable familiar room, glowing and warm in the dancing flames from the fire: at the big dark oak wardrobe and tall chest of drawers, at the wash-stand with its marble top on which stood a rose-patterned jug and wash basin with a matching soap dish, at the snowy towels which hung on brass rails on either side. On the painted iron mantelshelf stood the pretty china clock supported by dimpled cherubs that Gwen had always loved, and she realised with a start that the hands were already pointing to a quarter to nine.

The room was so cosy with the warmth from the fire

that she wished she could just curl up and go to sleep, but now Aunt Fan was standing in the doorway telling them they would have to hurry or they'd be late for school, and they hadn't even put their books ready yet.

Wind billowing their skirts and rain lashing their faces, the girls hurried past the neat grey stone houses with their dark green or brown front doors many of which flew open as they passed. Mrs Roberts was the first to call after them, 'How's yoeur mam and the new baby then?' and as they turned to answer her, Mrs Evans from across the road, the front of her hair still in curling rags, cried, 'Saw Mrs Dobbs early this morning, told me, she did, that you've got a new baby sister.'

By the time they'd reached the top of the street and were crossing Broadway they were very wet and very late, and picking up their skirts they began to run.

Chapter Two

'No more babies, no more keeping shop, no more rushing around doing two things at once.' Doctor Powell's message had been loud and clear.

'And how do I do that with a new baby?' Sarah Llewellyn asked herself aloud, weakness causing her warm brown eyes to fill with tears. Hearing her husband Tom's footsteps on the stairs she brushed them away hastily and managed a tremulous smile as he opened the door.

Three weeks it was since the day Lucy was born and she hadn't yet set foot out of bed. She was getting impatient with herself, for she'd been downstairs by this time with the other two.

'Your heart is tired, Sarah,' Doctor Powell had told her. 'You'll be able to lead a normal life so long as you take things easy.'

She'd never taken things easy. The hard work in domestic service before her marriage, finishing up as parlour maid, hadn't prepared her for sitting around.

'The girls are in the shop,' Tom told her. 'You'll have to make up youer mind, Sarah. Doctor says you should close it down.'

She didn't want to give it up and the girls were managing whenever they were home from school. Good girls

11

they were, both of them, opening up each afternoon when they came home and keeping open all day on a Saturday. Trade was down, of course, seeing that the shop stayed closed for most of the day, but she still hoped they could keep it going. It would be better when she was up and about. The regular small profit from the shop had always been more than useful, helping to keep the children nicely dressed and shod. She'd been saving for a pram and had been so looking forward to going outdoors to buy it. At this rate though it would be several more weeks at least before she could be churched. She knew she wouldn't have the strength to carry Lucy around welsh-fashion as most of the women in the neighbourhood did. She would just have to get a perambulator, and a new one was out of the question.

When I do go out, she thought, I'll try Ted Lewis's shop in Splott. If he didn't have a baby carriage in the shop, he'd probably know where he could come by a bargain.

Young Ted had made a marvellous job of the shop his father had left him. In old Mr Lewis's day it had been a typical second-hand shop with everything covered in dust – sofas with the stuffing oozing out of them, tables and chairs scratched and worn beyond their useful life – but his son had soon altered all that after the old man had died. The windows had been cleaned for the first time in years and polished until they shone. The shop had been scrubbed out and new oilcloth laid. Ted had learned his trade as a carpenter and soon formed a policy of buying only decent stuff, or something with the potential to be carefully repaired and french polished. Sarah knew that if Ted had a pram it would be spotless and in good condition.

But maybe Fanny could help her find a pram. She was a good sister, one of the very best, especially the way she'd

12

offered to stay with her while Tom was at work. Her own fiancé had died of a fever in 1884 while serving at Khartoum, and Fanny, brokenhearted, had vowed she'd never marry. And she never had. A dressmaker by trade, she lived alone in a couple of rooms in Broadway just around the corner from them. She always brought her sewing with her and her sewing machine had had to be delivered on a hand-cart for she had a living to earn and her customers couldn't be kept waiting.

Sarah didn't know what she'd have done without Fanny, the faint hum of the sewing machine downstairs was comforting to hear, for she knew her sister would come immediately she tapped on the floor with her stick. Tom had wanted her to keep Mair home from school, but the girl wasn't yet eleven years old and she didn't want her to have to empty slops and change and wash dirty napkins. Worked very hard the girls had, both of them. They seemed to enjoy serving the customers, especially young Gwen, and she was very glad for she didn't want to close the shop, not just yet anyway.

'Youer too soft with them girls,' Tom had said. 'Just think how you used to have to work at Mair's age.' And, remembering, Sarah had been thankful that her girls would be able to stay at school until they were thirteen at least.

Sarah had been only a year older than her eldest daughter was now when she'd left her home in Tonyrefail in 1876 to go into service in Cardiff as a scullery maid at a gentleman's house, though being the eldest girl of the family she'd known all about hard work long before that. Home had been a small overcrowded cottage where she and two younger sisters had slept together in one bed. She was really looking forward to having a room of her own, even if it was only a small box room in an attic.

Her mother had helped her pack the rush hold-all with the things she'd been told she'd need: a dark dress, high at the neck, two strong bibbed aprons and a holland one, a spare chemise, a flannel vest and some drawers, a warm nightgown, and handkerchiefs she'd hemmed herself. The boots she was wearing were the only pair she had, and long outgrown. By the time she'd tramped all the way up Penylan hill with her bag, her feet were throbbing painfully and she'd felt fit to drop, but she'd been expected to start her duties almost right away, as soon as she'd taken off her hat and coat and left her things in the tiny bedroom she'd found she was to share with two others.

Sarah seemed to spend most of that first year in a grubby apron, her sleeves rolled above her elbows, staring down into a deep sink full of scummy water, scrubbing endlessly at greasy, soot-blackened pots and pans, wishing with all her heart that she was back in the little bedroom at the cottage, sharing with her sisters.

A year later she'd been promoted to kitchen maid and had gradually worked her way up. When at last she'd glimpsed the rooms where the family lived she'd been enraptured, never guessing at such luxury: the beautiful brocaded curtains, velvet sofas, the soft thickness of carpets and rugs, porcelain and glass treasures glimpsed through the glass of ornate china cabinets, leatherbound books on shelves that reached the ceiling in the master's study. At first it had filled her with awe, then gradually she'd become fired with ambition. She wasn't silly enough to think she could copy her betters, but she resolved that when she got married she'd have pretty things about her and keep her home nice.

Sarah had started to save at the post office, buying a

stamp whenever she could, and her first acquisition had been the cherub clock when she'd attended an auction sale at a nearby house. It wasn't a valuable clock, the spring had been broken and she'd had to get it repaired, but it was a pretty thing and she loved it. The shop had been started to help provide the little comforts she wanted – pretty curtains, rugs for the floor, a small china cabinet in which to keep the best tea-set. She'd even managed to save enough for four dining chairs stuffed with horse-hair.

Faintly she could hear the hum of the sewing machine as Fanny got on with her work. When Lucy began a whimpering which quickly progressed to a full-throated roar, the machine stopped abruptly and within moments her sister was opening the bedroom door.

Chapter Three

'Just like new it is, Sarah,' Fanny said breathlessly as she unpinned her hat and sat down at the kitchen table. 'I wanted to ask Ted how much he was asking for the pram but he was that busy. Left me alone he did in the back room to look at the kitchen chairs, and there it was, covered over with a shawl. Pity you can't come with me now to look at it.'

Sarah shook her head. 'Promised Gwen I have that she can come with me when I buy one. Awful disappointed she'd be if I went without her. Anyway, I can't leave the dinner and everything, Fan, and it's too far to carry Lucy all that way.'

Sarah hadn't been further than the corner shops since being churched just over a month ago. She'd been slow getting her strength back after Lucy's birth, but at three months the baby was plump and rosy. With her deep blue eyes and tuft of fair curls she charmed everyone who saw her, and both Mair and Gwen were her willing slaves.

When Fanny had finished her cup of tea and gone home, Sarah waited anxiously for the girls to come from school, worrying in case the perambulator was sold before she could see it.

'If it's almost new it'll probably cost more than we can

17

afford,' she cautioned herself, feeling excited at the prospect of going to Ted Lewis's shop just the same.

When the girls came from school they carried the cradle to the back of the shop where Mair could keep an eye on the baby while she served, then Gwen was sent upstairs to put on her white muslin dress with the wide blue satin sash and fetch her leghorn hat, for although it was only May the sun was quite warm.

At first Sarah walked slowly but the fresh air was a tonic after being indoors for so long, and there was unaccustomed colour in her cheeks as she pushed open the door of the second-hand shop and stepped on to the shining oilcloth. When the brass bell that hung over the door had clanged loudly and Ted Lewis didn't come into the shop, she took Gwen towards the back room and looked inside. Then, seeing the wheels of the pram, she lifted the shawl that covered it and gazed in delight at the wicker body and cream-lined leather hood, touched the deep-buttoned interior caressingly, then stood back to view the gleaming wheels, two large and two small, with delight.

'Ooh, Mam! It's lovely,' Gwen breathed ecstatically. 'It's just like the ones those nursemaids wheel around the park. Are you going to buy it?'

'I'm afraid it's not for sale.' They hadn't noticed Ted Lewis come to the doorway. His face wore a sad expression as he told them, 'I only brought it down here while the chimney's being swept upstairs.'

And Sarah suddenly remembered the time about two years before when Ted's young wife died giving birth to a stillborn child. All contrition she cried, 'Oh, Ted! There's sorry I am. I didn't realise it belonged to you. My sister told me that she thought you had a pram for sale.'

'It's stupid of me I know, Mrs Llewellyn, but – well, I

just can't bring myself to part with it. Mary was so happy and excited on the day it arrived.'

Seeing the tears in his grey eyes, Sarah turned to her daughter.

'Go and watch the shop for Mr Lewis, Gwen, there's a good girl. And don't you touch anything, mind.'

'I've got something that might amuse you, young lady,' Ted Lewis said kindly, wiping his eyes with the back of his hand and following the child into the shop.

Opening a cupboard he brought out a polished wooden box with a ballerina on top. When he set it down upon the table the dancer pivoted round and round to a tinkling tune. Then he wound up a figure of a little drummer boy who marched about the table beating his drums until he too slowed down. When Ted saw Gwen looking longingly at the doll he'd left on the shelf of the cupboard, he brought it out and put it carefully into her arms. Looking down at the pretty china face, gently touching the ringlets that fell about the doll's shoulders, Gwen gave a long drawn out 'Ooh!' of delight.

'Beautiful, isn't it?' Mr Lewis was smiling down at her. 'You must be very careful with it. I'll put these things away when I come back.'

But as he turned Sarah reached his side, telling him regretfully, 'We'll be going now, Ted, seeing the pram isn't for sale,' and Gwen felt a sharp stab of disappointment at having to part with the doll so soon. But Mr Lewis replied, 'Let's go and talk about it, shall we, Mrs Llewellyn? There's no earthly reason for me to hang on to it. I've no chance of making use of it now.'

'You've got some lovely stuff here, Ted,' her mother was saying as they walked away. 'Where did the doll come from?'

'Well, I bought the contents of a house and the toys were in with it . . .' The rest was lost as he closed the door of the back room behind him.

Now Gwen turned her full attention to the doll, marvelling again at the shining curls, the brown eyes that stared at her solemnly as she stood the doll on her knees, the red lips slightly parted showing four tiny pearly teeth. And the clothes! The long sprigged muslin dress had a wide blue sash, almost the same colour as the one she wore herself. The tiny soft black kid boots were laced to just above the ankle and were almost covered as she let the lace-trimmed petticoats fall back into place.

A few minutes later Mr Lewis was wheeling the pram towards her with Sarah following behind. Reluctantly she laid the doll on the table and got up. When her mother said, 'Mr Lewis has sold me the pram after all, Gwen, so you'll have to wheel it home,' she felt really excited, but couldn't help noticing that although he was smiling, the man's eyes were sad.

People stared as they passed for such a pram was rarely seen in those parts. When they reached home, with her mother exhausted but triumphant, and Gwen had manoeuvred it past the parlour where Mair was serving a customer and attempted to get the pram into the alcove under the stairs, it wouldn't go and had to be left in the dark little passage that led to the kitchen.

As Gwen helped to set the tea Sarah said anxiously, 'I wonder what youer dada will say about that pram.'

She didn't have to wait long to find out for suddenly there was a commotion in the passage and Tom's voice yelling angrily, 'Christ Almighty! What blutty fool put that contraption there?' Sarah froze on her way to the door, her face registering disgust and surprise. She'd

20

never known Tom to swear within hearing of the children; she was quite sure that Mair would have heard him from the parlour, and the customers too.

Now Sarah moved towards the door but before she could grasp the handle it flew open to reveal Tom, his face contorted with pain, hopping about on one leg while nursing the shin of the other. As she put her arm about him and helped him to the sofa, he looked up sheepishly, saying, 'Sorry, girl, but it was a stupid place to leave a thing like that. I could have broken my bl— my neck falling over it.'

Sarah was bending down now, gently examining the bruised leg, calling for Gwen to bring warm water and a towel, admitting to her husband, 'I forgot it was there, Tom. I was in such a rush to get the tea.'

Gwen was sent to the passage to manoeuvre the pram through the doorway and into the kitchen, but there was only one possible place for it and that was right in front of the pantry door. Before many minutes had passed Sarah realised just how inconvenient it was going to be as the table was being set, especially when the butter dish was forgotten and the pram had to be pulled out once more to get it, then when they'd all sat down it was discovered that the pickle was still in the pantry and the pram had to be moved yet again.

Sarah didn't grumble. She knew by now that the pram was much too big for the small house, but it was a beautiful carriage and despite all the inconvenience she could hardly believe her luck.

By this time the shop was shut and Mair came into the kitchen, saying, 'Lucy's fast asleep so I didn't disturb her.' At which news Sarah sighed for she'd wanted the baby to stay awake until her bedtime.

When Mair saw the pram she exclaimed in delight, but it wasn't long before she too saw its drawbacks as, the meal over, she set about clearing the table.

'Well, there's nowhere else to put it,' Sarah told her defensively, but Mair knew there was a place much more convenient to the front door than the kitchen, a place where the pram would bother no one for the room was seldom used. Ever since the parlour had been made into a shop her mother had turned the middle room into the best room and made it a shrine to housewifely pride. The room was always cold and dark with the blind permanently drawn to protect the green velvet curtains and the Axminster carpet square from the sun.

When the dishes were washed and put away and Sarah was feeding the baby behind the screen, Mair crept along the passage to the parlour with a home for the pram in mind, but she knew in her heart that her mother would never allow it and that her father would be angry if she upset her mam by suggesting it.

Mair closed the door behind her and looked around the room. In the centre stood a large pedestal table and six dining chairs padded with horse-hair. The armchairs either side of the fireplace and the matching sofa against one wall were overstuffed and anti-macassared. There wasn't a pin's point between the ornaments on the mirror-backed overmantel below which a painted fan stood in front of the empty fire basket. Within the ornate brass fender stood a brass coal-bucket in the shape of a helmet and a matching companion set of shovel, brush, and tongs.

Mair glanced across at the what-not in the corner. This too was crowded with ornaments, tiny porcelain souvenirs, mostly with painted coats of arms. On the wall by the door was a pretty little organ with emerald green silk pleated behind its fretwork front, its top covered with family photographs.

Mair sighed as she realised there was no room for the pram after all. She was the only one Mama entrusted to dust these treasures but with no sunlight to find her out she would often just rub a duster along the edges of the shelves, and she never disturbed the aspidistra yellowed through lack of light, the plant that stood in a green china pot on a wicker table in front of the darkened window.

Closing the door quietly behind her she went back to the kitchen where Lucy was now being topped and tailed ready for bed. Mama was right after all. There was no other place for the pram.

Chapter Four

Sarah stood just outside the front door watching proudly as Gwen wheeled the pram up and down the long street, especially when she saw a neighbour stop to admire Lucy who at six months old was sitting up in a beribboned bonnet and jacket, her cheeks rosy, eyes wide and blue, smiling at everyone. Sarah knew to her cost that Lucy's moods could change quickly, the rosebud mouth turn down in a moment, while tears and tantrums would quickly replace the smiles and chuckles of a moment before. Young as she was, Lucy loved her own way.

I'll soon nip that nonsense in the bud, Sarah promised herself. It was all Tom's fault, of course. Fancy him telling the girls that Lucy was to be kept quiet at all costs. Mair had told her this when she'd remarked that the baby was becoming very spoilt. She knew Tom had been worried about her health at the time but giving in to the child as they had was a recipe for disaster.

Mair had always been such a good child, never giving them a moment's worry. At twelve years old she'd grown tall and was fast becoming an attractive young lady with her creamy skin and smooth dark brows, her grey eyes fringed with long silky lashes. Gwen was different in every way – warm-hearted and impetuous, often impatient, she quickly got bored, especially with the humdrum life of school and shop. Which was why Sarah had come out to watch her now, for Gwen had wanted to take Lucy to Waterloo Gardens, and who could blame her on such a hot sunny day? But Sarah considered Gwen much too young for such responsibility. Knowing her daughter would soon tire of walking up and down the street, she kept her eye on her in case she disobeyed her instructions and turned the corner.

Only last night there'd been a clear demonstration of how different the girls were. They'd been discussing the fact that Mair would be leaving school early next year.

'Things will be a lot easier for me then,' Sarah had told Mair. 'With you taking charge of the shop, I can devote my time to the house and the baby.'

'What will you do, Gwen, when you leave school?' Mair had asked.

'Gwen is to be apprenticed to the dressmaking like Aunt Fan was,' Sarah had replied for her. But Gwen had shaken her head emphatically and surprised them all by saying, 'When I leave school I want to work in Ted Lewis's second-hand shop.'

'You'll need to learn a useful trade, my girl,' Sarah had told her. 'Something you can fall back on if you need it.'

'But I don't want to make dresses and things,' Gwen had cried, tearfully rushing for the door. Sarah had dragged her back, telling her in no uncertain terms, 'If I say youer going to learn to be a dressmaker, that's what will happen, make no mistake, my girl.'

Ten minutes later, the incident seemingly forgotten, Gwen had been playing happily with Lucy on the mat. And while congratulating herself on her handling of the situation, Sarah was the first to admit that though Gwen was sometimes awkward, she never sulked or bore anyone a grudge.

A few days later Gwen was pressing her nose to the window, trying to see into Mr Lewis's shop. She had come straight from school, running full pelt through the side turnings, across Broadway, down a long street into Pearl Street and over Splott bridge. Breathless still from running, she was endeavouring to see what was happening inside. Shading her eyes she could see Mr Lewis standing at a table with an old lady who seemed to be dressed all in black. She was placing little parcels wrapped in newspaper on the table which Mr Lewis was quickly unwrapping, screwing up the newspaper and putting it to one side. Gwen watched excitedly, hoping to see some more toys or pretty ornaments, for ever since the day she'd come here with Mama to buy the pram, the shop had held a great fascination for her. There was another second-hand shop in the road but it was typical of its kind with shabby sofas and tables and chairs displayed on the pavement outside and things piled on top of each other in the shop itself, dust lying on everything. As she'd passed today she'd glanced anxiously at a battered-looking mantel clock that stood on a pile of old books in the window, before remembering that the hands were permanently stuck at half-past twelve.

As she watched Mr Lewis place the pieces of a child's tea-set on the table just the other side of the window she hoped he wouldn't look up or he must surely see her. Now she began to count. Twelve cups, twelve saucers, twelve plates, a sugar basin and slop bowl, a milk jug, and last of all the prettiest little tea-pot, all in blue and white. If only she had the courage to open the door and go inside so that she could take a good look at the set, but if she did the bell over the door would clang loudly bringing Mr Lewis quickly to her side, and when he enquired what she wanted, what could she say? She hadn't any money and she couldn't very well ask to see the doll and the toys again.

Gwen remembered her mother telling them that at the big house where she'd worked the children had a tea-set of their own with tiny cups and saucers and plates but it was kept in a china cabinet and very seldom used.

She hadn't noticed the lady coming towards the door with Mr Lewis hurrying before her to open it and show her out. Gwen moved quickly, but not quickly enough. He looked surprised to see her but smiled at her and asked kindly, 'Was there something you wanted, Gwen?'

When she shook her head, he said, 'Would you like to come in and see what I've just bought?' And as she followed him to the table and he began to pick up the pieces lovingly to show her, he said, 'Have you heard of Mr Dickens' book *The Old Curiosity Shop*, Gwen?' When she nodded, for Dada had bought several of Charles Dickens' books at a second-hand book store, he went on, 'Well, the scenes on this tea-set are from the illustrations in that book. And look at this.' He turned over a tiny plate for her to see the trade mark on the bottom: 'W.R.S. and Co. That stands for William Ridgeway Son and Company.'

Gwen nodded, wondering why Mr Lewis was looking so pleased. For once he didn't look sad at all. It was a lovely little tea-set, and she wished it could be hers. But who cared what it said on the bottom of the plate? She picked it up and stared politely.

'See that, Gwen?' he was saying excitedly. 'See that picture above the maker's mark? And read what it says –

Humphrey's Clock. Well, that was the weekly paper some of Dickens' stories were first published in, one episode each week. The factory that made this little tea-set was working only for ten years, between 1838 and 1848, so this tea-set is over fifty years old. Now what do you think of that?'

He was looking so happy, his eyes were shining as he began to arrange the tea-set on a shelf of the china cabinet. Gwen did her best to look as though she understood the importance of what he was saying. She loved the little tea-set in quite a different way, and wished that she could put a half a spoonful of tea into the tea-pot and pour on the boiling water, and have the milk jug brimming with creamy milk and the sugar basin filled with shining lumps of sugar, and borrow Mama's little silver sugar tongs. Over fifty years old, Mr Lewis had said, so perhaps it had belonged to the lady who'd sold it to him when she was a little girl. That's why she'd looked sad, of course, having to part with it after all those years.

Mr Lewis was telling her, 'You've got a treat in store when youer old enough to read Mr Dickens' books,' when she clapped her hand to her mouth as she realised that her mother would never believe she'd just been dawdling all this time.

'I've got to go now, Mr Lewis. Thank you for showing me the tea-set,' she said politely. And with a last look around, she hurried from the shop and ran like the wind towards home. Turning into Wilfred Street she wondered if she could get to the bedroom she shared with Mair without being seen. The front door was always open so long as they were serving in the shop. If she could get to the bedroom Mama might think she'd been home all the time.

The warm sunshine had brought people from their stuffy rooms. Women in long skirts, the sleeves of their blouses rolled above their elbows, stood talking in little groups.

'Hello, Gwennie.'

'Hello, Mrs Jenkins.'

'How's youer mama, Gwen?'

'A lot better, thank you, Mrs Jones.'

A group of children were sprawled on the pavement playing five-stones. A grubby small girl nursed an even grubbier rag doll. Some boys were shouting excitedly over a game of marbles, but above their cries she could hear shouting coming from the direction of her own house, and reaching the front door she knew there was no way of getting upstairs unseen, for Mrs Palmer from next door was standing in the passage, her face red with anger, shouting, 'I'll 'ave the law on you, Sarah Llewellyn. Told you before, I 'ave, you 'aven't got no right to run a shop 'ere. Like bedlam it is t'other side of that wall. All them boots tramping in and out, kids yelling, and customers laughing and joking with them girls of youers.'

The shop had been a bone of contention between the two women ever since it had been opened and Gwen knew how thin the walls between the houses were, for couldn't she often hear the springs of Mrs Palmer's bed squeaking? To say nothing of the rows that seemed to be a part of that household. Mrs Palmer was tall and thin but her husband was a tubby little man who always spoke pleasantly to them all.

Mabel Palmer was usually pale but now she was red with anger and her eyes were flashing as she cried, 'Get the bobby on to you, I will, Mrs 'Igh an' Mighty, if I don't get some peace. See if I don't!'

The flat cap she was wearing had slipped to the back of her head, loosening her bun which hung in coils by one hair-pin. As their neighbour stamped through the door-way Gwen glanced anxiously at her mam. If Mrs Palmer had been red, Sarah was a ghastly white. Gwen put her arm about her mam to help her to the kitchen and just then Mair came out of the shop on the heels of the last customer she'd served. Closing the front-room door and locking it behind her, she turned a frightened face towards them. 'She's right, you know, Mama,' Mair said with obvious effort. 'It is noisy sometimes, especially when lots of children come in and have to wait to be served.' But Sarah would have none of it. 'How about all the noise she makes when she's having a barney with her old man?' she asked.

Neither of them answered, knowing how upset she must be to make a remark like that.

Gwen knew the row wouldn't be mentioned to Dada, for it would just give him a fresh excuse to get the shop closed down, something he'd wanted to do ever since her mother had become ill after Lucy's birth.

The months flew and long before autumn her mother had found out from a neighbour all about Gwen's visits to the second-hand shop. It had been a Friday evening and Mair had been kept busy with the customers. It was late when Gwen finally arrived home from school. But, after the row because she hadn't been told about these little trips, seeing how happy this new interest was making her young daughter and how proud she was of all the things she'd learnt at the shop, Sarah decided, much to Gwen's relief, there was no harm in her daughter carrying on. For, as she told her husband, 'Ted's a real gentleman. A good father he'd have made too if the Lord had seen fit to let him. Our

Gwen still wants to work there when she leaves school, Tom. I don't suppose he intends to employ anyone, but even if he did it's no job for a young lady, is it?'

When winter came and the days grew short, much to Gwen's consternation the visits to the shop had to stop.

'It's dark just after you come out of school, child,' Sarah told her. 'I'm sure Ted wouldn't want you walking home in the dark.'

When he suggested she come on Saturday mornings instead the world was bright again, even though it meant her getting up very early to do her share of the chores: bath-bricking the knives and polishing the brasses.

When spring came and the evenings grew lighter she went back to calling at the shop straight from school on a Thursday for Mr Lewis usually went out on a buying trip on a Wednesday afternoon. Sometimes, when there were a lot of new things to unpack and exclaim over, Mrs Ball, the daily who cooked and cleaned for Mr Lewis, would come downstairs, smiling at Gwen so that her eyes would almost disappear into her plump rosy cheeks. Mrs Ball was a motherly soul, and in her opinion young Gwennie's interest in them old bits of china had done her employer the world of good.

'Time you washed youer 'ands the both of you,' she'd tell them. 'Teas on the table an' I'm just about to toast them pikelets.'

Now that Lucy was almost eighteen months old she was into everything and it was Gwen's job to look after her whenever she was at home, for Mair had her hands full with the shop. On the days she went to the second-hand shop Sarah would say, 'Don't stay too long Gwen, Lucy will need some fresh air.' The truth was that now the child was toddling, Sarah would get breathless rushing after her.

Gwen would walk her little sister up and down the street, stopping frequently as neighbours bent to pat her fair curls, and most were rewarded with an angelic smile – not always though. One day old Mrs Westacott who lived at the top of the street bent down to Lucy to ask: 'How many toosie-pegs have you got now, dearie?' and before Gwen could inform her that Lucy had almost a mouthful, the old lady had pushed a grubby forefinger into the child's mouth, which was quickly withdrawn with a blood-curdling yell as Lucy sank her teeth into the offering.

The new king was to be crowned on the 26th of June and all the children were hoping for a holiday from school. Some of the shops in Clifton Street and Broadway were beginning to arrange their coronation displays and Mair was sent to buy some crêpe paper and a large picture of the king, but before they could begin to dress the parlour window the poor man was taken ill with appendicitis and the ceremony had to be postponed until August 9th. The portrait of Queen Victoria, that had adorned the window on the sad occasion of her death, had by now been placed in a bamboo frame and hung on one of the crowded walls of the sitting room.

The hot summer went on and when school broke up at the end of July Mair left and devoted her time to the shop. Now it was open all day, Mrs Palmer's voluble complaints were much more frequent and the dissension between the families had filtered down to the children. Iris Palmer had once been Gwen's best friend, but just now when they'd gone out to view the window and Mair's back was turned, she'd poked her tongue out at Gwen who'd returned the insult. They'd often quarrelled anyway but what Gwen missed most was taking her turn with Iris's iron hoop, a hand-me-down from her brother. Sarah had soon made it clear that she didn't approve and forbade her trundling it in the street. So Iris had bowled it as far as the lane behind Broadway for Gwen to have her turn.

Now, while Mair went back into the shop, Gwen went through the kitchen to the wash-house where her mother was staring through the window. Following her gaze Gwen saw her father leaning on his spade talking to Mr Palmer over the garden wall, the two men laughing over something that had been said. Their wives' quarrel over the shop had made little difference to the men. Mr Palmer had always been a good neighbour. He was short and fat with a bristling moustache. Her father had a moustache too but his was black and silky and drooped at the sides, making his pale, thin face look even longer.

Suddenly the men burst out laughing again, and Sarah's lips clamped with disapproval as she stirred the fruit stewing in the saucepan, before saying, 'Another fuss there was this morning while you were at school. I wouldn't mind so much but Mair gets upset. You know she never could abide arguments. I don't know how youer dada can stay so friendly when he knows just what all these upsets are doing to us.'

'Where's Lucy?' Gwen asked, hoping to change the subject.

'Youer Aunt Fan came and took her to the shops.'

'I'll take her out for a while when they come back,' Gwen promised, feeling guilty that she'd intended slipping away to Splott as soon as she could. The second-hand shop still held a great fascination for her and Ted Lewis always seemed to enjoy showing her his latest purchases.

She'd once heard her mam say to her dad, 'I don't know how that Ted makes a living. Old Tom, his dad, used to do a lot of buying and selling around here. Scruffy his shop was, I know, but he sold what people could afford, and bought stuff from them, shabby or not, when they were in a fix.'

Ted had often told Gwen how his business worked. 'I buy good stuff,' he'd said. 'Sometimes it will need repolishing but I sell mostly to the trade. Occasionally I find something antique or rather special and put it in an auction where folks will know what they're buying.'

He always seemed pleased that she took such an interest. She loved it when there were boxes to unpack and he'd say, 'I wonder what we have in here?' He knew, of course, but it was wonderful that he let her delve into the packing case, bringing things out very carefully and unwrapping them. Few of the things were as old as the child's tea-set that he'd bought last year. Sometimes he'd show her pieces of furniture but she was much more interested in the things she helped to unpack. It wasn't always china, though most of this was beautiful. Some of the ornaments were lovely too, but the parasol she'd unwrapped last week had been really gorgeous, covered in periwinkle blue silk and adorned with painted butterflies.

Chapter Five

As the time for her to leave school drew near Gwen wished she could find the courage to ask Mr Lewis for a job. He'd taught her quite a lot over the past five years, especially about pottery and porcelain. She loved the shop and its ever changing contents, and the idea that she would have to work somewhere else and never have time even to call in as she did now was more than she could bear. Today at lunch-time her mother had said, 'We'll go to see Mr Cohen as soon as you know when you're leaving school, Gwen.'

She'd pressed her lips together, forcing back the exclamation of dismay that rose to them, and made up her mind to call on Mr Lewis as soon as school was over.

'You'd really like to work here?' he asked her in surprise. 'I thought youer mam wanted you to be a tailoress?'

'I'd die!' Gwen told him dramatically. 'I hate sewing. Made a real mess of it, I did, when my aunty tried to teach me to use her machine. I'd love to work here,' she added wistfully.

Ted smiled down at her, uncertain what to say. She'd been a quick learner and careful with the china. Already she was beginning to recognise some of the pieces made at the well-known potteries. She'd wondered if a cup that

37

had come with a basket of junk was Caughley, and that was before he'd turned it upside down and shown her the impressed 'Salopian' name mark on the bottom.

'Where did you say the factory is, Mr Lewis?' she'd asked.

'Was, Gwennie, was. John Rose of the Coalport porcelain works took it over in 1799, so that cup is over a hundred years old.'

Gwen knew she'd remember what he'd told her. It was funny because she never could remember the dates of battles in the history lessons at school.

Now he looked down at her eager young face. What should he say? He didn't want to upset Sarah Llewellyn and it seemed she had her heart set on the tailoring for this daughter. But neither could he dash the hopes mirrored in the child's eyes as she gazed anxiously up at him.

'You can come here to work, Gwen, but only if both your parents are willing.'

'Thank you! Oh, thank you, Mr Lewis.' He thought for a moment she was going to hug him, but she ended on a quieter note. 'Oh, I hope they'll let me come.'

Going home Gwen felt excited, thrilled with the prospect of working in the shop. Despite her thirteen years she felt like skipping along, but as she approached the house the feeling of euphoria left her and her spirits sank. Her mother wasn't likely to give in, was she? There'd be an awful row when she told her about the job Mr Lewis had offered her, and Dada would be mad at her for upsetting her mam.

Entering the kitchen she found Aunt Fan sitting at the table and her mother pouring tea. Before she could answer her aunt's friendly 'Hello, love,' her mother swung around, demanding, 'Wherever have you been child? You promised to hurry home to help Mair for a while before you go to that lantern lecture after tea.'

Gwen's hand flew to her mouth in dismay at her own forgetfulness, aware now that this was the worst possible moment to ask if she could go to work at the second-hand shop.

'Well, girl, has the cat got youer tongue?' Sarah asked impatiently. 'Still waiting to know where you've been, I am.'

Gwen licked dry lips and looked around the room anxiously before telling her mother haltingly: 'M – Mr Lewis has offered me a job!'

Sarah said sharply, 'Oh! he has, has he? Well, let me tell you, young lady, youer going to the tailoring. It's practically arranged.'

Sick with disappointment, Gwen pleaded, 'Please, Mama, please let me go to the shop!'

Sarah shook her head. 'Determined I am, Gwen, that you will learn something useful. Be thanking me you will one day, my girl, you'll see.'

Fanny put her cup down quickly so that it clattered in the saucer and pleaded with her sister, 'Just hear her out, Sarah. If Gwen is old enough to start working for a living, she's old enough to state her point of view.'

Sarah gave a short laugh. 'Was I ever asked if I wanted to go into service? Did you have any say about being apprenticed to the trade?'

'You know I didn't, and if our Jenny hadn't died of the diphtheria she would have had to learn her trade too, for as Mam often said, one of her children being in service and living away from home was quite enough.

'I hated that workroom, Sarah. The smell of wet cloth as the steam rose from the damp-rag, and the weight of those big tailoring irons as we carted them to and from the stove! On the hottest summer's day there was a fire in the stove so that we could heat the irons, and even on cold days the basement was stuffy with so many of us working there, the machines so close together you had a job to keep youer elbows to youerself.'

Fanny paused for breath but when Sarah didn't say anything, she went on, 'Shut away below ground level as we were, we rarely saw the sunlight. You hear tales of the conditions abroad, Sarah, but it was just as bad here in the eighties and nineties, and I don't suppose it's improved that much since my day.'

'But it wouldn't be like that at Cohen's,' Sarah protested. 'He's only got the one small workroom, and only about half-a-dozen girls.'

'He's well respected in the trade,' Fanny conceded. Then nodding towards Gwen, who was watching her mother's face anxiously, she said, 'She's just not cut out for it, Sarah, believe me. Remember what happened when I tried to teach her to use the machine? Let Gwen try working for Ted, see how she gets on. If it doesn't work out she could still be apprenticed.'

White-faced, clenching her hands until the nails bit into her palms, Gwen willed her mother to listen to Aunt Fan towards whom she felt a warm glow of gratitude.

'We'll see what youer father says,' Sarah told her at last. 'Now go and help Mair in the shop, there's a good girl.'

When Fan came into the shop to say goodbye, Gwen flung her arms about her and kissed her gratefully. But after they'd waved her goodbye she couldn't settle and kept glancing anxiously towards the door, wishing that her father would come through the passage.

'Mrs Davies asked for blacking, Gwen,' Mair admonished, and Gwen looked down at her hand to see that she'd been holding out a bar of brown soap.

At last Dada was waving to them as he passed on his way to the kitchen. If only they'd discuss it right away. Sick with apprehension, Gwen waited for the call. Supposing her mam hadn't really changed her mind at all? She knew her father would agree with whatever Mama wanted, believing as he always did that she would know best.

Lucy rushed passed them, flinging the kitchen door open and jumping straight into Dada's open arms. While Gwen waited, beside herself with anxiety for the verdict, Lucy was swung up high and hugged tightly, rosy cheeks pressed warmly against her father's, blond curls in delicious disarray. At last the child was settled on his knee, her expression one of smug satisfaction as Dada finally turned his attention to Gwen. He smiled at her and winked, immense relief surged through her and she knew everything was going to be all right.

'We've decided to let you try the shop, Gwen,' Sarah told her. 'See how it goes, 'cos if I don't approve of what youer doing, you'll still be apprenticed to the tailoring trade.'

Hugging both her parents gratefully, Gwen hurried back to the shop to tell Mair the good news but not before she heard Sarah remark: 'I hope we're doing the right thing, Tom. A funny job it seems to be for a young lady. Now if she'd wanted to work in a draper's I think I'd have understood . . .'

Gwen made up her mind to tell Mr Lewis yes before her mother could change her mind.

As soon as tea was over and the dishes washed and dried, she slipped on her coat and the floppy woollen tam she wore to school and left the house, sure there'd be no questions this evening for they knew she was going to a lantern slide lecture at the church hall. But she intended to go to the shop first and afterwards, although she'd be a little late, she could slip into the darkened hall and sit on one of the benches at the back. The lecture was about Egypt and the Pyramids, and they'd been reading about Ancient Egypt in school. Anyway, hopefully she wouldn't miss many of the slides or any of the lecture, for Dada would surely want to know what she had seen.

Mr Lewis looked surprised to see her after shop hours but led the way upstairs to his living quarters. Gwen looked around her with growing interest for she hadn't been up here before. She recognised several ornaments and a picture that she herself had unpacked and admired. There was the beautiful cabinet inlaid with brass that had at one time been on display in the shop and amongst the ornaments crowding its top was the pair of Coalport vases with domed lids that had beautiful birds painted on them by someone called Randall. She remembered Mr Lewis carefully unwrapping them himself and telling her who the artist was, and she remembered the painter's name because it was the same as one of the teachers at school.

'Lovely, aren't they?' Mr Lewis remarked, following her gaze.

Staring at the softly glowing colours, Gwen licked her lips then looked up at him. 'It's about the job, Mr Lewis,' she told him. 'My mam and dad are going to let me come to work for you.'

'That's wonderful, Gwen,' he told her, trying to hide his surprise. He hadn't expected any opposition from Tom but Sarah must be more easygoing than he had thought. He was glad Gwen was coming to work for him. She was glancing about her now in obvious appreciation and he was looking forward to teaching her what he knew.

His thoughts went to the time when he would have been about her age, and he could see his father again clearly in his mind – fustian trousers tied with string just below the knee, stained clay pipe clasped between his teeth, eyes screwed up against the smoke. A character his dad had been, and well liked by his customers; the long procession of men who'd walked at his funeral proved that.

He saw himself as a child delving amongst the bric-à-brac his dad had banished to the attic as unsaleable. Once, amongst these things, he'd found a tea-pot with a streaky chocolate-coloured glaze. It was no ordinary tea-pot for it didn't have a lid, not even an opening at the top, which was probably the reason for his father throwing it out. Moulded fruit hanging from branches decorated the body of it, and when he held it under the light of the lantern it took on a lustrous purple sheen.

The next day, the tea-pot wrapped carefully in news-paper, he'd walked into town to show his find to an antique dealer, for he had a feeling about the funny tea-pot, a feeling he couldn't explain. When his mother had been alive she'd taken him to this shop, tearful at parting with some small family possession to help make ends meet. He'd half expected to be laughed at, but instead the dealer had told him that it was what was known as a Rockingham Cadogan tea-pot.

'Who does it belong to, boy?' the man had asked sus-piciously, peering over small steel-rimmed spectacles, his white beard jutting aggressively from his chin.

'My dad,' he'd replied, knowing the man would never believe that it belonged to him. Then, seeing his still doubting expression, he'd added: 'Mr Lewis. He's got a second-hand shop in Splott.'

'Tom Lewis? Oh, well, I'll be down that way tomorrow.

Perhaps he'll have something else interesting for me. This tea-pot isn't very valuable, of course, more a curio it is, but I'd prefer to deal with him myself.'

Disappointment at not being given any money to pass to his dad was mixed with a feeling of elation at having found something the dealer could put a name to. When he'd told him, his dad had scratched his head thoughtfully. 'There's a book somewhere in the attic, Ted,' he'd told him. 'No use to me it isn't. Got pictures in it and writing all about old china.' And he'd nodded at his dad sympathetically, knowing that bright as he was where a bargain was to be had, he could neither read nor write . . .

Ted suddenly became aware that Gwen was looking up at him expectantly.

'Sorry, love,' he said smiling apologetically. 'I was far away. I'm very pleased that you can come to work for me, Gwen. When do you leave school?'

'Next weekend, Mr Lewis.'

'Well, you can start on the following Monday. I'll have to talk to your mam before that, get everything settled.'

'Thank you very much. I'd better be going now. I've got to go to a lantern lecture.'

When the side door had closed behind her, Gwen began to run. Reaching the church hall out of breath and with a stitch in her side, she entered the darkened room and slid on to the bench nearest the door, but she couldn't concentrate on the pictures as they were thrown upon the screen. Her thoughts would keep going back to the remarks her mother had made and she had overheard. Would she change her mind even now?

'Oh, no! She can't. She mustn't.' Gwen looked about her in embarrassment as she realised that in her agitation she'd cried the words aloud.

Chapter Six

On the morning that Gwen was to start work she pivoted in front of the cheval mirror, cheeks pink with excitement, swinging the mirror backwards and forwards in an effort to see the full effect of the new, almost grown-up, outfit Aunt Fan had made her. The dark grey serge skirt came to the top of her ankle boots, the pale grey blouse had three rows of pin tucks either side of the dainty pearl button fastening, and the high collar was stiffened with buckram and edged with lace.

She brushed her newly washed hair with even strokes until the chestnut glints gleamed in the sunlight slanting into the room, then pulled it back tightly from the forehead, fastening it at the nape of her neck with a large tortoise-shell slide. But as always a few tendrils escaped and curled becomingly about her face.

At Mair's, 'Gwen! You'll be late!' she took her purse and a clean lawn handkerchief and hurried downstairs to where her sister was standing, holding on to the knob of the banister.

After kissing Mam and Lucy, she hugged her sister quickly and made for the door.

'Gwen!'

Stopping in full flight at the sound of her mother's

voice, she turned her head inquiringly.

'Youer apron, girl.' Sarah held out a white holland bib pinafore, neatly ironed and folded, and Gwen's face fell at the thought of all the glory of the new outfit being hidden beneath it.

'Needing it you'll be, working in a place like that,' Sarah warned. 'How long do you think that blouse will keep clean,' she went on, 'when you unpack those things Mr Lewis is always buying?'

Resignedly Gwen draped the folded apron over her arm and waited while Mair unbolted the front door and placed the iron dog against it to keep it wide. Then, with a final hug for her sister, she was hurrying up the street.

Mair didn't feel at all envious as she watched Gwen go. The truth was that she was really thankful that she herself was needed at home to look after the shop. She'd often heard her aunt refer to her as a home-bird, but she'd always been painfully shy with strangers and never happier than when surrounded by family and friends and the familiar things of home.

Mair could still remember the awful apprehension she'd felt when, about the time that Gwen was born, her mother had arranged for her to stay with her grandmother in Tonyrefail. Living so far away, she had never seen much of her nan. Physically sick she'd been at the thought of leaving home. So sick she'd been unable to travel when the time came, but as soon as the threat of being sent away was over she'd made a rapid recovery. How she envied Gwen her lack of self-consciousness, the way she welcomed each new situation with open arms. She'd looked so vividly alive this morning, so pleased to be going at last to work at Ted Lewis's shop.

Gwen was turning the corner now after giving her another little wave, and leaving the front door open ready for business, Mair went into the shop to count the change in preparation for the day ahead.

When Gwen opened the shop door, setting the bell clanging, she looked around her with deep satisfaction. The outside blind over the window not yet having been drawn, the morning sun streamed in, setting the cut glass adazzle and the polished wood aglow. As she hung her coat up in the little back room she noticed with satisfaction the full packing case awaiting her attention, promising an exciting half-hour of discovery when she could play the guessing game as she unwrapped each item.

As she came back into the shop, she saw Mr Lewis coming downstairs.

'Good morning, Gwen. Did you see the case of stuff I bought last weekend?'

'Shall I unpack it right away, Mr Lewis?'

'We'll do it together,' he told her, wondering how he was to keep such an eager beaver occupied. Apart from his dealings with the trade, he wasn't ever exactly run off his feet, even on the busy days.

Gwen was already delving into the packing case, having remembered just in time to don her apron, and Ted watched her, enjoying her obvious pleasure in each item that she unpacked. Firstly she unwrapped a pair of pale pink vases decorated with white angels in pâte-sur-pâte, and in her mind pronounced the words the way she'd heard Mr Lewis say them, proud that she'd recognised what they were. Next came a little china cottage on a grassy plinth decorated with moulded flowers and shrubs.

'A pastille burner,' Ted told her as she placed it carefully on the table beside the vases.

Next was a lovely little wooden chest about twelve inches long, the hinged lid inlaid with mother-of-pearl. She opened it to find the chest contained two tea caddies, their tops also inlaid.

The clang of the bell made Gwen straighten her back and turn towards the door. As a middle-aged woman came into the shop, looking about her, Ted whispered: 'Go and serve her, Gwen. I'll be here if you need any help.'

Her heart beating fast, Gwen smiled as she went towards the customer.

''ave you got any odd cups and saucers, miss?' the woman asked, and relieved that she didn't have to test her knowledge so soon, Gwen led the way to the back of the shop where the everyday objects were stacked on shelves. When the woman had chosen, and the china was wrapped in newspaper and put into a straw bag and she had taken the money, Gwen returned to unpacking the case.

Now she unwrapped a cream jug in the shape of a cow, the mouth and tail forming spout and handle, then gave a little scream as in the darkness of the packing case the paper fell off a heavy pottery mug and she saw what she thought was a toad crawling up from the bottom.

Ted laughed as he bent down and brought the mug up into the daylight and she saw that it was only a china frog moulded to the inside. As she stared at it in amazement he told her it was meant as a joke to frighten someone who had perhaps already drunk too much.

The packing case was nearly empty when she took out a china figure of a young girl dressed in the fashion of the eighteenth century, the pretty head tilted slightly, the soulful eyes seeming to stare into her own. She stood in dainty black slippers on a low green plinth, her full skirts in layers of pale blue and mauve, the billowing white flounce at her waist sprigged with tiny flowers. The dress had long tight sleeves that ended well above the wrist in matching frills, and she held a garland stretched between her hands.

Gwen touched the waving hair tenderly and traced its moulded contours to where it was tied with a bow at the nape of the figure's neck.

As she turned the little piece around, admiring it from every angle, Ted asked gently, 'Do you like it, Gwen?'

Her gaze still on the figurine, she answered, 'It's lovely, Mr Lewis, really lovely.'

'Then I'd like you to have it,' he said, watching her cheeks flush with pleasure.

But she cried, 'Oh, I couldn't, Mr Lewis. It might be valuable.'

'Not very, I'm afraid, Gwen. It's Continental, could be any one of a number of factories. You'll notice there's no maker's mark on the bottom? But it's a pretty piece, and nicely made.'

'Thank you, Mr Lewis. It's a lovely present.' Then, stroking the figure fondly, she put it to one side and bent over the packing case once more.

Ted watched her, the expression on his face tender. Over the years he had come to regard Gwen as the child he had never had. He wanted so very much to give her things, to spoil her just a little, but knew he must be careful or his actions might be misconstrued. To him she was still a child. One who had brought new interest into his life at a time when he'd been feeling pretty low. He'd really enjoyed teaching her, watching her growing appreciation of fine things.

His housekeeper had grown fond of her too. Only this morning she'd suggested that Gwen stay at the shop for her midday meal.

'One more won't make no difference to me, Ted,' she'd assured him, and he'd agreed, providing Sarah Llewellyn was willing. He sometimes wondered who employed who for Daisy Ball wasn't backward in saying what she thought. But she was good-hearted and a wonderful cook, and although she didn't live in she was on the premises all day. Ted was glad of that, for he believed it was what had finally convinced Sarah that it would be proper for her daughter to work with him at the shop.

The very last item Gwen unwrapped was a pair of black and white spaniel dogs, eyes pleading, curly ears almost touching their paws. She set them on the table and then carried the packing case to the yard while Ted began to tie the little price tickets he'd made on to each item, and to tell Gwen where he wished them to be placed.

When she was asked if she'd like to take her midday meal with Ted and Mrs Ball, Gwen told him regretfully, 'Mama will be expecting me home today, Mr Lewis,' and he replied, 'Of course, Gwen. You must ask permission if you would like to have your meal here.'

At lunchtime, clutching her present, which she had already decided to place on the chest of drawers in the room she shared with Mair, Gwen turned the corner into Wilfred Street and was outside the Palmers' house when she saw a small figure pelting towards her, wearing a straw hat with cherries dangling from its brim which had slipped down over her eyes, and Mair, two unaccustomed spots of angry colour in her creamy cheeks, vainly chasing behind.

'Lucy, stop this minute!' Mair cried. But it was too late. The child collided with Gwen, knocking the hand that held the china ornament against the wall. Her heart sank as she unwrapped the tissue paper, giving a shriek of rage when she discovered the figure's head broken jaggedly away from the body.

By this time Mair had retrieved her best straw hat, the brim of which now hung loosely away from the crown, and with a little cry of despair had grabbed Lucy and was making for the house.

When Sarah appeared, having caught a glimpse of her youngest daughter leaving the house, she took in the situation at once, pulling the child towards her and marching her to the kitchen, crying, too angry to be conscious of the pun: 'This is the last straw! Youer father has ruined this child, giving in to her all the time as he does!'

Dragging the now screaming Lucy over her knee, she lifted her lace-trimmed petticoat and then a flannel one, revealing cotton drawers. And to the amazement of her elder daughters, she took off her slipper and gave the child two sharp slaps. But as her hand was raised for the third time she gave a little gasp and, dropping the slipper, clutched at her chest. Her breath was coming in short jerks. After a few moments, her face drained of all colour, she sank back against the cushion and closed her eyes.

Lucy lay on the rug sobbing loudly, but the elder girls' eyes were turned anxiously on their mother as Mair loosened her clothing and settled her more comfortably against the cushions.

'Get Doctor Powell, quickly, Gwen!' Mair told her, grey eyes filled with remorse. 'It's all my fault for chasing Lucy. But she's into everything these days, and Mama's usually too tired to notice.'

Doctor Powell came and went, issuing dire warnings about what would happen if they didn't close the shop for good, and ordering Sarah to have complete rest. He had helped get her to bed and left her some medicine and Dada had been sent for. Lucy, exhausted, was fast asleep on the sofa, her fair curls spread over the cushion, her face the picture of contentment, while the rest of the household wore strained expressions and crept quietly about, the broken ornament and the hanging brim of the hat silent reminders of what had started it all.

Chapter Seven

In spite of Mair's plea that the shop had had nothing to do with Sarah's collapse, it was closed down right away. Tom Llewellyn wrote out the notice himself and placed it in the front window, making arrangements a few days later for the corner shop to buy up the contents. And with Sarah now confined to her bed once more it was just as well, for Lucy was to start school when the autumn term began and would have to be taken to and fro, and for the foreseeable future it would have been difficult for Mair to cope.

Tom's eyes had blazed with anger as he'd carried on at the girls for their part in upsetting their mother, but the real culprit got off without a word of censure, their father as usual quick to defend her.

'Lucy is just a high-spirited little girl,' he'd told them, gazing fondly at his youngest.

Mair and Gwen had long noticed the way he played with Lucy whenever he was at home, bouncing her on his knee while he sang 'Ride a Cock Horse' or swinging her into the air and making her chuckle with glee. He'd always been a good father to them but had never played with either of them as he did with Lucy.

'I think it's because youer father knows now that he'll never have a son,' Sarah told them sadly. 'Making her into a real tomboy, he is, and it's getting more than I can handle.'

But no one could ever stay angry with Lucy for long.

'Sowy,' she'd say, looking up with those big blue eyes, then she'd bury her face in her mother's or sisters' skirts, and as they held her tightly all anger would melt away.

The day after Sarah took to her bed Mair was scrubbing the patch in front of the house when Mabel Palmer walked over to where she was kneeling, the wind swaying her many skirts so that she looked like a galleon in full sail.

'Mair,' she began, 'I know that youer mam and me 'aven't always seen eye to eye, but Sarah's ill now and we used to be good friends before that blast—before the shop was opened. Anything I can do, love, you've only got to ask.'

'Thanks, Mrs Palmer, but I can manage.'

'Our Willie's startin' school same time as Lucy,' their neighbour went on. 'Take them along together, I could, Mair. Save you it would, cariad. Awkward it's goin' to be if you've got to leave youer mam.'

Mair had been wondering how she'd manage when the time came. If only she could say, 'Yes, please!' But Mama would have a fit or worse just at the thought. But she didn't need to answer as Mabel went on, ''ow is she, love, today? There's glad I am youer dad 'as closed that shop at last. Tell youer mam I've been askin' after 'er, won't you?'

Although she had no intention of passing on the message and upsetting her mother, Mair nodded.

As she got off her knees and with the wet floor cloth wiped the front window ledge, her thoughts flew to Sunday and the class she took at the church. Oh, Gwen would look after things at home while she took her afternoon Bible class, but Ronald who took the boys' class had asked her to take a walk with him after evening service. She was eighteen and had never walked out with a young man, but she'd known Ronald since school. They'd often chatted after Bible class had finished. Like her, he was shy. Bright colour had come to his cheeks when he'd asked her about the walk. If she told him now that she couldn't come, he'd think it was because she didn't want to.

She pictured Ronald when he'd asked her out last Sunday, looking down at his shabby boots and the tight trousers that came well above his ankles. He was tall and thin, and his face was long and thin too. The fact that he was shy had encouraged her to forget her own shyness in concern for him, and to promise to go out, but that was almost a week ago and so much had happened since then.

Chapter Eight

'Please Dada! Please!' Lucy flung her arms about Tom and pressed her warm cheek against his.

'You know youer Mama doesn't want you to have a hoop.'

'But it's the only present I want and I won't go out of the street with it, I promise.'

'We'll have to see, Lucy,' Tom said, getting up to refill his pipe.

'It isn't youer birthday yet,' Sarah told her coming into the kitchen from the wash-house, 'and at nine years old I'd have hoped you'd want something more ladylike. Put on youer coat Lucy and help Mair get the washing in.'

Sarah disapproved heartily of her having a hoop and when Lucy had shut the back door behind her, she turned to Tom.

'You shouldn't have given in to her like that,' she told him. 'She's enough of a tomboy as it is.'

'I haven't given in Sarah, not yet.'

'You said you'd see, you know she won't let it rest. Iron hoops aren't for little girls, you'll be making her into a hoyden.'

'Ouer Lucy's a bit high spirited, that's all, Sarah and that's not a bad thing either, but she'll never be a

57

hoyden,' Tom said with conviction.

The arguments over Lucy were almost as old as the child herself. Sarah, staring out of the window to where Lucy was helping Mair gather washing from the line felt slightly mollified at the sight of her young daughter standing meekly while Mair filled her arms with clothes.

I'm probably worrying about nothing, Sarah told herself. The other two girls had never been allowed to own a hoop, not that Mair had ever wanted one, but she knew that as a child Gwen had deeply resented the fact.

Tom had wanted a boy so badly by the time Lucy was born, Sarah thought, looking tenderly towards him. Tom would give in to the child over the hoop, she was sure of that, but Lucy would soon tire of it just as she'd tired of everything else.

On the day she was given her new toy Lucy could barely spare time for her meals. She'd played with her present most of her lunch break and when she came home after school Sarah insisted she have something to eat.

'It'll be dark by then, Mama,' she cried in dismay.

'Sit down and have youer tea first,' Sarah insisted. 'It's bitter cold out there.'

With ill grace Lucy took a piece of bread and butter and dipped the spoon into her egg. A few minutes later while Sarah was refilling the kettle at the sink she pushed her half empty plate aside and made for the door.

When Sarah came back to the kitchen she rushed after her but by that time Lucy had joined a group of children at the top of the street.

On a wet blustery Saturday in spring, Gwen, now nearly seventeen, was holding her long-skirted coat down against the wind with one hand and her umbrella already threatening to turn inside out with the other, when she bumped into someone and apologised profusely. A tall young man immediately did the same. His round boyish face was topped by a shock of windblown hair the colour of ripe corn, and she found herself staring up into a pair of blue eyes that were smiling at her warmly.

'I'm sorry, miss,' the young man was saying, not looking sorry at all. Then as she struggled with the umbrella he took it from her, and holding it over her head, drew her towards a shop doorway where there was shelter from the wind and rain. Having straightened her hat, and feeling suddenly overcome with shyness at the situation, Gwen said quickly, 'I – I have to go. I'm late for work already.'

Goodness, she hoped no one had seen her being taken by the arm! Neither Mair nor herself was supposed to talk to strange men and she'd always obeyed her mother's rule, at least until now.

As she took the umbrella from him, he said quickly, 'I'm Charlie – Charlie Roberts,' and held out his hand.

'Gwen Llewellyn,' she told him, lowering her eyes, for what would Mama say about her introducing herself to a strange young man?

An overwhelming desire to stay and talk came over her, bringing a blush to her cheeks. The young man looked so friendly, but she was already late for work.

As Gwen opened her umbrella once more and prepared to leave the shelter of the doorway, he asked quickly, 'Please, when can I see you again?'

'I don't finish work until seven,' she told him. Oh, dear! Her mother wouldn't approve of this conversation at all.

'Where do you work, Gwen?'

'The second-hand shop further down the road.'

If he was surprised he didn't show it. Suddenly realising

that they were standing in the doorway of the other second-hand shop which was still closed for lunch, she looked now with disgust at the chipped ornaments and vases coated with grime, the scuffed chest of drawers with a knob missing, at the clock balanced on its pile of books, the hands permanently at half-past-twelve, and a blush rose to her cheeks once more as she remembered that she'd told him she worked in a second-hand shop. Oh, no. He'd probably think that she worked in one exactly like this.

'Is it because we haven't been properly introduced?'

'Is what because . . .?'

'That you haven't said you'll meet me again.'

Wondering what to say, Gwen looked at her watch anxiously, and following her gaze Charlie said, 'I'll walk along with you if you like.'

But she answered firmly, 'No, please! I must say goodbye now or I shall be late.'

Really, what would Mr Lewis think if the young man walked her to the shop and kept her talking in the doorway? Charlie was looking disappointed as she put up her umbrella and politely said goodbye, realising with a sinking heart when it was too late to turn back that in her rush to get away on her own they'd made no arrangements to meet again.

That afternoon as she worked Gwen couldn't get Charlie's face from her mind. Polishing the tables she saw it reflected there, his eyes smiling at her, the wind-tossed hair curled tightly from the rain. She'd been rude, she told herself, and because of it she'd probably never see Charlie Roberts again. Her heart sank at the thought. But Mama would have been horrified at such a casual meeting, and she knew nothing about him at all except for his name.

Gwen became aware that Ted was watching her with a puzzled look and suddenly realised that she'd been staring down at the table for a very long time.

'Penny for your thoughts, Gwen,' he offered with a smile, and making an effort to smile back, she replied, trying to make her tone flippant, 'They're really not worth that much.'

Try as she would to channel her thoughts in another direction, she'd end up thinking of the young man. Why hadn't she told him right away that she'd like to see him again? And she *did* want to see him, she was in no doubt about that. If only she'd given him a little encouragement instead of rushing off like that. Mama had them really scared about meeting boys they didn't know, but look how her parents had been about Ronald when Mair brought him home and she had known him ever since she started taking a Bible class. Got on their nerves Ronald had, just because he'd been nervous and talked all the time about the church.

'Can't you see that nothing can come of going out with him?' Sarah had asked. 'His family are dependent on him, Mair, he has to put them first.'

She had still gone out with Ronald but hadn't brought him home since.

Remembering what had happened a few weeks ago, Gwen sighed. Her mother had practically forced her to go out with the son of a friend of hers from the next street. Jimmy was a nice boy but she'd resented being forced into going out with him like that and at the end of the evening had told him she wouldn't be seeing him again.

There'd been ructions that night but Sarah had done all the shouting as, mindful of her mother's health, Gwen hadn't even raised her voice, which had made Sarah even more angry, for with no one answering her back she'd become more and more frustrated.

Gwen had come home early and without her escort.

'Where's Jimmy?' Sarah had asked.

'He's gone home, Mam. We won't be seeing each other again.'

'What did you say?' Sarah's voice had been deceptively calm, but Gwen had noticed the way she pressed her lips together disapprovingly.

'I like Jimmy, but there's no point in our going out together,' Gwen told her. 'We're still good friends, Mam. We haven't quarrelled or anything.'

'Oh! And I suppose you decided all this? Do you want to end up an old maid? Is that what you want? All you seem to think about, my girl, is that dusty old shop, and you'll be as old as most of the things Ted Lewis keeps there before you realise it. Only thinking of youer own good, I am. Someone's got to for youer head is just stuffed with nonsense.'

Biting her lip, Gwen had been making for the door when her mother caught her arm.

'Who's going to tell his mam then? Made a proper fool of me, you have. I don't know why I bother.' Sarah's voice had risen to a shriek, and frightened that she might collapse, Gwen had taken her arm and tried to ease her to the sofa. But Sarah had shaken herself free, crying, 'Take after youer father, you do, Gwen Llewellyn, acting high-handed just like he did when he closed down my shop.'

Sarah had never got over the shop being closed, for with it she'd always been able to find a shilling or so for the things she wanted to buy. Now it wasn't just money that was short but tempers too; Sarah's anyway as, her bodily strength often at low ebb, her forceful personality became more and more frustrated at all the things she could no longer do, physically and financially.

'Very absent-minded you are today, Gwen,' Daisy Ball said amiably, handing her a cup of tea and a plate of biscuits. Gwen smiled her thanks, and pulling herself together looked anxiously about the shop, but it was empty except for herself and Ted whom she could see was sitting at his desk in the back room. Sipping her tea she found herself thinking of Charlie again, wishing that they had made arrangements to meet.

It was just before closing time when the bell over the door clanged loudly, and turning despondently from arranging some ornaments, Gwen's eyes widened in delighted surprise as she saw Charlie closing the door. Then Ted Lewis was hurrying towards him, hand outstretched, smiling a welcome.

'Hullo there, Charlie,' he was saying, pumping his hand up and down. 'How's all the family? It's ages since I saw any of you.'

'Been working on my uncle's farm in Pembroke, I have. Back home again now, though. Got a job on a small-holding in Rumney.'

Ted was turning towards her, saying, 'Let me introduce my assistant, Charlie. This is Miss Gwen Llewellyn. Gwen, this is Charlie Roberts. Known his family all my life, I have.'

Gwen smiled happily up at Charlie and he gave her an impish grin. Well, she thought, we have been properly introduced now, even Mama would have to agree about that.

When ten minutes later she left the shop, Charlie left too, insisting on seeing her home. The rain had stopped but the strong wind behind them blew them over the bridge and along Pearl Street and in no time at all they were nearing Wilfred Street. Gwen stopped suddenly at the grocer's shop on the corner, holding on to the windowsill as she was buffeted by the strong wind, with Charlie instantly stepping behind her to shelter her from it.

'I'd rather you didn't come to the door with me, Charlie,' she told him, unsure of the reception her mother would give him.

Looking disappointed, he asked, 'When can I see you again, Gwen?' And when she hesitated he laughed down at her saying, 'We have been properly introduced now, you know.'

'Yes, but . . .'

'It's Sunday tomorrow. I could meet you at the Royal Oak if you like? We could walk along Newport Road to the country.'

'All right, the Royal Oak,' she agreed, happiness masking for a moment any misgivings about what Sarah would say. She'd already decided it was too soon for introductions anyway. Perhaps tomorrow she would take him home.

'Three o'clock be all right? Earlier if you like? I have Sundays off.'

'But what if it rains?' She voiced the thought that had been troubling her, breathing a sigh of relief as she gazed up at the sky and saw that the heavy clouds of earlier in the day had gone.

'It won't rain,' he laughed down at her, 'I've ordered it not to. Seriously, Gwen, bring youer umbrella. If it's wet we could take the tram into town from there.'

'Goodbye, Charlie,' she said, moving away into the street.

'Goodbye, Gwen. See you tomorrow.'

* * *

As Gwen and Charlie left the shop, Ted gazed through the window, watching them being blown along by the high wind. A strange feeling came over him as they went off together. He couldn't believe it was jealousy. Why should he be jealous? He was twenty years Gwen's senior, and over the years she had become the daughter he had never had. He loved her, of course he did, but with the tender love a father feels for his child. It was ridiculous to be feeling like he did; he should be feeling pleased that the young people had met. Charlie was a nice boy. He was obviously going to see Gwen home.

I hope he keeps the right side of Sarah Llewellyn, Ted thought. Look how she's always kept Mair at home. A pretty young woman like that should be out meeting people, enjoying herself. The young one, Lucy, won't be so easy to handle, though. Spoilt she is and always wanting her own way. Gwen doesn't say much, but reading between the lines . . .

Perhaps after all, he thought, a father does feel just like this when a daughter grows up and begins to live her own life. As much as any dad he wanted Gwen to be happy, wanted her to know the kind of love that he'd shared with Mary. Devastated he'd been when Mary died, and it had been young Gwen coming to the shop and taking such an interest in everything that had gradually brought him back to life.

'Youer dinner's ready, Ted,' Mrs Ball was calling from the landing, and as he climbed the stairs he was telling himself that he must be prepared for the time that would surely come when Gwen would get married and leave his shop for good.

As Gwen turned to face the street her heart gave a little

lurch as she saw that Doctor Powell's gig was standing in the road outside their house. Lifting her skirts she began to run, worry over Sarah uppermost in her mind. But Mama has been much better lately, she told herself. Perhaps Lucy's chill had got worse? Poor little Lucy had been coughing for days. Why only Wednesday Gwen had been sent to buy some 'Doctor Brown's Cough Mixture', but despite dosing Lucy with this excellent remedy, and her chest being covered with goose grease and a piece of red flannel, the distressing cough had persisted.

Lucy had still been in bed when Gwen had left for work this morning. Oh, she wished now that she'd called home after lunch at the shop instead of going to Clifton Street to buy thread for Mama.

When, out of breath, she reached the front door, it was slightly open. As she hurried down the passage and stepped into the kitchen her mother turned from gazing into the fire, her face pale and strained.

'Lucy's got a fever, Gwen,' she told her, her voice heavy with anxiety. 'I thought she was getting better but her temperature just shot up this afternoon. Mair's up there now with Doctor Powell. Have youer meal, Gwen, then take over from her for a while. The poor girl must be feeling worn out.'

'I'm not hungry, Mam. I had a cup of tea just before I left the shop and Mrs Ball always brings me a piece of cake. I'll take my coat off and wash my hands, then I'll go up.'

Upstairs Lucy lay with her eyes closed, fair hair spread over the pillow, cheeks two bright spots of colour. As Gwen entered the room Doctor Powell was snapping his bag shut. Then turning to the two girls he said, 'I'll be round first thing in the morning, but send for me before if the medicine doesn't begin to bring that temperature down.' Speaking to Gwen, he added, 'If you could come with me in the gig, Gwen, I'll make up a bottle at the surgery. She should start on the medicine as soon as possible.'

She nodded, and whispering to Mair that she would take over as soon as she got back, followed Doctor Powell downstairs. As she settled herself in the gig and he took the reins, he said, 'I'll give you some iron medicine for Mair while I'm about it. Anaemic she is. That girl doesn't get enough rest or fresh air.'

Gwen was surprised at his statement. Mair never complained and seemed to like working at home, endlessly cooking, washing, beating mats or scrubbing floors. Mama was able to do a bit more now. She made the bread and helped with the meals. She'd never relinquished her hold on things, ordering all the groceries and seeing to the housekeeping money, but still Mair must be doing too much for her strength.

While Doctor Powell made up the bottles of medicine Gwen sat on one of the scuffed chairs in the waiting room, feeling a little guilty because at that moment she'd found she wasn't thinking about Lucy at all but wondering how, without looking uncaring, she could get out of the house tomorrow afternoon to meet Charlie Roberts.

She must see him, if only for a few minutes to tell him of the crisis at home. The realisation that if she didn't turn up he'd think she didn't want to see him again filled her with despair. As she took the medicine from Doctor Powell and thanked him for the ride she prayed the elixir would quickly make Lucy better so that she could leave the house tomorrow with a clear conscience.

'Be careful crossing the main road, Gwen,' Doctor

Powell advised as he let her out by the side door, and looking up into his bluff, kindly face she felt a deep gratitude for all the care this doctor, who had brought her and her sisters into the world, had lavished on her family.

On the way home, her mind was filled with thoughts of Charlie again. She'd never felt this way about anyone before and yet she hardly knew him. She should be worrying about Lucy or Mair, not thinking about someone she hadn't even met until yesterday.

When the doctor came early the following morning, he was pleased that Lucy's temperature had begun to fall but warned that she must still be watched.

'If you're at all worried send for me,' he told Mair. 'Otherwise I'll be here tomorrow morning.'

When Gwen went downstairs to peel the potatoes for the midday meal, her mother said, 'I want you to take over from Mair this afternoon, Gwen, so that she can have a break. She can go round to Fanny's with those spools of thread you brought me.'

Gwen wanted to cry: 'Oh, no! Don't send Mair, I'll go for you.' For how was she to meet Charlie if she was confined to the house?

She made a pot of tea and took a cup upstairs to Mair, unable to find a solution to her dilemma. As she handed the cup to her sister, her hand shook, spilling tea into the saucer. Mair took the cup from her and placed it safely on the wash-stand. Then gently pulling Gwen down to sit beside her on the bed, she put an arm about her shoulders and whispered: 'What is it, Gwen? What's wrong?'

A tear escaped her tightly closed lids and rolled slowly down her cheek.

'Come on, love, it's plain something's upset you.'

'Oh, Mair!' The words came in a rush now. 'I was to

have met someone this afternoon at three o'clock. I know it's selfish, but I want to meet him so much.'

'Him, Gwen! Does Mama know?'

'No, but we have been introduced and I was going to bring him home when I knew him better.'

'Well, what's stopping you?'

'She wants me to take over here. You're to go to Aunt Fanny's for a break.'

'You go instead, I don't mind. You haven't seen Aunt Fanny for ages, Gwen. You're always at work when she calls round.'

At Mair's offer Gwen felt like dancing her around the room, but glancing at the invalid she remembered her mother's words and knew she'd never get away with it.

'Thanks for offering, Mair,' she said, shaking her head. Then anger welled up in her and she cried, forgetful of the invalid. 'No one else's mother makes such stupid rules. She's positively Victorian. Treats us like children. Anyway, you can't ask a boy to come and meet your mother the very first time he asks you out.'

Mair squeezed her shoulder sympathetically once more, saying, 'We'll both go out, Gwen, take it in turns. Mama always sleeps on the sofa in the parlour as soon as the dishes are washed. You can go out first if you like, providing you're not too long.'

But that afternoon just as Gwen was about to check if her mother was indeed lying down in the parlour, she heard Sarah's slow footsteps on the stairs. On tenterhooks she watched her mother come into the room and settle herself in the chair by the bed, putting her hand lightly on Lucy's forehead before turning to Mair and saying, 'You can go now, cariad. The spool of thread is on the kitchen table. Tell Fan there's no hurry for the blouse.'

Gwen followed her sister downstairs, whispering urgently as soon as they were out of earshot. 'Will you take a message to the Royal Oak for me, Mair?'

Horrified at the suggestion, she shook her head. 'Oh, I couldn't, Gwen. I just couldn't. He's a stranger. I might go up to the wrong young man.'

Seeing the disappointment in Gwen's eyes, Mair said quickly, 'I won't be long, I promise. Mama will go down to rest in the parlour quite soon. She always sleeps on Sunday afternoons.'

With a sinking heart, Gwen watched her go. But for Lucy's illness Mair would have been taking her Bible class at this hour of the afternoon.

As she opened the bedroom door and went back into the room, her mother said, 'Lucy's awake now, Gwen. Go downstairs and get the beef tea and a little jelly for her. We must get her to eat something.'

Downstairs she prepared the tray then went out to the safe on the wall in the yard for the jelly. Her father was talking to Mr Palmer who was in his own garden, resting his arms on top of the dividing wall.

'Hello, Gwen,' Eddie Palmer called in his usual friendly way, and when she'd greeted him and turned to go in the men went back to their conversation, which as usual was about politics.

'It's Lloyd George you've got to thank for bringing in the pension for the old,' their neighbour was saying.

'And not before time,' Tom replied. 'A crying shame it is, when a man has worked since he was a nipper, to have to depend on the charity of sons and daughters when he gets too old to work.' He had been a staunch Liberal himself until the formation of the new Labour Party.

Gwen closed the wash-house door and, her heart still

heavy with disappointment, took the tray upstairs. Mair had promised not to be long. As Gwen encouraged Lucy to eat she glanced across at her mother several times, hopeful for some sign that she was about to go downstairs, but Sarah was settling herself more comfortably against the cushions and a few moments later had closed her eyes.

When Lucy had finished the jelly and she'd put the tray aside, Gwen glanced anxiously up at the clock. It was almost ten past three. Charlie wouldn't yet have given up hope. She pictured him standing on the island where the tram stopped, watching out for her. As time went by he would realise she wasn't coming. Even if Mair came back right now she wouldn't be able to go, not with Mama dozing in the bedside chair.

A few minutes later, just as she heard the front door open and Mair running lightly up the stairs, her mother opened her eyes.

'I'm feeling quite dry, Gwen,' she told her. 'How about getting us a cup of tea? Bring the biscuits up, will you?'

Mair had come into the room, shooting Gwen a look of commiseration at finding her mother still there.

'Youer back soon,' Sarah said in surprise.

'Looks like rain,' Mair told her, 'I thought I'd get back before it started.'

Gwen went downstairs once more and was just putting the already hot kettle over the coals to boil when her father came in from the garden, saying, 'Starting to rain it is, Gwen. Big spots. It looks full of it.'

As he finished speaking there was a distant roll of thunder. Oh, she hoped Charlie would be home by now. Then she realised that she didn't even know where home was. Perhaps he lived in Rumney for that was where he worked. If it was all that way he'd be soaked going home, but the rain hadn't seemed to worry him yesterday, had it? What would he think of her for not turning up? Perhaps he'd think she didn't want to see him again. She'd just have to find a chance to explain for he wasn't likely to risk another snub, was he?

When she took the tray upstairs Mair had gone to their room to take off her hat and coat. Gwen poured the tea and handed her mother a cup, staring at her resentfully as Sarah broke a biscuit and took a sip from her cup. Didn't she realise that Gwen and Mair were grown women?

She treats us just like children, Gwen thought indignantly, knowing the hold their mother still had over them had come about because of her poor health. They'd never dared to thwart her because of the possible consequences. She knew her mother loved them, loved all her family dearly, but to her Mair and Gwen were still children she must guide and keep a watchful eye on. It seemed unlikely now that they'd ever be able to untie the apron strings.

Chapter Nine

'That girl is broodin' over something,' Mrs Ball remarked in her usual familiar way as on the following Tuesday she was dishing up Ted's evening meal.

He sighed, having already noticed the way Gwen watched the door every time the bell clanged. He'd thought at first that she was worrying about Lucy, but when he'd suggested that she took a few days off to be with her sister she'd seemed horrified at the idea, assuring him that Lucy was on the mend.

'I'm goin' to make 'er favourite steak and kidney tomorrow,' Mrs Ball told him now. 'Loves steak and kidney, Gwen does.'

But when Wednesday lunch-time came and they sat down to their meal Ted couldn't help noticing the way Gwen pushed the food around on her plate, her mind obviously elsewhere. She'd seemed happy enough when she'd left the shop with young Charlie Roberts on Saturday, he recalled, but nothing could have come of their meeting for she'd told him that she'd sat with Lucy most of Sunday to give Mair a break.

'Tired out, I wouldn't wonder,' Daisy Ball was saying as she scraped the food from Gwen's plate. 'Workin' 'ere all day then goin' 'ome to look after that spoilt young sister.'

'Lucy's not that bad, Daisy,' he told her. 'A bit head-strong perhaps, but she's a nice kiddie underneath.'

He knew it wasn't Lucy she was worrying about. If he didn't know differently he'd have thought Gwen was in love. But no again, for if she was in love she would be happy, wouldn't she? A bit absent-minded, perhaps, but happy with it.

Tomorrow he was going to an auction sale at a house out Marshfield way, and as was usual on these occasions Gwen was to look after the shop. For a long time now he'd had the feeling that she would dearly love to accompany him. She always wanted him to tell her every detail of what went on. Not many women attended these sales, a few of the dealers' wives perhaps, but Gwen would be with him, wouldn't she? There'd be plenty of room in the trap for her and any small things he might buy. The bigger items he always had delivered anyway.

After her lunch Gwen had gone to Clifton Street to get some silks for Mair's embroidery. When she came back, and before he opened the shop, Ted asked, 'How would you like to come to that auction with me tomorrow afternoon?'

'Oh, Ted, I'd love that, you know I would, but how about the shop?'

'We'll close it. I'll put a notice in the window right away. I always had to close it when I was on my own.'

'But that was nearly five years ago.'

'Well, they'll just have to get used to the idea again, won't they?' He'd made it sound as though it was going to be a regular thing. And why not? he asked himself, especially if she enjoyed herself. Already he was looking forward to having her company.

* * *

Sarah was feeling worried about Gwen as well. Something had happened to upset her, she was sure of it. The girl was acting strangely and Sarah couldn't put her finger on the reason. It couldn't be love; Gwen hadn't mentioned anything about a young man, or about bringing one home. She knew she'd have reason to worry if either Mair or Gwen became serious about a man for she hadn't told the girls anything at all. She hadn't been able to bring herself to mention the facts of life. Time enough, she'd tried to convince herself, when they were courting.

She'd been completely ignorant herself when she'd married Tom. Oh, she'd known a woman's belly swelled when she was expecting a child but she'd had no idea how the baby got there. That first night, when she'd shyly followed Tom to their bedroom in his mother's house, she'd undressed with her back to him, leaving her chemise and drawers on beneath her nightgown. She'd gone into his arms all unsuspecting, and when he'd begun to fumble with her clothes and she'd felt a sharp pain as he'd pressed her to him she'd let out a scream that had echoed throughout the house. In answer to his family's worried knocking, quick-witted Tom had opened the door a crack – she could see him now, his long flannel nightshirt flapping about his calves – telling them that she'd been frightened by a spider on the wall behind the bed. She'd heard his mother laughing, then they'd gone downstairs, leaving her to bury her scarlet face in the pillow while Tom tried to comfort her.

Their marriage hadn't been consummated until nearly a week later. Tom had been so loving and patient with her, telling her that if God had chosen this method for having babies then it must be all right.

She'd loved Tom dearly and she'd got used to it, though she'd never enjoyed what happened in the bedroom. Ten months later when Mair was born she'd considered herself the happiest girl in the world, especially when they'd managed to get the tenancy of the house in Wilfred Street. And later, with the help of the profit from the shop that she'd opened when Mair was two years old, she'd made it into a very comfortable home.

She sighed. If they were good girls they wouldn't let a man take any liberties anyway, and she was sure that both Mair and Gwen were that.

The letter for Gwen was delivered to the shop by the first post on Thursday morning. Her eyes lit up when Ted handed it to her. Reading it through quickly she called to him that it was from his friend Charlie Roberts, explaining to Ted when he came back to where she stood by the window that, 'He didn't know my address so he sent it here.'

Well, Ted thought, whatever Charlie has written has made Gwen very happy, that's obvious. How come he didn't know her address when he'd seen her home last Saturday? Anyway, the letter had certainly cheered her up, that was the important thing. He'd go now and write that notice to fix on the door.

As soon as Ted had gone into the back room Gwen whipped the letter from her pocket and read it through again.

Dear Miss Llewellyn,
Perhaps I shouldn't write to you for you may not have wanted to meet me on Sunday afternoon after all, but just in case there was some reason for you not being there, I felt I must get in touch with you again. I waited for you until about half-past three by which

76

time it was raining, then I sheltered in a doorway in Broadway where I would have seen you if you'd passed by. If you don't reply to this letter I will understand, but I do hope you will.

My job at the farm means I can only get away weekends when I could meet you again if you wish. I hope you don't mind me writing to the shop but I didn't know your address.

Truly yours,
Charlie

Oh, it was going to be a wonderful day, Gwen thought. First receiving the letter, and this afternoon the auction sale she was so looking forward to and which she'd enjoy all the more now that she'd heard from Charlie. She wished she had the time to write to him before she went, but anyway the auction would be something to tell him about in her letter.

She glanced at the address again: 2 Honeyridge Cottages, Rumney. What a lovely name. Gwen smiled at her thoughts, knowing that the way she felt she was prepared to find everything about Charlie wonderful.

That afternoon, as Bessie the pony clip-clopped along the country lanes, Gwen took deep breaths of the warm spring air. It was a sunny day and she was wearing her navy blue costume for the first time this year, together with the little straw hat she'd bought at a milliner's in town. It dipped becomingly over her forehead, and a posy of forget-me-nots nestled where the crown met the brim. When she'd stepped into the shop this morning she'd seen Ted's look of admiration and been surprised for she'd never thought he noticed what she wore. The long skirt had three rows of braid around its hem, and the fitted jacket was edged with the same. As soon as she'd known she was to accompany Ted to the sale she'd made up her mind to wear the costume provided it wasn't raining, for she didn't want to let him down.

The house, a fair-sized Victorian villa, was set in its own grounds and reached by a short lane bordered with high hedges. In the cobbled yard to the side of the house several flat carts were already drawn up together with a number of traps and gigs, and a man and some boys were looking after the horses and ponies.

As they entered the house Gwen noticed that it seemed to be full of people milling around, inspecting the things on display and consulting their catalogues. As she followed Ted into the largest downstairs room her eyes were bright with interest. She'd always dreamt about one day attending a sale like this, wandering through the rooms before the auction began, hoping to discover some treasure she would buy for a song. But she knew this would be very unlikely to happen, she wouldn't be bidding anyway, and even if she were the many dealers present would be a knowledgeable lot.

She found herself now in a long room, down the centre of which stood a massive dark oak table laden with china of every description. Ted had crossed the room to speak to someone he knew, and so, after watching people taking pieces from the table to examine them carefully, Gwen went over to do the same. The first thing she picked up was a Minton plate with pierced border, the centre of which was decorated with a view of the 1851 exhibition.

There were several large dinner services, one of which she was pretty certain was Bloor Derby, the china opaque and gaudily decorated in the Imari style. She couldn't wait to check the mark.

'I'm going into the next room to look at some furniture,' Ted called across. 'Would you prefer to stay here, Gwen?'

She nodded, eager to go back to the things on the table. When Ted had gone she remembered him telling her that he'd been asked to look out for suitable furniture for a four-bedroomed house a client had bought.

She moved a little way along the table and picked up a cup belonging to a Coalport service which was beautifully decorated against a background of rich maroon. Next to this was a set of three Mason's octagonal jugs with snake handles. But the auctioneer and his assistant were coming into the room, followed by a middle-aged lady who went over to a table cluttered with what seemed to be account books, an inkstand and some pens. Now the auctioneer climbed on to a chair while his assistant stood by, ready to lift any item that couldn't easily be seen.

She now found herself at the end of the table where ornaments, vases, and figurines were set in little groups identified by lot numbers. Suddenly Gwen could hardly believe her eyes, for amongst them was an exact replica of the figure of a lady that Ted had given her on her very first day at the shop. Although Dada had stuck the head on with fish-glue after Lucy accidentally broke it off, it had lolled to one side ever since. Oh, if only she could find the courage to bid on it.

The contents of the room were rapidly being auctioned. Gwen looked around anxiously for Ted who had already bid successfully on a number of items and was nowhere in sight. Soon they would come to Lot 204; she had noted the number when she'd picked up the figurine. If only Ted was by her side to advise her. As they began on the table, she licked dry lips.

At last the auctioneer was calling out 'Lot 204. Do I hear four and six?'

Gwen swallowed hard, waiting for someone to start the bidding.

'Half-a-crown,' someone offered, and Gwen remembered Ted saying that it wasn't a valuable ornament just one of many produced on the Continent, but nicely made all the same.

Someone had just bid three shillings and she couldn't afford much more than that herself.

'Three and six,' Gwen called, her voice shaking.

'Four shillings,' came almost at once.

'Four and six,' she cried desperately, knowing this must be her last bid.

'Going! Going! Gone! to the lady in the navy blue hat. Name please? Is there anything else down to you?'

Giving her name Gwen was sure that all eyes were upon her but it was worth it. She felt a warm glow of satisfaction at her success.

'You did well,' Ted told her when at last they met up. 'It's practically over now, Gwen, shall we pick up your lot number and settle up at the table?'

She'd picked up the little figurine but Ted was saying 'It's coupled with this Gwen, didn't you know? You bid on the lot number and these candlesticks are included.'

Gwen's cheeks were pink with pleasure as she took one of the pair of candlesticks into her hand crying, 'Oh Ted! they're lovely.'

They were made of china in pale blue and white and the prettiest cherubs clung to their stems. She would give one to Mama and one to Mair and buy Lucy a pretty hair ribbon as there wasn't one for her.

By the time they'd reached the kitchen the crowd had

thinned out and seemed now to consist mostly of people anxious to buy copper moulds or sets of saucepans and other kitchen equipment for use in their own homes. Gwen was hot and tired but had enjoyed the afternoon and the banter that went on endlessly between the auctioneer and his regular clients. But one thing she'd decided. Next time, if there was a next time, she would wear something cooler and more comfortable!

The auction over, they couldn't leave right away for Ted had to make arrangements for the delivery of the furniture that he'd bought. But at last they were outside, breathing the fresh country air, and soon Gwen was climbing into the trap that was already laden with boxes, promising her a busy but interesting day tomorrow.

Obviously pleased with what he'd bought, Ted was in good spirits, and as Bessie clip-clopped along the country lanes between high hedges, Gwen was grateful for the dappled shade. All too soon Ted was calling 'Whoah!' and pulling in the reins. Bessie waited patiently while Gwen stepped down from the trap. Having thanked Ted once again for taking her, she said, 'See you in the morning,' and with a little wave straightened her hat and turned to walk down the street.

Ted watched until she reached the house, a tender look in his eyes. He loved her, he had no doubt about that now, but he knew he must keep his feelings to himself or he would spoil the easy companionship they shared. Why, only this morning he'd seen how she'd reacted to the letter that Charlie had sent. The young man seemed so right for her in every way, and short though their acquaintanceship was, it was obvious Gwen was in love with him.

Ted sighed. He was twenty years her senior. Youth attracted youth and it was right that it should be so. He picked up the reins and urged Bessie into a trot, glad at least that his secret need never be known.

Chapter Ten

It was Saturday night and through the party wall the sound of harsh persistent coughing was keeping the girls awake.

'Mabel ought to see the doctor,' Mair said with a sigh, pulling the bedclothes tightly about her ears. Gwen yawned widely and did likewise as the coughing went on.

'Saw her pegging the clothes out yesterday, I did,' Mair remarked, wide awake now. 'Steam was billowing from their wash-house. She should never have been outdoors.'

'Pity their Iris is in service,' Gwen mumbled sleepily. 'She only gets home once a fortnight, doesn't she?'

The next morning when he came in from the garden Tom looked serious.

'Been talking to Eddie . . .' he began, when Mair broke in, 'How is she, Dada? How's Mabel?'

'Pretty ribby, he reckons. Says she can't afford to lose any weight and that cough is really pulling her down.'

Sarah had just come into the kitchen from the wash-house and Gwen watched her mother's face, knowing that she was wrestling with her conscience. Sarah bit at her bottom lip for a moment then went over to the cupboard at the side of the range and took out the shopping basket. Then she opened the pantry door and they could hear her moving things around. All eyes were focused on her as she stepped back into the kitchen with the half-full basket then went back to fetch an apple pie and a sponge cake from both of which she cut a generous slice, putting them side by side on a plate which she covered with a snowy white tea-towel.

Looking defiantly at her family, she said, 'Well, Mabel and me were good friends for years until all that silly fuss about the shop.'

Taking her shawl from the peg behind the kitchen door, she lifted the basket and went down the passage to the front door.

Tom looked at his daughters, a grin spreading slowly over his thin face.

'Some good's come of it anyway,' he said with satisfaction. 'It's about time they made it up.'

When nearly an hour later Sarah came back with an empty basket and an arm full of washing, she handed the latter to Mair.

'Mama's got a nerve, giving you that washing to do,' Gwen whispered, following her into the wash-house.

'Shh!' Mair put a warning finger to her lips. 'I don't mind, really I don't, Gwen. A bit of washing's a small price to pay for having them friends again.'

Later, when Doctor Powell was expected, Sarah tied a clean starched apron about her waist and went next door again, taking dinner for Eddie. As she closed the door behind her, Tom muttered happily that it was 'just like old times.'

The meal over, and with Sarah's dinner still in the oven as she hadn't yet returned from next door, Gwen and Mair got on with the washing-up, for Charlie would be here very soon.

She'd told Mama about Charlie with some trepidation.

'Why haven't you brought him home, Gwen? You know I'd want to meet him,' Sarah had grumbled. 'You oughtn't to make arrangements with strangers like that.'

'But I told you Ted introduced us, Mama. Charlie's a friend of the family.'

'It's such a lovely day,' Mair was saying, looking out of the tiny window at her father working in the garden. 'What frock will you wear, Gwen?'

'My voile with the cornflowers on it, I think. It's the coolest one I've got.'

While Sarah was eating a belated dinner, and Mair despite the fact that it was Sunday was hanging Mabel Palmer's washing on the line, Gwen carried a jug of hot water upstairs and started to get ready. The room was scented from the lavender soap in the dish on the wash-stand. She put on her clean chemise and petticoats, and had opened the door of the big oak wardrobe to take out her frock when she gave a cry of dismay as she noticed the frilly hem of the dress was torn away and hanging loosely to the floor.

'Lucy!' she screamed, forgetting for a moment in her anger that she'd vowed never to upset Mama if she could help it, in case it brought on one of her attacks.

As she put on her old dressing gown and charged downstairs, the ruined dress in her arms, tears of disappointment threatened to fall. Rushing towards her, Mair gave one look at the garment then at Gwen's stricken face and cried: 'Oh, Lord!'

'You knew about it?' Gwen cried incredulously.

'I didn't know she'd ripped it. I caught Lucy trying it on, Gwen. She must have pulled it off too quickly when I shouted at her to put it back.'

Mair remembered opening the bedroom door to see a

flushed Lucy parading in front of the mirror in the wardrobe door.

'Don't tell Gwen, please, Mair,' Lucy had begged, stumbling over to her and clutching her skirts.

The sleeves of Gwen's dress had completely covered Lucy's hands and her feet were hidden by the frilly hem.

'You be careful getting that off,' she'd warned.

'I wish I could have a dress like this,' Lucy had said wistfully, standing before the mirror again.

'You've got your white muslin,' Mair had told her, then her voice rose when Lucy showed no sign of removing the garment. 'Take that off, Lucy and put it away carefully. Now!'

As Gwen continued to stare miserably at the dress, Mair begged, 'Don't upset Mama, please, Gwen. She's so happy at being friends again with Mabel. She didn't hear you shout because she's in the garden talking to Eddie Palmer over the wall. Anyway, Aunt Fanny will probably mend it so's it won't even notice.'

'Well, Lucy's not going to get away with it,' Gwen warned darkly. Come to think of it, Lucy had been eyeing her warily for the last few days. Ten years old she may be but she'd like to put Lucy over her knee at this very moment and spank her hard! Sober reflection told her that she must bide her time for no good would come of having a row with her now, with Charlie expected so soon. And she mustn't upset Mama, especially not today.

Gwen hurried back to the bedroom and put on her cream dress with the two rows of coffee-coloured braid around the hem. The neck was high and trimmed with lace about her throat, and the sleeves were tighter than the voile. It was a warm spring day. 'Drat Lucy!' she said to her reflection, then hearing a knock on the front door, hurried downstairs to open it.

Charlie stood there smiling at her, and she smiled back at him warmly then took him to the kitchen where she introduced the family one by one.

'Gwen tells me that you know Ted Lewis very well, Mr Roberts,' Sarah began.

'Call me Charlie, please! Yes, Mam lived next door to his family before she was married.'

Sarah was about to ask his mother's maiden name when Tom said, 'Youer work is market gardening then, Charlie?'

'I work at a farm in Rumney. Are you interested in gardening, Mr Llewellyn?'

Tom put a lighted spill to his pipeful of shag, closing one eye against the sparks, taking a long pull at it before nodding, 'Come and see my vegetables, the peas are doing very well.' And they both went outside.

Sarah knew that next to politics, gardening was Tom's favourite subject and she sighed with disappointment knowing she'd have no chance of questioning the young man further. She could offer him tea when they came in from the garden of course, but Gwen was already tapping her foot impatiently, anxious to be off. As soon as they stepped into the kitchen she said, 'It's time we were going, Charlie, or we'll miss the tram.'

She smiled tenderly at Mair as they said goodbye. She would soon be leaving for her Bible class and last night had told Gwen in confidence that she was seeing Ronald again, going for walks every Sunday after class.

'Why don't you bring him home then?' she'd asked, but Mair had replied that it was obvious that Dada didn't like Ronald very much.

'Do you love him, Mair?' was Gwen's next question, love being the thing uppermost in her mind, but her sister had said quietly, 'No, I don't think so. I like him and he says he loves me, and I like walking out with him.'

Gwen felt sorry for her, thinking, She's wasted on that Ronald. If only Mair could find someone like Charlie . . . At that moment her thoughts were brought rudely back to the present for Lucy, who'd been dancing along the passage by Charlie's side, was begging him to take her with them.

Gwen opened her mouth to say, 'Not this time, Lucy,' but before she could utter the words her mother was saying, 'If Mr Roberts doesn't mind, it would do the child the world of good to get out in the fresh air.'

What could Charlie say but that he didn't mind? But Gwen noticed that the smile left his face.

She was absolutely furious. Was this Mama's way of making sure that she wouldn't be alone with a young man? It was Lucy herself who'd asked, but Mama had soon cottoned on, hadn't she? And now, as they walked along the street, Lucy was looking up at Charlie, her blue eyes pleading, asking him, 'Can we go to the country, Charlie?'

'No, we can't,' Gwen said crossly although the country was where she'd wanted to go herself. 'And it's "Mr Roberts" to you, Lucy.'

They reached the end of the street and stood irresolutely on the corner.

'Where shall we go then?' Charlie asked, and looking at his face Gwen thought miserably that this was the worst possible start to their friendship.

'We could take a tram to town if you like,' she suggested. 'There's a band plays on Sunday in Cathays Park.'

Lucy looked mutinous because she hadn't had her own way, and Gwen couldn't think of anything to say. They hadn't long to wait for the tram and the breeze was pleasant as they sat on the open-top deck. Glaring at her sister, Gwen vowed to make sure that Lucy stayed home next time.

There were crowds enjoying the sunshine, listening to the band. Looking around her, Gwen saw only a sea of parasols and straw boaters. Her feet tapping to the music, she was feeling better despite herself, but knew that she'd have to watch every word she said for Lucy would probably repeat anything she thought interesting enough. It was really offputting the way she hung on Charlie's arm and stared up at him, it seemed to Gwen, adoringly.

Presently they wandered into the town and along Queen Street, but with all the shops closed Gwen knew that it would have been much better to have gone along the Newport Road to the country. But she hadn't wanted to give in to Lucy's whims, had she?

Now, as they walked slowly along the hot pavements, with Lucy visibly sulking, she thought longingly of the shady country lanes and the springy turf of the fields beneath their feet. And Charlie knew so much about the country, didn't he? He would have told them the names of the wild plants they didn't know, and the names of the birds and the trees, and if Lucy hadn't been with them they would probably have held hands. Tears of disappointment and frustration stung her eyes but Gwen blinked them back determinedly.

When Lucy asked sulkily, 'When can we go home?' Charlie looked at his pocket watch, saying, 'It's just gone half-past four.'

'Now, if you like,' she answered Lucy, for what was the use of prolonging the agony?

As they were boarding the tram Lucy wanted to climb the stairs to the upper deck but Gwen, giving vent to her feelings, dragged her inside, sitting her down opposite

Charlie and herself where her sister glowered out of the window in silence.

As they neared Clifton Street, Charlie asked, 'When can I see you again, Gwen? Will the same time next Sunday be all right?'

'Yes, that will be lovely, but shall I meet you at the Royal Oak?' she suggested. That way she could be sure of Lucy not being foisted on them.

When they got up to leave the tram, Charlie rose too but Gwen told him firmly, 'You go on to your stop. It will be less of a walk for you to get home.'

Looking a bit crestfallen, he sat down again and Gwen wished that she'd let him walk them home but now it was too late. As the tram moved off they waved until it was out of sight, then as they started for home Lucy said petulantly, 'I wish I hadn't come. Thought we were going somewhere nice, I did.'

'We did go somewhere nice,' Gwen said without conviction. 'Anyway, I've got a bone to pick with you, miss.'

Lucy looked scared, all bravado gone. Lifting her skirts, she ran the rest of the way home.

Gwen knew as soon as she entered the kitchen that Mama had expected Charlie to see her home for the table had been laid with the best china and an extra place had been set. How was she to explain why he hadn't come back?

Before Gwen and Charlie could meet again, Britain and the world were stunned and shocked by the sudden death of the king. King Edward had returned late in April from a visit to Biarritz feeling unwell. Soon it became known that he was suffering from bronchitis, and on May 6th he suffered a series of heart attacks and shortly before midnight passed away.

Early the following day the paper boys were running the streets and the *Echo* carried the sombre headlines in large black print: **DEATH OF HIS MAJESTY.** DRAMATIC DEMISE OF OUR BELOVED AND REVERED SOVEREIGN. THE WHOLE WORLD MOURNS WORLD'S PEACEMAKER.

Sarah insisted that the girls dress the front-room window in mourning right away. When Gwen pointed out that it would be a sufficient show of respect simply to pull down the blind she didn't agree, and sent Lucy to buy black crêpe paper which Mair was instructed to drape as a background for the large portrait of the king they had last displayed at his coronation.

Chapter Eleven

The next day, Gwen left the house to go and meet Charlie, with strict instructions to bring him home, Sarah having made it clear that she approved of him. To her relief, Lucy didn't even ask to accompany her. They walked along the Newport Road and soon found themselves in shady Ball Lane where Charlie took Gwen's hand in his, pointing out and naming the wild flowers that grew in the hedges as they listened to birdsong from the trees and bushes. She hadn't know that she was capable of feeling so happy. The touch of Charlie's fingers clasping hers was sheer bliss. How could she have been so miserable last Sunday just because Lucy was there? Charlie looks happy, too, she thought. Every time she looked up at him he beamed at her, and presently he took his hand from hers to put an arm around her waist. They talked about the king dying and what it would mean to the country, and of Prince George who would now be crowned.

'Do you realise that we'll have lived in three reigns at least, Charlie?' Gwen asked, amazed herself at the thought.

'Queen Victoria's, King Edward's and now King George's,' he agreed. 'And who knows how many more?'

When at last they returned home the table was laid and a delicious meal of boiled ham, fresh lettuce from the garden, tomatoes and gibbons was waiting. There was a cut-glass bowl of fruit, a jug of cream, and one of Sarah's special sponges sandwiched together with raspberry jam. The tea flowed, and conversation too, and when the meal was over Tom took Charlie out to admire the vegetable patch, and the already colourful flower borders. While they were out there Eddie Palmer came to the wall and, the washing-up finished, Gwen went out to join them for all too soon Charlie would be leaving for home and a whole week would have to pass before she would see him again.

When he had gone Sarah went to the middle room to rest on the sofa, for what with her visits to the invalid next door, and having Charlie to tea, and then going back to see that Mabel was settled, she was feeling worn out. Before she went she told Gwen, 'I like youer Charlie, he's a very nice boy. And youer father has taken to him, I can tell.'

When later the two girls went up to their room, Gwen asked: 'Did you go out with Ronald, Mair?'

'Yes, we went for a walk but he couldn't stay long because his mother is a bit of an invalid. He's the sole supporter of the family, Gwen. His father died when he was a young child.

'I wish I could have brought him home like you brought Charlie,' she ended wistfully.

'Well, you could have, Mair, if Mama had known you were seeing him again.'

'No, I couldn't, Gwen. Dada didn't take to him at all. I don't think he could ever leave his mam anyway. He said tonight that if he married his wife would have to live with his mother and look after her.'

Gwen gave her sister a pitying look. Poor Mair, she thought, what a prospect! As far as responsibilities were concerned she'd just be stepping out of the frying pan into the fire.

Chapter Twelve

On the day Gwen went with Charlie to meet his parents the sun shone from a cloudless sky. She had prayed fervently all week that the day would be warm and sunny so that she could wear the voile dress that Lucy had ripped and Aunt Fan had repaired so beautifully you would never know where the rent had been.

Now, as she walked proudly on Charlie's arm along the Newport Road, up the hill and down towards the village, she was feeling a little nervous at the thought of meeting his family. But listening to the birdsong from every tree and hedge, and taking deep breaths of the fresh country air, she began to relax.

Soon they were nearing the cottage, and following Charlie up the narrow path between the flower beds she recognised many old favourites from the garden at home.

As he knocked on the door Charlie gave her an encouraging little smile. His mam must have been waiting for them as almost immediately the door flew open and a plump rosy-cheeked little woman beamed at Gwen. Her silver-grey hair was drawn back neatly into a bun, and her blue eyes were the image of Charlie's. She welcomed Gwen warmly, drawing her into the passage and along it towards a large flag-stoned kitchen that smelt deliciously

97

of spicy fruit cakes that were cooling on the scrubbed wooden table.

'Warm it is in this kitchen, Gwen,' his mother remarked as she bustled between the glowing range and the table, one end of which was draped with an embroidered cloth set with dainty china tea things. Pouring the tea and putting an assortment of cakes before them, she went on, 'It'll soon cool down now that I've finished the cooking. Why don't you and Charlie sit in the garden until teatime? There's a nice breeze coming from the Bristol Channel. We're not very far from the water here, you know.'

As they chatted Gwen looked about her. Blue gingham curtains stirred in the breeze from the open window where a set of three ruby glass vases stood on the deep ledge, the sunlight shining through them sending rosy fingers of light across the table-cloth. On the high mantelshelf brass ornaments twinkled: a pair of prancing horses, boots, spill vases, and tall twisted candlesticks either side of a black marble clock, nudging each other with barely an inch to spare.

The flag-stones, scrubbed white, were partly covered by two enormous rag mats, the predominant colour being dark red, one in front of the fireguard and the other between the table and a long open-ended green leather sofa.

Mrs Roberts wouldn't hear of Gwen washing up the cups, insisting on them going into the garden where a narrow path divided flowers from vegetables. There was a patch of shade by the fruit bushes, and when Charlie had brought out two wooden armchairs and some cushions, and his mother a tray of home-made lemonade and glasses, they settled down. It was cool and pleasant with the birds twittering and the scent of flowers, and presently Gwen's eyes closed and she slept, waking with a start when Charlie's father arrived home and they were called in to tea.

Gwen took to Mr Roberts right away as, his ruddy face wreathed in smiles, he talked to her as though they'd known each other all their lives. The table groaned under all the food: the salmon salad, dishes of stewed fruit and jugs of cream, the plates of thin bread and butter, the sandwiches, the assortment of cakes. The tea flowed from the big brown pot and they talked and laughed. One of the photographs on the mantelpiece was of Charlie's sister Hetty, and this was brought down and admired. Gwen looked down at the pleasant-faced dark-eyed girl, and Mrs Roberts told her that Hetty was in service at a big house in Devon but was hoping one day to find work in Cardiff so that she could live at home.

This time when the meal was finished Gwen insisted on washing-up and Charlie dried, after which they strolled in the garden until it was time for him to walk her home.

The following Sunday when they got back to Wilfred Street after their walk, Mair brought Ronald to tea just as Gwen had suggested. He seemed painfully shy and as he stood on the hearthrug next to Charlie Gwen couldn't help but make comparisons. Charlie was looking smart in his best summer-weight jacket and grey trousers, but the legs of Ronald's shiny trousers showed a good couple of inches of sock and the sleeves of his jacket were also much too short.

The talk once again was of gardening, a subject Ronald obviously knew little about. Both Tom and Charlie tried to draw him into the conversation but after one sentence he'd dry up. Poor Mair was looking more and more glum as her worst fears were realised.

Tea had been over about half-an-hour when, red with

embarrassment, Ronald rose to his feet and swallowing hard said, 'Thank you for inviting me to tea, Mrs Llewellyn, I did enjoy it, but I'll have to go now because my mam isn't well and I'll be needed at home.' His voice was low and his face getting redder by the minute and Gwen wished with all her heart that there was something she could say that would help.

Mair went with him to the door and when she didn't return to the kitchen, Gwen went in search of her. Mair was sitting disconsolately on the bed and as Gwen sat down and put an arm about her she said, 'Poor Ronald, he's so conscientious, he worries about his mother all the time. He can't afford nice clothes for himself like Charlie can, Gwen, he gives nearly all his money to his mam.'

Now, every Sunday, Gwen and Charlie would have tea at either his house or hers. Soon summer was fading and chill winds stirred the crisp golden leaves at their feet yet, still, when the weather was fine they took long walks in the country, their cheeks glowing and their eyes only for each other. With November and the shortening days they began taking a tram to town and wandered around, looking in shop windows dressed ready for Christmas, resplendent with holly and mistletoe, glittering gifts, and golden angels hanging from the ceiling, silently trumpeting the festive season.

It was towards the end of November when, on a day of dark clouds and sudden showers one of which had sent them hurrying for the entrance of an arcade, Charlie shook out his dripping umbrella and Gwen gave a little shiver, and at once his arms came around her. There was no one in sight and he bent down, his lips on hers, gently at first, then with growing passion. Suddenly, remembering that they were in a public place, he released her, his face red with embarrassment, saying, 'I'm sorry, Gwen,' then, in a firmer voice, 'No! Dammit! I'm not sorry at all. I love you, Gwen. If only we could get married.' His voice brightened as he went on, 'If I could only find a cottage to rent, even if it meant leaving my job to get a tied one, would you marry me, Gwen?'

'Yes, Charlie! Yes!' she told him breathlessly, but she knew in her heart that it wasn't for her to say, that until she was twenty-one it would be her parents who would decide, and she'd known Charlie for less than a year. Mama would never agree. But they could get engaged, couldn't they?

'At Christmas,' Charlie cried, delighted with the compromise. If he was lucky enough to get the chance of a cottage he could put it to Gwen's parents then, and being engaged would make it that much easier to ask for one.

But Gwen was so excited that she just blurted it out as soon as they got home. She and Charlie were to be engaged, if Dada would give his permission.

'Delighted,' Tom said when Charlie had asked him formally, and he went to fetch a bottle of parsnip wine from the pantry.

Gwen had seen a ring she liked in a jeweller's window on the way home. It had two small diamonds either side of a sapphire, in a pretty gypsy setting. Mair rushed to hug and kiss her, delighted at the news. The only curb to Gwen's happiness came when Charlie left for home.

'Youer not getting married yet my girl, not if I've got anything to do with it,' Sarah said. 'Charlie's a nice boy, none better, but youer too young to know youer own mind. When youer twenty-one will be quite soon enough.'

In vain Gwen reminded her that she herself had been married at eighteen.

'And we had nothing, just a second-hand table and

chairs and a bed my grandmother gave us. It wasn't until we managed to rent this house and I opened the shop that we were able at last to buy the things we needed.'

'But it's over three years before I'm twenty-one,' Gwen wailed.

'Then there'll be plenty of time for you both to save some money,' her mother replied, ending the conversation by leaving the room.

Gwen knew it would be no use appealing to her father but she told Ted who as always was sympathetic, although he added, 'Your mam's right about one thing, Gwen, it will give you time to get things together.'

He couldn't help feeling a little pleased at Sarah's decision. He'd been wondering how he was to bear it when Gwen got married and left the shop. It was quite usual for young married couples to have a baby by the end of the first twelve-month. Gwen would soon forget all about him with all her new interests. He felt ashamed at his relief over Sarah's decision for in his heart he wanted Gwen's happiness above all else.

Gwen discussed the situation heatedly with Mair, who was full of sympathy. She had long since told her parents that she was walking out once more with Ronald, and he now sometimes visited the house, but Mair knew that committed to looking after his family as he was, it would be a very long time before they could make any plans, even though she was now over twenty-one.

When Charlie called one Sunday there was an air of suppressed excitement about him, but it wasn't until they'd turned the corner into Broadway that he asked, 'Gwen, would you marry me right away if we had somewhere to live? Not with youer family or mine?'

She couldn't help feeling some of Charlie's excitement,

but with a voice full of bitterness and regret told him, 'You know I have to wait until I'm twenty-one. Mama would never give her permission.'

'But why, Gwen? Why have we got to wait? I've got a steady job, even though it isn't well paid, and I've managed to save a bit. There's a cottage that will soon be to rent. I wouldn't be the only one after it but I'd stand a good chance, living in the village all my life.'

'It's nothing against you, Charlie,' Gwen hastened to assure him. 'Mama likes you, I know, but she's determined I should wait until I'm twenty-one.'

'Bugger that!' he cried angrily. It was the first time Gwen had ever heard him swear.

She reached home determined to tackle Sarah again, after all, Charlie might have a chance of renting a cottage. But she'd hardly begun to explain this before Sarah sprung to her feet crying angrily, 'What's the rush, you haven't been engaged a twelve-month yet.'

Dada had given her a warning look at upsetting Sarah, telling her, 'Wait a while like she says girl and you'll have a good start. Youer mam's got youer best interests at heart, you know that.'

Nodding her agreement Sarah had taken up her sewing again to show that the discussion was over.

As the months passed their longing for each other grew. Walking together, they held hands, and their kisses left Gwen shaking and weak, determined to beg her mother once more to change her mind. But the result was always the same – a blank refusal on Sarah's part even to discuss the situation. She had done her best to convince herself that it was for Gwen's own good, remembering the early days of her own marriage with little in the way of furniture and precious little money for food. Mair had been a sickly baby and Sarah had often taken her tiredness and frustration out on Tom at the end of the day, but he'd been unfailingly gentle and understanding as he still was.

At the back of her mind she knew that it wasn't only for Gwen's sake that she'd insisted on her waiting until she was twenty-one. The money Gwen paid in was essential to help meet the bills. These days she found it difficult to manage on Tom's money alone. If only he hadn't closed down the shop. It all boiled down to that, didn't it? Lucy had another two years at school before she would be earning and then it would only be a pittance, and Mair was needed at home and anyway had never been trained to do anything else. Open the shop again she would, as soon as she felt strong enough. Sarah sighed wearily, knowing she'd been telling herself that for years.

Chapter Thirteen

Gwen and Charlie had become desperate to find a cottage they could rent by the autumn, for early in November she would be twenty-one. Her bottom drawer had long since spilled over from the chest she'd stored things in since her eighteenth birthday, until now she was putting things away in any nook or cranny she could find.

Charlie was still prepared to change his job if it meant getting tied accommodation, but that didn't seem very likely, and Gwen was contemplating something she'd always said she wouldn't and that was having rooms with her mother. There was no chance now of them going to live with Charlie's parents as his sister had now returned home, having been lucky enough to find a living-out job at a big house at St Mellons.

'Well, I'm not giving up my bedroom,' Lucy declared emphatically, having had the luxury of one to herself ever since she was small.

'You'll have to if we've got to live here,' Gwen told her, hoping desperately that it would never come to that, but determined also to marry as soon as she was twenty-one. Gwen had inherited Sarah's strong will and was definitely not looking forward to the prospect of living at home, for she knew that if it had been her and not Mair constantly with her mother there would have been frequent ructions between them. She knew also that because of her mother's fragile health, it was she who would have had to give in.

'I can't sleep with Mair. She'd keep me awake with that cough of hers,' Lucy was saying sulkily.

Mair had had a stubborn cough for ages but Gwen doubted if Lucy could hear it from her bedroom at the back of the house. It had grown steadily worse, despite rubbing her chest with goose grease, and the bottles of 'Doctor Brown's Cough Mixture' that had been purchased over the months had made little difference to it. Gwen had begged Mair to go and see Doctor Powell, for she was looking exhausted, with shadows beneath her grey eyes, but Mair kept putting off the visit, assuring her sister that she'd soon feel better.

Being desperately in love herself, Gwen wondered if Mair was pining. She and Ronald had been courting for years. Gwen had no doubt that her sister had come to love him but there was little hope of their getting married, not unless his mother miraculously got well and someone else was able to take on the financial burden of the family. She became increasingly worried about Mair. She would often wake to find the bedclothes damp to the touch, and Mair's nightgown clinging to her thin body with perspiration.

The sound of a distressing fit of coughing brought Gwen to her feet to hurry to the parlour where Mair lay exhausted against the sofa cushions, a hankie to her mouth, her eyes closed, her face as pale as lint.

When Mair opened her eyes it was to find Gwen anxiously bending over her saying, 'You can't go on like this, Mair, you'll have to see Doctor Powell.'

Mair didn't answer, for how could she tell Gwen that

she was too frightened to go? That she didn't want the doctor to put a name to what she feared was wrong with her?

'If you think it would be too much for Mama, I'll come with you,' Gwen went on. 'Perhaps we could go tonight?'

'Where could you go tonight?' her mother asked, coming into the room. 'I heard you coughing again just now. I'll have to send for Doctor Powell, Mair if you won't go to see him.'

That evening, feeling very apprehensive, Mair set out for the surgery with Mama one side of her and Gwen the other, and more than once on the journey she would have turned tail for home if they hadn't been there.

The waiting room was already three quarters full when they pushed open the door and as Mair looked around she took some comfort from the fact that, despite it being summer, several of the patients were coughing. It's probably summer colds she thought hopefully. Oh, if only Doctor Powell could put her fears at rest.

Her mother was sitting one side of her, breathing heavily, and Gwen the other as the waiting room rapidly filled up. Soon they were standing around the walls, several babies were wailing miserably, their mothers rocking them to and fro. A sigh of relief went around the waiting patients when, at last, the brown shutter in the wall flew up and the doctor cried, 'Come in please.'

Now they all moved up one place, on the scratched bentwood chairs, and Mair counted that they did this twenty times before at last it was their turn.

'Next please!'

'She's had a cough for ages,' Sarah was explaining while Mair was sent behind the screen to undress.

Doctor Powell had greeted them cheerfully, asking

after Sarah's health before beginning to examine Mair, but as the examination proceeded he grew more serious. He seemed to be taking ages, although he must have known his waiting room was, by this time, overflowing.

When Mair was once more behind the screen she strained her ears towards the murmur of voices, guessing that Doctor Powell had taken her mother aside. She couldn't hear what they were saying, but as soon as she was dressed for the street and had joined them once more the sight of their sombre faces made her heart sink, and before anyone could help her to a chair she cried, 'It's the consumption isn't it? That's what I've got.'

Doctor Powell sat down and took Mair's hands in his, saying, 'Yes, I'm afraid it is tuberculosis of the lungs, but I hope we've caught it early, Mair. You'll have to have complete rest and fresh air. It would be ideal if you could be sent to the country.' He turned to Sarah, 'Have you any close relatives in the country?'

Sarah was shaking her head and Mair knew there was only Nana living in Tonyrefail and that was hardly country. Anyway, poor old Nan needed looking after herself and her sister had gone to live with her.

'I'd like to have another opinion,' Doctor Powell said as he scribbled down an address in Cathedral Road. 'I'll get in touch with the doctor and let Mair know when she can see him. Now don't forget, open your bedroom window when the weather's fine. Rest and fresh air should work wonders.'

'There's no need for him to pretend,' Mair told them sadly, when they were on their way home. 'I've feared it was the consumption for a long time. That's why I was afraid to go to the doctor's.'

'If it is, they've probably caught it in good time,' Gwen

told her with a cheerfulness she was far from feeling. 'Lucy will have to stay home now and look after things, Mama, instead of that dressmaking apprenticeship you've been trying to arrange.'

Poor Lucy, Mair thought, knowing she'd set her heart on making pretty clothes.

By the time the second doctor had confirmed Doctor Powell's diagnosis, Sarah had already instructed the girls to move the bed that Gwen and Mair had been sharing into Lucy's small back bedroom, and Lucy's single bed had been installed in its place for Gwen and Lucy to share.

As Lucy gathered up her clothes from her own small wardrobe, to carry them to the bedroom she was to share with Gwen, there were two bright spots of anger in her cheeks, and, slamming doors as she went, she flung the clothes wildly on to her side of the bed. A moment later she was hanging her things to one side of the double wardrobe, carelessly pushing Gwen's clothes out of the way to accommodate them, muttering to herself, 'That room was mine, it just isn't fair.'

Later that evening when Sarah was trying to explain gently to her that she could no longer be apprenticed to the dressmaking, she cried, 'I will go! I will! I'm not going to stop home. Oh, Mama you promised that I could.'

'I'm sorry, Lucy, really I am, but there's no other way—' Sarah began, but Lucy was rushing upstairs with Gwen following her, flinging herself on to the bed and sobbing so loudly that Gwen's heart went out to her. When she put her arm about her sister to comfort her Lucy shook herself free, crying, 'It's all right for you isn't it? You don't have to give up your job, do you?'

And Gwen was remembering when she was Lucy's age

her own longing to go to work at Ted's shop and her excitement when her dream came true. Feeling deep compassion for Lucy's plight, she vowed to take as much of the burden on herself as she could when she was at home.

When Charlie came that evening, knowing nothing of Mair's visit to the second doctor, or the confirmation of her illness, he noticed that Gwen was looking very glum.

'I might have some news that will cheer you up, Gwen,' he began cheerfully. 'You know old Mrs James who lives next door to us? Well, she's going to live with her daughter soon and there'll be a cottage to let.' Then, seeing that Gwen's expression hadn't changed he added, 'Oh, I know there'll be others after it, but we do stand a chance.'

'It's no good, Charlie,' Gwen told him sadly, 'I can't leave home now. We can't even have rooms here—' and she told him that it had been confirmed that Mair had tuberculosis.

'Poor Mair, poor Ronald too. I'm so sorry.' But he was also thinking poor Gwen and me too. It was a bitter blow to all their plans. Surely there must be some way they could marry in the autumn after waiting all this time.

A few years before Charlie had bought himself a second-hand bike so that he could visit Gwen in the evenings. Now, he came every night of the week, sitting in the kitchen talking to Sarah or Tom. For after working all day at the shop and at home for most of the evening, coping with Lucy's tantrums and assuring a pale-faced and apologetic Mair that she was no trouble, Gwen had little time to spare. He'd talk to her father about politics and the possibility of a war in Europe, for he'd found himself getting interested over the years. When it was time for him to leave, Gwen would see him to the door, but before opening it they'd cling desperately to each other in the dark little passage, telling each other without much hope that very soon they must find a solution.

Propped against the lace-trimmed pillows in the tiny back bedroom, stuffy even with the window down on those hot early summer days, Mair seemed to grow even paler.

Ronald was now a constant visitor and her grey eyes would light up with love whenever he came into the room. He'd sit in the armchair beside the bed and cradle Mair's long slim fingers in his own while making plans for a future both of them knew was unlikely to come about. A lump would come to Gwen's throat whenever she took them a tray of tea, and she'd feel selfish and uncaring in her eagerness to marry Charlie and get away.

It was at Ronald's suggestion that they bought the second-hand bath-chair. Gwen scrubbed the wicker body and Fanny made bright new cushions for it. Now Ronald wheeled Mair out every fine Sunday afternoon and most evenings, and for a while her health seemed to improve as her skin took on a healthy look from all the unaccustomed sunshine and fresh air. She began to take an interest in what she would wear for the outings, even asking Fanny to make her a couple of new frocks. Over the years Tom had revised his opinion of Mair's young man, appreciating Ronald's devotion to Mair and his family.

Early in July Doctor Powell told them that Mair was now on the list for a bed at Brompton Hospital at Frimley in Surrey, which was a sanatorium for patients with tuberculosis. Everyone was overjoyed that she was going to have a real chance of getting well.

'It shouldn't be too long,' Doctor Powell told them hopefully, congratulating himself on pleading Mair's case successfully although he knew only too well that there might still be a fair wait for a bed.

The outings with Ronald continued, but as the summer went on Mair became listless once more. The little back bedroom was stiflingly hot, and when there were no visitors Mair would lie on the bed with the covers thrown back. Even draped as she was in a voluminous calico nightdress, Gwen saw with a pang of fear that she had become even thinner, the shadows beneath her fine grey eyes much darker. Persistent fits of coughing tortured her fragile body and Doctor Powell was unsmiling as he told them that he'd renew his efforts to get her admitted to the hospital quickly. No one realised at the time that a brief item of news that had appeared in the papers late in June was about to put an end to Mair's hopes of a place at Brompton, and to the hopes and dreams of countless others.

It was on the 28th of that month that Archduke Franz Ferdinand and his wife Sophie were assassinated while riding in an open car in Sarajevo, Bosnia, in the Balkans. The Archduke was not popular even with his own people but he was the heir to the Austro-Hungarian Empire. Few people at home realised the importance of the news they'd read in their paper, and even fewer would have guessed that it would be responsible for starting a world war. Probably most of those who read about it would have agreed with Eddie Palmer.

'Funny buggers, foreigners,' he'd remarked complacently, resting his arms on top of the garden wall. 'Blutty 'ot-tempered lot. You never know where you are with them.'

And Tom nodded his head in agreement.

Chapter Fourteen

August Bank Holiday 1914 dawned warm and sunny. Most of the neighbours in Wilfred Street were preparing feverishly for picnics at the tide-fields or in the countryside around St Mellons, while luckier ones with a little money to spare were off for a day by the sea.

As she busied herself with the chores, Gwen stopped to look out of the front bedroom window at the children impatiently waiting to be off. Little girls, their best clothes covered by starched broderie-anglaise pinafores, small faces shaded by wide-brimmed straw hats; and the boys unnaturally still in their Sunday knickerbocker suits, standing outside, mindful of the warning they would no doubt have received: 'Keep youerselves clean, mind, or you'll 'ave to stay home.'

Gwen smiled when she heard Lucy singing in the bedroom they now shared, glad she'd offered to look after things at home so that her sister could enjoy herself. The child seldom had any time off, and as Gwen had explained to a disappointed Charlie last evening: 'It's only fair, love. When I was her age I always went somewhere on Bank Holiday. Lucy never has any fun these days.'

Poor Lucy hadn't yet come to terms with having to stay at home instead of being apprenticed to the dressmaking.

Most of the time she went about with the air of a tragedy queen, and although she did her unenthusiastic best it had soon become apparent that housework was not her strong point.

'Does this frock look all right, Gwen?' She spun round in the doorway, the skirt of the sprigged muslin dress billowing around her. Her cheeks were bright, her blue eyes dancing, and Gwen thought once more that her own sacrifice was a small one to have brought such happiness.

'What time are they calling for you?' Lucy had been invited to go to Penarth in her friend's family's pony and trap.

'Gertie said to be ready by twelve o'clock. Gwen, can I borrow your new blue hair ribbon? It will go lovely with the sash on this dress.'

'It's in my top drawer,' Gwen told her. 'I think your hair looks nice loose as it is now.'

'It's sure to be breezy by the sea,' Lucy said happily.

When Charlie arrived early that afternoon, the first thing he asked was, 'Is your dad about? Have any of you seen the papers, Gwen?'

They hadn't, but Tom was in the garden talking as usual to Eddie Palmer over the garden wall. 'Putting the world to rights' Sarah was fond of saying. But today, as Gwen and Charlie walked towards them up the garden path, they were quick to notice that both men were looking very serious.

Charlie unfurled the newspaper he was carrying and pointed to the front page where the headlines declared in large black print GERMAN INVASION OF BELGIUM.

'Seems Germany has declared war on France,' he said.

'Shouldn't have any effect on us anyway,' Eddie replied confidently, but Tom wasn't so sure. 'Belgium's neutral,' he said. 'We may stick up for her.'

Just then Sarah called for Gwen to come into the house and she left reluctantly. Since Charlie had begun to take an interest in these discussions, she'd become interested herself and would have loved to stay and listen.

It was stifling indoors and she was all for wheeling Mair's bath-chair out to the shady part of the garden. Ronald thought it a good idea too, but Mair said it wasn't worth the bother of getting dressed, she was tired anyway and would prefer to stay in bed, so Gwen lowered the window a little more and drew it up at the bottom, but even then there wasn't enough breeze to stir the lace curtains.

At tea-time Tom and Charlie were still talking of the war that had started on the Continent.

'In the *Daily Herald* it said that the anti-war demonstrations in London were organised by the Labour Party,' Charlie said, knowing Tom was a loyal member of that party.

'Well, no one in their right senses would want a war,' he said with conviction.

The talk went on into the evening when Lucy came home, pink from the sun and excited about her lovely day out, insisting on changing her clothes right away and washing the supper dishes so that Gwen could take a stroll with Charlie in the warm evening air. There were lots of people still about, talking in little groups, and they stopped to chat to the neighbours around the Palmers' house, listening to the different points of view, the word war was on everyone's lips.

By the following day the tension had steadily mounted, the *Echo*'s headlines doing nothing to dispel their fears. BRITISH ULTIMATUM TO GERMANY stood out in bold black letters, and underneath: BELGIAN NEUTRALITY THE HUGE ISSUE. KAISER GIVEN UNTIL MIDNIGHT TO DECIDE.

It was hard to have to wait for the morning papers to know what would happen. That night few people were anxious to go to bed. The street was buzzing with gossip, the air cool and pleasant after the heat of the day. With something important to talk about, people stayed on and on.

Mair was settled for the night and Sarah and Lucy had already gone to bed. After she'd walked to the corner with Charlie and they'd said a lingering goodnight, he'd mounted his bike and ridden off and Gwen had turned for home. The Palmers' front door was wide open. The group who'd been outside the house were now inside. Gwen could hear her father's voice coming from the front room, and as she entered, the heat from so many people crowding in and the popping gas jet was overpowering. There was an air of gloom as they discussed the possibilities if Germany didn't agree to withdraw her troops, but the gloom was tinged with excitement, her father's voice alone in condemning any thoughts of war.

It was almost three o'clock when Gwen and her father went to their beds, and when morning came and she was roused from an exhausted sleep by the strident bell of the alarm clock, it was to find her eyes still stinging from all the pipe and cigarette smoke that last night had filled the Palmers' front room.

Downstairs Lucy was preparing breakfast, telling Gwen in an excited voice, 'Dada's just gone for a paper.' But before he could return Eddie Palmer came in to break the solemn news. Great Britain was at war.

Chapter Fifteen

Soon there were uniforms everywhere, servicemen crowd-ing the railway station, the trams and the streets. A whole way of life seemed to be passing when, the day after war broke out, crisp pound notes were issued instead of gold sovereigns. People's reactions were mixed but most thought it wasn't a fair exchange. As Eddie Palmer remarked, 'Feel cheated you will, Tom, getting a piece of paper in youer wage packet at the end of a hard week's grind.'

Young men flocked to the recruiting centres, anxious to do their bit before it was too late, for there seemed to be a general assumption that it would be all over by Christmas.

One Wednesday, Gwen was amused to see four small boys tagging behind a group of soldiers who were being marched along the road, taking huge steps almost at a run in their endeavour to keep up. They were a ragged lot, and the one beating a rusty saucepan bottom with a stick to the rhythm of the soldier's feet, had a bit of flannel shirt bursting through the elbows of his jacket, but their faces were earnest, eyes straight ahead, as they tried valiantly to keep in step.

Mostly, though, the war seemed far away. Gwen's mind was occupied with other things. A neighbour had told her there might be rooms to let in Broadway in a couple of weeks' time. As yet it was only a rumour so she hadn't told Charlie about it until she knew more. The house was only just around the corner. If they could get the rooms, she could still help out at home.

Mair was hoping for a bed at Brompton very soon; Doctor Powell had told them he was keeping in touch. Poor Mair. Her cough was getting worse, racking her thin body, and Gwen knew that it was only the hope of a place at the sanatorium that was keeping her going.

That evening when she took Mair's tray to the bedroom her sister was in the throes of an exhausting bout of coughing, a piece of the white rag kept for the purpose held tightly against her mouth. When it was over Mair tried to hide the rag under her pillow but Gwen had already seen the streaks of blood and her heart went cold with fear.

'How long has that been happening?' she asked as calmly as she could.

Mair shook her head and in a rare moment of self-pity said, 'If they don't send for me soon, Gwen, it will be too late.'

'That's nonsense, love. Have you told Doctor Powell?'

'No, I haven't. He might tell Mama and she's worried enough already.'

Gwen glanced at the clock on the mantelpiece. If she hurried she would get to the surgery before it closed. Putting the used tea things on the tray to take down, she said, 'I've got a few things to do before Charlie comes, love. Will you be all right for a while?'

But downstairs, with her hat and coat on ready to go out, she told Sarah, 'I'm just going to pick up Mair's medicine. I won't be long.'

'But that will do tomorrow,' Sarah told her.

'I'd rather get it tonight,' Gwen said firmly. 'I might meet Charlie on the way back.'

The surgery seemed to be full of coughing people and crying babies even at this hour of the day. Gwen stood just inside the door, waiting for a seat to be vacated, letting the worries crowd her mind. Poor Mair, poor Ronald. They were just made for each other, but Mair seemed now to be slowly slipping away.

When at last it was her turn and she'd told Doctor Powell about the blood on her sister's hankie, he looked serious, but admitted that he'd suspected as much. 'But she would never admit it,' he told Gwen. 'Mair is afraid of upsetting your mother, but she must be honest with me, Gwen, so that I can do my best for her.'

'But they'll be able to help her at Brompton, Doctor?'

He sighed, rubbing tired eyes with the back of his hand. 'Gwen,' he said, his voice filled with compassion. 'I really don't know how to break this to you . . .'

Heart plummeting, she waited for him to go on. Was he going to say that Mair was too ill – beyond help? But swallowing hard, he continued: 'It's this war, you see. It's going to make a difference to everything. It seems they want the beds at Brompton for the soldiers. I'm truly sorry, Gwen.' He put a comforting hand on her shoulder. 'I'm afraid Mair is a very sick girl.'

As she walked back along Broadway tears trickled unashamedly down her cheeks. How was she to tell Mair what Doctor Powell had said? Better to let her go on hoping, and that would mean keeping the knowledge from Mama as well. Before reaching the street she dried her eyes and tried to compose herself, telling herself that no good would come of dashing Mair's hopes. Her heart heavy, she turned the key and went into the house.

Sarah was coming downstairs. 'Where's the medicine?' she asked, staring at Gwen's empty hands.

Her hand flew to her mouth. 'I must have left it at the surgery.'

'What! And after queueing for it all this time?'

'You all right, Gwen?' Charlie was coming towards her from the kitchen, looking lovingly at her.

'Yes. I must have got a bit of grit in my eye,' she told him, anxious they shouldn't know that she was upset.

Seemingly satisfied with her explanation, Charlie went back to the conversation he was having with Tom, and Gwen went upstairs to take off her hat and coat.

When later she tapped the door and went into Mair's bedroom, Ronald was sitting by the bed holding her hand. Smiling at Gwen, he said, 'I've just been telling Mair that when she's well again, after she's been to Brompton, we may be able to get married. Our Tim should be working by that time, and my sister Lily should be in service and paying something in.'

'That would be lovely, Ronald,' Gwen managed to say before hurrying from the room.

It was very hard keeping the awful knowledge to herself, especially as the word 'Brompton' occurred so often in conversation as a message of hope to Mair.

Towards the end of the week, as she kissed Charlie goodnight, he said, 'I met an old schoolfriend of mine this morning, Gwen, Artie Shawcross. Used to live next door to us he did. Wants me to go to a meeting with him tomorrow night. You won't mind, will you, love? I'll be round to see you afterwards if it's not too late.'

'What sort of meeting, Charlie?'

'Oh, just a meeting about the war.'

'You're not going to join up, are you?' She held her breath, waiting for his answer.

'Of course not, but it'll be interesting and I can have a drink and a chat with Artie first.'

I mustn't be selfish, she told herself. Charlie hadn't had any close friends the whole time she'd known him. But she was remembering his mother mentioning Artie Shaw-cross. 'Used to get ouer Charlie into trouble at school, he did,' his mam had said. 'Always one for a lark was young Artie.'

Oh, well, Gwen thought, he's probably altered now he's grown up.

When Charlie had gone she went upstairs to find Sarah in Mair's bedroom, watching her while she slept, the expression on their mother's face heartbreaking to see. It was obvious that Sarah knew how ill Mair was without being told, but they'd all go on pretending that she would get well. And there was no one better at that than the invalid herself. The old pieces of petticoat and nightdress that she used as rags would be a sure giveaway, but it seemed no one had noticed the blood until Gwen had seen her coughing that day, and she hadn't seen any since.

'Have you stopped coughing up blood, Mair?' Gwen asked hopefully when she took up her supper.

'No,' Mair said regretfully. 'It's been like that for a while now.'

'What do you do with them then? The rags, I mean.'

'I've been burning them in the grate while you've all been at supper.'

Of course. The fire was lit in the bedroom every evening now for Mair found the evenings chilly.

As Charlie shuffled forward in the queue towards the entrance to the hall he laughed and talked with Artie. It had been ages since he'd gone out with anyone but Gwen, and that was the way he'd wanted it, but he'd really enjoyed having a drink and a chat over old times and old Artie had always been good company.

He was quite looking forward to this meeting. 'Explaining all about the war they'll be,' Artie had told him. And he meant to listen, for then he could have a friendly but knowledgeable argument with Tom who seemed to think that Britain should never have gone in. He'd better keep his hand down if they asked for volunteers tonight. He meant to join up, of course, but not right away. It wouldn't be fair to Gwen, would it, with them hoping to be married very soon, and with all the worries she had at home and all.

Charlie was beginning to feel uncomfortable. They'd been seated about an hour and one speaker after another had roused the audience to fever pitch. His eyes kept turning in the direction of the posters plastering the wall at his side. 'Your Country Needs You' was the message from every one, and from the largest poster Lord Kitchener seemed to be pointing his finger straight at Charlie. There was more clapping and Artie leaned towards him to tell him excitedly that he meant to join up as soon as they asked for volunteers.

'Better get in while we've got the chance,' he said. 'It'll probably all be over in a few months' time.'

The last speech was coming to an end, and the tumultuous applause had hardly died away when most of the audience were scrambling to their feet, stumbling over those still sitting down in their eagerness to reach the recruiting table. Suddenly Archie was on his feet too, dragging Charlie from his chair, crying, 'Come on, boyo, get a move on.'

The fever of patriotism was contagious. The blood was pounding in Charlie's ears. His heart was hammering as he jumped to his feet. By God! he thought. Artie's right. A man should fight for his country.

As he rushed after Artie and they stood in line he felt drunk with the emotions the meeting had evoked, but when at last it was his turn to stand before the recruiting sergeant he stood proudly, his voice calm as he answered the questions and signed the form that was put in front of him.

'How tall are you, son?' He easily topped the regulation five foot three by six inches.

Still in a state of euphoria, he left the hall with Artie. 'Fancy another drink, Charlie?' But he shook his head. The cold night air was having a sobering effect, melting the feeling of well-being away. Doubts began to plague him. What had he done? How was he going to tell Gwen that he'd broken his promise? Poor Gwen. She'd been so patient all these years, having to wait for her twenty-first, and now he was about to wreck her hopes.

Saying goodbye to Artie, he boarded the tram and soon it was rattling along the Newport Road. Filled with regrets, he stared miserably before him. Deep in thought, he missed the stop at Clifton Street, getting off at the Royal Oak instead. Heading for Broadway, Charlie's steps slowed to a halt and he stood there uncertain what to do. It was late to upset her, wasn't it? Perhaps he should let Gwen have one more peaceful night before he dashed all her hopes. Turning up his collar and hunching his shoulders, he turned in the direction of home.

Chapter Sixteen

'You did what?'

'I said I joined up, Gwen.'

'Oh, Charlie! And after you promised me you wouldn't yet.'

They stood in the passage staring at each other, their usual warm embrace forgotten. Seeing the tears of disappointment and frustration brimming in her eyes, Charlie wanted to fling his arms about her and hold her close, but he doggedly went on trying to explain, saying, 'I had to do it, Gwen. Everyone seemed to be joining up. You can't ignore the fact that we're at war.'

'Dada says there's no need for us to fight,' she said tearfully.

'Well, we're in it now and someone's got to go. Anyway, Gwen, it'll be over in a few months. We can get married then, love.'

Tom was calling and Charlie went through to the kitchen. Gwen was about to follow him but, suddenly realising that she could contain her feelings no longer, dashed upstairs and flung herself on to the bed. Still angry and hurt at what Charlie had done, a part of her as always understood how he must have felt. Perversely she couldn't help being a little proud of him, but disappointment was uppermost as she struggled to keep back the tears. It was the second blow to her plans that day for earlier she'd heard that the rooms in Broadway that she'd set her heart on getting had already been promised to someone else.

Rinsing her face in cold water from the flowered jug on the wash-stand, she went downstairs half expecting to hear Tom giving Charlie his point of view. But when she opened the door she was surprised to hear her father saying, 'Well, Charlie, seeing that we're in the war now, it's highly commendable of you to have joined up. I expect I'd have done just the same at youer age, boyo. When the Boer War started I already had a wife and two young daughters to provide for. If I'd been single like you I'd probably have volunteered myself.'

And if we could have got married when we wanted to a long time ago, we might have had children too, Gwen thought bitterly.

That night when she crept into the bedroom where Lucy lay sleeping her heart was heavy with disappointment. It was that Artie's doing, of course. It was a pity that Charlie had ever met up with him again. She could understand him feeling patriotic; she often felt like that herself when they sang '*Mae Hen Wlad Fy Nhad-au*' or 'God Save The King', but Charlie could have waited for a while, at least until they were married and had a place of their own. No one was storming Britain's shores, were they?

Gwen bit back the sob of despair that rose to her throat, worried in case she woke her sleeping sister.

Suddenly an idea came to her and she sat up in bed, hugging her knees. While Charlie was in the army they wouldn't really need a place of their own, would they? So long as they had somewhere to stay when he came on leave. Aunt Fan had a spare room she used only for sewing. There was even a bed against the wall on which she laid the clothes she'd made. Gwen felt sure that Aunt Fanny would let them have the room whenever Charlie came home. It would only be for the nights so it wouldn't affect her sewing. Her aunt had lost the man she loved at Khartoum all those years ago before even the Boer War. She would know how important it was that lovers should be together. She wasn't twenty-one until November but Gwen was sure she could get her mother to waive that condition now that there was a war, especially as she'd still be living at home.

Supposing Charlie was called up quite soon? Would there be time for them to marry before he went? She'd already chosen the style for her wedding dress from Aunt Fanny's book of patterns, but the material hadn't been bought as yet. Oh, well, if the dress wasn't made in time she could wear the white muslin she'd had last spring. A new hat would work wonders. Her mind racing with ideas now, Gwen saw the first pale fingers of dawn streaking the brightening sky before dropping into an exhausted sleep from which she was reluctantly dragged by the strident bell of the alarm clock.

As she went about the chores, thankful that it was Sunday morning and Charlie would be with her just after lunch, she nursed her wonderful idea. The more she thought about it, the more sensible it seemed. She wouldn't mention it to Charlie until they were in the country and alone. Gwen glanced through the kitchen window, thankful that it was a warm sunny day. She hadn't asked Aunt Fanny, of course, but was sure that it would be all right. Her aunt was such a generous soul and not at all embittered at being left a spinster by that awful war.

When Charlie came at last and Gwen had bribed Lucy with a bar of scented soap and a hair-slide to look after the house on her own, they set off on their walk. Charlie, relieved that she no longer seemed angry with him, tucked her arm in his, reflecting that Gwen's reaction to his joining up had been nothing to his mother's. She'd still been carrying on when he'd left the cottage.

He'd sensed an air of excitement about Gwen so wasn't really surprised when on reaching the path that led to the tide-fields, she said, 'There's something I want to talk to you about, Charlie.' He smiled at her fondly, waiting for her to begin.

'I think we ought to get married before you go away, love.' Gwen was looking up at him hopefully, but the smile had left Charlie's face. There was an awkward silence, and embarrassed by this, a blush crept over Gwen's cheeks. Why wasn't Charlie overjoyed as she'd expected? A lump had come to her throat and she stared miserably ahead.

Charlie's arm crept about her waist. His cheek close to hers, he said softly, 'Gwen, *cariad*, try to understand how I feel. I can't even begin to forgive myself for upsetting you like this, but there's no turning back now. The thing is, Gwen, I wouldn't know any peace of mind if we got married and I left you with no home of your own nor any hope of one. You'd have very little money to live on, and there's always the possibility of my coming home to you wounded or an invalid, perhaps for the rest of my life. I've thought of little else for days, love, I just couldn't do it to you.'

'But I'd manage all right, Charlie. I'd have my job.'

'And supposing you had a baby?'

'I'd love to have a baby,' she burst in.

Charlie's expression was serious as he said, 'Look, love,

apart from all the responsibility of looking after a child, have you thought that with Mair so ill with the consumption, it wouldn't be right to expose a tiny baby to the infection? You know how often I've asked you to be careful yourself. You always say that you're as strong as an ox.' He gave her a bleak smile. 'Well, there's little more you can do but take care, but a baby would be very vulnerable.'

As Charlie's voice trailed off, tears of disappointment streamed down Gwen's face. She'd set such hopes on his being delighted with her idea; had pictured them making plans for a quick wedding.

They were alone on this part of the tide-fields, the sun warm on their faces, the long coarse grass rippling about them in the breeze from the Channel. Taking a handkerchief from his breast pocket, Charlie tenderly wiped away her tears then drew her towards him. With arms about each other, their bodies straining to be close, their lips met. Hearts hammering, oblivious of everything but that they would soon be parted, they clung to each other desperately.

It was Charlie who broke away first with a deep sigh, saying, 'Oh, Gwen, I almost forgot what I've been saying to you.' Then, gazing towards the sullen waters of the Channel, he went on, 'God! I've made a real mess of things, haven't I? But it doesn't alter my decision. I couldn't expose you to the risk of my ending up losing a limb, or even worse.'

At his words the tears flowed faster, and gently he took her face in his hands. Then, smoothing back the damp hair from her forehead, he kissed the tip of her nose, tasting the salt of her tears, not trusting himself to put his lips to hers again.

With heavy hearts they retraced their steps to the

Newport Road, walking slowly towards Gwen's home where Charlie was expected to tea. She could hear Lucy coughing as she was opening the door. Her younger sister had caught a cold. When they entered the kitchen she was huddled in the armchair, obviously feeling sorry for herself. She looked up to tell Gwen, 'I don't feel very well. I think I'll go up as soon as we've had tea.'

When the meal was over Lucy went to bed, and as Gwen washed the dishes and her mother wiped, Sarah said, 'Seems worried about something, our Lucy. Sits and stares in front of her with a face like a fiddle, she does.'

'She hardly touched anything at tea-time. I think I'll take her a cup of tea.' And making a sandwich after cutting a thin slice of beef from the joint, Gwen laid a tray and went upstairs. She put the tray down to tap upon the bedroom door, but hearing muffled sobbing turned the handle quickly. The curtains were drawn tightly together and in the dim light she could just make out Lucy's tousled head upon the pillow. As Gwen set the tray down on top of the wash-stand and pulled back the curtains, Lucy sat up, her face blotched with tears.

Gwen sat on the bed, drawing her little sister close, whispering, 'Whatever's the matter, *cariad*?'

'I'm frightened, Gwen.'

'Frightened of what, Lucy?'

'Of getting the consumption. I've had a cough for days, Gwen, perhaps I've got it already.' Tears of self-pity welled in Lucy's eyes once more.

'Nonsense, love, you've just had a cold. That bottle of cough mixture I bought will soon put you right, you'll see. Anyway, Lucy, we always keep Mair's china and cutlery separate. Mama has always insisted on that.'

'Maudie Thomas says you can get it from handling the

sheets. Her sister died of it, didn't she?'

'Yes, she did, Lucy, but no one else caught it, did they? Anyway, we boil Mair's bedding and nightdresses in the copper with plenty of soda. Don't you ever let her know that you're worried, will you?'

Looking at Lucy's woebegone face as she shook her head, Gwen's heart went out to her. Her pretty looks were spoilt by discontent. She was only fourteen and hadn't got over the disappointment of having to stay at home now that she'd left school. Gwen bent forward to give her a sympathetic little hug.

'I'll do Mair's bedding from now on,' she promised. 'You just get rid of that cold and your cough will soon disappear.'

With Charlie gone she'd have plenty of time for extra jobs, Gwen reflected sadly. Lucy flung her arms about her and she was warmly hugged. When this threatened to go on for too long, Gwen unclasped her sister's hands and held them in her own, shocked at their roughness until she remembered all the stretches of oilcloth and stone floors the child scrubbed in a week. No wonder she was fed up.

Chapter Seventeen

It was mid-October before Charlie received his papers, together with a travel warrant to Exeter and instructions to report to the General Station by 10.00 hours. When Monday came, a day of low cloud and threatening rain, matching Gwen's mood to a T, she stood close to Charlie on the windswept platform, her hand clasped tightly in his. All about them were groups of people come to bid goodbye to new volunteers or hardened soldiers of just a few months, the ones already in uniform probably on a last leave before going to the front.

The air was heavy with emotion, one young girl clinging to an embarrassed-looking soldier and sobbing loudly while he tried to comfort her.

'Artie's cutting it a bit fine,' Charlie said, looking anxiously at his pocket watch. The train was thundering into the station and Gwen and Charlie flung their arms about each other, oblivious of those around them. The crowd surging forward pushed them this way and that, and Gwen opened her eyes to see Artie making for the carriage, a girl on each arm.

The train stood at the platform obscuring the leaden sky while steam billowed in all directions. Charlie pulled her to him once more but at the sound of the whistle their lips quickly parted. Grabbing his bag, he rushed towards the train, leaping into a carriage where Artie was holding the door, yelling, 'Come on, mun, the train's packed.' But Charlie made straight for the window, crying, 'I'll write tonight, Gwen.'

Now the train was moving and Gwen ran alongside it, straining to get a last glimpse, but soon it gathered speed and was quickly out of sight. A deep sigh seemed to pass through the people on the platform, wiping away the brave smiles of farewell. Hankies were fumbled for and eyes discreetly dabbed, some only to swim with tears again, like the couple Gwen was now passing, the woman's voice distraught as she said, 'It's for the trenches he'll be this time, Bert.'

The man put a comforting arm about her as Gwen passed by. Thank goodness Charlie will have to train in this country first, she thought. Perhaps the war would even be over before he could be sent overseas.

On the tram she felt bereft, as though something had been torn from her heart, but on arrival at the shop Ted, kind as always, made a fuss of her and Daisy brought her a cup of tea and some of Gwen's favourite welsh cakes she'd made especially, and insisted she sat at the table in the back room until she'd finished them.

That night as she turned the key and stepped into the passage Sarah came to meet her, telling her in a loud whisper, 'There's a lady waiting for you in the parlour, Gwen. Came here this morning she did, but I told her you wouldn't be home until now. She didn't say what it was about.'

Gwen quickly unpinned her hat and hung her coat on the hall-stand, then, curious to know just who it could be, she opened the parlour door but didn't recognise the plump, pleasant-looking lady who rose to greet her.

'Miss Llewellyn?' the woman asked, and when Gwen nodded she went on, 'I'm Mrs Read. Someone told me a little while ago that you were looking for rooms. I know it's been a long time, love, but I'd already promised them to another young couple. Now he's in the army and she's gone back to her mam.'

Gwen felt a sharp pang of disappointment. If only she could have had the rooms while Charlie was still home! But would it really have made any difference? He had been adamant. No marriage until he came home safe and sound.

Mrs Read was waiting for an answer so regretfully she said, 'I'm sorry, but you see my fiancé has gone away too.'

Heavy with disappointment, she saw her visitor to the door. She seemed such a nice woman, Gwen told herself, sure that they would have got on well.

Charlie's first letter told her little about where he was except that there'd been a long journey by truck to reach the camp after they'd left the train. It was deep in the country and he made a joke of the fact that after all the rain recently they were all wallowing in mud. He told her that she wouldn't recognise him with his hair cropped short, and when a week later a sepia photo arrived, she very nearly didn't.

Eddie Palmer remarked that wallowing in mud would be good practice for the trenches. Their Bert had been out there from the beginning. 'Saw a chap last week that got a blighty,' he went on. 'Thankful to get home he was, I can tell you.'

Charlie's letters came almost every day, full of love and longing and the hope of getting a leave by Christmas. She read them over and over, cried over them, and slept with them under her pillow. She in her turn wrote every night, pouring out her feelings until, drained and exhausted, she felt strangely at peace.

About a month later, turning into Wilfred Street, Gwen noticed with a sinking heart that every blind was drawn. This was an increasingly regular occurrence in the streets around, and she was wondering sadly who it could be this time when a girl of about ten and a small boy came out of a house almost opposite her own and, crossing the road, began walking towards her. When they were just yards away little Benjy Williams broke away from his sister's grasp and ran to Gwen, stopping in front of her to point proudly to the black arm band around the sleeve of his serge sailor jacket. Gwen's eyes misted as she looked down at the girl who now had her brother in tow once more. Jessie's eyes were red and swollen. 'It's Dada,' she told Gwen, her eyes brimming. 'Had a telegram we did.'

Before Gwen could voice her sympathy, they were going up the street with Benjy being dragged along protesting.

'Youer dinner's in the oven,' Sarah greeted her with one foot on the stair, a cup of tea for Mair in her hand. Then noticing the expression of sadness on Gwen's face, she added, 'You know then about Alby Williams? Poor Cissie. However will she manage?'

'I'll go over afterwards,' Gwen decided, 'see if there's anything I can do.' Being brought up in a house with a shop, she and her sisters knew everybody in the street.

'I'll pack a basket,' Sarah decided. 'That pooer girl will need all the help she can get. Mabel told me about the telegram hours ago but I've been on my own most of the afternoon. Lucy went round to help Fanny. She's rushed off her feet with all those uniforms to sew, even though

136

she's got Dolly Powell helping her.'

When half-an-hour later Gwen knocked on the Williams' front door it was opened by Jessie who showed her into the kitchen, and when a distraught Cissie looked up at her Gwen's arms went about her, and sitting beside her on the horse-hair sofa she smoothed the fine fair curls from the woman's damp forehead, holding her gently as one would a child. The youngest, a boy of about eighteen months, toddled over to rest his chin on his mother's knee and stare at her with solemn puzzled eyes as the tears fell. Gwen lifted the child to her lap and rocked him gently, and the other children crept forward to sit in a circle at her feet.

'Shall I help get them to bed?' Gwen asked, for it was obviously past the younger ones' bedtime.

Jessie replied, 'Mama always puts them in the tub, then washes some of their clothes for the morning. I'll have to put some coal on the fire first, though.' And taking the galvanised bucket that stood in the corner, she went out to the yard.

Soon the mats were rolled up and the tub was in place in front of the fire, and as Jessie bathed the baby with expert hands, Gwen held the towel ready to receive him and looked around the room. There was a wooden armchair either side of the range and colourful pegged mats almost covered the flag-stoned floor. A dark oak dresser held an assortment of china, and a red chenille cloth bordering the mantelpiece matched the one covering the table. Suddenly she became aware of the picture of a young man in army uniform, looking shy and proud. Poor Alby. Although he was older than her, she'd known him since she was a child.

Drying the baby, and watching Jessie put the next child

in the tub, she thought how like her father the girl was.

When presently Cissie rose and put the telegram into Gwen's hands she saw in her mind's eye the telegraph boy, smart in his belted tunic and peaked cap, coming to the door. Glancing down, her heart filled with pity as she read the words: 'Regret to inform you Lance Corporal Albert Williams was killed in action on 10th of November, 1914. Lord Kitchener sends his sympathy.'

Cissie gave a deep sigh, saying, 'The times I've watched them telegraph boys ride past. I was always thanking God they didn't come here, Gwen, and now they have.'

When it was Benjy's turn to be dried and dressed and Jessie attempted to take him up to bed, he would have none of it. Pointing to his clothes neatly folded on the sofa, he stamped his little feet, crying, 'Benjy wants – Benjy wants that!'

Lifting the black arm band that now lay on top of the sailor jacket, Jessie cried in consternation, 'You can't, ouer Benjy! You can't wear it to bed.'

He began to cry and Cissie, opening her eyes at the disturbance and taking in the situation, said wearily, 'Let him put it on, Jess. He doesn't understand. Take it off when he's asleep, you can.'

Closing her eyes once more she rocked gently to and fro, murmuring, 'Whatever will we do, Gwen? Whatever will we do?'

The simple cry touched Gwen's heart, and for the first time she understood Charlie's fears. It really was out of love for her that he'd wanted them to wait. Yet if he didn't come back she knew she would feel bitter and cheated. Oh, but he will come back! she assured herself quickly. Gwen's own cheeks were wet now as she thought of Charlie. Cissie was going to have a struggle to keep her family fed and clothed on the small army pension, but at least she would have her memories and the children to remind her of him. So many young women would be forced into spinsterhood having lost sweetheart or fiancé in this dreadful war.

There was a knock on the door and Jessie ushered two more neighbours into the kitchen. When a few minutes later a third arrived, the little room was crowded and Gwen slipped away, after promising to come again tomorrow. Mama would still be coping on her own and it was time to settle Mair for the night.

Chapter Eighteen

Over the years Tom had revised his opinion of Mair's young man. As he did every evening after work, Ronald had just gone up to her room, and when the kitchen door closed behind him Tom said to Sarah, 'That boy is a real brick, the way he's looked after his family and comes to spend every evening with Mair. He must know it's hopeless by now.'

She nodded, sadly aware that what Tom had said was true, but it was something that until now they had never put into words and she wished he hadn't said it. He was quite right about Ronald, though. He was a fine young man, and always so conscientious. It broke her heart to see him sitting by the bed, night after night, holding Mair's hand. She slept a lot now, exhaustion sometimes overcoming her even when someone was with her.

Unable to fool each other any longer, the young couple had stopped making plans, but their love was deeper than ever and heartbreaking to watch.

One evening towards Christmas Ronald confided his feelings to Gwen. Sarah was next door with Mabel, and Lucy was ministering to Mair's needs. Suddenly Ronald burst out with, 'I feel awful about not joining up, Gwen, but what can I do? Who would look after my mam and the kids? And there's Mair. Now she knows she can't go to Brompton, she seems to have given up hope.'

'You're needed here, Ronald,' Gwen assured him. 'Your mam could never manage on her own, and they rely on your money to live on, don't they?'

He nodded. 'I don't really see how I could go, but everyone else seems to be joining up.'

'Mair looks forward to seeing you so much. It would break her heart if you went away,' Gwen told him.

Just then Lucy came into the kitchen and Ronald went upstairs. Gwen sighed, knowing how cruel some people could be to any young man not yet in uniform.

It was less than a fortnight to Christmas but there was little of the Yuletide spirit in her heart. With Mair so poorly, Charlie away, and Lucy feeling sorry for herself – though Gwen had to admit, not without cause – there seemed little to celebrate. It was the first year the house hadn't been decorated with paper chains, but with no guests expected and so much to do it had seemed a waste of time. Sarah had packed a parcel of goodies for the Williams family, and Gwen had decided that her sacrifice would be to take on most of the chores over Christmas and let Lucy enjoy herself for once. She loved company so. Gwen had another surprise for her young sister, for despite being busy sewing uniforms Fanny had found the time to make Lucy a new dress from material Gwen had bought a few weeks before.

There was an ever increasing number of walking wounded in the streets, most on crutches and often in hospital blue, an empty trouser leg or sleeve pinned up telling its own tale; others with bandaged heads. These were the presentable wounded, thankful to be home, anxious to forget the carnage and horrors of the trenches, thankful that they'd never have to go back.

Seeing these men, some of whom she knew, would sometimes trouble Gwen's conscience. She was already doing voluntary work at the church hall two evenings a week where she rolled bandages and packed comfort parcels, knitting balaclavas and socks in any spare moment, but she felt she should do more – perhaps become a tram conductress to release a man for the forces, or go to work at the munitions factory? Ted was always saying he couldn't manage without her, and she had taken on all the book-keeping, and anyway where would she find another job where she could take time off whenever Mama was poorly as she so often was these days?

Charlie was expecting leave early in the new year and it was pretty certain to be embarkation leave when it came, for people had long since given up predicting that the war would be over very soon.

As Christmas approached and Lucy received the usual invitations from her friends, Gwen told her to her delight that she could accept.

'But it isn't fair on you, Gwen,' she protested half-heartedly. 'You work all the week yourself.'

'Well, you can make it up to me when Charlie comes home,' Gwen told her.

Suddenly the smile left Lucy's face. 'What can I wear?' she wailed. 'I haven't had anything new for ages.'

'Perhaps we can alter one of your dresses, sew on a new collar or something?' Gwen suggested, hugging to herself the knowledge that Lucy's new dress would be hanging in Fanny's wardrobe right now.

Two days before Christmas the weather turned bitterly cold, the back gardens wearing a mantle of white frost, and the roofs too, except around the chimney pots from which smoke billowed. Towards evening a blanket of freezing fog came down, muffling the sounds of footsteps and horses' hooves alike.

Late on Christmas Eve, with the fire roaring up the chimney, Gwen was putting mince-pies to cool and Lucy was washing her long fair hair in the wash-house, preparing excitedly for the festivities ahead.

'You haven't altered my dress yet, Gwen,' she reminded her worriedly for the umpteenth time.

'Don't worry, I won't let you down,' Gwen assured her, and Lucy, now combing the tangles from her curls at the mirror over the kitchen mantelpiece, said, 'I'm really grateful. I haven't been anywhere for ages.'

When Lucy went upstairs to wrap her presents, Gwen sat staring into the fire. Sarah was sitting with Mair as she did more and more now, whenever Ronald wasn't there, and Dada was with Eddie Palmer. Gwen was remembering last year when she was looking forward so much to spending Christmas afternoon and evening at Charlie's home. The weather then had been similar, bitterly cold, with white frost icing the roofs and roads and pavements, giving the illusion of snow. As they'd made their way through the village their breath had steamed and mingled in the frosty air.

The cottage had looked festive with home-made decorations, and she'd donned a white apron and helped Charlie's mam with the final preparations for tea. The cold chicken and ham, both from a neighbour's farm, were delicious, as was the sherry trifle, and of course she had to sample the heavily fruited Christmas cake and mince-pies. The little cottage had generated love and contentment, and with the non-stop chatter and the sparkling home-made wine, the evening had passed all too quickly.

The only dampener on the horizon at that time had been the fact that Sarah wouldn't let them get married. Gwen hadn't seen Charlie's parents for a few weeks, she decided she'd visit them on her next half-day, Lucy's partying would be over by then.

Her own home had been a happy one. Despite a persistent cough, Mair had seemed quite well. Lucy's pretty head had been full of all the parties she was going to. There'd been no inkling at all that long before another Christmas arrived the world would be plunged into war.

A knock at the door brought Gwen hurriedly to her feet. When she opened it she stared in dismay at Ronald who stood there, his face a ghastly white, obviously very upset.

'What's wrong?' she asked apprehensively, fearing something might have happened to his ailing mam. Then she saw the white feather clutched so tightly in his hand that the knuckles showed as white as his face.

Burning anger rose in Gwen; anger against any of her sex who would do such a horrible thing as indiscriminately distribute these emblems of supposed cowardice. Only last week she'd been told of one being handed to a soldier still on sick leave who'd been glad to get out of uniform for a few hours. He'd been angry about it but she could see that Ronald was devastated for he was sensitive about not yet having joined up.

Gwen sat him down at the table, and before drawing the kettle over the fire, gently prised the white feather from his fingers. Lifting the cover she threw it on to the coals. Soon with a steaming cup of tea between his hands, Ronald turned to her with a look of deep hurt in his eyes and said, 'It's what they're all thinking, isn't it? But I'm tied hand and foot, Gwen. Dear God, I just wish I could go, then I'd feel that much better about myself.'

'Nobody thinks like that, Ronald, only the stupid woman who handed you the feather. It's women like that who haven't any guts. People around here know about the sacrifices you've made all your life, and how much you're needed now.'

The hot tea had brought some colour back to his cheeks when Sarah opened the kitchen door, saying, 'Oh, there you are, Ronald. Mair thought she heard you come in.'

The one bright spot of Christmas Day was Lucy's excitement over the coming parties and her joy when she discovered the new dress in the wardrobe she shared with Gwen. She hugged her sister over and over, trying the dress on, eagerly twisting this way and that in front of the mirror crying, 'Oh, Gwen, and I only bought you a bottle of scent.' Then she dashed off to thank Aunt Fanny for making it.

Gwen did her best to make this Christmas just like any other. The chicken and roast potatoes were cooked to a golden brown, the plum pudding with its sprig of holly was just right. It was all ready to serve when Tom carried Mair downstairs in the warm rose-pink dressing gown that he and Sarah had given her, the pretty shade bringing a semblance of colour to her cheeks. As they sat down to the festive meal Lucy chatted excitedly, her mind on her presents and the pleasures ahead. Sarah was watching as Mair listlessly pushed the food about her plate, her expression sad. Mair looked so weary as she lolled against the back of the chair, and Gwen bent forward to say, 'Try to eat some of the chicken, cariad, it will do you good.'

The house was quiet once Lucy had left for her party. Mair lay in her room in an exhausted sleep, and Sarah was resting on the sofa in the parlour. When the dishes were washed and dried with Tom putting them away, he brought out the rhubarb wine and poured two glasses. Looking at Gwen tenderly he said, raising his glass, 'Let's drink to Charlie's health. May he come home very soon.'

As Lucy unlatched the gate at her friend's house she was shivering with excitement as well as cold. It was just like the old days, she thought excitedly, dressing up like this and going out. The atmosphere at home had been so drab and miserable, and for the last few months it had seemed to be nothing but chores. But fancy Gwen getting a dress made for her like that. Gwen was good, she meant to make it up to her. Waiting for the door to open Lucy unbuttoned her coat to look admiringly at the pretty blue silk dress.

Her friend Susan opened the door and, taking Lucy's hand, drew her inside, admiring the dress with just the right amount of envy as Lucy took off her coat. The wide hall was decorated with coloured streamers and chinese lanterns. It was wonderful to listen to everyone laughing and talking at once. A girl was playing the piano and they all stood around it singing, but soon it was time to go to the dining room where a roaring fire greeted them. The table groaned under so much fare, the centrepiece an iced Christmas cake decorated with fir trees and little sleighs.

Lucy thought of Gwen, busy at home, washing the dishes and ministering to Mair, trying to bring a little of the Christmas spirit into their day, and a warm feeling of gratitude came over her.

After the meal, when the carpet was rolled up, a few couples began to dance. The pianist, who by this time had been introduced as Susan's cousin, was playing a medley of Strauss waltzes. When Susan's brother David came up to claim a dance and took Lucy's hands in his she blushed with embarrassment as she remembered that, despite the 'Snowfire' she'd rubbed into them all last week, her hands were still rough to the touch. But nothing could really spoil the pleasure of the party, and there was another one tomorrow. The waltz having finished she hugged herself at the thought.

Charlie was expected home during the second week of the new year, and with Christmas over Gwen's excitement grew. As she approached the station on the morning he was expected there were a number of ambulances drawn up outside and drivers and attendants lifting empty stretchers to take inside.

She hadn't been on the crowded platform long when the train steamed in. Charlie looked different in uniform and with his hair shorn but she recognised him right away as they rushed towards each other.

They embraced ecstatically, oblivious of the jostling crowds. Presently he held her away from him and looked lovingly into her eyes, saying, 'I've dreamt of this moment, Gwen.' Then their lips met again in a long kiss.

At last they were leaving the station. The ambulances were still there, only now the wounded, their faces grey with fatigue, were being carried on stretchers towards them. Gwen saw Charlie glance at them, his face full of pity. Now the walking wounded were shuffling out, some on crutches, and the sight of their blood-soaked bandages made Gwen shiver. Tightening her hold on Charlie's arm, she glanced up into his face and the look he gave her in return seemed to say, 'Now do you understand how I feel?'

Loving him as she did, she linked her arm in his and squeezed it reassuringly.

Chapter Nineteen

It was wonderful having Charlie home, especially as Ted had given her the afternoons off to be with him. The days were cold and wet but nothing could dampen their joy at being together. Lucy was as good as her word, persuading Gwen that she could manage on her own, telling her to go and enjoy herself. Charlie met her from work at lunch-times and they would go to the cottage in Rumney for tea, that way his mam and dad could enjoy Charlie's company too.

Charlie's parents had got quite friendly with Gwen's over the years and now Dora Roberts said, 'Tell youer mam, Gwen that I'd love them to come to tea again when they can manage it. I know it's not easy with an invalid in the house.'

Charlie and Gwen made wonderful plans for when the war was over, and Gwen wondered wistfully if Mrs Read would still have the rooms to let. Everyone had been so sure that it would be all over by Christmas, surely it couldn't last much longer?

On several evenings they took a tram to town to see a show, but first Gwen ran her finger down the entertainments column in the *Echo*, complaining, 'Honestly Charlie, they're all about war. The Olympia's showing *The Fringe of War* and it's *By the Kaiser's Orders* at the Castle. Oh but Vesta Tilley's at the Empire, we could go there.'

They sat in the stalls, hands tightly clasped, listening to Vesta Tilley singing patriotic songs. There was no way of forgetting the war, but they were together and happy, as happy as anyone could be while counting the hours until they had to part.

As they walked home together Gwen clung to Charlie's arm as though she could never let it go and in the darkness he pulled her gently into a doorway and their kissing was long and intense.

Another night they spent at the music hall and Gwen was humming the new song 'Sister Susie's Sewing Shirts For Soldiers' for days afterwards.

On the day he was due back there were ambulances outside the station again, but the doors were closed with no sign of either drivers or stretcher bearers.

Hearts heavy at the thought of parting, arms entwined, they waited for the train that would take Charlie away, conscious that this time he'd be going overseas and that the parting might be a long one. As the train was coming into the station, hissing to a stop, they clung to each other desperately until Charlie had to tear himself away, dashing at the last minute for a carriage. As she hurried after him the whistle blew shrilly and the train began to move noisily away. Keeping her eyes on the carriage, she waved a hankie until it turned the bend then found she needed it for a more urgent use as the tears rolled slowly down her cheeks.

Dabbing her eyes, Gwen made for the stairs and saw, a few steps in front of her, a girl whom she had noticed with Artie on the platform. She looked a quiet little thing, not his type at all. Gwen was wondering whether to introduce herself when, seeing a gap in the crowd, the girl rushed forward and was lost to sight.

As the train had gathered speed Charlie too found his heart heavy at the thought of the long months of separation ahead. He closed his eyes, picturing Gwen's face as she'd waved him goodbye, seeing her warm brown eyes brimming with unshed tears. How he wished he could have forgotten his principles and got married before going overseas, but the memory of soldiers who had come home minus limbs or badly shell-shocked reminded him of why he hadn't. He loved her so much, had waited so long – far too long, he told himself, knowing that Gwen shared his need. It wasn't fair to her to have joined up just when they were planning to marry at last.

When Charlie opened his eyes it was to see the usually garrulous Artie staring out of the window, his face thoughtful. As though aware that he was being watched, he turned to Charlie, saying, 'Did you see her? The girl who came to the station with me? It's the real thing this time, I swear it is. I've never met anyone like her. She's different to all the others, all right. Wants me to write regular, she does.'

They had been back at the camp for only a few days when they boarded lorries to take them to the port. On the troopship they were packed like sardines; elbow room would have been a luxury. As the ship nosed out into the Channel the increasing swell soon made Charlie queasy. Artie, standing a few yards away, was talking cheerfully to anyone fit enough to listen, but as the swell increased even those who considered themselves good sailors were thankful to sink down to the crowded deck. Presently Charlie slipped into an uneasy sleep, to wake with a mouth like sandpaper and a thirst he had no hope of satisfying, just as the ship was approaching Boulogne harbour.

They disembarked on the dark quayside to be once more packed into lorries that trundled first through ghostly silent streets, then along dark deserted lanes, quiet except for the occasional bellowing of a bull.

A cold grey dawn was breaking when at last they turned into a field of tents. Being near the tailboard and anxious to feel firm ground beneath his feet, Charlie jumped down eagerly – straight into a patch of squelching mud, splattering himself to the eyebrows.

When Gwen got back to the shop at the beginning of the following week, Ted was in the process of buying some ornaments from a customer. She shook her head sadly when she saw him passing money over for a pair of late-Victorian vases decorated with fat pink roses. Hideous they were, he'd never sell them. But he had no intention of selling them, he'd made that very clear. Ted would soon be broke, she told herself, the way he was going on. The shelves in the spare room had rapidly filled up with the things he'd bought, things that were practically unsaleable, and every single item was tabbed with the name of the customer he'd bought it from. He'd given a solemn promise that people would be able to retrieve their treasures after the war.

The first time Ted had bought something that she knew wouldn't sell, she'd remarked, 'But this isn't the stuff you usually buy,' and he'd replied, 'Well, you have to try and help these people, Gwen. Steady jobs their men have left to fight for their country. An army allowance doesn't go far with a family to feed.'

'But you paid as much for that cracked tea-pot as you would have for a perfect one.'

'The value is all in the mind, Gwen. To Mrs Hopkins that tea-pot is a family heirloom. Pride of place it had in a glass cupboard at the side of the parlour fireplace. Showed it to me she did when I went there once. It's eased her conscience at selling it, knowing she can buy it back after the war.'

Gwen glanced at Ted. He was always so thoughtful of people's feelings, putting himself in their place, knowing how best to help. The spare room was already stacked with all sorts of lame ducks. Victorian china of the sort that had been cheaply made for the masses, and better quality things, badly cracked or chipped. Ted must know they would probably never be reclaimed but he seemed happy that he'd given the owners badly needed money and the hope of buying back one day.

At home life was becoming more and more gloomy, especially since Doctor Powell confided to Sarah that he thought Mair's illness had been too far gone to benefit from a stay at Brompton anyway, especially as at that time she would have had to wait a little while for a place.

'What a pity the war came when it did, Doctor,' Sarah had remarked. 'If she'd gone away we might have seen a big improvement by now.'

But he had shaken his head and told her what he thought, adding, 'That's not to say you're going to lose her, Sarah. With good nursing she could go on for years.'

Now Gwen would arrive home each evening to find her mother staring into the fire, unless she was upstairs with the invalid. A disgruntled Lucy would be feeling sorry for herself, endless washing and scrubbing and running up and down stairs having lined her pretty face with discontent, and the long, fair curls that once had been her pride and joy were now often tangled and untidy. Gwen was always willing to take over so that she could go out, but with a martyred air she'd declare herself much too tired to wash and change. Her father too was looking strained and tired. He'd go up to sit with Mair as soon as Ronald left, and come down with his eyes moist, pretending he needed to blow his nose.

One evening she was just about to tap on Mair's door which was slightly open when she heard Ronald saying, ' . . . that's nonsense, love, you're going to be with us for a very long time.'

Mair's reply was low. 'It's not nonsense, Ronald. I'd like to think you'll get married and have a family. It's my one regret that we couldn't do just that. I love you so much, and I want to think you'll be happy.'

'I could never love anyone as I love you, Mair,' he was saying, 'and we're going to be together for a long time yet.'

Gwen had stood as though transfixed. Now she tip-toed away to the bedroom she shared with Lucy, her eyes burning with unshed tears. As she flung herself on to the bed they began to fall, and she buried her face in the cool pillow and sobbed for the hopelessness of their situation.

Chapter Twenty

Charlie would never forget his first glimpse of the trenches. On a wet spring dawn they'd left camp to march with full kit through sleepy villages and silent towns and along country lanes, often in driving rain. In one small village, shuttered for the night, a casement flew open and a night-capped head appeared briefly to cry, '*Bonne chance, Tommy. Vive les Anglais*!'

On the second day the sound of guns came to them like distant thunder, growing ever louder as, wet and weary, they trudged towards their goal, the kit they carried growing heavier by the minute.

Even the cloying mud of the camp they'd left two days before hadn't prepared them for the boot-sucking stuff Charlie and his mates found themselves in that first day in the trenches; the boards they walked on almost submerged, the place pervaded by a strong smell of decay. And nothing he'd ever seen in his whole life had been half as desolate as the wide stretch of No Man's Land that separated the barbed-wire entanglements of either side. Here the earth was blackened and riddled with craters and the debris of battle and shells of once proud trees, blasted by gun fire, threw grim silhouettes against the sky.

The trench he found himself in was about three feet

wide, and perhaps six and a half feet deep, with a fire step running its length, but he soon learnt to keep well down, for if a head popped up or even the glow of a cigarette was shown for a moment, it would attract a hail of bullets.

They seemed to be under almost constant bombardment and at first his stomach churned with fear, but the concentration required as they returned fire soon calmed him. Two evenings later he made his first sortie into No Man's Land, wriggling on his belly like an eel, watching for the sergeant in front to wave him on. Suddenly, in the darkness, he found himself falling into a shell-hole, landing on something soft and warm, horrified to feel stickiness spreading over his hands. Pressing hard on the edges of the crater, he heaved himself out, and steeling himself, his eyes now accustomed to the gloom, turned the body over, gasping as he recognised, even though his face was contorted, the young officer who'd spoken to his group that morning.

As the weeks passed and Charlie grew more dirty, dishevelled and flea-bitten, he spent his spare moments as did the others squeezing the seams of any of his clothing he could reach in a vain attempt to be rid of the lice that day and night tormented him.

Often his thoughts flew to Gwen. The sweet, fresh look of her, the glowing cheeks and warm brown eyes. He thought longingly too of his home; his mam bustling about in her starched white apron on baking days, the kitchen filled with a delicious smell as the scrubbed table groaned under cooling bread, pies and cakes. But what he thought about increasingly now was the zinc bath drawn up in front of a roaring fire, with snowy towels draped over one end of the guard and a clean change of clothing at the other. In his imagination he'd draw three buckets of hot water from the brass tap in the boiler at the side of the range, adding it to the cold already in the tub. The memory was like a mirage that appeared whenever he was at his wettest, coldest and dirtiest. For a moment he would allow himself to luxuriate in the thought, until the reality of his filthy existence took over, or the almost constant bombardment started up once more.

On a warm evening early in May just as it was getting dusk, Gwen was looking through the front bedroom window down to the street below when her eye caught that of Jack Hopkins the lamplighter. He called up to her, but she had to lift the window before she could hear what he was saying.

' . . . trouble around Mabel Street,' he yelled, after putting down his pole and cupping both hands around his mouth. 'There's a German woman lives round there. Leastwise, her dad was German.'

'That'll be Helga Thomas,' Gwen cried. 'Just a minute, Jack, I'm coming down.'

Opening the door, she went to stand by the gate where the lamplighter was waiting, asking, 'Was it because of that liner the *Lusitania* being sunk? I thought there'd be trouble over that.'

Jack Hopkins nodded. 'Daft, I call it. She's as Welsh as any of us. Born in the valley, she was. Her father's been naturalised an' all. What could she have to do with any sinking?'

'It's awful,' Gwen said. 'Billy her husband has been at the front since the beginning. What did they do this time?'

'Pushed lighted paper through the letter-box. The child was screaming, so her neighbour told me. Poor little soul. By the time the fire engine got there they'd put the fire out, but a lot of her stuff was ruined with the water.'

'Poor girl!' Gwen cried. Helga had been in the same class at school, a quiet girl with a lilting Welsh accent for they'd lived in the valleys until she was eight when her father brought the family to Cardiff where he'd found work.

It was awful about the *Lusitania*. It had been sunk yesterday off the coast of Ireland with the loss of about 1,500 lives. It was a terrible tragedy and it was only natural as the Germans were to blame that people were going to feel bitter towards the Hun, but Helga had never set foot in Germany, and her father had seen fit to emigrate.

These outbreaks of hostility were getting more frequent. In other parts of the country there'd been trouble whenever the Germans had dropped bombs. The first had fallen harmlessly, so the papers said, on Dover last December, but in January two Zeppelins had dropped more than twenty bombs on Great Yarmouth and King's Lynn in Norfolk, killing four people and injuring many more. And there'd been other raids too, and each time, although these must be naturalised subjects for all other Germans or Austrians had already been interned, the wrath of so-called patriots had been vented against anyone bearing a German name.

Jack Hopkins sighed. 'Well, I'd better be getting along,' he said, 'the lamps won't light themselves.'

As he bent to pick up his pole Gwen told him she meant to go around right away to see what she could do, but he turned to her anxiously saying, 'I'd leave it, girl, if I was you. Darned unfair it is, I know, but they'll have it in for anyone who helps.'

As he moved towards the next lamp-post Gwen reflected on his words, but Helga was a friend. She hadn't seen much of her since she'd left school but they'd got on well then. The poor girl must be terrified being in that house with just the child. Her parents had returned to the valleys long before the war.

Gwen lifted her coat from the hall-stand and pinned on her hat. Mama was sitting with Mair. She was just wondering whether to call up to her when she heard the bedroom door open and Sarah appeared at the top of the stairs.

'You going out, Gwen?' she called down in surprise. When she reached Gwen and was told about Helga, she said worriedly, 'Better stay out of it, cariad, you'll only bring trouble on yourself and we've got enough to cope with now Mair is so poorly.'

'I'll just see if there's anything I can do,' Gwen told her, and Sarah nodded. Then, as Gwen opened the door, Sarah put a hand gently on her arm, saying, 'Take care. Don't court trouble if you can help it.'

As Gwen took the couple of turnings that would bring her to Mabel Street she wondered what she might find. The house was about halfway along and as she approached it the smell of burning grew stronger. Lifting the latch of the gate she saw by the light of the lamp outside that a charred hall-stand had been tipped up in the front garden, together with some burnt oilcloth that was ripped into pieces. The door itself was scorched in places. Lifting the knocker, she banged on it several times but no one answered.

Helga will be afraid to answer the door, she told herself, especially after dark. Looking around to make sure she wasn't being watched, Gwen lifted the letter-box and called: 'Helga! Helga! It's Gwen – Gwen Llewellyn. I've come to see if I can help.'

At first there was no sound, but when she'd called again

and stood wondering what to do next, the door opened a crack and a voice whispered hoarsely, 'You'd better come in quickly.'

Inside, the smell of burning wood and oilcloth was strong. Gwen looked about her in the dim light from the open kitchen door. The boards now bare of oilcloth were badly charred; the walls also were blackened and still wet where neighbours had attempted to put out the fire. Following Helga, she stepped down into the kitchen where everything seemed as usual, but one glance at her friend's face belied this impression.

'Is the baby in bed?' she asked, noticing the little garments on the airing line strung across the kitchen just below the ceiling.

'Yes. Mary's safer upstairs, Gwen. I sometimes put her to sleep in the parlour but I won't from now on.'

Helga shuddered, and Gwen put an arm about her, saying, 'What you need is a strong cup of tea.'

Putting the kettle over the coals, she set about laying the table with cups, saucers, sugar bowl and milk jug. Helga sat hugging her knees, staring into the coals, the expression on her face one of despair.

'Have you had anything to eat today, Helga?'

When the girl shook her head, Gwen said, 'You must eat to keep your strength up. I'll get something, shall I?' But apart from the heel of a loaf, a tin of condensed milk, and the remains of a pot of jam, there was little that could be turned into a meal, and the safe on the wall in the yard yielded only a small piece of cheese, some margarine and an egg.

'That's for the baby tomorrow,' Helga explained when Gwen brought in the egg. 'I've been afraid to go to the shops. They're maniacs, Gwen. What do they think I've done? I'm as disgusted as anyone about that ship being sunk. I've come to hate my name. I used to like it when I was in school because it was different from everyone else's but I really hate it now. I just wish I was called Helen or Nell.'

'You could call yourself Nell . . .' Gwen began, but Helga shook her head, saying, 'Everyone knows me around here. When I went to the shops last week some man called me "that German bitch".'

As a sob rose in Helga's throat Gwen's arms went about her. Huddled against her, the girl went on brokenly, 'I wanted to keep a home for when Billy comes back, but I'm scared, Gwen, especially after what happened today.' She shivered, rubbing her hands together then stretching them towards the fire.

'I must get something for you to eat,' Gwen told her, 'I'll just slip home for some soup that was left over. It won't take me long to get it from the safe, and it'll warm you up.'

Seeing the fear in Helga's eyes at being left alone, she hugged her to her saying again, 'I won't be long, love.'

Putting on her coat and hat once more, she went through the passage and closed the door softly behind her, looking up and down the street anxiously. But it was deserted. Hurrying along, she wondered what her mam would say if she suggested staying the night with Helga? Sarah would be anxious to avoid any trouble, but not at all costs. Her mother was a compassionate woman. But supposing her actions did bring trouble upon them? Things weren't easy for any of them now with Mair so ill. But she couldn't turn her back on Helga, could she? They'd just have to face it if it came.

Feeling uneasy at the thought, Gwen knew that if

trouble came she would be responsible.

When she entered the kitchen Sarah was sewing the seam of a sheet she was turning. Raising her eyes to Gwen, she said simply, 'Well?'

'She's in a bad way, Mam. The place is a shambles, especially the passage and the stairs. It's a miracle they weren't burnt. If they'd been in bed and not noticed things smouldering they might have died. They've got nothing in the house because she's afraid to go to the shops.'

'Have you managed to help her? Is there anything I can do, cariad?'

'I came back to take her that soup that was left over. I – I – may have to stay the night, Mam.'

Sarah was already on her feet and getting the wicker basket from the cupboard. She began bringing things from the pantry to put in it, saying in a worried voice, 'I know you have to go, but be careful, Gwen.'

This time when she arrived at the house in Mabel Street the door flew open at the first knock and she was drawn quickly inside, then it was shut again and the bolt shot home.

The soup heated, Gwen watched Helga spoon it up ravenously, and vowed that in future she'd do the shopping for her. Surely it would blow over? They wouldn't repeat the unprovoked attack? Who were they, these people who perpetrated such atrocities in the name of patriotism? They weren't Helga's immediate neighbours anyway for they'd been kindness itself. If there were more Zeppelin raids around the country would it all start again? It was a worrying thought.

When at last they got to bed Helga couldn't seem to rest, sitting bolt upright at every little sound and begging Gwen to listen. She dozed fitfully, waking twice to find

Helga hugging her knees and staring before her. The third time she woke to find her standing at the window looking out. It was obvious that Helga needed to have someone with her. But I can't stay with her every night, Gwen told herself worriedly, it wouldn't be fair to Mama and Lucy.

'I've made up my mind, Gwen,' Helga told her, coming to sit on the bed. 'I could go to live with my mam and dad if I could find somewhere to store my stuff. I'd have to find somewhere for when Billy comes home, but we can't stay here.'

'Would you be welcome in your parents' village? I mean, well, no offence, but they are German too.'

'Oh! But my mam is pure Welsh. They lived there years before we came to Cardiff. My dad's naturalised, of course, and he lived there before they were married. Homesick they were for the place, that's why they went back.'

'In that case, it seems the best thing to do,' Gwen told her.

'Do you know anyone who would store our things? I could manage a little every week.'

Gwen shook her head. She'd ask Ted, and if he couldn't perhaps he'd know someone, but it was best not to raise Helga's hopes.

At about three o'clock the baby began to cry. Gwen went downstairs to heat milk. She brought it upstairs and the child soon drained the cup, but when her mother took her back to her room she screamed so loudly they ended up with the child in bed between them, Gwen's expression softening when she saw the silky lashes fanning cheeks still wet with tears.

Gwen dozed fitfully through the remaining hours of the night and left the house in time to call home before going to work. As she turned into Wilfred Street she was surprised to see her parents standing outside the house, staring down at the pavement. As she drew near she could see something printed there in large white capitals. Oh, no! she thought. Not already. Then as she drew level she could make out the words: ROTTEN BITCH! HUN LOVER!

Gwen looked from her father's drawn face to Sarah who seemed to have aged since last night, and said simply, 'I'm sorry.' But her father put an arm about her, saying, 'We don't blame you, Gwen. What else could you do?'

When they went into the kitchen Lucy gave her a look which told her plainly how she felt, hissing at her as soon as they were alone, 'Your fault this is, our Gwen. How am I going to face my friends now?'

When Gwen didn't answer she went on, 'I don't know why you went round there. You only knew her from when you were in school. She wasn't a real friend like the ones I've got, asking me to their houses and that.'

What Lucy said was perfectly true, of course. Because of the shop she and Mair had never been able to have any real friends. They'd been expected to come home from school each evening to serve customers, there'd been no time to play with other children. Helga was the nearest she'd come to having a friend, sharing a desk together, managing to sit with each other even when they moved class. But even if she'd been a complete stranger Helga had needed a friend last night, hadn't she?

At work Ted kept giving her concerned glances, but it took Daisy Ball to ask outright, 'Had a bad night with youer poor sister, Gwen? There's peaky you look this morning, cariad.'

And so the story came out, and Ted's face, and Daisy's too, became more and more angry as she told it. And when she came to the part about Helga needing someone to store her furniture, Ted said, 'We could find room here if we push things up a bit.'

'But won't you make yourself a target then?' Gwen asked anxiously. After all, Ted had a business. He couldn't afford to upset people.

'No, I don't think so, Gwen,' he told her. 'If anyone saw me bringing things away they'd think I'd bought the stuff. Oh, and tell her there won't be anything for storing it. Only too pleased to be able to help, I am.'

Deciding when her lunch-break came she'd give Helga the good news, Gwen hurried around to Mabel Street, feeling sick with apprehension when as she approached the house she saw the message painted in large letters on the wall.

BLOODY HUN. GO HOME.

Gwen knocked on the door, waiting anxiously for it to open, but there was no reply. She was knocking again when a neighbour's door opened and a middle-aged woman came out, wiping her hands on a sacking apron, saying, 'I was hoping you'd come, miss. Mrs Thomas gave me a message. Left with the baby she did, soon as she saw that.' She pointed to the wall, shaking her head in disgust. 'Goin' to take a bit of gettin' off that is. Must 'ave been the last straw. Said to tell you she'd paid the rent 'til the end of the week, and she'd be very grateful if you could find somewhere to store the furniture. Told me to give you the key but she wouldn't say where she was going, only that 'er uncle will come here Friday night, an 'e'll pay you then for your trouble.'

'I'll probably be able to make some arrangements,' Gwen told her. She certainly wasn't going to get Ted into any bother by saying he'd store the furniture for nothing.

Chapter Twenty-one

For weeks Gwen went about looking over her shoulder, terrified at the slightest sound, but thankfully there was no more trouble. Helga's attackers were obviously satisfied at running her out of town. Not knowing her new address, Gwen delivered a note from Ted to her uncle when he came on the Friday night. Ted had written assuring Helga that her things would be taken care of until the war was over, and at no cost to herself. Luckily the writing outside Gwen's home had been written in chalk and easily washed away. Even Lucy seemed to be pacified when it was gone.

The war was dragging on and on. Although not yet rationed, food and coal were becoming short. No one now believed that it would soon be over. There was an increasing number of wounded on the streets, and since the battle of Ypres, where the Germans used gas, victims of this new and terrifying form of warfare could be seen, ashen-faced and with bloodshot eyes. These were the lucky ones who'd made it home, for many victims of gas died in agony in the trenches, frothing at the mouth and struggling desperately for breath.

As the year wore on Mair became even thinner, her legs like sticks, the fine grey eyes sunken into her head, her cheeks often bright with fever. But still she clung to life.

Every evening Ronald climbed the stairs to her room and cradled her hands in his, talking to her in a low, gentle voice. It was almost as though he willed her to live for him, as though some of the strength flowed from his hands to hers, for Doctor Powell had several times predicted that she wouldn't last the week but each time she'd rallied and taken a slight turn for the better.

As 1916 came in there was little to celebrate either at home or on the battle fronts, and with most families having one or more members at the front, and many having already lost a loved one, the new year brought little joy. Each day Gwen waited anxiously for the post for yet another of Charlie's letters to swell the number in her top drawer. He told her little of what he must be going through, his letters were full of love and his longing to be home with her. In return she would sit down and pour out her heart to him. As the months went by with heavy losses on the battle fields and an inevitable slowing up of volunteers, there were rumours about conscription being introduced, but when in May it was announced, it was restricted to batchelors.

It was June before Ronald received his call-up papers. He brought them with him when he came straight from work.

'I'd be glad if it wasn't for leaving Mair,' he confided to Gwen. 'My brother and sister are old enough now to give our mam a hand, and they'll have my army pay to help them out. It's Mair I'm worried about. How shall I break it to her, Gwen?'

'Don't worry, Ronald, we'll look after her for you,' she assured him, knowing in her heart that nothing they could do would make up for Ronald's devotion to her. Gwen was under no illusion about the effect his going could have.

'When do you have to go?'

'Next Tuesday. Oh, Gwen! How am I going to break it to her?' he asked again.

'Well, I expect you'll get a leave after your training, Ronald, before you go overseas. Tell her about that. It will be something for her to look forward to.'

On the day before he was to leave Ronald came early in the evening and went straight upstairs. Whenever Gwen had occasion to go to her bedroom she could hear his low murmuring as she passed the door, and pictured him gazing at Mair lovingly, holding her hands in his.

When at last he came downstairs his eyes were moist. Stepping down into the kitchen where Sarah and Gwen were busy knitting balaclavas, he said in a voice husky with emotion, 'She's a bit upset. I don't like to leave her like this.'

'It'll be all right, Ronald,' Sarah said, getting up and putting a hand on his arm. 'You look after yourself, son. As Gwen was saying, you'll probably get a leave in a while.'

When Ronald had gone, at a nod and a glance ceiling-wards from her mother, Gwen rose and went upstairs. Pushing the bedroom door open quietly she went over to the bed where Mair lay, propped against the pillows. Two bright spots of colour stained her cheeks down which silent tears were rolling.

'He'll have leave in a couple of months, Mair,' Gwen said comfortingly, taking her sister's hand. 'You've got that to look forward to, cariad.'

'I shan't be here then.' The voice was little more than a whisper. 'Look after Ronald for me, Gwen. Tell him I want him to be happy. He'll know what I mean.'

'Of course, love, but you'll be able to give him the

message yourself. You'll feel much better when his letters start to arrive.'

Mair's tears only flowed faster.

On a hot night towards the end of August it was Lucy's turn to keep watch at Mair's bedside. Someone had been with her night and day for weeks as her strength had faded then rallied, and they'd all waited anxiously for Ronald's letter about his expected leave. But when, that morning, one had arrived it had brought a cry of despair from Mair and tears had slowly rolled down her cheeks. She'd handed the letter to Gwen, pointing to the first paragraph and as Gwen read it she cried, 'Oh, it just isn't fair! Ronald's to go overseas immediately, without coming home.'

'Can't anything be done? Compassionate leave perhaps?' Sarah asked quietly, drawing Gwen to one side.

'That letter was written two days ago Mam. Anyway, I think you've got to be a close relative to even apply.'

'There's been a lot of casualties on the Somme,' Tom said bitterly when he was told. 'They can't even afford the time to train them properly now.'

'But he'll get his leave eventually won't he?' Sarah asked anxiously. 'After all, they owe it to him, don't they?'

Tom had given a mirthless laugh. 'Some hope,' he said. 'The army doesn't work like that.'

'But he said in the letter that he hopes to be back before too long.'

'That was for Mair's benefit, Sarah. I'd be very surprised if he was.'

Sitting in the armchair at the side of the bed, Lucy was reading a book, when a sudden change in Mair's breathing made her turn quickly towards her. Her sister's eyes were closed, each breath seemed to be torn from her with effort. Her heart cold with fear, Lucy ran to the head of the stairs calling anxiously, 'Mama! Gwen!'

Tom had just got in and as the three of them hurried to the bed he said, 'I'd better fetch Doctor Powell.'

Gwen sat on one side and Sarah at the other while Lucy, her eyes wide with fright, stood at the foot.

'Ronald,' Mair's voice was barely above a whisper. Gwen took Mair's hand in hers, saying gently, 'It's Gwen, dear.'

'Tell him—' There was a long pause, then the low voice went on, 'Tell Ronald to be happy.'

The bedclothes were rising and falling with the effort Mair had made, but after a while her breathing became even shallower.

'Why doesn't Doctor Powell come?' Sarah fretted anxiously, Mair's other hand clasped gently in her own. She bent closer to smooth back the hair from Mair's forehead whispering tenderly, 'Oh, my love! My little girl.'

Mair's eyes were closed, her face pallid. There was fear in Sarah's eyes as she said, 'Pass me that mirror from the dressing table, Lucy.' But even before she held it towards Mair's face she knew that her daughter had gone.

It fell to Gwen to break the news to Ronald. The letter proved difficult to write, there was no way of softening the blow, and her own tears stained the pages long before it was finished.

The mourning outfits were bought at David Morgan's drapery store in the Hayes, for Fanny, already burdened with an ever-increasing number of uniforms to make, couldn't have completed even one of the outfits in time.

It was a sombre occasion as they left the house to take

the tram to town. Their arms about their mother, the girls walked her slowly to the store, but even supported by them Sarah had to stop several times just to get her breath. Doctor Powell had been pleasantly surprised at the way she'd borne her loss, he'd been fearful of the effect it might have on his ailing patient, but Gwen knew it was the inevitability and the long preparation for Mair's death that had helped her to come to terms with it.

Lucy had never been in this fashionable drapery establishment before, and she gazed about her in wonder at the array of outfits displayed on tailor's dummies. Then an assistant was approaching them, smiling at them sympathetically when she saw the black arm bands. Ushering them over to where mourning outfits were on display, she helped them choose several to try on. Then they were on their way to the dressing rooms, the assistant almost hidden under the garments she was carrying.

Just over an hour later they were leaving the store with Gwen and Lucy carrying the many parcels, and even so managing to keep an arm through Sarah's as they made their way slowly to the tram stop. The girls had both chosen costumes with the fashionable long jacket, the full skirts almost to the ankle. Both chose black crêpe-de-chine blouses, Lucy's with a lace collar, Gwen's with a high neck edged with narrow black lace. Sarah, with her ample figure, had chosen a dress and coat. They had visited the millinery department for a wide black straw hat apiece, but luckily only Lucy had needed shoes.

The weather was humid, the trying on of clothes had been exhausting, but when Sarah remembered the mourning jewellery they had to retrace their steps to the arcade. Sitting in the jeweller's shop waiting while he put coils of Mair's dark hair into each of the brooches they had chosen, Gwen looked at her mother anxiously for Sarah was grey with fatigue.

'A cup of tea would do you good, Mam,' she suggested when at last they came out into the arcade, and it seemed an excellent idea as they entered the cool interior of the tea-shop and sat down at the table. But soon Gwen wasn't so sure for the hot liquid was making her feel warmer than ever, and she thought longingly of the sprigged muslin dress and pretty straw hat that she would normally have worn on a day like this but which were totally unsuitable for such a sombre occasion. As they left the tea-room and headed once more for the tram stop the sun was at its hottest. Red with heat, Gwen struggled with the parcels and helping Sarah along, while Lucy in her cool linen duster coat, which happened to be grey, stayed cool and pretty.

The day before the funeral, as food was becoming short, neighbours brought their offerings to the house to help Sarah provide refreshments for the mourners, a ritual that could always be relied on.

On the day of the funeral, despite so many men being away at the war, the older ones and young boys formed a procession to walk behind the hearse and single carriage. It stretched to the end of the street. The glossy black horses stood proud and patient while the coffin was slid into the hearse and piled with wreaths. Then the undertaker's men in their tall hats with black streamers closed the glass doors of the hearse and soon it was drawing slowly away. In the single carriage Tom stared sadly from the window, remembering happier days with the daughter he'd lost, while Sarah, Fanny and the girls dabbed their eyes with black-edged handkerchiefs.

The service at the church where Mair had taught Bible

class was very moving as Father Davies extolled her many virtues and bemoaned the fact that her life had been so short. Glancing often at her mother's ashen face, Gwen was thankful when they'd sung the last hymn and the women could go back to the house while the men went on to Cathays cemetery.

The next morning Sarah instructed the girls to clean and polish Mair's room from top to bottom, putting clean linen and blankets on the bed. Lucy was almost in tears.

'She's going to say that I've got to sleep here, Gwen, I know she is, and I'm scared of getting the consumption!'

But it soon became apparent that Sarah had other ideas. Mair's photograph was sent to be enlarged and hung on the bedroom wall over the fireplace in an ornate gilt frame. Little trinkets of their sister's were arranged on the chest of drawers.

'What became of that pretty cloth that Mair embroidered when she was a little girl?' Sarah asked, and when it was found and washed, starched and ironed, she laid it on top of the chest of drawers, arranging the knick-knacks on top of it.

'Don't worry, Lucy,' Gwen told her, 'Mama isn't going to ask you to sleep there. It's being made into a shrine for Mair.'

When finally everything was to Sarah's satisfaction and fresh curtains were hung at the window, she would sit in there by the hour until Gwen began to be worried for her. But soon Sarah found another interest that worried the family even more, for now she began to send for stonemason's catalogues, with a view to having a marble statue of an angel for Mair's grave. Tom was worried, confiding to Gwen that they didn't have that sort of money, and what was wrong with the small granite urn? He'd had engraved upon it the words:

THE SISTERS

To which Sarah replied that there was nothing wrong with
it, it was very nice, but a marble angel, just a small one,
would be more appropriate, and she would scrimp and
save until she got one.

Tom was very alarmed. 'Mair would be the last to want
us to put ourselves in queer street for that,' he told
Gwen. 'I don't know what's got into youer mother. She
did all she could for Mair while she was alive.'

But Sarah began scrimping on the grocery order, which
was restricted enough already by the shortage of things in
the shops, and the stone-mason's catalogue, always to
hand, was getting to be an obsession.

It was mid-September and still there was heavy fighting
on the Somme. Charlie had told Gwen in his last letter
that he'd recently met up with Ronald who was taking his
loss very hard. When Gwen thought of Charlie it was
always his smiling face that came to mind; the laughing
eyes, the ready grin, the infectious good humour. She felt
that the solemn young man in army uniform who gazed at
her from the photograph on the mantelpiece wasn't really
Charlie at all. Well, of course, there wasn't much to laugh
about just now, but these awful times would pass and then
the old Charlie would be back.

On a Monday evening late in September she'd just got
home from work when there was a knock at the door. She
opened it to see a small boy who looked vaguely familiar
standing there hastily rubbing his eyes with the back of
one hand while he held out a note with the other. When

175

he took the hand from his face she recognised one of Ronald's young brothers, and when she saw the black arm band she felt cold with apprehension.

Beckoning the boy into the passage she turned up the gas jet and opened the letter with shaking fingers, swallowing hard as her eyes scanned the words.

'Sorry to have to tell you ouer Ronald's been killed in action. The telegram came this morning.'

Taking the boy to the kitchen, she said to Sarah, 'It's bad news, I'm afraid.' And when her mother had read the message she cried, 'Oh, the pooer soul! We must go round right away, Gwen, see if there's anything we can do.'

Short as groceries were, especially since she'd been saving, Sarah got out the wicker basket and began putting things in it, saying to Gwen, 'Even with there being no proper funeral, there'll be people dropping in.'

Gwen was pinning on her hat again, telling the boy 'Run along and tell your mam we'll be round in a minute.'

When he'd gone she looked at Sarah anxiously, saying, 'Are you sure you feel up to coming, Mam?'

Sarah's eyes had filled with tears. 'He'd become like a son to me, Gwen,' she said simply. 'That pooer, pooer woman. Whatever will she do?'

The same boy who'd brought them the note opened the door and took them to the parlour where his mother lay in bed propped against the pillows, her eyes red with weeping. She was a thin woman, and her face was pale, but it held a gentle expression as she said, 'My Ronald used to talk about all of you. Like home youer place was to him, and youer Mair was his world. Shattered he must have been getting the news out there, but they're together now.' A sob rose to her throat and Sarah's arms went about her, her voice breaking on the words as she said, 'That's the one consolation.'

Gwen turned to a girl of about fourteen who had come into the room, saying, 'Shall we make a cup of tea?' and picking up the basket, she left the room.

Presently, with a cup of tea in her hand, Sarah looked about her with approval. The room was spotless and smelt of lavender; the sheets and pillowcases on the bed were snowy white. The girl who'd taken Gwen to the kitchen was handing her mam a cup, together with one of the Garibaldi biscuits Sarah had brought. She wished now that she'd got to know Ronald's family better, but he'd been with them in Wilfred Street such a lot and talked of them so often she felt she knew them.

'I don't know what I'd have done without ouer Ronald when the children were small, Mrs Llewellyn,' his mam was saying. 'I've got good children, thank God. I've been lucky that way.'

'How will you manage now?' Then, putting her hand to her mouth, Sarah went on, 'I'm sorry, I didn't mean to pry.'

'Well, Tim got a job on the trams when he left school in August. Learn to be a driver he will in time, and Lily here is hoping to go into service when she leaves school. Our Mary will be ten by then so we'll be able to cope.' Her voice trailed off.

'Is there anything we can do?'

'No, but thank you, Mrs Llewellyn.'

'Sarah – call me Sarah. I'd really like to help.'

'I'm Agnes. I'd like us to be friends.'

When about an hour later Gwen and Sarah returned home, the first thing Sarah did was to pick up the memorial catalogue. But she didn't browse through it as usual. To Gwen's astonishment she ripped the booklet in half and threw it on the fire, saying, 'Youer father was right, Gwen. A waste of money it would have been. I just felt I

177

should make some sacrifice for Mair.'

'She wouldn't have wanted you to do it, Mam,' Gwen began, but Sarah went on, 'Oh, but I've thought of something much more useful to do, Gwen, for her and for Ronald. I'm going to see that Agnes and the children don't go short. One of us must go round from time to time. That's what friends are for.'

Gwen smiled at Sarah's words, knowing just which one of them it would be.

Chapter Twenty-two

'Lucy's late again, Gwen. Where does that girl get to?'

'They've probably missed the tram and had to wait for the next. She was going with Vera to the music hall, wasn't she, Mam?'

Vera was Lucy's new friend. About a month after Mair died Lucy had at last been apprenticed to the tailoring trade, and Vera had started work there on the same day. A fair proportion of the work was still the making of uniforms and would be until the war was over, but Lucy was happy to have got a start.

It was the summer of 1917 and they had been out of mourning for about three months, but long before that Lucy had been grumbling about having to wear black. She lost no time in starting to enjoy herself once she was able, and then it was as though she was feverishly trying to make up for lost time. And who can blame her? Gwen thought, remembering how lucky she herself had been to be able to go straight from school into a job she loved.

When the door opened and they heard Lucy's light step in the passage, Sarah gave a sigh of relief. Then Lucy came into the kitchen, eyes bright with excitement, humming a song everyone had been singing for years: 'Keep the Home Fires Burning'. Gwen marvelled once again at the transformation in her young sister in the last few months. With her wide blue eyes and the long fair hair rippling in waves down her back, and especially with some bright colour in her cheeks, she looked pretty and carefree, as she should at her age.

'Did Vera see you to the door?' Sarah asked anxiously. Vera was a year older than Lucy and had served an apprenticeship with another tailor before going to McClelland's to work.

'Yes. Isn't it lucky it's on her way home? The music hall was marvellous. You should go sometimes, both of you. We all joined in the songs. They held a board up with the words but everyone knew them. They sang, "Goodbye Dolly, I Must Leave You", and "Pack Up Your Troubles", and "Tipperary".'

'It's a good job you were in before Dada got home. He's gone to a meeting in town.'

'I'm nearly seventeen, Mam,' Lucy protested. Anyway, she thought, I know how to get around Dada all right. Hadn't he given her the money to go the music hall in the first place? She only had to fling her arms about him and kiss his cheek.

When Tom came in she did just that, and sang them some of the songs from the show. Her father patted her cheek and called her a minx but she knew he was loving every minute of it.

Gwen found herself humming 'Keep the Home Fires Burning' under her breath as she went upstairs. The music had been composed early in the war by Ivor Novello, a talented young musician who'd been born and brought up in a house in Cowbridge Road in Cardiff. Now, in the quiet of the bedroom she hummed the tune softly, her eyes on Charlie's photograph on a small table at her side of the bed. The sentiments of the song almost moved her to tears for they echoed the feelings of everyone with a loved one away in the war.

Suddenly Gwen put her hand to her mouth in dismay. She still didn't have a home or hearth to welcome Charlie back to. They'd waited so long to be married, must they still wait when he finally came home? The thought was unbearable.

Lucy was downstairs, entertaining Sarah and Tom. She was a born mimic and would keep them amused until her mother insisted she go to bed.

Gwen lit the lamp and stared into the cheval mirror on the low chest of drawers. I'm beginning to look like an old maid, she thought sadly. I feel like one anyway, her thoughts went on. I'm twenty-four, practically on the shelf.

Then she rounded on herself for such thoughts. She was engaged to Charlie. How could she think herself an old maid? Oh, if only this awful war was over.

She had spent the evening with her mother at Agnes's house, and been forced to admit to herself that she'd been quite wrong in thinking she would be the one to do all the visiting, for Sarah had gone regularly to see Ronald's mother ever since the day the telegram arrived. Gwen always went to see her there and back safely. They took their knitting with them, balaclavas, socks or gloves for the comforts fund, and soon Agnes had started knitting too, saying she found it very satisfying to be able to do something, however small, for the boys.

At first Gwen was amazed at the way the two women talked about Ronald and Mair. It was as though they'd emigrated to some foreign country instead of both being dead.

'They'll be happy together now,' one of them would say, and the other would answer, 'It's such a comfort knowing they're with each other.'

It wasn't always the same words, but the sentiments were the same.

Despite things being in short supply they usually managed to take a small treat to have with a cup of tea. Today it was a sponge cake Sarah had made that morning. The cake looked delicious, especially as it was sandwiched together with home-made raspberry jam that had been made last year when the bushes in the garden had been weighed down with fruit.

'Sorry the sponge hasn't risen as it usually does, Agnes,' Sarah had said when she'd put it on the table. 'One egg isn't nearly enough. I used to use three.'

'But it looks lovely, Sarah. You shouldn't keep bringing us things. One egg is a big sacrifice these days, especially with all the other things you have to put in. Let me give you one of ours to make up. I've got two in the safe in the yard.'

'No, Agnes. Definitely not. You need all the good food you can get to keep youer strength up.'

The conversation went much the same way every time but Sarah would never take anything in return. It was her little sacrifice. She was glad to be able to do it, and hoped Mair and Ronald knew what good friends she and Agnes had become.

Food and practically everything else was getting short, and there were long queues at the coal-yard. They were lucky to be able to borrow an old pram from Mabel Palmer that was kept for the purpose. Before Mabel had acquired it they'd borrowed a soap box on wheels that belonged to her youngest son. White bread had long disappeared from the shops and the National loaf was a dirty brown, though the government assured everyone it was good for them.

As the war went on people were getting more and more depressed about it. There was a lot of bad feeling over the way food was being distributed and angry scenes in queues that seemed to get longer every day. At first the Llewellyns had missed out on things in short supply, for, with both Gwen and Lucy out at work all day, Sarah wasn't fit enough to stand for hours on end. The butcher, grocer and greengrocer with whom they'd traded for years, realising their plight, saw that they had a fair share. Gwen and Sarah knew only too well that if one of the neighbours found out, with the exception of course of Mabel, who was a good friend, there would be ructions.

Tom, in common with most of the men still at home, had taken on an allotment to which he departed every fine evening as soon as he'd finished his meal, bringing home enough vegetables and salad in spring and summer to keep them going, and Fanny too, any surplus being sent across the road to Cissie Williams who, with her husband lying in a grave in France, and a family to feed, was finding it difficult to cope on the pittance she received.

Eddie Palmer had the next allotment to Tom's and in the long summer evenings the men would set off together, airing their grievances about the war and their hopes for a Labour government one of these days, a government they both thought would really represent the working classes. They'd come home with colour in their cheeks from all the fresh air, proudly carrying their offerings, having the look about them, as Sarah often remarked to Mabel, of men who'd put the world to rights.

Sundays were taken up for Gwen with cooking the

midday meal, then, leaving the washing up to Sarah and Lucy, she'd go with her father to Cathays cemetery to lay flowers on Mair's grave. Sarah had accompanied them at first, but after a bout of bronchitis, Doctor Powell had insisted she wait until she was really fit.

In the spring, when she had been getting over the attack, Sarah had wanted to visit the grave, but Gwen had been sure it would prove too much for her, for besides the walk to the tram stop they would have to change trams. When Ted had heard of Sarah's wish he'd offered to take them in his pony and trap. They'd set off on a Wednesday afternoon with Sarah still in deepest black. They'd reached the grave and Gwen was putting daffodils into the vase when her mother collapsed. If Ted hadn't been standing beside her she would have fallen to the ground.

It was now the end of the summer and Sarah was often upset still. It would seem to come over her suddenly. She'd sit for hours in Mair's room, rocking herself to and fro in the old rocker with the red plush seat and back that Tom had brought up from the middle room. Gwen didn't disturb her when she was in these moods for the sessions seemed to do her good.

When winter came and produce from the allotment became scarce the food problem grew worse for a time, but then rationing was introduced, a fairer system all round. First sugar, followed a little later by butter and margarine, tea, jam, and bacon – and of the latter the ration was quite generous.

It was the autumn of 1918 and with the coming of Spanish 'flu people were exposed to an enemy far more terrifying to most civilians than the war had ever been. Sarah was worried about Gwen and Lucy going out to work each day, especially since she'd read in the *South Wales Echo* that the local authority was closing all elementary schools in view of the large number of child victims of the virus. They were also considering closing down all places of entertainment in an effort to check its spread.

'You'll need to hold a hankie over youer nose and mouth,' Sarah said, getting two large ones from the drawer.

'Don't worry, Mam,' Gwen told her, 'I've bought us some of those Formamint tablets anyway.'

'What's Formamint? I remember seeing that advertised in the paper.'

'It's a throat tablet that kills germs.'

When she got to the shop, Ted said, 'I was reading in the paper this morning that this awful 'flu is sweeping the world.'

Daisy Ball, coming into the shop just then with cups of tea, said, 'Terrible, it is. A woman in the next street to me got taken ill last week and now she's dead.'

Gwen was needed in the shop just then and the customer was staring at her as she approached. It was awful now the way people looked at you anxiously to see if you were ill, but you could hardly blame them. No one wanted to die.

About a week later a girl of about ten came into the shop and handed Gwen a note. Business had been very slack, people weren't going out and about unless it was for necessities. The child looked pinched with the cold. This one looks more like a seller than a buyer, Gwen thought, opening the note.

'My mam can't come 'erself. Wants to sell something she does 'cos we 'aven't got any coal. Mrs Roberts said you'd keep things 'til after the war so we can buy them back.'

'Well, your mam hardly needs to send a note with a messenger like you,' Ted said, coming over and gently ruffling the girl's hair. 'Where is it, this thing you're wanting to sell?'

'Mama wouldn't trust me with them. Valuable they are.'

Ted smiled indulgently. Everyone seemed to think that of their bits and pieces.

'Where do you live then, and when can I call?'

'Today, please! We 'aven't got any coal.'

Ted looked down at the child, at the pale face and thin coat, saying, 'I have to wait here for a dealer to call. I'll come as soon as he's been, but it may be late.'

'Will the coal-yard still be open?' the girl asked anxiously.

'I'll see to it if you like, Ted,' Gwen put in quickly. 'I could go with her now.'

She followed him to the back room where, tipping some coins on to the table, he selected a few and put them into her hand, saying, 'See what it's worth, but in any case give them enough to get some coal.'

'But supposing it's just rubbish?' she asked, putting on her coat.

'It won't be, Gwen. It mightn't be of much value but she's a tidy body. I'll leave it to your judgement.'

As she was about to leave the shop with the girl, Ted dashed to the door. 'Don't forget to hold that hankie to your mouth, Gwen,' he told her, and she did so self-consciously, the child's eyes upon her.

As they approached the house which was in a street off Splott Road she saw that the brass letter-box and knocker had been polished till they shone, and a half-moon patch in front of the door had been scrubbed white. The girl pulled the key on a string through the letter-box, letting them in, then led the way along a narrow passage to the kitchen.

When the door was pushed open Gwen saw there was a bed against one wall and on it lay a woman of about thirty. Gwen had removed the hankie as she was entering the house. Now she wished she had the courage to put it to her mouth again for the woman looked so ill, her face the colour of alabaster. Without raising her head from the pillow she was resting against, she said in a voice hardly above a whisper, 'Take the lady into the parlour, Esme. And be careful with them, mind.'

'Has your mother seen the doctor?' Gwen asked anxiously as they went along the passage once more.

The girl looked at her pityingly, saying, 'We can't afford doctors, miss. My dad got killed in the war.'

Gwen felt apprehensive. Did the woman have Spanish 'flu? She didn't really seem ill enough, being able to talk, but perhaps she was sickening for it?

Next moment she forgot her fears as they entered the parlour and the girl went over to a glass cupboard at the side of the fireplace and brought out a beautiful porcelain plate displayed on a wooden stand. Then she brought out the others, one at a time. There were six in all and Gwen stared disbelievingly at them. She knew what she thought, and hoped, they were. The porcelain was soft paste, heavier than most and truly white, and the name Billingsley was on her lips as she took the plates one by one to the light, the better to see the lovely roses and other flowers exquisitely painted on every one.

Trying to conceal her excitement, she thought, They must be Nantgarw. What other porcelain could be heavy yet translucent, and so white? Certainly none of the

Continental factories. And the painting was Billingsley's style, and hadn't he started the factory there in 1813? Of course, it could have been Baxter or Pardoe who'd painted them but that would have been after the factory was transferred to Swansea, and there they'd altered the beautiful soft paste . . . Her thoughts were interrupted when Esme asked impatiently, 'Well, do you like them?'

Turning over one of the plates and seeing the expected impressed 'Nantgarw' mark, she nodded, saying, 'They're beautiful, but Mr Lewis will have to see them for himself.' Ted would be over the moon if they were genuine, and there was every sign that they were. But how did a family so obviously poor as these people come to own such lovely things?

As though anticipating the question, the girl was saying, 'Pretty, aren't they? My mam was in service at a big house until she married my dad. She started there when she was ten. But in the end, before she left to get married, she was looking after the old lady who was ill in bed.'

'And she gave your mother the plates?' Gwen prompted.

Esme nodded. 'The old lady thought her relatives were taking stuff, and she was very fond of my mam. She said, "You take these, Elsie, while you've got the chance. Something to remember me by".'

When they went to the kitchen the woman lay with her eyes closed, her face almost as white as the pillow she rested against.

The girl shook her mother gently, saying as she opened her eyes, 'Mam, the lady's seen them. I told her you don't want to sell them for good. Mr Lewis is coming around later to see them.' Then, suddenly remembering, she cried, 'Oh, Mam! How about the coal? We haven't had our ration for last week yet.'

Gwen put five shillings on the table, asking, 'Will that be all right to go on with? Mr Lewis will probably be here before they close.'

'How much will they be worth, miss?'

'I don't really know,' Gwen told her. 'He'll tell you when he comes.'

She almost ran back to the shop, eager to tell Ted of her find. He'd be so pleased.

But he didn't look it as he opened the door for her, crying, 'Where's your hankie, Gwen? I thought you'd promised your mam you would cover your mouth with it?'

'I was so excited, Ted, that I forgot.'

'Excited about what? You know how serious it could be if you got the 'flu.'

'The woman I went to see – she's got six Nantgarw plates.'

'What?' Ted's look of surprise was comical to see.

'She was in service with an old lady. It was a big house, the child said.'

'And she was given the plates?' He sounded as though he didn't believe the tale.

'Well, apparently she nursed the old lady.'

'What's happening about them, then?'

'I told them you'd go round sometime today. I gave them five shillings to get some coal and things with. They seem pretty desperate for money.'

'You had a good look at the plates, Gwen?'

She nodded, telling him, 'I don't think she wants to sell them outright. She's heard about you keeping things until after the war. This place gets more like a pawn shop every day, Ted, except that you give them much more than things are worth and allow them longer to redeem them.'

He laughed, saying, 'That's a pretty good description, Gwen, but it's just my way of helping.'

Ted went to see the plates, handling them with reverence and delight. He was sure they were genuine, but decided to have them valued by an expert he knew of. He probably wouldn't be able to give her what they were worth. But if she still wanted him to keep them until after the war, he'd see she had a fair deal.

In the *Echo* most nights there were pieces about the influenza epidemic, with advice on how to treat it and suggestions that might help to prevent it. Also a number of advertisements for various health foods, all claiming special powers for keeping the 'flu germ at bay. That night was no exception, warning readers that the virus was spreading with alarming rapidity, and to take every precaution against it. This spread of the illness had become only too evident locally for when Sarah had ventured as far as the corner shop that morning, it was to find it closed with a notice on the door explaining that both Mr and Mrs Morgan were ill with 'flu and the shop would remain closed until further notice. They soon found that there were many other small businesses in the area in the same boat.

It was two days later when Gwen was dusting shelves and rearranging ornaments that she began to feel really out of sorts. There was a sickness in her stomach and a sudden greyness in front of her eyes which grew darker until she lost consciousness and fell to the floor before Ted could prevent her. He carried her to the sofa in the back room and Daisy hurried to fetch a blanket to tuck around her while a worried Ted rushed to get a cab to take her home. Then he'd gone for Doctor Powell, while Sarah, trying to quell her fears, had got Gwen to bed and watched over her anxiously.

When Doctor Powell arrived he was grey with fatigue. Sarah settled the kettle over the glowing coals for tea before following him upstairs. After examining Gwen, he followed Sarah down to the kitchen where Ted was waiting anxiously for news before going back to the shop.

'It is influenza,' the doctor confirmed, 'but she's a strong girl, Sarah. Now don't worry, I'll be back tonight.' He drank some tea gratefully before asking, 'Can anyone come with me to pick up the medicine? I'm going back to the surgery to see who else wants me to call.'

Ted volunteered, and when she'd watched the gig move off, Sarah took a bowl of water and a flannel to the bedroom to bathe Gwen's face.

That night the lamp was left burning on the chest of drawers. Sarah sat dozing in the armchair by the side of the bed, and Lucy slept on the sofa downstairs until it was time for her watch.

Gwen lay twisting and turning, feverishly muttering. She was a child again in a starched white pinafore. She could see Mair's face so clearly: the grey eyes, the gentle smile. And gentle fingers were smoothing back her hair. Mair's fingers. But when she opened her eyes it was her mother bending over her. Sarah was looking at her so tenderly, and there were tears trembling on her lashes.

'Thank God!' she whispered to Tom. 'She recognised me, I'm sure she did. She's been somewhere. She was talking to someone.'

Gwen didn't know but Ted had sat with her all that first evening, sometimes taking her burning hand and holding it tenderly. And he'd been there the next evening just as soon as the shop was closed. Doctor Powell had been twice on this second day, and when Ted appeared again they could tell him the fever had gone. It was the secondary infection that often occurred that Doctor Powell was afraid of for it sometimes led to pneumonia. It was this that was causing so many deaths. Gwen must be watched over carefully.

'He loves her, you know, Tom,' Sarah said as soon as Ted had drunk his tea and gone up to the bedroom.

'Who loves who? Don't talk in riddles, woman.'

'Ted Lewis. He loves Gwen, I'm sure of it.'

'You must be imagining things, Sarah. She's engaged to Charlie.'

'Yes, and I wish now I'd let her marry him. I was wrong, Tom, but I thought it would just be until she was twenty-one. I never dreamt the war would go on all these years. She'd hate me, you know, if anything happened to Charlie.'

'Nonsense! Gwen couldn't hate anyone.'

'And I'm right about Ted, too,' Sarah burst in. 'I think he's loved her from the time she was a little girl visiting his shop. But don't worry, Tom, Ted won't make any trouble. He'll always want what's best for Gwen.'

'I think you're imagining it, cariad,' he said, shaking his head.

But she knew that she wasn't.

Chapter Twenty-three

'I ought to be well, Mam, with all the things you're buying,' Gwen said picking up Sarah's newest purchase from the table. 'Chymol, the food that builds.'

There were so many things advertised to help combat the 'flu and Sarah seemed to have tried them all. Chymol was her latest attempt to, as she put it, 'perk Gwen up'. It must be costing a small fortune, she reflected. Sarah had bought the largest size of this latest pick me up, two and ten pence it had cost her, and whether it was any good or not remained to be seen.

Everyone was spoiling her since she'd been ill. Only this morning Lucy had bought her a present of Icilma cream, but it would take more than just rubbing that into her face, Gwen thought sadly, to improve her complexion, which, ever since her illness, was sallow and inclined to be dry.

'It's what you put into yourself not on yourself that improves your colour,' Sarah told her for the umpteenth time. 'Start to eat well again and you'll soon look better, cariad. You ought to make an effort. Charlie could be home very soon.'

Since the beginning of November the papers had been hinting that the war could be over quickly. On the 9th the headlines of the *Echo* shouted in black capitals: VERGE OF SURRENDER. PEACE IS CLOSE AT HAND. Yet in the same paper there were still long lists of casualties, with several paragraphs about each one and a photograph supplied by the grieving relatives. They all began the same way, only the name, rank and service number were different: 'The parents of – have been notified'. And looking at the fresh young faces in the photographs, Gwen was only too conscious of the awful grief and sadness felt for each one.

Charlie's letters were full of plans for when he got home. Gwen, on her very first trip out, put a notice in a shop window in Broadway which began: 'Wanted urgently, two rooms'.

If she could get a place soon, hopefully she could decorate it ready for when Charlie was demobbed and they got married. The 'flu had left her feeling tired and listless despite all Sarah's remedies, but the thought of Charlie coming home at last was just the tonic she needed.

When on the 11th of November Germany finally surrendered, the crowds went mad with joy – with the exception of those laid low with 'flu, for the epidemic was still raging, and those who had recently lost a loved one. The heartbreak notices would continue in long columns in the *Echo* for a very long time to come.

Today the headlines of the special edition of the paper read: GERMANY SURRENDERED THIS MORNING, (BRITISH OFFICIAL) ARMISTICE SIGNED. FIGHTING OVER AT 11 TODAY

In common with everyone else Gwen felt a tremendous surge of relief at those printed words, but at the back of her mind was a niggling fear that a yellow telegram could still arrive at Charlie's home. It was a morbid thought and she blamed it on her recent bout of 'flu. Determined to enjoy the wonderful news, she put on her hat and coat and went outdoors.

The noise was deafening as neighbours sang and danced non-stop. Bunting had been hurriedly slung across the street and all the children seemed to be waving flags like mad. Snatches of song came to her. Someone nearby started to sing 'Goodbye Dolly, I Must Leave You' but was quickly shut up with, 'A goin' away song, that is, ouer Martha, not a welcome 'ome one.'

Someone else was singing 'Tipperary' and the crowd took it up. Then they started 'Pack Up Your Troubles in Your Old Kit Bag', followed by 'Keep the Home Fires Burning', which seemed the most appropriate of the lot on this cold November day.

'Pity is, Gwen, that the fighting will have gone on to the last minute,' Mabel Palmer said, coming to her side. Mabel and Eddie had two sons on the Western front now, and her words resurrected Gwen's fears, but their neighbour was taking her arm and pushing through the crowds to where Cissie Williams's youngest, the baby boy who had clung to Gwen's knee on the day the telegram had arrived to tell them his dad had been killed, was standing on a wooden kitchen chair, waving a Union Jack nearly as big as himself and singing 'Take Me Back To Dear Old Blighty' in a loud but lisping voice.

Everyone clapped and cheered the little mite, then Gwen caught sight of Cissie's face as her son was lifted from the chair. She looked so proud, but there was a haunting sadness about her eyes and Gwen's heart went out to her. Although she was celebrating the end of the war with everyone else, there would be no banner with 'Welcome Home, Albert' over her door.

That evening Gwen decided to go to the shop to tell Ted that she would be returning to work the following Monday. Pearl Street, and every side street off it, had rows of Union Jacks flying in the breeze. Light was streaming from most of the houses as curtains and blinds remained undrawn. Little groups of people were still singing and dancing to accordion or mouth organ, and as she passed people called out friendly greetings to her.

Knocking on the door, she wondered if Ted too would be out celebrating but almost at once it was opened and Ted stood there, looking pleased and surprised, crying, 'There's lovely to see you, Gwen, and looking so well too.'

As he helped her take off her coat she remembered waking when she was so ill to find him holding her hand, and a blush rose to her cheeks. It had just been his usual kindness, she told herself. Ted was like that.

When they'd climbed the stairs and she'd entered the parlour she looked around her for the Nantgarw plates. They were displayed in Ted's elegant early-Victorian glass-fronted cabinet, colours glowing in the warm light from the gas mantle in its apricot glass shade. They were beautiful, and she fully understood their owner's reluctance to part with them.

'Lovely, aren't they, Gwen?' Ted's eyes had followed hers to the cabinet. Now he carefully lifted out the plates one at a time and stood them on the polished table. She went over, and taking one gently in her hands, gazed down at it, fingering the beautiful porcelain lovingly.

'She sold them to you?' She looked at Ted questioningly.

'No. I'm afraid there are strings attached. She wants the chance to buy them back one day.'

'She got over the 'flu then?'

He looked puzzled for a moment, replying, 'Mrs Evans didn't have the 'flu, Gwen, she's an invalid. What made you think she did?'

'She looked so ill that day I went there, Ted, I thought afterwards I might have caught it from her.'

'The poor woman suffers from a serious form of anaemia, Gwen, which makes her very weak. She used to take in washing but lately she's been too ill even to do her own. I went with the girl to put what I gave her into a Post Office account. It's hard to think she doesn't have enough to pay her way when her husband gave his life for this country. Still, she should be all right now.'

Suddenly he smiled at her, saying, 'Whatever am I thinking of? The war is over at last and Charlie will be home. You must have lots of plans.'

'We have to find somewhere to live, Ted, that's the first priority. We can't make arrangements for the wedding until we do.'

'Didn't you say your Aunt Fan is making your wedding dress?'

'Yes. It's nearly finished. She has to make Lucy's dress then for she's to be bridesmaid.'

'Jenny Lucas will be going to Portsmouth to live as soon as her husband comes home from France. He's from those parts and he's got a job to go back to.' Ted was stroking his chin and looking thoughtful as he went on, 'I wonder if her mother would consider letting the rooms?'

'Where do they live?' Gwen asked excitedly.

'The house is in Railway Street. But hang on, Gwen, hold your horses. She might not want to let. It's different with your own daughter, isn't it?'

'Can we go and see, Ted?' she pleaded. 'Supposing someone else asks first?'

People were still celebrating as they walked down the long street of terraced houses, calling to Ted to join them for everyone seemed to know him, but he laughingly shook his head and they pressed on, Gwen's heart beating fast with hope.

When they reached the house Ted saw Mrs Lucas talking with a group of neighbours, and when she hurried over and he'd explained that he was wondering if she'd have rooms to let when her daughter went away, she said, 'Well, I wasn't really thinking of letting the rooms, Ted. A daughter living with you is different. It's family.' Then she looked at Gwen and asked kindly, 'Desperate, are you, love?'

When Gwen explained that she must find rooms so that she and Charlie could get married when he came home, she added, 'We'd both be out all day at work.'

'Come and see them anyway,' Mrs Lucas said. 'Ouer Jenny won't mind. Over the moon she is today, the war being over.'

As she opened the door and they stepped inside, Gwen's heart lifted. The passageway smelt of lavender polish and there were two long carpet runners in a red Turkish design on top of the gleaming oilcloth. Jenny occupied the middle rooms upstairs and down. Both were high-ceilinged and quite large, and everywhere was spotlessly clean.

When they were once more downstairs Mrs Lucas said, 'I'm not promising, mind you, I'd have to see what Mr Lucas has to say. But I'll tell you this – no one else shall have them. Anyway, it will be a while before my daughter leaves. I shall miss her, that's a fact, but young people have to live their own lives, don't they?'

'Thank you, Ted.' Gwen's voice was warm with gratitude as they walked away from the house.

'She hasn't said you can have them yet,' he cautioned, but he knew she wasn't listening. 'Supposing Charlie comes home before Jenny's husband?' Gwen went on. 'We could wait a week or so, I suppose.'

Ted tried again. 'Don't count on it, Gwen. I'd hate to see you disappointed.' But the warning fell on deaf ears. Gwen was already totting up how much she'd saved in the Post Office, and what it might buy in the way of furniture and things. And Charlie had quite a bit put by as well.

'I forgot to ask Mrs Lucas how much the rent would be,' Gwen said regretfully, and Ted shook his head, knowing he'd been wasting his time.

Chapter Twenty-four

On the December day Charlie came home, Gwen had been on pins for hours: rushing to the door at the slightest sound, combing her hair when it didn't need combing, unable to eat for excitement. She flitted about the house, rearranging ornaments and straightening pictures, until Sarah would have lost patience with her if she hadn't known the strain her daughter was under.

When at about half-past-three a knock came, Gwen rushed along the passage to open the door, narrowly missing the aspidistra in its brass pot. Charlie stood there, his arms outstretched, and next moment they were about her as the door closed behind them. Their lips found each other's like homing pigeons, but not before she'd noticed the change in him – his face thin and pale where it had been plump and ruddy; the suit he'd been measured for five years before hanging loosely about him. But the biggest change of all was in his eyes, which ever since she'd known him had twinkled with merriment. Now, despite the love that shone from them, they held a haunted look, as though the horrors of war were still with him.

When at last they tore themselves apart she thought she must have imagined it for he was smiling at her and then beyond her to where Sarah, having allowed a decent

interval to elapse, was coming towards him, arms outstretched in welcome. Then she was calling, 'Lucy! Lucy!
Look who's here.' And turning to Charlie she said, 'She's
in her bedroom titivating, I expect.' But Gwen thought,
Sulking more likely, for Lucy had been moody for weeks,
bursting into tears at the slightest criticism. She's in love,
was Gwen's opinion, and it didn't seem to be going right.
For from going out with Vera nearly every evening, she
now seldom went out at all except to work, but her friend
had called for her several times so they obviously hadn't
quarrelled.

Lucy was coming downstairs slowly and it was clear
she'd been crying, but she managed to smile for Charlie.
Then they were all seated at the kitchen table, the tea
poured and the welsh cakes being handed round, and
when they'd finished Sarah said, 'I expect you and Charlie
have lots to talk about, Gwen. The fire's wasting in the
parlour so go on in. Lucy and I will do the washing-up.'

They didn't talk right away but went into each other's
arms once more, and when at last they moved apart Gwen
had to get her breath before she told him, 'We're having a
welcome home party for you, Charlie, just your family
and mine. Unless there's someone you'd like to invite.
Artie, perhaps?'

Charlie laughed. 'Artie will be much too busy,' he said.
'Real serious he is about that girl he met on his last leave
before we went to France. Gone to Penarth to meet her
parents he has.'

'Oh, I'm glad,' Gwen began, but Charlie broke in with,
'There is someone I'd like to ask. He only lives a few
streets away from here. Rotten luck he's had, Gwen. His
wife left him just after he went abroad. Cheer him up it
would, I'm sure, and I'd really like you to meet him.'

'Yes, of course. The party's to be on Saturday. What's your friend's name?'

'Ben. Ben Wheeler. You'll like him, Gwen. Will it be all right with your mam?'

'She'll be pleased if he's a friend of yours. Oh, Charlie! You should see those rooms I wrote to you about. We can have them as soon as Jenny goes away. Her husband should be home any time now. Then we can make plans for the wedding.'

At the mention of the wedding they clung to each other again and only the sound of footsteps approaching made them part. But it seemed Sarah was only passing to go to the front door, and when they heard Mabel Palmer's voice, and then the kitchen door close, their lips met again.

Before Charlie left to get the last tram they'd made plans to have the banns called as soon as possible so that they could be married in about a month's time. Charlie had to have a suit made for he had nothing that fitted, and they had the furniture to choose and all the other things they needed.

When Gwen told Sarah of their plans, her mother said, 'Don't you think you should wait until the girl actually moves to Portsmouth?' And she'd replied, with no doubt in her heart now, 'Oh, Mam! Her husband's bound to be home by then.'

'All the same,' Sarah persisted, 'it could leave you married with no home of your own.'

Mama's right, Gwen thought grudgingly, but she was so tired of waiting. Aloud she said, 'Well, we could go to see the Vicar, but perhaps it would be better not to call the banns until we know for sure.'

Gwen's wedding dress hung in the wardrobe with

Lucy's dress beside it, and Fanny, now that she could go back to dressmaking, was making a soft grey gaberdine coat and skirt for Sarah, together with an elaborately pin-tucked blouse.

Gwen would open the wardrobe door many times a day to finger the white crêpe-de-chine dress with its hem a good two inches shorter than she'd ever worn before, and which would show a little of the fine white stockings and elegant white bar shoes she'd bought. She'd lift down the hat-box and try on the long lace veil, to be held in place by a circle of orange blossom.

When Saturday came Gwen was up early to do a little more cleaning, burnishing the grate until it shone and dusting the ornaments, and by mid-afternoon had washed and changed into her best dress and put on a starched bibbed apron to protect it. Now she brought the piece of ham that had cost them three weeks' bacon ration, from the meat safe in the yard, and began to slice it thinly to make sandwiches. There was a delicious smell from the batches of cakes and fruit pies cooling on the scrubbed wooden table to complement the large fruit cake that had been made for Christmas but saved instead for this special occasion. Half the marble shelf in the pantry was taken up with dainty trifles in their little glass dishes, and there were two dozen sausage rolls, admittedly more pastry than sausage, but the pastry was light and glazed golden brown.

The two china tea-pots stood ready to be filled, and on the flag-stoned floor of the pantry, beside the herb and ginger beers, were four assorted bottles of home-made wine which Mabel and Eddie Palmer had generously given. Mabel, good friend that she was, stood by Gwen's side now, buttering bread and cutting it into dainty triangles.

Half-an-hour later, with everything ready, Charlie and his parents arrived. Gwen kissed his mam and dad warmly and soon they were chatting easily with Sarah and Tom, both families delighted at the coming wedding.

When the food was ready and the fires in both kitchen and parlour attended to, Charlie went to call for his friend.

'Where's Lucy?' Sarah asked. 'Went upstairs to change she did ages ago.'

Gwen reached the bedroom to find her sister lying fully dressed on the bed. She could see that Lucy had been crying.

'What's wrong, love?' Gwen put a comforting arm about her.

'Nothing. I just don't feel very well, that's all. You go down, Gwen. I've got a headache. I'll splash my face with water and take a daisy powder. It'll soon go.'

'I'll bring you a glass of water. I won't say anything to Mama, all right?'

It was ages before Lucy came downstairs, but Sarah, busy talking with her guests, didn't notice.

Gwen took to Charlie's army friend right away. He wasn't as good-looking as Charlie, she decided, but he had steady grey eyes and a friendly smile. His dark hair stood on end, short and bristly, and his suit fitted him after all the years – which was more than Charlie's did.

They had finished the meal which was much praised and enjoyed, especially in view of the rationing, and Gwen and Lucy had washed up when Sarah suggested they all go to the parlour where the chairs were more comfortable.

'Do you think anyone would mind if I went to the pub for an hour, Gwen?' Charlie asked her presently. 'Ben wants me to meet his father and a few friends.'

She didn't want him to go, of course, but what could she say?

'You go along,' she told him. 'If anyone misses you, I'll do the explaining.'

Dora Roberts was the first to notice and she wasn't too pleased when she heard where they'd gone.

'He shouldn't have left like that,' she said. 'And after your mam taking all this trouble for him an' all.'

'He'll be back soon,' Gwen said with conviction. After all, like his mother had said, the party was for him.

When Fanny arrived after completing a rush order, they had a sing-song with Eddie Palmer playing the accordion. He went from one popular song to another, but as the evening wore on Gwen became more and more worried about Charlie. He was thoughtless and ungrateful, she told herself, and it seemed that his friend's company was more important to him than his family's. The home-made wine, especially the parsnip, had mellowed everyone. She could see that Charlie's dad was having a wonderful time, throwing back his head and singing lustily, but his mam seemed unhappy and kept looking uneasily towards the door. Then she voiced her concern again, turning to Gwen, saying, 'I thought you said the boys weren't going to be away very long, cariad?'

Hearing, Sarah turned to Tom. 'Go around to that pub and see what's happening, will you, love?'

But Tom didn't want to go. 'They're both grown men, Sarah,' he told her. 'It will only embarrass them.'

Annoyed and concerned at the way the party was turning out because of Charlie and his friend, Gwen was also disappointed for she'd planned to take the rug up in the parlour when the sing-song was over so that they could dance. She'd heard Eddie play a medley of Strauss waltzes before and she'd been really looking forward to dancing with Charlie. They'd all have enjoyed it, she told herself, Lucy and Ben perhaps, Charlie's parents, and she knew Dada would have partnered her mother and Fanny in turn. But where was Lucy? She'd gone from the room a while back and hadn't returned. She hadn't been her usually bubbly self for weeks. Young love, Gwen told herself with a shrug. Well, she had problems herself tonight. She'd have something to say to Charlie when she got him on her own!

When the clock on the mantelpiece chimed the hour, telling them that it was ten o'clock, Charlie's mother looked so unhappy that Gwen thought, How could he behave like this, spoiling everything? At a word from Sarah, Tom said grudgingly, 'Better go round there, I suppose. Fancy keeping me company, Joe?'

Mr Roberts rose with alacrity, but his wife warned, 'No going in for a drink, mind. You've had enough with all that wine. We've got to catch the last tram, so don't be long.'

The men were just making for the door, when, with the accordion silent now, noises came to them from the street. Someone was singing 'Tipperary' loudly, and another voice was warning, 'Shhh! Charlie. Shhh! Youer voice is enough to wake the dead.'

Next moment Tom and Joe went out to steer Charlie homewards, helping Ben one side and a burly man the other. As they brought him into the house and along the passage to the kitchen, everyone from the parlour followed them, with Charlie's mother now red with shame at his behaviour, apologising over and over to Sarah.

'Never seen him like this before, I haven't. I just can't understand . . .'

'Don't worry about it, Dora,' Sarah reassured her. 'The boy's been under a lot of strain.'

Gwen was loosening Charlie's collar, the expression on her face a mixture of love and annoyance at the spoilt evening, while Ben, red-faced, was saying, 'I'm very sorry, really I am. It was all my fault. Charlie's not much of a drinker and we only meant to be about half an hour. Wanted him to meet my dad, I did.' He nodded towards his companion. 'The trouble was, everyone knew me. They kept on bringing us pints, because we were in the army it was. Well, I refused quite a few, but Charlie thought it looked ungrateful, and – well, it didn't take long to get him like this. We been trying to sober him up at home but it's hopeless.'

'We'd better be off, son,' Ben's father was saying. 'I think we've caused enough trouble for one night. Heartily sorry I am that it turned out like this.'

When they'd gone, with Ben apologising all the way to the door, Dora Roberts looked up at the clock and wailed, 'Oh, Joe! What are we going to do? We'll miss the last tram if we don't go soon. How are we going to get him home?'

'Oh, but Charlie will stay here,' Sarah assured her. 'Don't you worry, Dora, we'll look after him. It wasn't his fault after all.'

'I'll come to the tram stop,' Gwen told them, 'see that you get it all right.'

'Oh, no, Gwen. That would mean you having to walk back on your own.' Charlie's mother shook her head emphatically.

'I'll go with her,' Fanny said, 'I could do with some fresh air. I've washed the dishes, Sarah, all except those last few glasses, so you can go up to bed.'

'Whatever will your mam think of our Charlie?' Dora wailed as they went up the street.

'Don't keep on, woman, it wasn't his fault.' Her husband's tone told her plainly that the subject was closed.

When the tram had gone, Fanny and Gwen walked slowly back along Broadway.

'I thought all that excitement would have been too much for Sarah, but she seemed to revel in it, didn't she?' commented Fanny. 'She looked a bit tired towards the end, though. And what was the matter with Lucy? She went up to bed while we were still singing.'

'I don't know, Aunt Fanny.' Gwen's voice was troubled. 'She's been like it for weeks.'

'Perhaps she's in love, Gwen. It's time she was courting. She is nearly eighteen.'

'Well, Mama thinks she just goes out with Vera, but . . .'

They had reached Fanny's home and Gwen stopped, saying laughingly, 'No need for you to come back with me or I'll have to take *you* home.'

'Goodnight then, Gwen. Don't be mad at Charlie.'

'I'm not. I know it wasn't really his fault.'

Turning the next corner, Gwen was soon home. When she'd closed the door behind her and taken a few steps into the passage, the kitchen door opened and Gwen was surprised and shocked to see Lucy come out clad only in her long flannelette nightgown, the candle she held casting shadows over her face.

'What – why are you – ?' Gwen began to stutter, and Lucy told her, 'I just wanted a drink.'

'Well, you could have gone through the side door in the middle room. Why aren't you wearing your dressing gown?'

'I didn't know Charlie was there, did I?' Lucy answered crossly. But Gwen was thinking, I remember seeing you looking over the banister while they were carrying him in.

Lucy gave a little shiver, saying plaintively, 'I'm cold, Gwen. I'm going back to bed.'

She watched her sister take the stairs two at a time, the candle casting huge shadows before her. Then, when the bedroom door had closed, she stood in the darkness, puzzling over what she'd seen. It wasn't just that Lucy had come from the kitchen – it was possible that she had forgotten when she went for a drink of water. It was the way she'd come out as soon as Gwen had shut the front door. It was as though she'd been waiting for the signal, almost as though she'd *wanted* Gwen to see her. And she hadn't seemed embarrassed at all at only wearing her nightgown. Lucy was becoming very strange.

Chapter Twenty-five

Charlie was very subdued and apologetic to everyone next day but Gwen felt there was something troubling him besides his having spoilt the party by having too much to drink. Whenever he and Lucy were in the same room he seemed embarrassed and she remembered again with some trepidation seeing her sister coming from the kitchen.

A few days later, when she and Charlie were alone, Gwen tried to discuss the coming wedding plans again but his thoughts were obviously elsewhere.

'What is it, Charlie? What's wrong?' she asked worriedly.

Turning to her, he swallowed hard before replying, 'Something very embarrassing happened to me the other night, Gwen. I've been wondering how to tell you because it concerns Lucy.'

'What about her?' Surely Charlie wasn't going to tell her that he'd seen Lucy as she'd gone through the kitchen to fetch a glass of water? He should have kept that to himself so's not to make things worse for Lucy, who'd probably forgotten he was there. But if that was true why did she have the feeling that Lucy had wanted to be seen?

Charlie was licking dry lips so she asked again, 'What about Lucy?'

Then he began to tell her how on the night of the party, having drunk too much, he fell into a deep sleep. 'When I woke,' he told her, 'I remembered I was dreaming about you, Gwen. I – ' He seemed to be finding it difficult to go on, but after swallowing hard again, he said, 'Well, I could hardly believe it myself, but Lucy was with me on the sofa. I – well, in my dream I'd thought it was you, Gwen. We had our arms about each other, we'd been kissing passionately – that's what woke me up. I was horrified to find it was Lucy I had my arms about.'

Gwen could hardly believe what she was hearing. 'You're sure you weren't still dreaming?'

He shook his head. 'If only I had been, Gwen, but why did she do it? Even when I woke and pulled away from her, she still clung to me.'

'But you must have known it was Lucy!'

'I didn't, honestly, Gwen. I thought it was all part of a wonderful dream and that my arms were about you.'

'Oh, Charlie! This is awful. I knew she was smitten with you when she was a child but – well, this is disgusting!' Hot anger towards Lucy burned in Gwen and she cried, 'Just wait until I get her on her own! Mama's always been very strict where men are concerned. If she heard about this she'd have a bad turn, or even worse.'

'Don't say anything to Lucy, Gwen,' Charlie begged. 'It can only stir up trouble. It's embarrassing enough as it is, but if everybody knew . . . And like you said, it could have a serious effect on your mam.'

He looked so shamefaced, her heart went out to him. She flung her arms about him and kissed him before saying, 'Don't worry, love, nothing can come between us now. But, oh, Charlie! I just wish those rooms were vacant so that we could be married right away.'

How was she to be in the same room as her sister and keep her tongue still? Yet she knew she must. If Mama ever found out what had happened, she'd send Lucy away. They still had relatives in the valleys. She'd probably send Charlie packing too. He was right. She must keep what she knew to herself at all costs.

The weeks passed uneasily with Gwen hardly speaking to Lucy unless she had to for fear of what she might say. And at night, sharing the same bed, she slept as near the edge as possible to avoid contact with someone whose behaviour had shocked her deeply.

One Thursday night just before closing time she was overjoyed when Mrs Lucas came into the shop to say they could have the rooms from the following Monday. Gwen could hardly wait to tell Charlie. Now the banns could be called, and the rooms furnished ready for them to go back to after the wedding reception.

As she entered the house and hurried towards the kitchen, longing to share her good news, she became suddenly aware of Fanny's voice anxiously calling Sarah's name, and above this the sound of abandoned weeping. Her heart went cold as she flung open the door and took in the scene before her. Her mother, white to the lips, was lying back against the cushions of the armchair, her eyes closed, moaning and clutching her chest. Fanny's face was pale too and her eyes anxious as she endeavoured to undo the buttons of Sarah's high-necked blouse. Turning to Gwen, she said, 'Better get Doctor Powell, I think. She's been like this for a while.'

Sarah must have heard for her eyes fluttered open. Pleading with Fanny, she said, 'No, Fanny. No! We don't want anyone knowing our business. Beginning to go it is now – the pain, I mean.' She closed her eyes once more, and Gwen saw tears glistening on her lashes before rolling slowly down her cheeks.

Lucy huddled on the sofa, her face blotched with crying, great sobs shaking her body. But such was her animosity towards her sister now, Gwen felt no compassion. Mama must have found out, she thought, and if she had, what about Charlie? Would anyone believe him? She was quite unprepared for Fanny's next words.

'Lucy tells us she's going to have a baby, Gwen. She says it's Charlie's.'

Gwen sprang towards Lucy but Fanny held her back, saying, 'You'd better hear her out, cariad. Go on, Lucy. Tell her what you told us.'

The tears flowed faster as Lucy shook her head, mumbling under her breath, 'I can't. I can't tell her. She'll kill me, you saw her just now.'

It was a nightmare. She'd wake up at any minute. Gwen looked from one to the other in disbelief. As Lucy's sobs and sniffling increased, Fanny asked, 'Shall I tell Gwen?' and Lucy nodded.

Gwen sank to a chair as Fanny began. If only Charlie were here to stand up for himself. Lucy must be lying, of course. She wouldn't put anything past her these days. In her mind she saw Lucy again, her nightdress billowing about her, coming from the kitchen, the candle held aloft. But Charlie had explained about that; had admitted they'd put their arms about each other. Who would believe him when he told them he'd been dreaming? But she must listen to what Fanny was saying . . .

' – and she went down to get a glass of water, not knowing that Charlie was sleeping on the sofa.'

'That's a lie!' Gwen yelled. 'She did know. I saw her looking over the banister when the men brought him in.'

'She says,' Fanny went on, as though Gwen had never interrupted, 'that she went across to the couch to look at him, surprised to find him there. He was breathing heavily and she sat by his side to make sure he was all right. Suddenly his arms went about her and he pulled her down by his side and began kissing her.'

'Why didn't she stop him?' Gwen cried. 'Perhaps it was Lucy who put her arms about him. She's a liar, Fanny. A born liar. You can't believe a word she says.'

'Well, she isn't lying about having the baby, Gwen, more's the pity. Your mam's been watching her for days, caught her being sick this morning, she did, but when Sarah went to tackle her she dashed off to work. We both went to meet her there this evening.'

'It isn't true,' Gwen protested. 'It was Lucy who put her arms about Charlie. Ashamed of herself she should be! He told me all about it. Real embarrassed he was.'

'So he admits it then?' Sarah opened her eyes to stare at Gwen.

'There was nothing *to* admit. It wasn't his fault, he was fast asleep.'

'A likely tale!' Sarah was shouting now, struggling to get up, and Fanny pressed her back into the chair, warning, 'Calm yourself, Sarah. You've already had one turn tonight. Thank goodness Tom will be here soon.'

'He'll marry her,' Sarah was shouting, 'and right away too.'

'He will not!' Gwen yelled, suddenly cold all over. 'It's me he's going to marry. Thank goodness the rooms are ready for us now. I was going to tell you as soon as I got in. We won't wait for the banns to be called. The Register Office will do.'

'You would still marry a man who could do this to youer

sister?' Sarah asked incredulously.

'Lucy's making it up,' Gwen was still yelling, but Sarah, ignoring her words, went on, 'They deserve each other. And once they're married, I never want to see either of them again.'

When Lucy burst into fresh tears at her words, Sarah told her forcefully, 'You might well cry, for all the trouble you've brought to this house! It's terrible what you've done to youer sister, and her waiting for him all these years. Still, it seems she's well rid of him. As for you, madam, youer a disgrace to our name, but I'll have no bastards in this family. You'll marry him as soon as possible, and then, as I've said, I never want to see you again.'

Face as white as lint, Sarah was staring at Lucy, bosom rising and falling rapidly with the effort to breathe. Gwen was about to defend Charlie once more when her mother swayed and would have fallen if Fanny's strong arms hadn't come about her. Between them they carried her to the bedroom, and fear adding to her misery now, Gwen ran for Doctor Powell.

'No need for him to know what this is all about. She's just had a turn, that's all,' Fanny had whispered at the door.

Doctor Powell came and prescribed bed rest once more.

'And absolutely no worries,' he added sternly. 'Whatever has upset your mother, and something has, must be shelved for the time being. Do you understand?'

When they nodded, he went on, 'It's absolutely vital that Sarah remains calm.'

Looking from one to the other for assent, his eyes rested on Lucy's blotched face and he said to her, 'Whatever it is that's upsetting you, girl, don't burden your mother with it.' He patted her on the shoulder, and Lucy looked up at him and nodded as Fanny and Gwen had done. It was obvious that Doctor Powell didn't know the predicament they were in. How could any of them remain calm, especially Sarah?

When Tom arrived home and was told what had happened his expression grew serious. 'I'll go up to the bedroom right away,' he said. 'Pooer Sarah, she's not long got over the last bout. I can't believe it of Charlie, though. He's been like a son to me.'

Ignoring Lucy, he went to the bedroom and sat by Sarah's side, holding her hand, telling her in a gentle voice, 'We'll weather this together, cariad. So long as we've got each other, we can face anything.'

'He'll have to marry her, Tom. Pooer Gwen. She's waited for him so long, and it's all my fault.'

'Shhh, love. We'll talk about it in the morning.'

Charlie would be knocking at the door any minute, and Gwen was longing for, yet dreading his arrival. Perhaps he could put things right? But it was a forlorn hope, seeing he'd already admitted that they'd been together that night, their arms about each other, and admitted kissing Lucy too, although he'd explained he'd been dreaming of Gwen. She could just imagine her parents' reaction when he told them that!

It's hopeless, she told herself. Oh, why had Charlie gone out that night? Why had he got drunk? None of this would have happened if he hadn't. But there were other questions that took even more answering. For instance, why had Lucy sat by his side wearing only her nightdress? She was the real culprit, with more than a little explaining to do.

Chapter Twenty-six

Later that evening Charlie still hadn't arrived. He's in for a shock when he does come, Gwen told herself miserably. But he wouldn't allow them to bulldoze him into marrying Lucy, she was sure of that. Her spirits rose at the thought, but next moment, remembering her parents' determination to get Lucy married and avoid a scandal, they plummeted again. Charlie would have to admit, wouldn't he, that, however innocently, he'd had his arms about Lucy and had kissed her? But you didn't have a baby through kissing, did you?

She felt on edge, going to the window and looking out every few minutes. But Charlie had returned to his job on the farm a few weeks before. He'd have gone home for a meal and to wash and change before coming to see her. She twitched the parlour curtains aside once more, and seeing him approaching the house, dashed for the door.

Before he could put his arms about her, she cried, 'Oh, Charlie! Something awful has happened.' Looking concerned, he asked, 'What is it, Gwen? Can't we have those rooms after all?'

Oh, if only that was all, she thought. But before she could even tell him about the rooms being vacant, her father was coming towards them.

'I want to have a little talk with you,' he told Charlie. 'I think we'd better go to the parlour.'

Gwen went to follow them in but her father, about to close the door, said firmly, 'No, Gwen. This is men's business.'

'It's my business too, Dada. I want to come in.' But her father shook his head, saying, 'No, Gwen, this is between me and Charlie.' And he shut the door firmly.

She felt like pushing it open and demanding to stay, but Charlie would soon put her father right, wouldn't he? He'd tell him how Lucy had behaved, the shameful little hussy! Ever since Charlie had told her what had happened she'd wanted to give Lucy a good shaking and ask her just what she thought she was doing, but after what had happened this evening hatred for Lucy was welling up inside her. What if Dada believed Lucy and not Charlie? Later, hearing the parlour door open, she hurried into the passage to see her father going upstairs, but it was Charlie her eyes were upon, and seeing that he looked white and shaken, Gwen's heart sank.

'They say I've got to marry Lucy, Gwen,' he told her incredulously. 'I couldn't deny that I'd had my arms about her, but I was pretty sure nothing could have happened. She says she's having a baby, but she can't be, Gwen. Do you think she could be making it up?'

'We'll get married ourselves right away, Charlie. We'll go to the Register Office. We've waited all this time . . .'

But Charlie was shaking his head.

'I've had to promise your dad. He said if I refused it would kill your mam. She's ill again, isn't she? He told me the doctor says she mustn't be upset.'

'Oh, no, Charlie. You can't marry her! You mustn't!'

'But I couldn't deny she was with me on that couch.'

'You were dreaming of me, Charlie. You told me so.'

When he sat down and rested his head in his hands, he looked so miserable she thought she couldn't bear it, especially when he said, 'It would have been better if I'd been killed in France in the trenches, Gwen. I'll just be changing the hell out there for another kind of hell, only worse. I never liked Lucy. I think you know that.'

Her father was coming downstairs now and Gwen glared at him as he stopped to tell Charlie, 'I'll go with you to the Register Office first thing tomorrow morning about the licence. Sarah's very relieved, I can tell you.'

'He can't marry Lucy, Dada,' Gwen cried. 'We're engaged. The rooms are ready now, we can be married –'

'Admitted being with Lucy he has, Gwen. Where's youer pride, girl?' Her father went to the kitchen, shutting the door behind him.

She flung her arms about Charlie then but he put her gently aside, saying, 'It's hopeless, love. No one will believe it was innocent. I wouldn't ever have touched Lucy if I'd been awake, Gwen. And it sounded really daft when I said I was dreaming it was you. Your father didn't believe it, I could tell. He said, "When the drink's in the wit's out, boyo, and you can't deny you were drunk, can you?"'

The tears were rolling down Gwen's cheeks now. Putting an arm about her, he drew her close, saying, 'God, what a mess! I'll love you dearly, cariad, as long as I live. Why did I have to go out that night, Gwen? Why did I get drunk? I could have refused those drinks, but I wanted to be good mates. Now look what I've done to you. To both of us.'

When Charlie had gone Gwen sat on in the parlour, the blinds drawn and the gas-light turned off. Feeling numb and hopeless, she stared before her, rocking herself to and fro. Thinking of all the long, lonely years she'd waited for Charlie, she told herself now that those years hadn't been so bad after all for at least she'd had hope then. There'd always been something to look forward to during those long years of war, his letters, the plans they made and wrote to each other about, the love they poured out on the written page.

It was cold with the fire unlit. She began to shiver, but still she sat on. No one came to see if she was all right. Only her father was up, and he thought she was well rid of Charlie anyway. She ought to go upstairs to see if her mother needed anything, but still she sat on, hugging her knees for warmth, rocking to and fro. She wasn't going to sleep in the same bed as Lucy tonight or ever again, she'd made up her mind about that. She would get a blanket and pillow and stay down here on the sofa.

There was a tap on the door, then it opened and Tom stood there, letting in a shaft of light from the passage.

'Could you settle youer mam for the night, Gwen?' His tone was apologetic, as though he thought he might be asking too much.

She rose without a word. When she reached the door he put a hand gently on her arm, saying, 'Don't upset her, cariad, not tonight'. And she nodded before taking the candlestick and matches he held out, and having lit the candle and watched its flame grow strong, went upstairs.

Next morning Tom Llewellyn was up early. When Gwen left the parlour, still fully clothed from the night before, he was already dressed in his best dark grey suit, and his thick melton overcoat was draped over the head of the sofa ready to put on. When an hour later Charlie still hadn't arrived, he paced up and down, glancing frequently at the clock, finally bursting out angrily: 'By God! I'll go and fetch him if he doesn't come soon.'

In a daze Gwen prepared her mother's breakfast and washed up the dishes. Now she was wondering however she was to face going to work, for Ted, knowing her so well, was bound to sense that something was very wrong. Just then she saw Lucy scuttling down the passage and heard the front door slam, and realised it was she who was expected to stay at home and look after Mama. And although she was relieved to have an excuse for not going in, she was consumed with anger at the way everyone took her for granted.

The Palmers must have heard the row last night, Gwen thought, but when ten minutes later Mabel came in she said nothing about it, only asked right away, 'Who's ill, Gwen? Mrs Evans saw Doctor Powell knocking last night. Only just told me she has.'

'Mama's had another of her turns, Mabel. I have to let Ted know that I won't be coming to work. Would you be able to stay just while I go?'

'One of the boys will take a note for you, Gwen. Write it out now and I'll take it with me. I'll come back to see Sarah when he's gone. All right is she now, cariad?'

'She's got to stay in bed.'

Gwen looked so unhappy that Mabel felt like putting an arm about her, but she sensed the girl didn't want to share her trouble, whatever it was. She'd be worried about Sarah's health, of course, but that wouldn't explain the sadness in her eyes. And what had all that rumpus been about last night? There had been far more noise than when they'd had the shop. She hadn't made out anything that was said but one of the girls had been crying. Sarah must have been taken bad afterwards for they'd never have carried on like that otherwise.

It's no business of mine, Mabel told herself. But when, just as she was opening her own front door with Gwen's note in her hand, she saw Tom, dressed in his best, pop his head out and look up and down the street, her lips formed an 'Ooh!' of surprise. She'd never known Tom to lose a day's work, not in all the years she'd lived next door.

Gwen felt relieved that she didn't have to face Ted right away. However was she going to explain? Anyway, perhaps Charlie had changed his mind about his promise? She felt hope rise in her at the thought. Dada was like a cat on hot bricks. She wondered what he'd do if Charlie didn't turn up.

Half an hour later she answered a knock on the door to find a subdued-looking Charlie and his father standing there.

'Come to see your dad, I have, Gwen.' Joe Roberts' voice was belligerent.

'Look, Dad, I asked you to leave it to me,' Charlie implored. 'Only make things worse you will.'

Then Tom was striding towards them, saying, 'We'll talk in the parlour, shall we? We'll have to go to the Register Office soon. Lucy's going to get time off from her work. We can call for her on the way. I believe a special licence means waiting only a day or two.'

Tom was closing the parlour door behind them as he spoke, and Gwen felt angry with herself for not insisting that she be in on the discussion. It was her life they were destroying. Why didn't she push open the door and tell them so? She was twenty-six but Dada still treated her like a child, expecting instant obedience. Still, Charlie seemed to have come to his senses. Raised voices from the parlour proved he wasn't giving in easily to Dada's demands.

She was still standing at the foot of the stairs, her hand resting on the knob of the newel post, when the parlour door burst open and Mr Roberts stormed out, his face red with anger, crying, 'I'm darned if I'm going to let my boy marry your Lucy and ruin his life!' And her father, his face equally red, yelled after him, 'You can't stop him, Joe. Charlie's a grown man. He promised me last night.'

'I'd like to talk about that promise.' Charlie's father was walking back into the parlour now. 'Knock me down with a feather you could have last night. Afraid to refuse he was, in case of what might happen to your missus.' Before the door shut once more she'd caught a glimpse of Charlie's face. He'd looked awful, like a man who'd been condemned to life imprisonment or worse.

By the time the door opened again Gwen was a bundle of nerves, biting her nails and pacing to and fro. When they did come out of the room Charlie didn't look at her, and she heard his father say, 'Well, put like that I suppose he'll have to marry her, but it's a rum do. I'd like a word with that girl myself.'

'You'll see her when we pick her up at the workrooms. Gwen is home looking after her mother. Well, shall we go and get that special licence?'

Suddenly, Charlie seemed to come to life. He cried, 'And what if I refuse?'

'Then it would kill Sarah,' Tom told him. 'She'd never get over the disgrace. We've never had any scandals in this family. Good girls we had. Anyway, you've admitted to me –'

'All right! All right!' Charlie was yelling now. 'Let's get on with it. But in my book good girls don't go around sitting on men's beds in their nightgowns, do they?'

Tom's face was red, his eyes bulging. Gwen saw he was about to hit Charlie, but as he lunged forward Joe Roberts caught his arm, saying, 'Can't it wait for a day or so, Tom? The Register Office, I mean.'

'No!' Tom's voice shook with anger. 'The girl's pregnant, isn't she? The quicker they get married the better. You know what neighbours are like. They'll be counting the months.'

Gwen had been watching this exchange from the foot of the stairs. Now, as Charlie put on his cap, she sprang to life, crying, 'No, Charlie. Don't do anything until your dad talks to Lucy. It's all a mistake – it must be!'

Just then her mother called her name plaintively, and resentfully she went upstairs. By the time she'd calmed Sarah and given her her medicine, for she'd heard the row and was in an agitated state, and had gone downstairs to make a cup of tea, there was no one about and her father's bowler had gone from its peg on the hallstand.

Chapter Twenty-seven

It was like some awful dream as plans were quickly made for Lucy's wedding. Gwen could hardly contain herself when her sister announced that she would wear the pink bridesmaid's dress to be married in. But Sarah put her foot down firmly.

'It's hardly a time for flaunting yourself,' she told Lucy. 'You can get married in your best hat and coat, and I for one will be glad when it's done. Lying here in bed I've had plenty of time to think about youer wickedness, Lucy. I'd never have believed it of a daughter of mine. Haven't you any feelings for Gwen at all? And you can turn off the waterworks! Crying isn't going to help any of us now.'

On the day itself there was no reception planned for when they returned from the Register Office. Charlie was going straight there with his witnesses; his parents had refused to accompany him even to the short service. And Gwen, not wanting to be at home when they returned, had accepted Mabel's offer to stay with Sarah and had gone to work.

'Pooer girl,' Mabel had said to Eddie only that morning. 'It must be awful for her, knowing he'll be at that Register Office marrying her sister, and after waiting for him all that time.'

'You found out why he's marrying the other one yet?' Eddie had looked up from his breakfast to ask.

'No. Sarah's acting like a clam about it and I didn't like to ask outright.'

Gwen had waited until yesterday before visiting Mrs Lucas to tell her she wouldn't require the rooms as she was no longer getting married, and the good soul, seeing the girl's distress, had refused to take the week's rent Gwen insisted she owed for messing her about. Telling Gwen how much she'd looked forward to them coming to live with her, she'd made a cup of tea and put a few tactful questions, but Gwen was not to be drawn, having decided that the best thing was not to satisfy anyone's curiosity except Ted's. Let them think what they like, she told herself. It won't be any worse than the awful truth.

She had tried to avoid Lucy as much as possible since that dreadful night, but thank goodness it wouldn't be necessary for very much longer. Joe Roberts, knowing how embarrassing it would be all round, had arranged for Charlie to go back to Pembroke to work on his uncle's farm, where fortunately a small cottage was available. This suited everyone for Sarah hadn't changed her mind. She'd barely spoken civilly to Lucy since the night she was taken ill, except frequently to remind the girl that once she was married she wanted no more to do with her.

For the week they were to remain in Cardiff after the wedding Lucy was to stay at home, and Charlie with his parents, for neither family would have them both. Gwen knew that she should be glad that they were going away but her feelings about it were mixed. She still loved Charlie deeply for none of what had happened had shaken her faith in his innocence. To her he was the victim of her sister's selfishness. She had no doubt that Lucy had fancied she loved him and that was what it was all about. But if Lucy had got what she wanted, it hadn't brought her much joy. She looked as unhappy as the rest of them.

It was a few days after the wedding, and Sarah, now out of bed, had gone with Tom to spend the evening with Fanny while Lucy was at her friend's saying goodbye.

Gwen was sitting staring into the fire when the knock came. When she opened the door and saw Charlie her eyes lit up, but only for a moment as she reminded herself that he was Lucy's husband now.

'No one's in except me,' she told him. And he said, 'I was hoping to talk to you, Gwen. I feel so awful about everything. Oh, my love, how could I have let it happen?'

He looked so unhappy that, drawing him into the parlour, her arms went about him, and suddenly all the pent-up emotions that she'd suppressed over the years rose in her and she clung to him, her lips on his. When Charlie would have pulled away, crying, 'No, Gwen! Oh, no! We mustn't!' her arms tightened about him and her lips pressed against his. They kissed passionately, their need of each other desperate now. He pulled her gently to the floor and they came together in a loving ecstasy that dulled the pain of Gwen's initiation. It seemed so right after all the years of waiting that when it was over and she lay in Charlie's arms, she felt no shame.

He kissed her mouth, her eyes, her hair, then suddenly said, 'Oh, Gwen, what have I done? Supposing . . .'

Her lips on his smothered his words, but presently he drew away, and sitting up now, his head in his hands, said, 'As though I haven't caused you enough pain already, but I love you so I couldn't stop myself.'

'Lucy cheated you into that marriage, Charlie. Can't you get out of it in a while?'

'There's the child,' he said. 'I'd never have married her, however compromising the situation, if it hadn't been for that.'

There was silence which he broke, saying, 'I'm going away next week, Gwen. Perhaps it's just as well, the way we feel.'

His arm about her once more, he smoothed her hair, murmuring, 'What have I done to us, cariad? What have I done? Oh, Gwen, I pray nothing will happen. Tonight mustn't ruin your life.'

It's ruined already, she thought, but at least I'll have something to remember.

Charlie got up then, saying, 'I'd better go to the kitchen in case anyone comes home.'

'I'll be there in a minute,' she told him, making for the stairs, conscious that the pins had fallen from her bun and that her blouse was undone.

Upstairs she poured cold water into the flowered basin on the wash-stand and splashed her hot cheeks. After drying her face she went across to the cheval mirror and gazed into it. The pupils of her eyes were large and dark and her heart beat fast as she thought of what had just happened. It had seemed so right, so natural, but she knew nobody else would see it that way. Supposing, like Lucy, she had a baby? For a moment excitement rose in her at the thought of carrying Charlie's child, to be instantly dashed by the hopelessness of the situation if it did happen. But she would have to wait until the end of next week to find out.

She stood there deep in thought until she heard Charlie's voice calling, 'Gwen, are you all right? I think I'd better go soon before anyone comes home.'

Hurriedly now she pinned up her hair and fastened her

blouse, then straightening her skirt she hurried downstairs.

When Charlie had gone she was on edge. Sarah and Tom would be home soon. Surely they would see that something momentous had happened to her? She wanted to be somewhere quiet where she could think about the events of the evening. I'll go to bed, Gwen decided. It was early yet but she could always plead a headache.

Closing the bedroom curtains she undressed quickly and slipped between the cool sheets, then lying on her back she stared up at the ceiling, her mind in a whirl.

So that is what marriage is about, she thought. That was what she'd heard women say had to be endured. They couldn't have loved their husbands as she loved Charlie, that was for sure. But on Monday he was going away with Lucy. Would what had happened make that any easier to bear?

Like Aunt Fanny she would be a spinster now, a maiden aunt to Lucy's child. Would the memory of tonight help her to face the barren years ahead?

Hearing the front door open she turned on to her side, and pulling the bedclothes tight about her shoulders, closed her eyes, feigning sleep.

Chapter Twenty-eight

The cab taking Charlie and Lucy and their luggage to the station had just turned the corner. Gwen dropped the lace curtain back into place and swallowed hard. Charlie had already been in the cab when it arrived and she'd kept out of sight, for no good could come of seeing him now.

She had gone to the parlour while her mother urged Lucy quickly to the door where her two straw hold-alls waited. She'd heard Sarah shut the door as soon as Lucy had got into the cab. Her mother was upset, she knew that, but Gwen was in no mood to go to the kitchen and commiserate with her.

She could hardly bear the thought that Charlie and Lucy were now husband and wife, and ever since the night that the news had broken, had been unable to stay in the same room as her sister. One thing she'd soon realised, though, and that was that without Lucy all the chores they'd shared ever since her sister had gone out to work would now fall on her. It was a dreary prospect but she was too unhappy to care. Perhaps working so hard she might fall into an exhausted sleep instead of lying awake wondering how she was going to get through the rest of her miserable life.

When she went through to the kitchen Sarah was sitting

at the table, her head in her hands. She looked up pitifully to say, 'That's the second daughter I've lost, Gwen. But I won't change my mind. I meant it when I said I wanted no more to do with the pair of them, especially after what they've done to you.'

Ignoring the latter remark, Gwen asked, 'Shall I make a cup of tea before I go to work? I only asked for an hour off.'

It hadn't been out of any feeling for Lucy that she'd asked to start an hour later. She'd been afraid of the effect the parting might have on Sarah, particularly if she were alone. She'd got up early to blacklead the range and light the fire, knowing the rest would have to wait until she came home. The washing, particularly when it involved lighting the boiler, would have to be done on a Wednesday when she was home mid-day. Her mother she knew would be able to do the cooking, ironing, and dusting but that still left a great deal to be done.

'Perhaps I've been too hard on Lucy,' Sarah said as they drank their tea. 'But I can't help it, Gwen. She's my own daughter but it's fair turned my stomach, the way she's behaved. The little hussy!'

Only too aware of how her mother would view her own behaviour with Charlie, Gwen kept her silence.

Taking the cups to the wash-house, she glanced at the clock. Sarah called after her, 'Leave the dishes, Gwen, it will be something for me to do.'

Putting on her hat at the mirror set in the hall-stand, she marvelled that she didn't look any different from this time last week. There were deep shadows under her eyes, unhappy eyes that wore a worried expression and would do, she knew, until at least the week-end, for then she should know if there were to be any consequences. And what would she do if there were, with Charlie already married? She'd been a fool to take the risk, only it had seemed so right at the time.

Every night since she had tossed and turned until the small hours, fearful of the possible outcome. I'm probably worrying about nothing, she told herself. I don't suppose it will happen the very first time. But it had with Lucy, hadn't it?

When she arrived at the shop Ted was talking to a dealer friend, but Daisy Ball, showing her sympathy, clucked around Gwen like a hen with its chick. All Daisy knew was that the long engagement was off, and she was sure it couldn't be Gwen's fault.

In Daisy's book the panacea for every ill was a cup of tea, and this was quickly forthcoming. As she sipped it Gwen wondered what Ted had told her was the reason for the hour she'd taken off, for Daisy knew nothing at all about the marriage or of Lucy and Charlie going to West Wales to live. She's bound to find out in time, Gwen thought miserably, but for the present anyway it was one less embarrassment to face.

When the dealer had gone Ted came over to where Gwen stood dusting the shelves.

'Was your mam all right afterwards?' he asked. Then glancing at her and noticing her pallor, went on, 'I can manage if you don't feel up to work today.'

'I'd rather be here, Ted,' she told him with conviction.

'We'll unpack those things I bought on Saturday, if you like.'

She nodded and Ted followed her to the back room where, lifting her apron from its peg, she went over to the packing case. Ted had been to a house sale on Saturday. He'd brought the things back with him but it had been too late to unpack them then.

Despite her unhappiness she felt some of the old

excitement as she lifted out each item and unwrapped it. There was the usual collection of better quality vases, one with the Minton mark for 1863–72, and a Coalport vase of about the same period. Next she brought out a Parian group made by Copeland; two little sisters clinging to each other, their arms dimpled and rounded. There were three ribbon-threaded wall-plates, each painted with a view of a royal house: Balmoral, Windsor and Osborne.

Unwrapping the next object she found it was an ornate brass oil-lamp, its shade a globe of rich burgundy glass, a garland of flowers painted around it. Gwen held it towards the light from the high window, conscious that she would have liked to buy it if they had married and taken Mrs Lucas's rooms. Her eyes began to sting with tears at the thought and she delved deeply into the crate.

'Not bad for a small house sale, Gwen,' Ted was saying. 'There's some nice little pieces that should sell.'

'I like the lamp, Ted. It's very pretty.'

'You can have it at cost, Gwen, if you want it.'

But she shook her head and he went on, 'Well, I'm not going to sell it. I'll put it upstairs. I can do with another lamp.'

As day followed day her hopes fluctuated. In the despairing moments she told herself that she had only herself to blame. Charlie wouldn't be able to help her now, she would have to face the consequences on her own. And if anything happened to Mama because of the disgrace then she'd have to live with that too. Their love making no longer seemed romantic, no longer even seemed justified by the fact that they'd been engaged so long and would have been married if it hadn't been for Lucy.

By the time the weekend came her nerves were taut

almost to breaking point. Was Charlie also worrying about what might happen to her? She would never know for with the families estranged she'd probably never see him again.

By the following weekend Gwen was frantic with worry, crying into her pillow each night at the situation she found herself in.

'Let me know if you ever need me,' Charlie had whispered before they'd said goodbye. But what was the use? He couldn't help her now, could he? Marriage was the only thing that could put things right.

She couldn't eat, couldn't sleep. The shadows had deepened beneath her eyes, and Sarah said to Tom, 'Taking it hard she is, pooer girl. Go into a decline, she will, if she goes on like this.'

Hoping her mother wouldn't guess her trouble, Gwen washed out the clean pieces of hemmed flannelette she should have used, taking care her mother saw her folding them to put away, but it was only delaying the awful moment for she was convinced now that a baby was on the way.

The strain she was under and the lack of food was making her feel ill but she still hoped desperately that something would happen to put her mind at rest.

It was on the Saturday after a week of worrying that, while she was standing by the shop door staring miserably out at the street, a greyness came before her eyes, and as it darkened she sank to the floor in a faint.

When she opened her eyes she was lying on the sofa in the back room, and while Ted was tucking a blanket around her, Daisy was waving smelling salts about under her nose.

With a sigh of relief Ted said, 'That Charlie's got

something to answer for.' Her eyes flew to his in alarm, but he couldn't possibly know, could he? When Daisy had gone upstairs to make a cup of tea, Ted went on, 'Marrying Lucy and going away! No wonder you're in such a state.'

'He had to marry her, Ted,' she reminded him.

It was almost closing time and when Daisy came down in her hat and coat to tell Ted that his tea was ready, she turned to Gwen, saying, 'There's enough for you an' all, love. Best get something inside you before you go. How are you feeling now? Forget 'im I would, if I was you.'E's not worth it, cariad. Breaking it off after all these years . . .' And she shook her head as though it was beyond her comprehension.

'I'll take her home in the trap after she's had some tea. Don't worry, Daisy, I'll look after her.'

When the side door closed behind Daisy, Ted said, 'Do you feel fit enough to come upstairs, Gwen? Have some tea with me and then I'll take you home.'

When they reached the room where a meal of cold meats and pickle and a plate of cherry cake awaited them, she sat on the small velvet sofa and sank thankfully back against the cushions. Ted didn't go straight to the table to pour the tea, but paced to and fro on the hearth-rug before coming and sitting beside her, taking her hands in his.

'I don't know how to put this to you, Gwen,' he began. 'If what I'm going to say upsets you, just forget it. Perhaps it's too soon . . .'

Fear rose in her again. Had he guessed after all? A blush rose to her cheeks as she asked, 'What is it, Ted?'

Looking at her earnestly, he began. 'You know I've had a high regard for you since you were a child, Gwen? Well, for a long time now it's been rather more than that. It's been hard sometimes keeping it to myself, and there was Charlie, and I'm so much older than you. Anyway, I knew I didn't stand a chance. But I do love you. Will you marry me, Gwen?'

Her lips parted in surprise. Of course she'd always known he was fond of her, but she'd thought that was all it was. Now she would have to tell him what was troubling her and shatter his dreams, for he wouldn't want any more to do with her when he knew what she'd done. She was very fond of Ted and valued his opinion of her. If only she didn't have to tell him! If only she could pack her things and disappear out of their lives, all of them – Mama, Dada, Aunt Fan, Ted. She'd thought of it more than once over the last few days, she had a little money saved. But where would she go? And if she found a job, she wouldn't be able to keep it. But they'd try and find her, thinking it was because she was upset over Charlie, and when they found out what was wrong it would break her mother's heart.

Ted was looking at her, his voice sad as he said, 'Well, I think I've got my answer. I should never have asked. Of course, I'm much too old for you.'

'It isn't that, Ted.' Oh, she'd hurt his feelings and that was something she hadn't wanted to do, but he didn't understand, and wouldn't unless she told him why she couldn't marry him. Tears came to her eyes and brimmed over. Ted's arms went about her and he said, 'I didn't mean to upset you, cariad. It must have been a shock to you, my asking like that, but with Charlie married . . .'

'I can't!' she began.

But he burst in with, 'Forget I ever asked you, Gwen. Of course you're still in love with Charlie, but he's married now, you've got to come to terms with that.'

It was then she blurted out, 'I think I'm having a baby, Ted. That's why I can't marry you.'

If she'd hoped to shock him into silence she succeeded, but only for a moment. Then his arms went about her again and he asked tenderly, 'Haven't you told Charlie?' And when she haltingly explained why she hadn't, he took her face in his hands and asked, his voice firm now, 'Will you marry me, Gwen? Oh, I know I'm taking advantage, but it could be quick, by special licence. No one need ever know.'

'But you would, Ted. *You'd* know. It was after Lucy sprang that bombshell. We loved each other so much.' Her face was scarlet with embarrassment, but Ted was smiling at her. He was sure in his heart that she'd been a victim of circumstances. Now, if Gwen agreed, Charlie need never know. He didn't give much for the boy's chances married to Lucy, especially as he didn't love her. But Gwen hadn't answered his question. He'd ask it again.

'Will you marry me, Gwen?' he asked her gently. 'We could get a special licence. You can't be very far yet so they'll believe the child is mine.'

Relief was flooding through her. But was her fondness for Ted enough? And was it fair to him? She remembered the day they'd first met when she'd gone to his shop with Mama to buy a pram for Lucy – the pram he hadn't wanted to part with because it had been bought for his own child, lost at birth and his wife too. A feeling of tenderness rose in her and she said, 'I'd like to marry you, Ted, and I'm very grateful. I've always been fond of you . . .'

His lips seeking hers stopped her words, but as she returned his kiss it remained gentle. Then he held her at arm's length, saying, 'You won't regret it, Gwen, not if I can help it.'

And she answered him with, 'I know I'll never regret it. And thank you, Ted.'

'Sarah will be wondering where you are. I'll bring the trap around. But first there's something I want you to have.'

He went across to the walnut bureau and opened a drawer. Taking out a small leather box he brought it over and put it into her hands, saying, 'I bought this a while back, Gwen, because it was beautiful. But if you'd rather choose a ring from the jeweller's?'

'Oh, no. Oh, Ted, it's lovely!' She had opened the box and was staring in wonder at the sapphire and diamond cluster. She had removed Charlie's engagement ring on the day he'd married Lucy. Now Ted took the ring from her and slipped it on her finger, covering the white mark where Charlie's ring had been for so long. He was saying, 'If it doesn't fit, I'll get it altered'. But it fitted perfectly.

Ted was helping her on with her coat, and overwhelmed with relief and gratitude she kissed his cheek warmly, wondering just what Sarah was going to say.

When they arrived at the house and he'd knocked on the door it flew open almost at once and her mother cried, 'Thank goodness youer all right, Gwen. I've been that worried. Sitting by the front-room window I've been for ages, waiting for you to come.'

When they entered the kitchen, Tom, who'd been smoking his pipe and staring into the fire, raised anxious eyes.

'There's pale you look, girl,' Sarah was saying, 'and Ted having to bring you home in the trap an' all.' Then turning to him she went on, 'She's not eating anything. Go to skin and bone she will. He's not worth it.'

'Letting youer tongue run away with you again, Sarah,' Tom warned.

It was then that she noticed the ring, her eyes widening as she looked to make sure it was on the third finger of Gwen's left hand. Her mouth opened in surprise as Ted told them, 'I suppose I should have asked Tom first but Gwen has agreed to marry me.'

Tom was pumping Ted's hand and Sarah's joy was obvious. Gwen found herself glancing towards the gap on the mantelpiece where Charlie's photo had been until he fell from grace. She'd never forget him, she couldn't however long she might live. But she'd never knowingly hurt Ted and would try to make him a good wife. He'd saved her from unbearable disgrace and she'd always be grateful.

Now Ted was telling her parents that he and Gwen were to be married as quickly as possible. The smile leaving her face, Sarah cried, 'But why all the rush? You must have a proper wedding, not a Register Office affair.'

'But it will be a proper wedding, Sarah,' Ted told her. Then he chuckled. 'Want to make sure of her I do, in case she changes her mind.'

'Church weddings are best.'

'Well, I promise you this, Sarah.' Ted was laughing now. 'All your grandchildren will be christened in church.'

'Oh, Ted! Youer making Gwen blush. But whatever am I thinking of? We've got a bottle of parsnip wine in the pantry. Get the glasses, Gwen, and we'll drink to youer happiness.'

When Ted had gone and Gwen was upstairs getting ready for bed, Sarah said, 'I'll have another go at them tomorrow, Tom. About getting married in church, I mean.'

'Why can't you leave things as they are?' he asked. 'Can't you see why Gwen doesn't want all that fuss? She and Charlie were to have been married in church, with a bridesmaid and lots of people coming here to the wedding breakfast. I don't expect she could bear to go through all that with Ted, knowing people were pitying her because Charlie had let her down.'

'I never thought of that, Tom. The pooer girl!' Sarah sighed. 'Oh, well, we'll have to make the best of it, I suppose.'

Chapter Twenty-nine

Four days later when Gwen and Ted were married she wished the small wedding breakfast could have been held at her new home, for the neighbours at Wilfred Street, curious to know why Gwen was marrying her boss instead of the boy she'd been engaged to since before the war, were out in strength to watch for their return. Anyway, Sarah had set her heart on having the breakfast at home, although it would be only Daisy, Mabel and Eddie besides themselves and Fanny.

Ted had no near relatives except an elderly aunt and uncle who lived in North Wales. It would be a long way for them to come, especially if the weather was bad, and it was rather short notice. 'I'll write and tell them afterwards,' he told Gwen. 'Perhaps we could visit them sometime?'

She agreed, knowing that if the ties of the shop had prevented Ted from seeing them all these years it was very likely they would in the future too.

When at last they were ready to go home, Gwen kissed Sarah, saying, 'I'll be round tomorrow evening to do some of the housework, so don't you try to do too much.' And Sarah told her with a happy smile, 'There's no need, cariad. Fanny's coming to live with us. It was only decided last night and I haven't seen you on youer own today. There's plenty of room here now with you girls all gone, so she can have the middle room for her sewing.'

What a generous soul Aunt Fanny is, Gwen thought. It was a great weight lifted from her mind. As she hugged her warmly as they said goodbye, she said, 'Thanks, Aunt Fan, for coming to live with Mam.'

Her aunt laughingly replied, 'Well, it'll be company for me an' all, Gwen. It works both ways, you know.'

Later that night when they were getting ready for bed, they were both very quiet, with Ted seeming as nervous as Gwen herself. It would have been so much easier with Charlie, loving him as she did, and the marriage had been so sudden. She lay stiffly in the bed, the sheet pulled up to her chin, while Ted turned off the light in its pretty frosted shade then climbed in beside her, to lie as stiffly as Gwen herself.

This is awful, she thought. She must have given him the impression that she wanted to be left alone, and of course a part of her did, but she wanted to make him happy too. A wave of gratitude swept over her and impetuously she turned towards him and kissed his cheek. Then his arms came about her and he whispered, 'Is it all right, Gwen?'

She put her lips to his reassuringly, cutting off his words, and when his body responded she put her arms about him. Ted was so gentle, so loving. It was nothing like the fevered ecstasy that she had shared with Charlie that night, and that had resulted in the baby she was now certain she was carrying, but she was grateful to Ted for being kind to her.

Afterwards she slept with his arm about her, and when morning came, for the first time in ages woke refreshed.

'We have to get up, Ted, if we're going to open the

shop,' she told him regretfully, snuggling deeper into the warm bed.

He held her face in his hands and kissed her, laughingly telling her, 'Your nose is as cold as a puppy's.'

But as the days went by Gwen found it wouldn't be easy to forget her love for Charlie, the longing that she knew she'd carry with her always.

'Shouldn't you go to see Doctor Powell, Gwen?' Ted asked. It was a month later, about seven weeks since Charlie had found her alone that night. Would Doctor Powell know when he examined her? she thought worriedly.

They'd been married just over two months when Gwen confided to Daisy that a baby was on the way, having told her mother the evening before. Sarah had been overjoyed at the news.

'At least one of my daughters has brought me happiness,' she told Gwen, making her feel guilty at the undeserved praise.

Gwen was glad now that Charlie was living away for she was sure that sometimes she wouldn't have been able to resist the deep longing she had to see him again. Did he still care about her in the same way? He'd never tried to find out if she was all right, had he? And if it hadn't been for Ted she would have been in a desperate position by now, an outcast both at home and with the neighbours. Oh, some of them would have been kind, but it would have been out of thankfulness that it hadn't happened in their families. Now, thanks to Ted, she was respectable, and although it was in a different way to Charlie, she did love him and want to make him happy. But it was a love that knew no peaks of joy.

As Whitsun approached, Ted suggested she had some

new dresses. Fanny made them in a loose-fitting style, together with a silver grey suit with a wrap-over skirt and a straight hip-length jacket to accommodate her already swelling figure.

Gwen and Ted were lucky to enjoy the same interests. She loved to accompany him to the auction sales, sharing with him the anticipation of maybe finding something special, but as the summer wore on and her body grew more cumbersome she was glad instead to draw a chair to the window in the sitting room above the shop and watch the people passing by.

It saddened her to see the tall thin young man selling matches on the pavement opposite. The tray containing the boxes hung from a string about his neck so that he could balance on his crutches, for the empty leg of his trousers on the right side was pinned up above the knee.

A little further along the pavement another young man stood selling boot laces. He shook perpetually, a legacy of the shell-shock he'd suffered during the war, and Gwen's heart went out to them both. Surely a grateful country could do better for them than this? Ted had a stock of boot laces and matches for he would never pass without putting his hand in his pocket. But there were so many wounded about the streets, a constant reminder of the tragic aftermath of war.

Chapter Thirty

'You're imagining it, Lucy.'

'I'm not! I'm not! They all hate me. They know we had to get married. They know you should have married Gwen.'

Charlie sighed. Lucy was right. His aunt and uncle hadn't taken to her at all, and Lucy hadn't helped matters either, finding fault with everything in the cottage, comparing its drawbacks with the amenities she'd enjoyed back home.

'There's no gas lighting,' she'd cried in horror on the day they arrived, 'not even downstairs like we had.' And then a few minutes later, 'What have I got to do to get water out of this tap?' And when he'd showed her how to work the pump, she'd yelled, 'What a dump! I'm not staying here.'

He'd wished she would pack her bags and leave him, but if she did her mother would only send her back. Charlie was glad that his work took him away from the cottage from morning until night; his uncle's land spread over a large area. Lucy was bored as he'd known she'd be, a fun-loving town girl shut away in the heart of the country like this, but he could feel no sympathy for her. All his sympathy was for Gwen. At least it had been until his mother wrote and told him that she'd married Ted. The news had hurt him deeply. She hadn't taken very long to find solace. He'd been worried up till then about what had happened between them, had wondered if there was any way he could get in touch to find out if she was all right. Her marriage to Ted, and especially so soon, had been a blow to his ego.

His mother had quarrelled with Gwen's parents so the news hadn't come direct. What difference could it make now anyway with him tied down by marriage himself?

It was as he was calling at the farmhouse before going home to the cottage that he heard his aunt's voice from the open kitchen door.

'Bone idle she is,' Aunt Betty was saying. 'Called to see how things were going with them, I did, and she was sat in the armchair reading a book. And with all that needed to be done, baking day an' all! Told her I did that if she wanted something to do she could keep hens like those who lived there before her.'

When she noticed Charlie standing in the doorway she clapped her hand to her mouth in dismay, but he couldn't fault her description, Lucy was no country girl. But it was the only job he'd been trained to do, and the only one that came with somewhere furnished to live.

'She wants to get away before the baby comes,' he told his aunt.

'But where would you go, Charlie?'

He was shaking his head when his uncle said, 'Well, I know someone who's needing a general hand for his farm. Met him at the market I did, yesterday. It's a farm in North Wales. I can understand how the girl feels, Charlie, us knowing all about you both. Be a fresh start for you anyway.'

'Is there a furnished cottage?'

'Yes. Told me he had the gas put in when his son was living there. Running water from the tap, too.'

'How about you? Won't I be letting you down?'

'No, boy. We'll manage. It's not working out for youer wife, is it?'

Less than a fortnight later their few possessions were loaded on to the cart when his uncle went to market. Lucy seemed excited about the move. It was May and her pregnancy was beginning to show. Charlie allowed a little pity to creep into his feelings for her. She was still such a child and had had so little out of life. All those years at home looking after Mair and the house, a couple of years of going out to work, and then this.

Lucy was looking pretty this morning, her eyes bright with excitement bringing warm colour to her cheeks, the blue of the cotton dress she wore reflecting the clear colour of her eyes. He noticed for the first time that her dress was stretched to its limit about her figure. He rarely saw her without her apron. When she noticed him looking at her she pulled the grey alpaca coat about her self-consciously, then put on her straw hat with its wreath of flowers about the crown, settling it becomingly on top of her fair curls before jamming in the hat-pin.

Farmer Rees greeted them kindly enough, but he was sparing with words, English ones anyway, for as Uncle Arthur had said on the journey, his was a Welsh-speaking community. Charlie told himself he should have realised.

While the two farmers concluded their business at the market, Charlie, taking pity on Lucy's plight, took her into a drapery emporium they were passing and to her joy paid for two new loose-fitting dresses. The money, he reflected sadly, he'd saved to marry Gwen.

'Perhaps I could get a second-hand sewing machine later on?' Lucy told him eagerly. 'I could make things for the baby as well.' And he felt mean because he couldn't share her enthusiasm.

They met Charlie's uncle for a meal and to say goodbye, and afterwards joined the farmer for the journey to their new home.

They sat on a bench at the back of the cart. When a silence descended on them, Charlie was worrying how they would communicate when the farmer turned his head to say: '*Dych chin siarad Cymraeg?*'

Charlie had heard this phrase before and answered in an apologetic voice, 'No, I'm sorry, we don't speak Welsh, but I mean to learn.'

For a while there was only the sound of the horse clip-clopping along the country lanes, then the farmer said in English, 'It's a nice day, isn't it?' And when they both agreed, with Lucy adding, 'It's quite warm, almost like summer,' he went on in the rich strong accent of North Wales, 'Hope you're going to be very happy with us, I do.'

At last it was time for him to point out his farmhouse in the distance. It was a large solid-looking grey stone building with a steep slate roof, set against a back-drop of green hills.

Lucy perked up when she saw the cottage they were to live in. It was some distance from the farmhouse and built of the same grey stone: a small two-up, two-down, with a well-tended front garden surrounded by a low stone wall. Farmer Rees dropped them off outside the gate, and giving Charlie the key, told them to come up to the farm for anything they needed.

The garden was already colourful with spring flowers – primulas, foxgloves and iris. Buds on shrubs and trees were bursting open to reveal glimpses of yellow and fiery red new foliage.

When Charlie had turned the big iron key in the lock, Lucy quickly unpinned her hat and ran excitedly from room to room, coming back at last to the kitchen, her eyes bright and cheeks pink with excitement. The kitchen was cool at this time of day, its window in shade. There was a new-looking deal table on which stood a welcoming vase of flowers, and on the black and red tiles were two rag mats in soft tones of beige and brown. A fire-guard topped by a brass rail surrounded a range that had been black-leaded until it shone, and the fire had been laid ready to put a match to. On the high mantel brass ornaments jostled for a place either side of the black marble clock which now struck four.

Lucy sank against the cushions of a long open-ended sofa and looked around her happily, while Charlie lowered himself into the wooden armchair at one side of the fire and stared about him.

If only I was sharing this with Gwen, he thought wistfully. But Gwen was a town girl too. Would she have been happy in the heart of the country? Anyway, he'd never have come here if it hadn't been for what had happened.

In her eagerness to explore the cottage, Lucy had left the front door open. Now a voice came to them from the doorway. 'Hello! Anyone in?'

A young woman stood there. She was plump and rosy-cheeked with a mass of fine dark hair wound into a loose bun and smiling brown eyes. But it was her accent that brought them quickly to the door for it had the musical inflections of the South Wales valleys.

'I'm Megan Rees,' she introduced herself. 'We were in this cottage until yesterday. Dilwyn and me have lived here for three years, been very happy too. But now we're buying a farm of our own with his dad's help. Swansea way it is, so I'll be near my folk again. Dad offered us to take any of this stuff we wanted, furnished this he did for us, but the kitchen's huge where we're going, and we've bought some of the furniture with it.'

'When are you moving to your farm?' Lucy asked, wishing with all her heart that this young woman was staying.

'The beginning of next week, and I can't wait! I'll be able to visit my family then, and they can come to see me.'

Lucy's euphoria with her surroundings didn't last. At first she polished, scrubbed floors, cooked delicious meals, cut flowers from the garden to arrange indoors. But she quickly became exhausted, and with no visitors to appreciate her work, grew bored with it. Charlie tried to interest her in going out but she wouldn't venture any further than the gate. Even when she ran out of eggs on baking day she waited for Charlie to come home then made him trail all the way back to the farmhouse for them.

'They won't understand me,' was her favourite excuse.

'Of course they will. They understand me, don't they? You ought to go over and make yourself known, Lucy, you'll be needing friends when the baby arrives.'

'Well, I can't go in these shoes. The lane's still mucky.' She lifted her feet one at a time in their dainty bar shoes.

'Perhaps we could get you something stronger to wear?' Charlie's savings were dwindling but there was still some money left.

She shook her head, saying, 'I don't want to go, anyway, I don't like farms, you know that.

'Could you get me some books next time you go to the market?' she asked, changing the subject. 'I've read all the ones I brought. I remember seeing a second-hand book stall in the general market before you come to the livestock.'

'How would I know what to get?' he said doubtfully.

'I like a good love story. Something romantic.'

'You ought to be making some baby clothes.'

'I've got some. Your aunt and uncle gave them to us before we came here. If I was home Aunt Fan would be making a layette,' she ended wistfully.

Looking at her, Charlie wondered for the umpteenth time how he'd got himself into this mess. He'd racked his brains trying to remember what had happened, but he'd been so drunk that night through the generosity of Ben's friends at the pub that anything could have happened. But one question had remained unanswered. What had Lucy been doing there anyway dressed only in her nightgown? Oh, she'd explained of course that she hadn't known he was there, but surely when she saw that he was, she could have gone back for her dressing gown, or entered the wash-house for her drink of water by going through the middle room and into the yard? Instead she'd come and sat down beside him. Gwen had said she'd thought Lucy was in love with him, and sometimes she was quite affectionate, like the day he bought her the dresses and again when she'd been pleased with the cottage. But he didn't love her; in fact she still irritated him like she had when she was a child. Why, the very first time he'd taken Gwen out she'd tagged along and spoilt things for them.

Charlie gave a deep sigh. He'd have to make the best of a bad job for the baby's sake at least, and Gwen was married herself now, there was no turning back.

As the months passed Lucy became increasingly frightened of what lay before her. It's all Mama's fault, she told herself. Sarah hadn't told any of them what to expect, obviously thinking it sufficient to warn them to be good girls and never to let any man take liberties. She would never have let it happen if she'd known. Now the baby was inside her and she was terrified wondering however it could be born. Did they cut your tummy open? she wondered, sick with fear at the thought. She couldn't bring herself to ask Charlie. He was her husband but she hardly knew him. Perhaps it was different if you'd been in love for years.

Lucy carried her fears with her through the lonely summer days. She had never become friendly with anyone from the farmhouse. Charlie had told her that they always spoke to each other in Welsh. He'd been begging her for ages to go into the village and see the midwife, but she'd kept on putting it off. Myfanwy Pryce, she'd been told, didn't speak English either so she wasn't going to receive any enlightenment there, was she?

It was a hot July morning and the mud in the lane had dried to a powdery dust. When Charlie was leaving for the farm he said, 'Why don't you take a little walk later on? You ought to get out more, Lucy, for the baby's sake.'

Pegging clothes in the garden, she remembered his words. Birds were singing in the hedgerows and the sun was warm on her back. She'd take a little walk along the lane that led to the village. It ran past the farm and she might see Charlie about. Although it was hot she put on the old grey alpaca coat over her dress to cover her bulging stomach but could no longer do up the buttons. Putting her hand to the small of her back in an attempt to ease the ache, she walked with cumbersome steps along the path to the gate and out into the lane.

She found herself worrying as usual about how the baby

would arrive. There was no one here that she could talk to, though the farmer's wife had done her best to be friendly, inviting her to come up to the farm whenever she wanted. Only she hadn't wanted, telling herself at the time that she'd only feel uncomfortable with them all babbling in Welsh. She hadn't meant to be rude but after a while they'd stopped asking. Now there was no one to turn to, with Charlie away working most of the day.

The hedge was low enough in places to see some of the farm buildings, but apart from a bull in the nearest field she saw no one about. Perhaps Charlie was with the lambs that she could see dotting the fields on the higher slopes? Staring upwards, she became aware of the bull trotting towards her. A moment later it had broken into a gallop, head down menacingly.

There was a five-bar gate between them, with high hedges either side, but Lucy didn't stop to think. Turning about as quickly as she could, her cumbersome body slow to respond, she tried to run. Suddenly the toe of her dainty shoe caught in a rut and she was pitched forward. As she hit the ground a searing pain engulfed her and she cried out, but there was nobody to hear.

As the pain eased for a moment, all the fears she'd been harbouring for months took over. What if it was the baby trying to be born? If there was no one to cut her open and take the child away, would she burst? Lucy had long come to the conclusion that this was the only way a baby could come into the world. But suddenly a stronger pain was making even thought impossible, twisting her face with sheer agony, forcing scream after scream from her lips.

Hearing running footsteps, she opened her eyes to see Charlie rushing towards her, his face white and set, turning to urge the boy behind him to hurry to the village for the midwife. Then, lifting her gently, her head limp against his shoulder, he made his way home.

'What's wrong, Lucy? Did you fall?' But his words were lost to her as another bout of pain rendered her insensible.

'It's much too soon for the baby,' he muttered to himself worriedly.

Lucy was writhing on the bed, still fully clothed, moaning into the pillow, when the midwife arrived and took charge. She herself was red with exertion, her plump cheeks wobbling as she took charge of the terrified girl. Charlie was remembering with embarrassment that she hadn't even been booked. But right away the professional took over, and as she eased the clothes from and then examined Lucy, with deft and gentle fingers, she murmured to herself in her native tongue.

A few minutes later, Mrs Rees, spurred by the garbled version of affairs given her by the young farm-hand, knocked on the door, and was soon busy boiling water and carrying it up, finding baby clothes and the hemmed pieces of flannelette that Lucy had made for napkins, and putting them over the guard to air.

Charlie hovered about downstairs, seeming to get in everyone's way, his face puckered with worry for the child hadn't been expected until late in September. He made up the fire and filled the kettles yet again, then at Mrs Rees's suggestion went back to the cow byres.

Lucy lay huddled in the bed, her face gleaming with sweat, pulling hard on the rolled-up sheet the farmer's wife had tied to the brass rail at the foot after putting the other end into Lucy's hand. 'Pull, cariad, pull,' she told her when the pain got bad.

'Push, cariad, push!' the midwife ordered a little while later. 'Pu-sh!' It was one of the few English words and stock phrases she kept for foreigners, as she thought of anyone not from her part of Wales. She'd seldom needed to use them, and never in the village, but they were useful to know just in case.

When Lucy felt the baby moving she screamed aloud, sure it was going to rend her apart. Her pain was double-edged with worry: would she be able to convince Charlie that the fall had been responsible for bringing on her labour? The midwife wouldn't be telling him anything – well, any words that he'd recognise – so it would be left to her to make him understand.

A quarter of an hour later she was looking down at the baby boy who, after being washed and dressed, was put into her arms. It was red and wrinkled, and she didn't feel any great love for it, not yet anyway, just relief that it was born and she was still in one piece. If ever she had a girl, she told herself, she'd tell her the truth when she was old enough. The truth wasn't half as bad as her own terrible fear of the unknown had been. But what was she thinking of? If she had a daughter . . . No more babies for me, she vowed. Never again!

Ten minutes later Charlie was in the room, gazing down at the wrinkled bundle in her arms. The farmer's wife had warned him that it was not very strong. What could have gone wrong? Why had it come so soon? Was it the fall she'd had in the lane?

Lucy hadn't been eating or sleeping properly for months. She'd been worried about something, probably the birth of the child; she wasn't much more than a child herself and her mother had cut off all ties. The sight of the baby, so helpless, stirred tender feelings. He wanted to bend down and take it in his arms, but although he'd washed his hands he was still in his farm clothes.

The baby was sickly at first and cried almost non-stop.

Lucy had trouble feeding it and finally, in desperation, in case it starved to death, it was put on the bottle. The only other child Charlie had seen just after birth had been plump and rosy, and had cried lustily when hungry. Well, perhaps given time to make up for being born so early, his son would too. Meanwhile the baby seemed to him to save its crying for the nights. Charlie would get wearily out of bed before dawn when the alarm clock shrilled out, bleary-eyed through lack of sleep.

Mrs Rees at the farm was kindness itself, bringing baby gowns she'd stored away years before, and tempting dishes to bring back Lucy's appetite. The day after the baby was born she sent a girl over to look after them both, and although there was little verbal communication Lucy got on with her quite well. One of a large family herself, Glenys took entire charge of the baby, singing him Welsh lullabies in a voice that seemed to caress.

There was one song that soothed Lucy too as Glenys sang it in her sweet voice while rocking the baby gently.

> *Cys-ga di-fy mhlen – tyn tlws*
> *Cys-ga di-fy mhlen – tyn tlws*
> *Cys-ga di-fy mhlen – tyn tlws*
> *Cei gys-gu tan y bo-re*
> *Cei gys-gu tan y bo-re*

It was a haunting little tune. Glenys would sit on the low wooden stool, her dark eyes filled with tenderness, singing the same words over and over. Lucy wished she could learn the lullaby for it quickly soothed the fractious baby to sleep.

A few days later when Megan Rees paid a brief visit to her in-laws at the farm, she came over to the cottage to see the new arrival. When she was settled with a cup of tea Glenys took the whimpering baby from Lucy, and nursing it Welsh fashion in the fine flannel shawl the farmer's wife had given them, began to sing the lullaby to soothe him. Megan, putting down her cup, sang the English version in a clear strong voice while Glenys stopped to listen:

> Slumber softly baby dear
> Slumber on and never fear
> Those who love you will be near
> We'll wake you in the morning
> We'll wake you in the morning

'Oh, it's lovely!' Lucy cried. 'Look, it's sent him to sleep. I must learn the words, Megan.'

'I'll write them down for you, cariad. Now, what are you going to call the baba?'

'Daniel, after Farmer Rees. Charlie says we should, they've been so good to us at the farm, and I like the name.'

'He'll be very pleased about that, but how about your own relatives?'

'We're putting in the two grandfathers' names as well. He'll be Daniel Thomas Joseph.'

'I have to go home tomorrow morning,' Megan told her, 'but we'll meet again soon, cariad. I'm so glad you're happy here.'

When Megan had gone, promising to call in again before she left for home, Lucy felt sad. It had been wonderful to talk to another woman in her own tongue. If only she could go home to Cardiff. She pictured herself dressed in her best, taking the baby to show proudly to all her friends. There was nowhere to go here, no one to dress up for. The dusty road to the village, or a walk over the fields to the farm, were the only places she could take him. It would be September before she could be churched, and beyond that stretched the winter she'd been dreading, for Megan had told her how bleak it was here, often with snow on the ground for weeks on end and a cutting wind bearing all before it.

As winter set in, with the skeleton branches of the trees swaying restlessly, Lucy's discontent grew. The baby was now plump and pink, but even the walk to the village became impossible as gales lashed the branches into furious dances and the narrow lane became a quagmire.

Lucy thought longingly of Cardiff's paved streets, and the gas light streaming from the shop windows in Broadway and Clifton Street. And she thought longingly too of her friends. But would they still be her friends after they'd heard of what she'd done to Gwen? Often she'd lain awake at night plagued by guilt. In vain she tried to tell herself that Gwen couldn't have been that heartbroken or she wouldn't have married Ted so quickly. Wasn't it more likely that, embarrassed by the situation, she had married Ted rather than spend the rest of her days an old maid?

For months she had been trying to persuade Charlie to look for another job. 'Any job,' she told him, 'so long as it's in an English-speaking town.'

'But they've been so kind to us, Lucy. Besides, the only work I've ever done has been on the land.'

'You could try, Charlie.'

'We wouldn't have anywhere to live even if I could get a job.'

'We could get furnished rooms,' she pleaded.

He sighed heavily. Who would give him a job that he wasn't trained to do? But he knew Lucy wouldn't give in easily. She would just keep on and on until she got her own way.

Chapter Thirty-one

Gwen and Ted had been married several weeks short of nine months when her pains started. Leaving her with Daisy, Ted rushed for Nurse Ellis, the midwife. In between the contractions the devoted old lady regaled her with tales of her own pregnancies, telling her encouragingly, 'Ouer Timmy was the quickest. Only about an hour in labour I was with him.'

As the pains grew stronger Daisy helped her into bed. Saucepans of water were already boiling on the kitchen stove, and the layette, nappies and fluffy white towels hung over the brass rail of the guard.

Suddenly Gwen was remembering that night long ago when she'd been a child, the night that Lucy was born. She smiled to herself, recalling that it had seemed quite natural to her to believe that the midwife had brought Lucy with her in her shabby brown bag. The sound of hurrying footsteps on the stairs put an end to her reverie and as another strong contraction began Nurse Ellis was by her side. Deftly her fingers moved over Gwen's swollen body, then she smiled encouragingly, saying, 'It won't be very long now, Mrs Lewis. You're doing splendidly.' She chatted pleasantly as she prepared Gwen for the birth, giving her a hand to grip when the pains were at their strongest.

Daisy was downstairs fetching more water when the baby's first cry was heard.

'It's a little girl,' the midwife told an exhausted, but happy Gwen, 'Bonny she is too.'

Daisy was rushing excitedly into the room, minus the kettle she'd gone to fetch, and Gwen could hear Ted's voice on the landing, but Nurse Ellis was shooing him away assuring him that his wife and baby daughter were fine.

The baby was washed and dressed and put into Gwen's welcoming arms, and as she looked down lovingly at the pink, slightly puckered face, tears of happiness rolled slowly down her cheeks. When Ted was allowed in he looked so pleased and relieved, and as he bent to kiss Gwen tenderly, murmuring, 'Thank God,' she realised he'd been thinking of that other time when he'd lost both wife and child.

'She's lovely, Gwen,' he said, kissing her cheek, 'We're a real family now.' And tired as she felt, she hugged him with a sudden surge of love and gratitude.

When the baby was tucked up in the bassinet and Gwen settled for a long sleep, Daisy drooled over the child, telling Nurse Ellis with an approving smile, 'In a hurry she was to be here. Never can tell with the first.'

Ted went over to Wilfred Street to tell Sarah the good news and brought her back with him.

'Youer Dad will be surprised when he comes home tonight,' she told Gwen. 'Thought it would be a few more weeks I did. Still, thank goodness she's here.'

'Daisy says you can never tell with the first,' Gwen murmured, watching her mother with some trepidation as she bent over the bassinet. Supposing she was so like Charlie that Mama might guess? But as Sarah was quick to point out, she was Gwen all over again.

'Lucy will have had her baby by now,' Sarah said wistfully.

'Why don't you write to her, Mam? I shan't, but there's no reason why you shouldn't.'

There were tears in Sarah's eyes as she replied, 'I can't, Gwen.' Then, looking a little shamefaced at breaking her word, she confessed, 'I did write to her a while back, I was that worried, but someone else was living in the cottage and they sent the letter back with a line to say the young couple had moved away.'

'Moved away? Why would they do that?' Gwen asked, suddenly anxious for Charlie.

'I don't know.'

'Why don't you ask Charlie's mam?'

'What! Ask Dora? Not after all the things she said. She came down while you were at work to try and stop the wedding, you know. No, of course, you don't. I didn't want to upset you any more than you already were. Lucy had to marry him, didn't she?'

Gwen ignored this remark. She had lost Charlie and it was difficult to forgive her mother her part in it. But, after all, she had so much to be thankful for, hadn't she? Ted, the baby, a nice home and respectability. But Ted wasn't Charlie . . .

'Have you decided on a name yet?' Sarah broke into her thoughts.

'Well, we both like Nancy, and Sarah for her second name.'

'Nancy Sarah Lewis! Oh look, Gwen. She's waking up, the pretty love. I think I'll have another little cuddle before Ted takes me home.'

As the weeks went by, Nancy became plump and

dimpled. She had wide brown eyes, and a sheen of red-gold hair, and Sarah was always saying she was just like Gwen as a child. It was plain to see that she could twist Ted around her little finger, he would dash up from the shop the moment she whimpered, and he showered her with gifts she was far too young to appreciate. Already there was a rocking horse, with a fine leather saddle and a mane of silky black hair, in the small bedroom they'd made into a nursery, and a child's armchair upholstered in pink velvet, on which rested the lovely Victorian doll Gwen had so admired as a child.

'You'll spoil her, Ted,' Gwen protested.

'Nonsense,' he said. 'I won't spoil Nancy any more than I was able to spoil you.' And he put his arms around them both and gently kissed the top of the baby's head.

Chapter Thirty-two

'I've finished the dusting, Gwen. I can go and fetch her,' Daisy cried, quickly untying her apron and hurrying to the mirror to pin on her hat.

Gwen smiled to herself. It was the same ritual every school day. No sooner would she glance at the clock or pick up her coat than Daisy would beat her to it, rushing to put on her hat to prove she had nothing better to do.

A warm rapport had grown between the old lady and the child. Nancy, now six and a half, loved to listen to Daisy's tales of when she was young, and whenever she was working about the flat the little girl would follow her from room to room.

Just after Daisy had left, the bell on the shop door clanged. As she hurried downstairs Gwen's heart sank for it was someone else with a parcel wrapped in newspaper, and this almost invariably meant they had something they wanted to sell.

Only that morning she had viewed the spare room with dismay. Once again, as during the war, it was filling up with objects that, although of great sentimental value to their owners, had little or no commercial value.

It was the end of May 1926. At the beginning of the month there had been a general strike that had practically brought the affairs of the nation to a standstill.

The TUC had called the all-out strike in support of the miners, who, already doing a hard and dangerous job for very little money, had been asked to work even longer hours for less pay. Soon the whole country had come out in their support. Mr Baldwin's government had used special constables and troops in an attempt to keep essential services going, and just eight days after it began the miners were left to continue the strike alone.

The woman unwrapping the newspaper parcel asked hopefully, 'Is Ted around?'

'No. He's away at a sale,' Gwen told her.

Looking disappointed, the woman asked: 'Do you think he'd buy this on the same terms as before?'

The last piece of newspaper had been whisked away to reveal the same tea-pot with the hair-line cracks that Ted had bought during the war, and that had stood on a shelf in the spare room until sometime last year when it had at last been reclaimed. Knowing that Ted would want to buy it back again to help the woman out, Gwen sighed and went to the till.

More and more people were being told of his generosity, but they were going through a bit of a bad patch themselves now, and with far more buying than selling, things weren't going to improve.

The woman had gone and when the door clanged again it was Daisy and Nancy arriving home. As Nancy rushed towards her and planted a warm kiss on her cheek, Gwen's arms went about the little girl and she hugged her tightly.

She was a lively child with big brown eyes and warm chestnut-coloured hair cut in the fashionable bob. Ted had been her devoted slave since the day she was born. If he was in the shop on her return from school, she would dash to greet him joyously, hanging on his arm and every word.

This evening, when he came into the shop and saw the tea-pot on the counter, his expression was rueful. 'Oh dear!'

'You started it,' Gwen replied, but she was laughing. 'Seriously, though, we'll have to get a bigger place if we go on like this.'

'Things are bad, Gwen. People thought it was going to be Utopia when the war finished. It's terrible to see the poor beggars, men who served in the trenches, hanging about the street corners with their toes out of their boots. Awful it is to see the look of hopelessness on their faces. Makes my blood boil it does.'

Ted was such a good man, and over the years Gwen's love for him had grown, but even so Charlie still had a place in her heart. Her feelings for him no longer evoked any of the passion she had once felt, but he'd been a part of her dreams and hopes for so long that she couldn't easily forget him.

Soon, though, she hoped to have news for Ted that she knew would make him want to shout with joy. She had been hoping for weeks that a second baby was on the way and now she was certain in her mind, but would see Doctor Powell before telling Ted.

His longing for a child of his own was obvious, and she'd been hoping for a long time to satisfy that wish, but when once she'd mentioned to him that she regretted it hadn't happened, he'd replied, 'I have a daughter, Gwen. Nancy is mine in my own eyes and everyone else's. No child of my own could be dearer to me.'

The world was changing rapidly, especially where

women were concerned, with skirts worn now just below the knee – some wore them even shorter – and it was so much more comfortable without a corset pulled in so tightly at the waist that you were hardly able to breathe. More and more women were having their hair cut short, and some smoked cigarettes in public, just like the men. To all this Sarah threw up her hands in horror. When Gwen took Nancy's class photo round to show her, Sarah brought out one of herself taken in a studio in town at about the same age.

Nancy, in the front row of the photo taken in the playground, beamed from the picture, her round dimpled cheeks framed by short bobbed hair, her dress just above the knee, and a small leather purse on a strap slung across her chest. She wore dainty ankle strap shoes and white socks to the knee, but a number of children in the picture still wore boots, hand-me-downs from older brothers and sisters, and some wouldn't have been in the picture at all, having neither boots nor shoes to wear, for this was a common reason of non-attendance at school.

Sarah's picture showed a solemn little girl with long hair falling to her waist, wearing a high-necked dress that came halfway down her button boots.

It was the antics of the 'bright young things', the young people of the upper classes, that bothered her the most, especially when she'd just read about their goings on in the paper. She made remarks like 'Brazen young hussies' or, 'When I was a girl youer betters were expected to set you a good example'. And when she'd read an account of a pyjama party that went on all night, she'd said, 'Disgusting I call it! Parading around in what should only be worn in the bedroom. Why, even now, Gwen, I always turn my back on youer father when I'm undressing. Courting trouble they are, if you ask me.'

In the years that had passed, Sarah had become more and more unhappy about the rift with Lucy, yet try as she would she couldn't find it in her heart to forgive. Often while Fanny treadled the sewing machine in her room downstairs, Sarah would sit in the bedroom that had once been Mair's, rocking rhythmically to and fro, thinking nostalgically of when the girls were little. She had never really got over losing Mair so young, but at least she could remember her eldest daughter with deep pride, love and affection, and everyone agreed she'd been a very sweet-natured girl. She'd lost Lucy too but in a different way. Her memories of her youngest daughter were bitter even now and still brought tears to her eyes. Her feelings towards her youngest were a hard knot of pain.

As Sarah rocked the chair she wished with all her heart that she'd been able to forgive, but she was still shocked and horrified to her very soul at Lucy's behaviour. She had never been naive enough to believe it had been all Charlie's fault, far from it. What had a respectable girl been thinking about, wandering around in a state of undress like that? And what Lucy had done to her sister was unforgivable. Poor Gwen. After waiting all those long years to be married. Sarah was really thankful that things had turned out all right for her in the end.

'We're going to have a baby, Ted,' Gwen told him just after she'd returned from Doctor Powell's. His look of joy told her all she wanted to know before he wrapped his arms about her and kissed her tenderly. Then he insisted she sat on the sofa with her feet up while he prepared a meal, but after he'd put the vase of flowers he'd just removed back on the table and the milk jug on the side-board, she thought she'd better take over, for in his present state of excitement he seemed quite incapable of concentrating on anything.

On April the 21st a little girl had been born to the Duke and Duchess of York, fuelling within Nancy an enthusiasm for babies. In May, when the little princess was christened Elizabeth Alexandra Mary, she promptly christened her latest doll with the same names. There were many pictures of the bonny little royal baby in the newspapers. Her face wearing a puzzled expression, Nancy asked, 'Why doesn't she look like the pictures of princesses in my story books, Mam? They're all grown up with long wavy hair and pretty dresses.'

'This one will be like that when she's older, cariad,' Gwen assured her. 'They've all got to start as babies, you know.'

She hoped Nancy's enthusiasm would last until the end of the year when the new addition to the family was expected. Ted had wanted to tell the child right away that she was going to have a little brother or sister, but Gwen thought it much too soon. Having to wait five or six months could seem an eternity to a child. Nevertheless the subject of babies remained very much in Nancy's thoughts.

Splott Road was much too busy with traffic for her to play outdoors unless it was in the yard at the back, but she never seemed bored, taking a great interest in everything that went on around her. She loved to put on the headphones to listen to Children's Hour, twiddling the cat's whisker on the crystal set like she'd seen her parents do, or scrambling up on to the table to sit beside the big horn of the gramophone listening to her favourite tunes, like, 'Yes, We Have No Bananas', or one that had just come out: 'Bye, Bye, Blackbird'. She loved helping in the shop too, and just like Gwen before her would dive excitedly into the crates Ted had brought back from a sale, unwrapping the things she removed as carefully as any adult.

On visits to Wilfred Street Nancy would make straight for Fanny's sewing room, for her great aunt would keep all the scraps of pretty material that were left over and show a delighted Nancy how to make doll's clothes in the latest fashion.

'Which doll have you brought today, cariad?' Aunt Fanny would ask, taking the tape measure from around her neck to measure it. However busy Fanny happened to be, she would always find time to cut the little garments out and tack them together, ready for Nancy's eager fingers to sew running stitches over the tacking. She was delighted when at last she could turn the sewing inside out and pull it over the doll's head.

It was a Saturday towards the end of summer when Ted brought Nancy home in the trap as usual after her visit to Wilfred Street. Eyes wide with what she had to tell, she dashed upstairs.

'Nana was crying,' she announced importantly, 'and Aunty Fan told her she shouldn't upset herself after all this time.'

'What was wrong, Nancy? You've been a good girl, I hope?'

'She was crying about Lucy. Who's Lucy, Mam? I heard her saying, "To think ouer Nancy has a cousin and we don't even know if it's a boy or girl".' Unconsciously she'd been giving a fair imitation of her grandmother's tone, but now she continued in her usual voice, 'Have I got a cousin, Mam? It would be lovely to have a cousin of my own.'

Perhaps I should have told her that she had an Aunt

Lucy and an Uncle Charlie, Gwen reflected sadly, but the rift had been so deep between the families there hadn't seemed to be any point.

Now she satisfied her daughter that, yes, she did have an aunt and an uncle she'd known nothing about, and very probably a cousin too. And to a further question from Nancy: 'No one knows where they live now.'

Gwen's mind went to Sarah. What had brought this old hurt to the surface, or had it ever really gone away? She knew her mother found hard to bear the fact that she hadn't been informed when the child was born.

It wasn't surprising really that Lucy hadn't been in touch. She could be as stubborn as her mother, and had been told over and over by Sarah that she never wished to see her again. Gwen had no wish to see her sister either but she'd better go round after tea and see if things were all right.

It was a lovely early summer evening and to Nancy's delight Ted had promised to take her for a drive in the country in the pony and trap. They would drop Gwen off at Wilfred Street on the way.

When Fanny opened the door, she nodded towards the kitchen, saying, 'Getting these moods a lot lately she is, Gwen. Guilty she feels about sending Lucy away like that. I can't think why. That one deserved all she got.'

Sarah looked up glumly when Gwen stepped into the kitchen, then rose to put the kettle over the coals.

Gwen drew her to the sofa, and putting an arm about her shoulders, said, 'Why don't you write and ask Dora Roberts where she is, Mam?'

'Lucy knows where I live, Gwen, she could have got in touch before now. It's over six years. And that child's my own flesh and blood, and not a word, not even to say if it's a boy or girl!'

'Well, one of you will have to swallow your pride,' Fanny told her, echoing Gwen's own thoughts. But Sarah's jaw jutted stubbornly and they knew they were wasting their time.

On the way home in the trap Nancy wouldn't keep off the subject of the cousin she'd just discovered she might have. Gwen wished she'd never heard about her Aunt Lucy and Uncle Charlie, for far from being the cousins that everyone except she and Ted thought they were, she was only too painfully aware that the two were much more closely related than that. Now she was thankful after all that she hadn't had the chance to confide in Charlie. With only Ted and herself knowing the truth, their secret should be safe.

Chapter Thirty-three

It was a Wednesday afternoon in the autumn of 1932 and the shop was closed when Gwen opened the side door to a breathless Fanny.

'A letter from Lucy,' she gasped, handing Gwen an envelope. She took it with mixed feelings. It could rake up a past that she was anxious to forget.

Even as she read the contents, Fanny was telling her, 'The boy is coming to stay with us. Danny his name is, and to think we didn't even know 'til now which she had.'

'But why now, after all this time?' Gwen asked. And her aunt replied, 'Who knows? There's no mention of Charlie in it, is there? It's as though he doesn't exist.'

'The boy is proof of that, Fanny. How's Mama taking it?'

'Excited she is. Wondering if she'll have time to get the back bedroom decorated.'

'But you sleep there.'

'Oh, I've got that spare bed in my sewing room Gwen. Sarah wouldn't want to disturb Mair's room. Still goes in there she does. Rocks in the chair by the hour.'

'Well, she'll feel better when she sees the child. It's been a grief to her for years not knowing about the baby. Sit yourself down, Fan, I'll make a cup of tea.'

'Isn't it quiet here with both the children at school? Little Teddy seems to have taken to it all right, doesn't he? Does Nancy still like the High School?'

'Yes. She's got lots of pals there now, and it's lucky her friend Joan passed the exam as well.'

Fanny had followed Gwen to the scullery which had been transformed out of all recognition from a junk room at the back of the flat. Ted had had it wired for electricity and the plumbers had brought water to a deep white porcelain sink. A new electric boiler with a wringer on top had been installed in the corner, and an electric cooker on four legs with a white enamel door on which was written the word 'Magnet' stood next to it. Now as Gwen filled the kettle and put it on one of the electric rings, Fanny looked around her at the cupboards which Ted had built against one wall and the deep shelves on which stood saucepans and other utensils. The walls were painted cream, and as Gwen set the tray on a table covered with a blue checked cloth Fanny was comparing it with the wash-house at home with its built-in brick boiler, old-fashioned gas cooker, and the long scrubbed bench on which to rest the bath of water on wash days.

'Wish we had this lot,' she told Gwen with a smile.

'Well, I've offered to do the bedding for Mam many times,' she replied.

Fanny hastened to tell her, 'I didn't mean that, cariad. You've got plenty to do with two children and a shop to look after.'

'Come and see the new fire Ted has bought for the parlour.' Gwen picked up the tray. When Fanny opened the door she cried, 'Oh! It's lovely, Gwen. Electric, eh? That's going to save you some work.'

Gwen put the tray down and bent to flick on a switch. A

red glow from the two bars brightened the room. They'd had the shop and flat wired for electricity the previous year, but the fire had only been delivered last week. It would be a boon for when Nancy did her homework, or practised her scales, and when young Teddy set up his Hornby train set on the rug in front of the guard. The fire stood in front of a copper panel and gave out a good warmth.

Now the subject of Lucy's boy could be put off no longer, but Fanny was picking up a picture of Teddy from the sideboard, saying, 'Isn't he like Ted?'

'More than you think, Fanny. More than you think,' Gwen replied with a smile. 'Give his toys to anyone, he will, and sees good in everyone.'

'Have you finished reading the letter Lucy sent?'

Gwen nodded. 'It's funny that she doesn't mention Charlie at all, just says that she takes in sewing and can't come herself but that she'd like the boy to get to know his grandparents. So he'll be coming Saturday week?'

Fanny nodded, saying, 'Look, I'd better get back. Youer mother will be turning the place upside down. Spring cleaning will be nothing to this.'

'Look, Fan, you can borrow my new vacuum cleaner. It will clean all the rugs without taking them up and beating them, and you can run it down the curtains too. It will save a lot of work, believe me. Ted will bring it round in the trap.'

'Thanks, Gwen, I wasn't looking forward to banging all those rugs on the line. We ought to try and get one of those but I don't think Sarah trusts any of the new gadgets.'

Nancy had been very interested in the mysterious cousin that she'd heard her grandmother mention from

time to time, but Gwen decided against telling her about
the letter until she'd seen Sarah. But her mother had no
more light to shed on the matter; the letter had been as
much a surprise to her as to everyone else. Gwen
wondered if perhaps she'd written to Lucy again but her
mother assured her she hadn't. She did write back now,
though, to say that they'd be delighted to have the boy to
stay.

They'd all been puzzled by the address at the top of
Lucy's letter. Cwm-Mawr was a village in the valleys, and
the last address they'd been given had been Charlie's
uncle's farm in West Wales.

'I wonder what happened, Gwen?' Sarah mused. 'Mind
you, I could never see ouer Lucy settling down on a farm.'
Then she sighed before adding worriedly, 'Hope there's
nothing wrong, I do.'

It was early in October and Nancy would soon be celebrating her thirteenth birthday.

'Why don't we have a family party for them both?'
Sarah suggested. 'Danny can't be much older than Nancy,
can he?'

'They've probably had a party for him at home,' Gwen
told her. 'Still, it wouldn't hurt to have another, I suppose.' Gwen answered as casually as she could, but her
thoughts were in turmoil. Supposing Lucy decided to
accompany the boy after all?

When Nancy was told about the visit she was very
excited, counting the days until Danny arrived. Gwen
wondered if he would be like Charlie? He'd probably be
fair anyway, with Lucy's hair being light gold.

Ted offered to go to the station to meet him, and the
children being in school, Gwen went with him, going up
the platform while Ted stayed with Bessie and the trap.

282

On the platform she waited anxiously for the train to arrive. Would seeing the boy bring back all the old bitterness? But no, she told herself, he's just a child and responsible for none of it.

Wreathed in steam, the valleys train was pulling into the platform. Gwen went towards it, scanning the carriages as doors were flung open and people spilled out on to the platform. There were only two boys of about that age unaccompanied. One was in school uniform with a satchel over his shoulder; the other was tall and wore long grey flannel trousers that he was obviously very proud of, for he gazed down at them and brushed them with his hand before picking up a battered cardboard case and looking about him.

That's him, Gwen decided as they walked towards each other. 'Are you Danny Roberts?' she asked when they'd met up. And he put his case down and lifted his cap, raising blue eyes to hers. He was fair, though not as fair as Charlie had been. His hair was wavy and fell over his eyes. Now he shook it back impatiently and pulled on his cap once more.

'I'm your Aunty Gwen,' she told him. 'Uncle Ted is waiting with the trap.'

He had a nice smile but it didn't remind her of Charlie's cheeky grin.

'Mama said that I'd be staying with my grandma,' he said.

'You are, Danny,' she told him. 'We've just come to take you there.'

When he'd been introduced to Ted and had helped her into the trap before climbing in himself, he put his cap back on once more. He seems a nice boy, Gwen thought, polite and well-mannered.

'How is your mother?' she asked to make conversation, feeling pain even now at mentioning Lucy.

'She's well, thank you. Busy with the sewing she is.' He spoke with the accent of the valleys so they must have lived there for some time.

'And your father?'

His eyes clouded and he looked away and swallowed hard before answering, 'Been away ages he has. I haven't seen him since before Christmas.'

'Working away, is he? You must miss him a lot.' And Danny nodded and dropped his gaze.

Why would Charlie go away to work? she wondered. The boy obviously missed him very much. He probably wouldn't have been able to get a job in the valleys with so many men out of work. But Charlie had always worked on the land. Why would they move from the country? But the boy was saying, 'I was born on a farm in North Wales but Mama never liked the country. Hates farms she does, and especially that one. The people all spoke Welsh.'

'But I thought they were living at your father's uncle's farm in West Wales?'

'They moved from there before I was born. Mama didn't like it there either.'

Gwen was remembering Lucy of old when she didn't get her own way. The marriage didn't seem to have been easy, but the boy was talking again, saying, 'In the cottage in North Wales we were sometimes snowed up and couldn't get to the village for weeks. Mama couldn't stand it. Dada still had his work to do but there was nowhere for her to go. We've only got a couple of rooms where we are now. Dada was on the dole. He's gone back to working on a farm somewhere.'

Didn't they even know where he was? Anyway, why

hadn't Lucy and Danny gone with him? But they were turning into Wilfred Street, bringing an end to the conversation.

Sarah hugged the boy warmly then held him at arm's length. 'The image of ouer Lucy he is,' she pronounced, but Gwen couldn't see the likeness. He was fair like Lucy, but his chin was firm and he seemed old and wise for his years. There was a sad look in the blue eyes when he was in repose, a look that wouldn't be there, Gwen felt, if his father was at home. She'd never been able to picture Lucy on a farm. Lucy with her love of pretty dresses and dainty shoes, and her desire for company and a good time, would have resented every minute of it.

When Sarah broached the subject of Danny celebrating his birthday with Nancy, they were in for another shock.

'But I had my birthday in July, Nana. I didn't have a party. Boys of my age don't. My mother made me these long trousers then.'

'July, did you say?' Sarah couldn't keep the surprise from her voice, and Danny replied, 'Yes. I was born early. They weren't expecting me until late in September. They said Mama was frightened by a bull.'

The colour rushed to Sarah's cheeks. Fancy a boy of his age talking like that! Came of living on a farm, she supposed, but what did he mean 'early'? 'Premature, you mean?' Fanny was asking the question for her, and Danny nodded. Sarah, the colour drained from her cheeks, cried, 'Oh, that pooer, pooer girl! And her all alone without her family.'

'Dada was always saying how good the farmer's wife was when I was born. He often said he wished he was still working there.'

Nancy was very impressed with Danny wearing long

trousers and with his grown-up air. She made any excuse to spend as much time as possible at her grandmother's house, and he would usually accompany her back home. Danny certainly hadn't been spoilt. This was borne out by his willingness to lay fires and run errands. Gwen could easily see Lucy expecting him to wait on her instead of the other way round. She liked Danny, but was worried about Nancy's infatuation with him. As she put it to Ted when they were undressing for bed: 'He's her brother, isn't he? And only you and I know it. Whatever are we going to do?'

'We'll do nothing, Gwen. He'll be going home soon. She'll soon forget him, you'll see, love.' Then, noticing her expression of disbelief, 'Well, perhaps not right away, but she thinks of him as her cousin. Anyway, they're not full brother and sister.'

'They have the same father, and Lucy and I are sisters. That's just as bad.' Gwen saw all sorts of problems before them. But next day, looking at Nancy she thought, She's such a child still. I'm probably worrying about nothing.

When Danny went home, Fanny made arrangements to take Sarah to see Lucy, just for the day. The bitterness that she'd nursed all these years over Lucy's treatment of Gwen seemed to have dissolved into thin air as Sarah packed a basket to take with her, telling herself that it must have been a terrible shock for the poor girl, the baby coming before its time like that and with no mother or sister to turn to for help.

The day was overcast, and soon from the train window they watched a landscape of slag heaps, and a pit wheel standing stark against the leaden sky.

'That's where I'm going to work when I leave school,' Danny told them.

'Youer going to be a miner?' Sarah asked in surprise. 'Is that what you want to do, Danny?'

He shook his head. 'No, of course it isn't, but there aren't many other jobs here, and I'm lucky that Ianto Davies has promised to take me on.'

'You should have tried for the scholarship like Nancy,' Fanny told him, 'then you could have gone to Grammar School.'

'I did sit for the scholarship, and I passed, but Dada wasn't there by that time and Mama couldn't afford for me to go.'

'Maybe we could help?' Sarah began. But as Fanny nodded Danny replied, 'Thanks all the same, it's too late now anyway, and Mama will be glad of the money.'

When they arrived at the house where Lucy had rooms, it was an emotional meeting between mother and daughter. Pretty soon, however, Sarah was looking around her. She'd have sworn that Charlie Roberts would have made a good provider but the room, although spotlessly clean, was sparsely furnished with table and chairs that didn't match, a built-in dresser, and one armchair piled with frilly cretonne cushions, matching the curtains at the window.

Seeing her mother's expression Lucy hurried to explain, 'We had a furnished cottage when we lived on the farms. All this stuff is second hand but I had to buy new beds and a wardrobe on credit. I've nearly paid for it now.'

'But why did you come here, Lucy? Surely you'd have been better off living on the farm?'

'Mrs Jones, that's the landlady, is a distant relative of Charlie's. It's my fault, Mam, I kept on at him to leave the farm. I couldn't stand it there, and she got him a job on a smallholding about a mile away.'

'Well, where is he now?' Sarah stopped as she saw the tears brim over and run slowly down Lucy's cheeks.

'We had a row. An awful row. It was over something I said.' She sniffed and fumbled for her hanky before adding, 'He'll be back, Mam, don't worry.'

'You're coming home with me, cariad,' Sarah said firmly, clutching Lucy to her.

'I'll never come back to Wilfred Street.' The words were muffled against Sarah's shoulder, but then Lucy pulled away to say, 'I couldn't, Mam. They'd all be talking about me. I just couldn't face it.'

'Well, how are you going to manage?'

'Charlie sends me money, all he can afford, and Danny will be working next year. The sewing's picking up too. I should get more orders with Christmas coming.'

'That Charlie Roberts, a fine husband he turned out to be!'

'It was all my fault. I tell you, Danny and me will be all right.'

The next day when Gwen called at the house, Sarah confided her worries.

'I can't believe that about Charlie,' Gwen said. 'I'll bet Lucy nagged at him all the time or he wouldn't have packed in his job at the farm.' And seeing she was in no mood to be sympathetic, Sarah changed the subject.

Chapter Thirty-four

It was Sarah's seventieth birthday. Cards from family and friends were lined up like soldiers along the mantelpiece and the table was set with a festive birthday tea. She was looking pale, having recently recovered from a bout of bronchitis, which with her weak heart had caused the doctor some concern. Doctor Powell had long given up, and Doctor Lloyd who had taken over the practice, though not as familiar with the family as his predecessor, had been very attentive to her.

Danny was expected at the celebrations and was to stay the night. Nancy was looking forward eagerly to seeing her cousin again.

She'd visited her Aunt Lucy several times over the last four years, accompanying her Nan and Aunty Fan. The first time had been just after Danny had started at the mine. They'd been sitting at the table in the living room drinking tea when he'd arrived home from the pit. Black as the ace of spades, was how Sarah had described him later, and as soon as he'd stepped into the room, his pit boots in his hands, Nancy's romantic little heart had missed a beat. The blue eyes had gazed at her from the coal-blackened face, making his teeth look dazzlingly white as he smiled a welcome at them all. Aunt Lucy had

289

ushered them into her bedroom while a zinc bath had been brought from the yard and set in front of the fire. Later Danny had come to them, his face pink now from a vigorous rubbing with the flannel and hot soapy water.

'Pity you can't get a house, Lucy,' Nana had said. 'Awkward it must be for you with the boy needing a bath every day.'

Now they were renting a house, for the sewing was going well and Danny had been working at the pit for over three years. No one asked any longer about Uncle Charlie coming home; even Lucy had given up pretending, for everyone knew they were having a divorce and that it would be through within the year.

Before Danny arrived Nancy heard her father's car and hurried down the passage to open the door. Poor Bessie had been put out to grass at last at the end of 1932. She was old and, as Ted had said, the traffic was becoming too much for her. They often went to see her in the field she shared with two other ancient horses on a farm on the outskirts of Rumney. Bessie always nuzzled up to her when she held out the lumps of sugar, and when the treat was finished would stay with them by the gate until it was time for them to leave.

Now, as Nancy opened the door to her mam, she hugged her then looked beyond to where her father was getting out of the blue Austin Seven.

'Is Nana enjoying her party? Did you tell her we'd be here as soon as we'd closed the shop?'

'Yes, Mam. She liked the vase I gave her. Danny hasn't come yet. Nana says she wishes Aunty Lucy would come as well.'

Gwen's eyes clouded at the mention of Danny. She knew only too well how fond Nancy was of her cousin.

'Of course I care about him,' Nancy had told her. 'He's family, isn't he?' But Gwen had noticed with a sinking heart how her eyes lit up at the mention of his name.

'Where's Teddy? Is he behaving himself?' Gwen asked now as they made their way to the kitchen.

'Oh, he's in the garden with Grandad and Mr Palmer.'

Sarah looked up as they stepped down into the kitchen and Gwen's arms went about her, hugging her tightly as Ted put a brightly wrapped parcel on the table in front of her.

'Oh! You shouldn't have. I had those flowers from you this morning, and you bought that birthday cake.'

'Open it!' Ted commanded, smiling fondly at her. And opening the parcel she drew out a velvet dressing gown from the tissue paper inside, and held it against her, the deep cherry colour lending warmth to her pale cheeks. She was hugging them again, expressing her delight, when the knocker banged loudly and Nancy dashed to open it. Gwen's face had lost its smile, but she forced one to her lips again as Danny came into the room.

He'd grown into a good-looking young man, tall and strong. How did Nancy feel? She'd said it was only cousinly love but talked of him incessantly. And how did Danny feel about her? He was fond of her, there was no doubt about that, but to Gwen he seemed slightly patronising, as though she were three years the younger instead of just three months.

Nancy had left school and was an assistant on the lingerie counter at David Morgan's store. She was becoming quite the fashion conscious young lady. She would describe to Fanny some style she'd seen at the shop, and her aunt would make it up in a different material for just a fraction of the cost. Most of her wages went on the pretty underwear she sold, dainty vests and lace-trimmed cami-knickers, a natural reaction against the liberty bodices and navy blue school bloomers she'd had to wear for so long.

She looked very smart and grown up today in the new Macclesfield silk dress made in the popular shirt-waister style, and Gwen noticed that Danny's eyes were admiring. Just then the back door opened and Tom and Eddie Palmer came through the wash-house to the kitchen, still talking animatedly.

Eddie was saying, 'I remember when the Prince of Wales came to the valleys, and what did he tell the miners? "Something will be done for you," he said. "I'm going to help you," he said. And what did he do? Sweet bugger all, that's what. Sweet . . .' Suddenly becoming aware of the women in the room, his face grew red. Muttering his apologies, he sat down.

'Discussing the Prince of Wales coming to the throne we were,' Tom said. 'Eddie doesn't think he'll make a good king.'

Early in the year King George V had died and there'd been a lot of controversy about the new king as yet uncrowned, especially when it became known through the American press that his prospective bride was a Mrs Wallis Simpson, an American divorcée.

Sarah's face still wore a look of disgust at Eddie's faux pas, and Gwen asked quickly, 'Where's Teddy, Dad? Is he still in the garden?'

'No. It got nippy out there. Gone in with Mabel he is, to see the new kittens.'

When Teddy came back with Mabel Palmer he was holding a small black and white kitten. His eyes bright with excitement, he said: 'Mrs Palmer says I can have this kitten if you'll let me, Mam.'

'Well, it wasn't exactly like that, Gwen,' Mabel hastened to assure her. 'Teddy said he'd like one of his own and I told him that living upstairs as you do, you mightn't want him to have a cat.'

'Can I, Mam? Can I?' Teddy pressed the soft fur against his cheek. He had grown tall, and at nine years old was getting more like his father every day.

'You'd better ask Dada, love.' But she knew already that the kitten would be going home with them.

They were having a sing-song in the parlour with Eddie playing his accordion and Tom accompanying him on the mouth organ when Gwen missed Nancy. Looking around again she noticed that Danny wasn't there either. Fanny saw her anxious expression and said, 'Just gone for a walk they are, cariad, to get some fresh air, see.'

In a second Gwen was at the front door and looking up and down the long street. Fanny had followed her from the room, saying, 'I don't know why you get so het up about that boy, Gwen. They're cousins and fond of each other, that's all.'

Well, perhaps that's all they were on Danny's part, but she'd seen the look in Nancy's eyes when he'd come in tonight. Hero worship it was. She'd have to have another word with her, tell her before it went too far that she'd better not get involved; that cousins shouldn't marry. Oh, but perhaps that was going a bit too far? They were both only seventeen, they'd hardly have marriage in mind yet. But remembering how quickly her feelings for Charlie had grown, Gwen was filled with apprehension. If Nancy had known they were brother and sister none of this would have happened but she couldn't have told her; wouldn't have been able to bear the look of disgust in her daughter's eyes when she realised that if it hadn't been for Ted marrying her mother she would have been illegitimate, while Danny had taken his rightful place as Charlie's son.

Gwen had gone white at the thought. Nancy loved Ted dearly. What would it do to her after all these years to know that he wasn't her dad after all? It didn't bear thinking about.

Then she saw them turning the corner. Nancy was smiling up at Danny. She heard their laughter ring out. Now the girl was running forward and, linking her arm in Gwen's, saying in a worried voice, 'Why didn't you put on your coat? Come on, let's go in and have a cup of tea. I'm starving anyway.'

As the two young people set about the sandwiches that had been kept fresh between two plates on the larder shelf, Gwen sipped the hot tea, thinking, Perhaps I'm worrying about nothing. But at the back of her mind was the memory of Nancy's adoring look when Danny had first arrived.

'What's eating you up, cariad?' Fanny asked gently when they were washing up together. 'Why can't you forgive and forget, Gwen? It's not Danny's fault, and it was all such a long time ago.'

When Gwen didn't answer she went on, 'Lucy's not a happy person. Whatever she did didn't benefit her much.'

But Gwen was unrepentant. Fanny didn't really understand. How could she? She would have found it difficult enough to forgive Lucy anyway, but no one knew the torment she felt at their children being attracted to each other. She could forbid Nancy to visit Lucy with Sarah and Fanny, but no one would understand her motives and it would only cause more trouble.

When they were leaving, Nancy said lightly, 'I'll be at work all day tomorrow, Danny, but as your train is at half-past-one I can pop over to the station to see you off. It isn't far from David Morgan's.'

Unsmiling, Gwen said her goodbyes. What was it Fanny had said? 'There's no harm in their liking each other, Gwen.' Well, when she was young she'd had cousins living in the valleys but she could never remember being *that* fond of them!

At last King Edward VIII's involvement with a twice-divorced American woman broke in the British press. The king was given an ultimatum, the throne or Mrs Simpson, and he chose her. The country was divided in its opinion. Families were divided too. Ted's was a lone voice in their household for he believed firmly that the king should have put the crown first.

In his view the fact that Mrs Simpson was a divorcée raised serious doubts about her suitability as wife for the king.

'I think he should be allowed to marry the woman he loves,' Nancy said with conviction. 'If he's forced to give her up, it will break his heart.'

'Well, I think he should remember his duty,' Ted said heatedly.

Gwen's opinion was, 'If he loves her I don't see why they shouldn't be married, so long as she doesn't become queen.'

'How long is this soppy conversation going on?' Teddy asked in disgust. 'Mam, can Ronnie come in to play with my train set this afternoon?'

As she nodded absentmindedly Gwen was thinking, That's Nancy all over, putting love before everything. And she wasn't just thinking of her daughter's plea for the king.

Mrs Wallis Simpson was granted her second divorce at Ipswich in October, and in November the king discussed his position with Queen Mary. Now there was only the abdication agreement to be signed. Once this was done he would no longer be king. When a copy of the document was printed in the newspaper it began:

'I, Edward VIII of Great Britain, Ireland, and the Dominions beyond the Seas, King, Emperor of India, do hereby declare my irrevocable determination to renounce the Throne for Myself and for my descendants . . .

'Whatever will they do with all the souvenirs they've made?' Gwen asked. 'Lots of manufacturers could come a cropper over that.'

'Not necessarily, love. Just think – it's a historic event that didn't happen. In time these pieces could become more sought after than if he had become king. Some of them are already in the warehouses and shops.'

Ted bought up a couple of crates cheaply, for warehouses and factories alike were anxious to cut their losses to make room for fresh souvenirs for the coronation of King George VI who was to be crowned on May 12th, 1937, and with less than six months to go they would have to work all out to produce them.

Nancy helped Gwen unpack the crates, and soon the table was groaning under the weight of the souvenirs. There were vases, plates, cups, saucers, all emblazoned with pictures of Edward in full Coronation regalia.

'The heirlooms of tomorrow,' Ted said with a grin. And looking at the sheer bulk of what he'd bought, Gwen hoped he was right.

Chapter Thirty-five

For the second time within twelve months the war clouds were gathering and now it seemed that nothing could stop them. Last autumn during the crisis the British fleet had been hurriedly mobilised and the auxiliary air force put on alert. Trenches were dug in the parks as makeshift shelters when Britain had seemed to be on the brink of war. Then Neville Chamberlain, who had already met Hitler twice in the pursuit of peace, the first time on the 15th September at Berchtesgaden, and again on the 22nd when he went to Bad Godesberg, was invited to meet Hitler in Munich when Mussolini would be present and Daladier the French Prime Minister was also expected.

Tension was high as the outcome of the talks was eagerly awaited, and hopes seemed to be realised when Mr Chamberlain returned waving a piece of paper at the crowds, an agreement which Hitler had signed and which the Prime Minister triumphantly told the cheering throng meant 'Peace for our time'.

Most people sighed with relief and got on with their lives as though nothing had happened, but there'd been a price to pay in return for his pledge of peace. Hitler was allowed to take the German-speaking areas of Czechoslovakia.

Tom had been sceptical from the beginning.

'Buying time, that's what Hitler's doing,' he cried, thumping his fist on the table. 'I wouldn't trust that bugger any further than I could see him.'

'Tom!' Sarah protested indignantly. 'There's no need for that.'

'Oh, yes, there is, love. What's happening in the world is enough to make anyone swear. By God it is! We haven't heard the last of Herr Hitler, you mark my words.'

Next day the headlines in the paper seemed to bear Tom out. Five thousand British troops were to be sent to Sudetenland, and the betrayed Czechs were anxious to fight for their country.

By the spring of 1939 the peace had become increasingly uneasy. In March Hitler took the rest of Czechoslovakia. In April Britain announced plans for military conscription, having promised Poland support if she was attacked.

'What did I say, Eddie?' Tom cried triumphantly. 'I told you that bit of paper wasn't worth bringing back.'

'We weren't ready for war then, Tom. It's given us some time to prepare. I reckon it would take a miracle to keep the peace now.' He stroked his chin thoughtfully, adding glumly, 'Another war doesn't bear thinking about.'

By the end of August the news was grave. On the 1st September German troops, massed on the frontier between Germany and Poland, opened fire. Britain immediately despatched an ultimatum, and people held their breath.

As though it was a foregone conclusion the papers were suddenly full of advice on making the shelter comfortable and hanging the black-out curtains. On that fateful

Sunday morning people everywhere huddled around their wireless sets to listen to Mr Chamberlain. As the clock struck a quarter past eleven and he was introduced, the sad voice began:

I am speaking to you from the cabinet room at 10 Downing Street. This morning the British Ambassador in Berlin handed the government a final note, stating that unless we heard from them by eleven o'clock that they were prepared at once to remove their troops from Poland, a state of war would exist between us. I have to tell you now that no such reply has been received, and that consequently this country is at war with Germany.

Upstairs over the shop Gwen was near to tears while Ted's expression was solemn. Only Nancy felt a tinge of excitement at the unknown. Teddy looked from one to the other questioningly, and Gwen thanked God that he was only twelve.

It was a Saturday night in November. The black-out curtains had long been drawn and Fanny and Sarah were getting ready to go to Clifton Street for some last-minute shopping.

'There's not much pleasure going to the shops these days,' Sarah was saying, 'with everything blacked out, and bumping into people every few minutes.' She was remembering wistfully Clifton Street as it used to be years ago with the gas light streaming from shop windows, especially this time of the year. There would have been holly and mistletoe decorating the windows, and paper chains hanging above the displays, and people jostling each other round the butcher's doorway hoping for a bargain when he auctioned the leftover meat, and the greengrocer shouting to you as you passed that the cabbages were going for half price, and how about a couple of extra oranges for the shilling?

Now you had to slink through the doorway and round a screen and even then the interior would be bathed in gloom. Still, Sarah thought gratefully, there's little else to tell you there's a war on save an Anderson shelter sunk into the earth of the back garden where Tom's cucumber frame used to be. This morning when she'd opened the door to look inside it had smelt damp and clammy, still it was reassuring to have it there.

As they stepped out into the foggy night she gripped her sister's arm. She always felt nervous when she stepped on to the darkened street, but on a night like this with no stars it was even more difficult to get your bearings, with not a chink of light from any window. The eerie blackness quickly enveloped them. Anxiously she felt for walls or windowsills and, reassured, stepped out with a little more confidence, thankful that Fanny at least had a good sense of direction.

As they turned into Broadway and barely discerned figures passed silently, their steaming breath mingling with the foggy air, she thanked God for the day that Fanny had come to stay. In fact, with Gwen married and Lucy living away, she didn't know how she would have managed otherwise. She would never have gone to Clifton Street on her own, not in the black-out anyway.

'We must mind that wall where the shops finish and the houses with the gardens begin,' Fanny was saying. 'It's just past the next corner.' And they both thought of poor

Mrs Lloyd whose black eye just after the black-out began had been the source of many a joke at her innocent husband's expense.

Broadway was like a ghost town and as they turned into Clifton Street it was little better. Where once they would have lingered to look into festive windows, dawdling from shop to shop, now it was straight to the butcher's and the greengrocer's and then back home.

As they turned again into Broadway, their eyes accustomed now to the gloom, Sarah said, 'I wonder if ouer Nancy knows Danny's volunteered for the air force? I expect he wrote and told her, same as us.'

'She'll be upset about it,' Fanny predicted. 'Strange, isn't it, how those two young ones took to each other right from the first? Ouer Gwen never seems very pleased to see the boy, though.'

Sarah sighed. 'To think they'll both be twenty-one next year! Gwen is forty-seven, and if Mair had lived, bless her, she'd have been fifty.'

Fanny laughed, saying, 'Well, it doesn't seem any time since the girls were little and I was making them muslin dresses for the Whitsun treat.'

'Putting on weight, ouer Gwen is, Fan. Always a bit on the plump side she was. Bonny, Tom used to say. Comes of women not wearing proper corsets any more. When I think how tightly laced we used to be. A waist like a wasp I had.'

'Well, I think it's much better the way they dress today, and you can still get laced-up corsets if you want.'

'Ouer Nancy only wears one of them suspender belts. It's a wonder she doesn't get a chill.'

They were at the door now with Fanny quickly opening and closing it behind them. She fumbled for the light switch but through the darkened shade the low-wattage bulb was dim.

Sarah sat down wearily on a kitchen chair and took off her shoes, saying, 'This bunion's giving me gyp.' At seventy-three her hair was iron grey and she still wore it in the 'earphones' she'd adopted in the twenties. She had put on weight and her breathing was laboured after the unaccustomed exercise, her chest rising and falling rapidly with the effort.

Fanny said gently, 'Here, give me youer hat and coat. The kettle's on for a cup of tea. It won't take long on the gas.'

She could do with losing a bit of weight, Fanny told herself worriedly as she went effortlessly up the stairs with an armful of coats. But then, Sarah had never been slim since her first child. She herself never put on an ounce of weight. 'Thin and wiry', that's what people said. Scrawny, that's what I am, she told herself with a smile. But she rarely got out of breath and still took in the odd bit of sewing.

Gwen locked the shop door and finished pulling the blackout curtains. It was a waste of time keeping open once it got dark. Few people would brave the black-out for the things they sold and most of their trade was with other dealers for the quality furniture that Ted bought and restored. One thing that had been gaining interest just before the war was the collecting of small items of Victoriana, like Goss armorial souvenirs bearing the arms of towns, colleges and other places interesting enough. Made in fine ivory porcelain, the earlier pieces bore the mark 'W.H.G., c. 1858 +', but the factory was still open and pieces could be picked up cheaply enough, especially

when house contents were sold. Young Teddy had a collection of his own and loved to attend jumble sales in
search of his treasures.

Gwen herself had been really pleased when the child's
tea-set in blue and white with the illustrations from
Charles Dickens' *Old Curiosity Shop* had come back to
them last week. She wouldn't part with it again. Who
knows, she thought, we might have a grand-daughter one
day? But thinking of Nancy she shook her head, her
expression sad. What was to happen to her, besotted as
she was with Daniel?

An old maid she'd end up, pretty as she was, the way
she treated the other young men she knew. She belonged
to the tennis club run by the YWCA. They'd been given
permission to use the tennis courts in the grounds of the
big house on Newport Road near St Mellons, called Witla
Court. One of the girls had a brother who gave Nancy a
lift on the pillion seat of his motor-bike but she never
asked him in. It was just: 'Thanks, Ray. Goodnight then,
see you next week.' And she'd wave until he was out of
sight.

Gwen had to admit that Danny didn't really act as
though she was his girlfriend. He was fond of her and
obviously liked her company, but he treated her as though
she was years younger than himself. When Gwen had
suggested that Nancy introduce her to the young
man who gave her a lift, she'd cried, 'Oh, Mam! not
matchmaking again. I've told you, Ray is just a
friend.'

Gwen sighed and went upstairs to prepare the tea. She
missed Daisy and her cheerful ways. The old daily had left
them last year when her legs had begun to swell and the
doctor had told her she must take her weight off them.

But Ted picked her up in the car every Friday and brought her round to tea. Although she always protested, Gwen saw that she left with a full shopping bag. She would never be able to repay Daisy for all her kindness over the years, and she had been with Ted so long he thought of her as one of the family.

As she put the kettle on and set the table Gwen's thoughts went back to Nancy. When a letter had come for her this morning she had taken it up to her room, but not before Gwen had seen the postmark and noticed too that when Nancy came down to breakfast her face looked glum.

'Danny has volunteered for the air force,' she told them. 'He could have waited a while. Still, I suppose it must be awful working underground. I know he only sticks the job for Aunt Lucy's sake. Says he's the bread-winner of the family. Always makes a joke of it he does, but it's true, isn't it?' The expression in her eyes said: Isn't Danny wonderful? and Gwen felt a lump come to her throat. If only Nancy would get interested in someone else.

Now she watched her daughter as she got ready to go to work. She combed her wavy hair before picking up the gas-mask in its cardboard box and slinging it over her shoulder. Finally she came across to kiss Gwen on the cheek. She looked very smart in the well-cut suit which hugged her slim figure. Nancy had lost her puppy fat at around seventeen. Now, as she put on a little felt hat, the mirror reflected warm brown eyes and creamy, rose-tinted skin. There hadn't been any shortage of interested young men over the years but Nancy would have none of them, and the reason of course was Danny. Something would have to be done, and soon, Gwen thought urgently.

What a pity if Nancy wasted her life hankering after the boy. If only she knew the truth – and Gwen hoped fervently that she'd never need to – she would realise that nothing could ever come of her feelings for him. Then Gwen saw with a sinking heart that in Nancy's hand was yet another letter to post.

Chapter Thirty-six

It was May 1940. On the day Winston Churchill succeeded Neville Chamberlain as Prime Minister, Germany attacked Holland and Belgium, and, as the weeks passed, pressed on through France, forcing the British army back towards the beaches of Dunkirk. Gwen listened to every news broadcast on the wireless, her face glum. But worrying as the war news was, she was preoccupied with troubles of her own.

The evenings had turned chilly and Gwen sat by the fire, her fingers busy with knitting, the khaki wool in a ball at her feet. Ted had lowered his paper and was watching her with love and admiration. Her cheeks were still smooth and her skin glowed. The wavy chestnut hair, worn now in a long bob, had a few silvery strands, but her neck was firm and youthful and he marvelled as he often did that she loved him for she was still a very beautiful woman, while at sixty-seven and so much older than her he felt that he was already an old man.

Ted was very glad that Gwen had never succumbed to the slimming craze that had swept the country a few years ago. Many women of her age were happy to be just bags of bones with scrawny necks in order to achieve their goal, but Gwen had never seemed to worry about such things.

She was plump and beautiful with it and he adored her.

As Gwen looked up their eyes met and she smiled, saying, 'Penny for them, Ted?' But he didn't answer, for a moment before her expression had been anxious and he knew the unwitting cause of her anxiety was Nancy.

Young Danny had been in the air force now for more than six months and on his last leave in January, despite the bitterly cold weather and the leaden sky threatening snow, Nancy had gone to Cwm-Mawr on the Sunday and again on her half-day. She'd gone alone for Sarah was finding the journey too much for her lately, and even Fanny had been put off by the weather. Danny had brought her home on both occasions, staying the night with Sarah and Tom. On the Sunday night as they'd come into the living room Nancy's eyes had been bright, her cheeks glowing. Watching her, Gwen had come near to despair. Her daughter looked so happy and Gwen knew it was a happiness that couldn't last.

When Danny had gone and Nancy was in bed, Ted had put an arm about Gwen, saying, 'Have you noticed the way he treats her, cariad? It's as though she's a child he was fond of, the way he teases her.'

But though he said little about it, Ted was worried too. If it ever came to telling Nancy that he wasn't her father, would she hate him for deceiving her all this time? He'd always thought of her as his daughter; had walked the bedroom with her cradled in his arms when she was teething, and later when she was toddling he'd been her faithful steed, crawling on all fours, with a chuckling Nancy patting him and calling him 'Bessie' after the pony she loved. As a little girl he'd swung her to his shoulders so that she could pick the most luscious blackberries, and later had taught her to swim at the baths in Tressilian Terrace, and on summer days he'd raced her to the sea at Barry Island. But would any of this count if she knew about Charlie?

Gwen had got up and was putting her knitting away in the drawer. He noticed with pity how she wrung her hands before straightening the sideboard cloth that didn't need straightening. She came across to him and said piteously, 'Oh, Ted, what are we to do?'

'Nothing, love,' he said with a confidence he didn't feel. 'It'll all blow over, you'll see.'

The war news was worsening. By the 14th of May German tanks had crossed the River Meuse and were sweeping north, hoping to trap large numbers of British troops in Northern France and Belgium. Less than a week later they'd reached the Channel and plans were hurriedly made for the evacuation of the British Expeditionary Force. The operation, called 'Dynamo', began on the night of the 27th of May and by the time it ended on the 2nd of June some 338,000 troops, of whom about 225,000 were British, had been rescued from the beaches of Dunkirk. The Royal Navy did a wonderful job, but even more wonderful was the way the little ships, from fishing boats to Channel steamers, aided them, sailing through hazardous seas to bring the men home.

People were drawn to their wireless sets to listen anxiously for news of what was going on.

'It's a miracle the way all those men were saved,' Gwen said when it was over.

'Yes, thank God! But we're alone now, Gwen. Their planes will only have to cross the Channel.'

It was a sobering thought and one that was soon on everyone's mind. On the first Sunday evening after Dunkirk, straight after the nine o'clock news, J.B. Priestley began his fifteen-minute broadcast to the nation. Anxious as most people were, it was comforting to hear his gravelly, North country voice helping to bring a little sanity into a desperate situation, rallying their spirits and encouraging people's patriotism. But no one could ignore the fact that invasion could be imminent as barbed-wire entanglements cut off the beaches from pleasure seekers, in a desperate effort to deter the enemy.

Three days before France signed an Armistice with Germany, Winston Churchill spoke on the wireless, saying: ' . . . the battle of France is over. I expect that the battle of Britain is about to begin.'

Worrying as the news was, Gwen's personal troubles became uppermost in her mind once more on the day that a new letter from Danny brought a look of joy and happiness to Nancy's face; a look that couldn't be ignored.

'What is it, love? Is he coming on leave?' Gwen asked, trying to sound casual.

'Yes, he's coming home next weekend,' Nancy told her happily. 'But how did you guess the letter was from him?'

'I recognised the post-mark. It isn't the first letter you've had from him, after all.'

When Nancy had left for work Gwen went to tidy her daughter's room, her heart once more filled with foreboding. She was dusting the top of the chest of drawers, putting each little knick-knack back as she found it, when she saw the edge of a letter sticking out of the top drawer. Instinctively she gripped the knobs to pull the drawer open and release it, but stopped suddenly. It's Nancy's private property, she told herself, remembering how angry she'd been at her daughter's age at her own lack of privacy. She stared at the edge of the letter, wondering what could be in it to have brought such a look to Nancy's face.

Days passed and Nancy's happiness seemed to increase. Was it just that Danny was coming on leave? No, Gwen was sure there was something more. She sometimes called herself a fool for not finding out while she'd had the chance. Nancy did tell them that he was coming to Cardiff on the following Saturday, and on the Friday evening, before washing and setting her hair, said she was going around to Wilfred Street to see if her nan had had a letter. From the window of the sitting room Gwen watched her go with a sinking heart. Of all the boys in the world, why did it have to be Danny that she'd fallen in love with? She felt that the time had come to tell Nancy the truth, yet she was fearful of the effect it might have when she found out that she and Danny shared the same father. Nancy had never seemed to be put off by the fact that Danny was her cousin. Once when Gwen had brought it up, she'd said, 'Well, I don't see why cousins shouldn't marry if they want to. If they're worried about having children in the circumstances, well, they haven't got to have them, have they?'

Ted had just come upstairs. He put his arms about Gwen, saying, 'Come on, it can't be that bad, love.' And suddenly the tears were rolling down her cheeks as she said, 'We'll have to tell her, Ted. This can't go on.'

A few minutes later they heard the door slam and footsteps running up the stairs. Gwen was wiping her eyes hurriedly with the hem of her apron when the passed the sitting room and Nancy's bedroom door banged loudly. A few seconds later there was the sound of muffled sobbing.

Gwen and Ted stared at each other in dismay. What could have happened to have changed their daughter's mood so quickly? Anxiously, Gwen went to tap on the door but there was no answer, just the sound of abandoned sobbing. It tore at her heart.

'Nancy love, can I come in?'

Still there was no answer. Beside herself with worry, Gwen turned the handle gently and went into the darkened room. The black-out curtains had been drawn earlier in the evening so Gwen went to the bedside table and fumbled until she found the switch of the lamp, looking anxiously towards the bed as it was suddenly bathed in soft light.

'Whatever is it, cariad? Is Nana all right?' But even as she asked she knew it wasn't Sarah's health upsetting Nancy for she would have come and told them right away.

The girl raised a tear-stained face to her.

'It's Danny – I hate him! I do, Mama. I hate him.'

A fresh burst of sobbing ended her words. Gwen's spirits had lifted at this unexpected outburst, but still it wrung her heart to see Nancy like this. She sat down and pulled the girl into her arms, smoothing back the wavy hair and kissing her forehead. When at last the sobbing was spent, Nancy sat up and looked at Gwen woefully. Taking the handkerchief her mother offered, and dabbing at her tear-stained face, she said, 'I knew how you felt, Mam, so I didn't tell you, but Danny said in his letter that there was something special he wanted to ask me when he came on leave, and he hoped I'd agree.' The handkerchief went to her eyes again, but swallowing hard she continued, 'I thought I knew what Danny wanted to ask me. I thought he loved me.' She gave a sad little sniff. 'Nana told me tonight what it was he was going to ask. He wrote to tell her that he was getting engaged to a girl he met at his base and they're planning to get married soon.' Then, her voice becoming a wail, she cried, 'They wanted me to be bridesmaid, that's what he was going to ask. Oh, Mam! I thought he loved me, I really did.'

As Nancy buried her face in the pillow once more, Gwen's feelings were a mixture of relief and sadness at her daughter's misery. If it had been anyone but Danny who had dealt this blow she would have been so angry, but now relief was flooding through her. He'd get married to this girl, the danger was over. No need to tell Nancy the secret she and Ted had kept all these years. Was it possible that Danny didn't know that Nancy's wasn't just cousinly love? Ted had always said that the boy treated her as though she were a child he was fond of. Had Nancy mistaken his feelings? After all, what did she know about love? But there'd been no mistaking her feelings for him, had there? Perhaps it had embarrassed Daniel, especially as he was in love with somebody else.

Nancy arranged to be out when Danny and his fiancée called next day. Gwen watched her get ready to visit a girl she worked with at the store, her face pale and sad.

The girl Danny introduced as Sally was pretty and vivacious, and like himself wore a blue uniform. When he was told that Nancy wasn't at home, he looked rueful, saying, 'I hope she isn't too upset, Aunty Gwen.'

'Oh, no!' Gwen lied. 'It was a previous engagement, she couldn't very well get out of it. She sends her love and best wishes.'

Danny said, 'You'll like my cousin, Sal. We've been pals a long time. She's a good sport.'

Danny and Sally had been gone for over an hour when Nancy arrived home and went straight up to her room. Feeling anxious, Gwen tapped on the door to tell her supper was ready.

'I don't want any, Mama.' Nancy's voice sounded muffled with tears.

'Come on, love. Shall I bring you a cup of tea?'

'No, thanks. I don't want anything.'

'But, Nancy!'

'Go away, please. I'm – I'm all right.' The sob in her voice belied Nancy's words. Gwen went in and with Nancy's tears damping her shoulder, held her close, thankful her own worries were over but mindful of Nancy's despair. First love could be devastating when it wasn't returned, and Nancy had thought that Danny loved her in the same way she loved him.

I must be gentle with her, Gwen thought, hugging her and smoothing back the damp tendrils of chestnut hair. We'll laugh together about all this one day I expect. But glancing at Nancy's woebegone face, that day seemed a long way off.

Chapter Thirty-seven

When she wasn't at work Nancy wandered like a lost soul about the flat, often shutting herself in her room for hours on end, looking so miserable the whole time that, relieved as she was at the turn of events, Gwen's heart went out to her. Then, just when she was beginning to despair, Nancy seemed to get over the upset, and though looking just as miserable as before began to go out every night with a girl she'd met at work.

'You don't know her, Mam,' she told Gwen in answer to her question. 'Brenda only started at the store a few weeks ago.'

There was now an ever present threat of air-raids, and every time the siren went Gwen worried in case Nancy couldn't get to a shelter in time. She almost wished the girl was still at home sulking in her bedroom.

Gwen was puzzled. Nancy didn't look happy, yet night after night she went with Brenda to the cinema or a dance held in a nearby church hall. It was as though she was forcing herself to seem to be having a good time, perhaps to prove to everyone that Danny's engagement meant nothing to her.

Brenda was a plump, good-natured peroxide blonde who giggled incessantly. They've nothing in common, the friendship won't last, Gwen told herself. But it did, and as summer waned and the cold dark nights of winter began, and the siren wailed earlier in the evening, Gwen sat on the bench in the shelter with only Teddy for company, for Ted was on fire-watching duty.

On one particular night Nancy had mentioned that she wanted to see a film called 'The Lion Has Wings', with Ralph Richardson and Merle Oberon, but had confessed that she didn't think that Brenda would enjoy it. 'She likes a good laugh, Mam,' Nancy told her. 'She prefers George Formby or someone like that.'

So Gwen didn't know for certain where Nancy had gone and it was very worrying. When the all-clear went at last and she clambered out to make a much-needed cup of tea, she took her worries with her. Later Ted came in, rubbing eyes red with weariness. The first thing he did when he found Nancy wasn't there was to look up at the clock.

At that moment they heard the side door slam and foot-steps on the stairs. When Nancy came into the room her face was glum.

'Where have you been?' Gwen began, 'we've been worried sick about you.'

'As it happens we spent the whole evening in Brenda's shelter,' Nancy told them in disgust.

'And the best place too, with the planes right over-head,' Ted assured her grimly.

Soon it was Christmas and Brenda came to tea in a maro-cain dress with a deeply plunging neck-line, that looked as though she'd been poured into it. She giggled her way through afternoon and evening. Everyone was relieved when at last Nancy took her to visit one of her friends who lived a few streets away. When they'd gone, Teddy let out a long and very expressive: 'Phew!'

'And what does that mean, exactly?' Gwen asked.

'It's that girl, Mam, she's nuts. What does our Nancy want to go around with her for?'

'She's Nancy's friend – ' Gwen began, but Teddy said quickly, 'She's soppy, Mam. She giggles for nothing.'

But Gwen was remembering gratefully that the girl had got Nancy over a very bad time.

New Year came in with little in the way of celebration for, as Ted said, with backs to the wall, who knew what might happen next? German bombs had already brought devastation to some cities. London had been under almost constant bombardment. On the 29th of December alone around 1,400 fires had raged, and there'd been a terrible raid on Coventry in November when around 50,000 homes and the Cathedral were destroyed. Would Cardiff's turn be next?

On the wireless Lord Haw-Haw's claims were becoming more and more bizarre. Far from undermining people's spirits as he was meant to do he gave them some much needed light relief and a jolly good laugh at his expense. His programme, preceded by the now familiar cry 'This is Germany calling', was listened to by many, but few if any took it seriously.

Gwen had begun to worry about Nancy in other ways now. There were lots of men in uniform about the streets who were bored and looking for female company. Did she meet these men at the dances she went to with Brenda? It seemed hardly likely that two attractive young women would dance together all night. Gwen was thankful that she had told her the facts of life as soon as she'd reached her teens, but that didn't ensure there wouldn't be heart-break. But Nancy had told her mother on one of her rare nights at home, 'Don't you worry about me, Mam, I'll never get serious about any boy again, not after the way Danny let me down.'

Gwen didn't have the heart to tell her that Daniel's love, other than family affection, had been just wishful thinking on her part.

January the 2nd was a cold frosty night with a full moon. Just after the warning siren had died away searchlights began to sweep the sky, and as Gwen and Teddy rushed through the yard to the shelter incendiaries were already beginning to fall, burning with an eerie yellow glow. The barrage of heavy gun-fire could be heard above the drone of planes as they closed the door.

Gwen reached up to the shelf above one of the benches to switch on the lantern, and they sat there in its sickly glow while the racket above them went on and on. Now shrapnel rattled nearby, but Gwen's anxious thoughts were with Ted and Nancy.

With all the incendiaries, her husband would be kept busy. Nancy was at a party given by one of her friends at work, to celebrate her engagement to a soldier who was home on leave. Gwen was sure she'd mentioned Grangetown but Teddy had put doubts in her mind by saying he thought it was the friend who lived in City Road who was having the party. Anyway, they'd have to insist on Nancy staying at home if there were to be many more nights like this.

It was already freezing, and growing colder. Gwen pulled the blanket she'd brought down tightly about her, listening anxiously to the racket above them, mumbling to herself, 'Oh, God! Please let Nancy and Ted be safe.'

'What d'you say, Mam?' Teddy asked, looking up from his comic. 'Can I look out a minute?'

'Not until they give the all-clear.' Then, seeing his look of disappointment, she said, 'Oh, all right then. But just a peek while it's quiet.'

As he pushed open the door the sky seemed to be aflame and the smell of burning and acrid smoke, reminiscent of childhood bonfire nights in Wilfred Street, made Gwen slam the door quickly. A few minutes later she gripped the seat as planes droned overhead, and then came the whine of falling bombs, seeming very near. Teddy's teeth were chattering but to show he was no coward he pulled his mouth organ from his trouser pocket and began to play the tune 'We're Gonna Hang Out the Washing on the Siegfried Line'.

During a lull, it seemed hours later, there was a sharp rap on the door. When Gwen opened it, Ted climbed quickly inside, asking, 'You both all right?' But she answered him with, 'Where did Nancy say she was going, Ted?'

'Grangetown, wasn't it? I don't think she should go out these evenings, Gwen. It's a bad one tonight, lots of fires.'

In the patchy light of the lantern she could see that his face was streaked with dirt, and his bloodshot eyes looked tired. He was rising now to leave the shelter, saying, 'Better get back. All hell's let loose out there.' Before she could answer, he was gone.

'Did you bring anything to eat, Mam?' Teddy asked hopefully.

'Only those pieces of bread and butter left over from tea,' she told him. 'Sorry, love, but we came down so early tonight. I did put some jam between it, though.'

Teddy ate hungrily, undeterred by the shrapnel showering the shelter at intervals. Gwen munched a jam sandwich slowly. They'd been down here since about twenty to seven. She was stiff with cold, and the thermos had been emptied hours ago. She thought longingly of the warm kitchen, hoping the fire which she'd banked down would stay in. If only she could be sure that Nancy had found shelter. And Ted – what was he doing now?

Nancy had met Brenda at the bus stop. They'd pooled together to buy an engagement present and Nancy carried the glass fruit set carefully.

'Linda's the same age as us,' Brenda said wistfully. 'I liked that soldier I danced with the other night. He and the one you were with wanted to meet us again. Why is it you won't ever go out with the same boys twice?'

'I don't want to get serious with anyone, Brenda, not ever again,' Nancy had confided in her months ago, told her all about Danny. But Brenda had said, 'It's just as well, Nancy. Cousins shouldn't marry anyway.'

'It's not really a party,' Brenda said now. 'I think there's only one couple coming besides us.'

'Will we know them?'

'I shouldn't think so. She said they lived next door. Linda would have liked to have a few more from work but it's the rationing, and her Gary staying with them for the week and all.'

A fair young man in khaki opened the door to them and they recognised Gary from the photos Linda had shown them. It was freezing cold outside and when they were shown into the middle room where the table was set ready with plates of sandwiches and sausage rolls and cut fruit cake, they both went over to sit by the roaring fire and eye the table hungrily, for neither had spared the time for a proper meal.

They'd admired Linda's ring, gold with five chippings of

diamonds set in platinum, and were sipping the glass of wine that had been poured to toast the happy couple when Pat and Don arrived from next door and were introduced. Nancy had just reached for another sandwich and was settling again in the chair by the fire, one side of her face already toasted pink, when the siren began to wail. Then Linda's mother was at the door, her face anxious, saying, 'Come on, all of you. Down that shelter quickly. Dad and I are going in next door to give you room.'

'The baby!' Pat was crying, already halfway to the door. 'We'd better go.'

'You stay here, love. Youer mam and me will see to Tony. Hurry up now, before anything starts.'

Nancy and Brenda were looking hungrily at the table where hardly anything had been touched.

'Grab a couple of sandwiches,' Linda told them. 'Come on, I've got to put the lights off and shut all the doors.'

The moon was bright and a white rime shone like silver in the frosty air. As they ran down the path flares began to fall, and before they'd clambered into the shelter incendiaries were falling too and searchlights sweeping the sky. Within minutes there was the heavy drone of planes which seemed to be directly overhead. Sandwiches held uneaten, they listened intently, faces pale in the light of the lamp. Brenda was the only one to have brought her wine. Now she downed it in one gulp and giggled, saying, 'Mustn't let it spoil the party, must we?'

But the party spirit had gone. Pat and Don sat in the corner and she said over and over, 'I should have insisted on going home. He'll miss us, Don, he'll be frightened.' Then turning to Nancy and Brenda, she said, 'He's only eighteen months. I shouldn't have left him.'

Gary had his arm about Linda, and Nancy and Brenda

sat opposite each other, listening intently to the noise overhead. To cover her fear Nancy suggested they have a sing-song, but before they could start there was a terrifying whoosh of air and an almighty bang, the sound of which seemed to reverberate around the shelter.

'God! What's that?' Gary cried, and they all fell silent, remembering with horror that the gas works and gas holders weren't very far away.

Pat, beside herself with worry, got up determinedly, saying, 'I'm going home. Tony will be terrified, poor little mite.'

'Wait until it's quiet again,' Don told her, drawing her down beside him. 'It would be madness for us to go in this.'

'I'm starving,' Brenda said. 'When Pat and Don go, I'll slip up and get some sausage rolls and things.'

'It's best you stay put,' Linda told her. 'Promised my Mam, I did.'

But when, about half-an-hour later, things seemed to be quiet again and Pat and Don got up to leave, Brenda did the same, taking no notice of everyone's protests.

'I won't be a tick,' she told them. 'We'll have a party when I get back. I'll bring a bottle if I can manage it.' And she gave a little giggle.

'I'd better come with you,' Nancy said half-heartedly when she saw Brenda was determined, but she was already through the door, running after Pat and Don, calling back, 'Stay there, Nancy, I'll be quicker on my own.'

As Nancy closed the door searchlights were once more sweeping the sky and there was the faint drone of planes, growing louder by the minute. The sky seemed to be on fire and Nancy's worried thoughts were with her mam and dad and Teddy.

The minutes passed and the throbbing noise seemed to be right overhead. Guns were pounding non-stop now and shrapnel falling like rain. The throb of the engines and the noise of the guns seemed to fill the shelter. But where was Brenda? Oh, why had she been foolish enough to go?

'She'll probably wait until this lot's over,' Gary was saying, trying to ease their fears.

The throbbing engines seemed to stop suddenly. A powerful rush of air shook the shelter as though it was cardboard, sending the lantern crashing to the floor. As the light went out there was the sound of an explosion that seemed to threaten to pull the shelter apart, but at last it stopped quaking and now instead was being showered with heavy debris. When at last things stopped falling, Nancy cried in a trembling voice, 'Brenda! Where's Brenda?' and rushed to open the door, but it wouldn't budge. Hysterical now, she threw her weight against it, but Gary put her gently aside and threw himself at the door. Then, when Linda joined him and it still wouldn't move, they sat in the darkness and began to call.

Later there was a scraping noise outside and voices shouting their names. When they'd answered and the digging went on, Linda took Nancy's hand then drew the shivering girl close, whispering, 'Brenda will be all right, you'll see.'

The diggers were through at last. The shelter door could be opened just a few inches, and those inside could see steel-helmeted figures bent almost double as they dug or pulled the last obstacles away. It was when Linda looked up towards the house that she gave a piercing scream, for as far as the middle room the house was just a shell and kitchen and scullery had gone.

Despite the raid being still on there seemed to be people everywhere. They were carried through the rubble

to a waiting ambulance to find Linda's parents and neighbours already inside, the baby whimpering in his shocked
mother's arms.

At the church hall the WVS were waiting with scalding
cups of tea. After the first grateful sip, Nancy, still in a
state of shock, stared about her at her fellow rescued,
hoping against hope to see that Brenda had been brought
in. No one had said anything but in her heart Nancy knew
there was little hope if her friend had been in that kitchen.
A long agonised cry broke from her lips. When a comforting arm slid about her, she turned hopefully, whispering
Brenda's name. The woman in the WVS uniform asked
gently, 'Your sister, is it, cariad?'

'My friend,' Nancy gulped, choking on her tears.

The lady went across to the red-eyed ambulance men
who were about to leave. Coming back, she took Nancy's
hands in hers, saying, 'You must be brave, my dear,
they're still searching the rubble. But whatever was she
doing inside the house?'

What chance would Brenda have had with a direct hit
like that? Nancy asked herself. She was dead, wasn't she?
They were just being kind.

Chapter Thirty-eight

It was not until four-fifty the following morning that the all-clear went at last and Nancy was taken home. Some of the shelterers at the church hall weren't fortunate enough still to have homes to go to. Linda, her family and their neighbours were among those who had to stay until something could be arranged.

Ted had found out Nancy's whereabouts earlier in the night but had been strongly advised to leave her there until the raid was over, though he'd lost no time in getting a message to Gwen.

When Nancy was brought in she looked white and shocked. Before she'd left the hall her worst fears had been realised. Brenda was dead. Held tightly in Gwen's arms, she was remembering how happy they'd been last night, going to the little celebration. She thought of the glass fruit set with its frosted ivy leaf pattern. It must have been smashed to smithereens. But what was she doing thinking about a fruit set when Brenda was gone? A sob rose to her lips and tears spurted once more from her eyes. Gwen pulled her down to the sofa and held her tight, murmuring, 'There, there, cariad,' as though she was still a child.

Dawn was beginning to break when Gwen put the

empty tea-cups on to a tray to take to the scullery, saying, 'I'll just carry these out then I'll see you into bed, love.'

Nancy was shaking her head, telling her, 'It's not worth it, Mam. It will be time to get ready to go to work soon.'

'You're not going into work today, girl, not after what happened last night.'

Nancy looked at her mother. Her eyes brimmed with tears as she said, 'Perhaps it will help me forget.'

Gwen tried again. 'I'll go up and switch on the fire in your room, shall I?'

'Mam! I'm going to work.'

It will help me to forget, she'd told her mother, but she knew it wouldn't. She had the feeling that nothing could erase from her memory the shock of seeing the shell of the house she'd entered so happily only hours before standing black and desolate against a sky on fire, and knowing that somewhere beneath the mounds of rubble her best friend was lying.

It was lunch-time when they brought her home in floods of tears. Gwen put her to bed and sent for Doctor Lloyd for she knew that Nancy was in shock at the loss of her friend, and more than that, was blaming herself for having been unable to stop Brenda from going up to the house.

'Don't worry, it'll pass,' Doctor Lloyd told Gwen. Since this war began he'd had to be a psychiatrist as well as a doctor. So many tragedies. Mams and dads who'd lost sons, or had them return crippled or an invalid; young girls who had lost sweethearts; wives who'd lost husbands and grieving children who'd lost fathers. It would take far more than a bottle of medicine to put them on the road to recovery. War was crazy. It wasn't just bodies that had to be mended.

Nancy, stony-faced and pale, lay staring up at the

ceiling after he'd gone. Doctor Lloyd had assured her that there was nothing she could have done. 'We take our own decisions, Nancy,' he'd told her. 'When your friend decided to go up to the house, she made up her own mind. She didn't really think it would be bombed or she wouldn't have gone. She was very foolhardy. You tell me you asked her not to go, and it wouldn't have helped if you had gone with her, now would it?'

This morning she had thought it better to go to work and face the day, but the sight of the haberdashery counter where Brenda had worked, and the empty seat beside her at morning break, had broken her heart. Everyone had commiserated with her, everyone had talked about Brenda. The hard lump of pain in her chest had melted into a deep well of tears that spurted from her eyes at every mention of her friend, and a silent scream seemed to come from her heart. Though it never passed her lips she could hear it ringing in her head.

Despite Doctor Lloyd's kindly words she found herself constantly regretting what she hadn't done. Could she have stopped Brenda? Tried to hold her back? Brenda had seemed to know no fear in her determination to bring the party to the shelter. Sometimes she would think she heard Brenda's infectious giggle, and the tears would flow again.

It was almost a week before, pale and sad-eyed, she went back to the store. And now, whenever the siren went, she would hurry to the shelter, her face anxious, hands gripping the edge of the bench, listening, always listening. In vain Teddy tried to get her to join in a sing-song.

'We should be quiet or we won't know what's happening,' she told him. 'Why don't you read your book?'

The raids continued throughout the spring, but Gwen found herself more worried about Nancy's health. The girl was losing weight, the big brown eyes seeming huge in the pale face. And she never ventured out after work. Whereas before she had been out night after night, taking risks, worrying them all, now she would take none.

Then one summer evening when there hadn't been a raid for several nights Nancy arrived home from work with a tall young man in khaki uniform. Gwen thought there was something vaguely familiar about him, and then Nancy said, 'This is Ray Thomas. Do you remember when he used to give me a lift home from the tennis club on his motor-bike?'

Gwen remembered plainly those evenings when she'd watched from the window as Nancy bid the boy a hasty goodbye, for in those days she'd only had eyes for Danny.

Nancy had met him on the tram on her way home from work. Over tea they chatted easily. He'd been in this country since coming home from Dunkirk. Funny he'd never seen Nancy before for he'd been home on leave a number of times. He'd been engaged to be married but while he'd been in France she'd met somebody else. Although Ray made a joke of it Gwen saw the hurt in his eyes.

Nancy's face had lost its frightened look, she hadn't even been listening for the siren as she usually did. Ray stopped for tea and supper, refusing at first because of the rationing until Gwen managed to convince him that the corned beef and vegetable pie had been very economical to make.

After Nancy had seen him to the door she came back to the room with a little colour in her cheeks, her eyes shining.

'We're going to the pictures tomorrow night, Mam. Don't worry, we'll go to a shelter if there's a raid.'

This from the girl who'd been so cautious for months! Gwen was thankful for the change even though she was worried about her safety, but that night the siren didn't go and Nancy came home to tell her excitedly, 'I'm going to Ray's house to tea tomorrow, otherwise his mam won't be seeing much of him. He has to go back Saturday.'

'Where does he live?'

'Newport Road. It's a big house but his nan and grandad live with them.'

'Well, it won't be far for you to go then.'

By the time Ray went back from leave Nancy seemed a different girl. She'd got on well with Ray's family, and with both of them having had an unhappy love affair they found a common bond. Now there were his letters to look forward to and answer every single night. When, on his very next leave, Ray told her he was going overseas, they decided to get engaged, but remembering that awful night of the raid Nancy didn't want a party to celebrate.

Chapter Thirty-nine

'I can't get Sarah to have the Doctor, Gwen. She's as stubborn as a mule. Tom's tried until he's blue in the face. It's a waste of time.'

'I'll come round tonight as soon as the shop's closed,' Gwen promised. 'Doctor Lloyd told her to take care. Constant coughing will put a strain on her heart.'

It was more than halfway through May 1943 and the war was dragging on and on. Gwen had been pleasantly surprised that Sarah's health had stood the raids so well, for a damp shelter wasn't the best place for someone with bronchial trouble and a tired heart.

The fear of invasion which had seemed imminent during the dark days after Dunkirk had gradually faded, especially when in June 1941 Hitler had launched a surprise attack on Russia. Later in December of the same year fate had taken another twist when the Japanese had attacked the US navy at Pearl Harbor, bringing the United States into the war at Britain's side.

The brighter nights were a big relief to everyone although for a while now, with so many accidents caused through the black-out, in some places dim lighting was allowed and a torch could be used providing it had several layers of tissue paper over the bulb and was directed at the ground.

Ted would be seventy next birthday and Gwen wished she could persuade him to give up his fire-watching duty, but he wouldn't hear of it. Apart from looking tired after so many broken nights, he never complained. Which brought her thoughts back to Sarah and tonight's visit. Gwen shook her head for her mother could be so stubborn when she liked.

After tea Nancy was going to see Ray's mother. When she came into the living-room wearing a new utility dress which her mother had given her the coupons for, Nancy having used all of hers in one grand spree, Gwen thought how well it suited her. The dress was made in a silky green material with a smart revere collar and a straight skirt just to the knee, the soft green emphasising the warm chestnut glints in her wavy hair. She looked so happy these days. The two of them had made such plans in their letters, and she'd accumulated quite a lot of things ready for when they were able to marry and set up home. Even that had been settled for the young couple were to have two rooms and a conservatory in Ray's parents' house now that the grandparents had moved to a cottage in the Devon countryside, away from all the air-raids.

Nancy was now working at the ordnance factory in a bid to help the war effort and had made friends with a girl whose fiancé was abroad like Ray.

Gwen was putting on her hat and coat ready to go to Wilfred Street.

'I'll come and walk you home,' Ted told her. 'It'll be dark before you get back.'

As soon as Fanny opened the door she could hear her mother coughing, and as she stepped into the kitchen Sarah was holding a handkerchief to her mouth, her face purple. A deep rumbling sound was coming from her chest.

'Oh, Mam!' Gwen cried. 'You should have had the doctor before now.'

Sarah's eyes were bulging with the effort of coughing. Fanny rushed to the tap to get her a drink.

'Pig-headed, that's what she is,' Tom was saying, his face concerned. 'If she doesn't send for Doctor Lloyd in the morning, I'll carry her there myself.'

'Give over, Tom,' Sarah managed to splutter. 'Go in the morning I will if I'm no better.'

Gwen looked at her worriedly. Sarah was seventy-six and still overweight. The coughing had worn her out. Now it had subsided she sat back in the chair, fighting to get her breath.

'Has she got anything to take?' Gwen asked.

'Lord, yes! She's been taking cough mixture all day but it doesn't seem to do any good.'

'Do you think perhaps we should send for Doctor Lloyd?'

'No, Gwen,' Sarah said firmly. 'The pooer man's rushed off his feet anyway. It's only a cough. I've had it before.'

When Ted called for her, Gwen was helping Fanny get Sarah into bed.

'I'm quite capable myself,' her mother was protesting after yet another bout of coughing. Earlier Fanny had switched on the electric fire which stood in the grate and the room was warm. Looking around the once familiar bedroom, which apart from the fire hadn't seemed to change much from when she was a child, Gwen was remembering the night Lucy was born and how the following morning she'd lain across this very bed, staring down at the new baby. The room had been so cosy on that winter's morning with flames leaping and dancing in the grate, then Aunt Fan had come to fetch them and send her and Mair reluctantly to school.

Sarah was resting against the embroidered pillows now, her eyes closed. Gwen whispered, 'I think we'd better send for the doctor,' but her mother's eyes flew open and she cried, 'Don't you dare, my girl, not unless you want to upset me.' It was as though she was a schoolgirl again instead of a woman of nearly fifty.

Gwen sat down and waited until her mother was asleep before following Fanny downstairs, saying anxiously, 'What do you think?' And Fanny answered, looking equally anxious, 'Well, you know what she's like if she's crossed, Gwen. Best leave things for tonight unless she gets worse.'

Going home with Ted, she confided her worry.

'Perhaps a good night's sleep will do her good,' he said. 'I'll pop round first thing to see how she is.'

Nancy came in with yet another present for her bottom drawer.

'Really, Mam,' she said, 'Mrs Thomas is always wanting to give me something. She says, "What do you think of this, Nancy? Do you like it?" And if I say I do – and it would be rude not to, wouldn't it? – she insists I have it. Didn't you have a pair of vases like these in the shop once? I think they were almost the same.'

'Wouldn't it have been better to have left them in the rooms you're going to have?'

'Yes, I'm going to, but I brought them home for you to see. They're really pretty, aren't they?' And she held one of the pale blue vases up to the light to admire the deep blue cornflowers and bright yellow marigolds painted on the front. Then, putting the vase down on the table, she asked, 'How was Nan?'

When Gwen told her, she said, 'Oh, I wish I'd come with you now. I thought it was just a cough.'

'Well, a cough can be serious when you're as old as Nana,' Gwen told her. 'But I didn't realise myself until I saw her. Anyway, cariad, you can go around tomorrow evening.'

When she went to bed Gwen tossed and turned, wondering if she should have overruled her mother's objections to having the doctor, but then she would have had Dada to contend with as well for with Tom, as always, Sarah's word was law.

She had just dropped into an uneasy sleep when the siren wailed and at once she was alert, pulling her dressing gown quickly about her. Urging Ted to hurry and get dressed, she banged on Nancy's door and then Teddy's. When she was sure they were awake she grabbed an armful of blankets and hurried down the stairs with Ted behind her, but they parted with a quick kiss at the side door where he waited impatiently for Teddy to join him to go on to their fire-watching post.

Gwen urged Nancy through the back door to the garden, thinking now of her mother, telling herself anxiously that getting out of a warm bed and going to the damp shelter was the worst possible thing in her condition.

They'd no sooner closed the door than the raid began and continued without respite, the noise deafening as high explosives and parachute mines were dropped on various parts of the city. The gun barrage was non-stop, and through it all Gwen found herself still worrying about her mother. Would they take her down the shelter tonight? And if they didn't, would it be safe to stay in the house? Nancy, sensing her thoughts, said, 'Poor Nan. She could have done with a quiet night, couldn't she?'

As the raid went on Gwen's thoughts turned to Ted and

young Teddy, out there at their post. Teddy had left the High School at the end of last year to join his father in the business. She had wanted him to go on with his education but he'd been so keen, and hadn't she been the same about the shop at his age? Teddy had been accompanying his father to sales for a long time now. If only the war would finish before he could be called up. At going on for seventeen he was just over six feet tall. He'd already joined the Army Cadet Force and was looking forward to getting into the real thing.

Gwen could see Nancy was becoming more and more agitated, gripping the edge of the bench and biting her bottom lip, and knew that the girl was reliving the raid on Grangetown when her friend had been killed. She put an arm about her and held her close.

It was almost four o'clock when the all-clear sounded, and the sky was once again red with the reflection of so many fires. Thankful it was over, Gwen climbed stiffly from the shelter with Nancy and hurried indoors. Stirring the dying embers of the fire into life, she filled the kettle and put it on the gas stove, then began to pile cups and saucers, milk jug and sugar basin, on to a tray.

Where was Ted? They should have been in by now. She was always thankful to see them come through the door after a raid. Presently, to her relief, she heard the key in the lock and footsteps mounting the stairs. She poured their tea then turned as they came into the room. Although Ted's face was streaked with dirt she could see that underneath the flesh was grey-looking, and that young Teddy was looking sombre too. He'll have to give it up, she told herself anxiously. He's done his bit anyway.

But Ted was coming over to her. Putting an arm about her, he said gently, 'It's your mam, I'm afraid, cariad.'

Gwen's heart froze, and she cried, 'Oh my God! It's Wilfred Street. They've been hit.'

'No, Gwen love. Sarah collapsed after she got to the shelter, Doctor Lloyd's with her now. Insisted, she did, on getting out of a warm bed and going down there, and in her condition too. Fanny and your dad wanted to stay in the house with her but she was convinced it wouldn't be safe. Fanny said she was warmly wrapped in her dressing gown and blankets, but the effort was too much for her. Get your coat on, cariad, you too, Nancy, if you want to, there's some petrol in the car.'

Fanny opened the door to them, her eyes red with weeping, and Gwen's heart went cold. Falling into Gwen's arms she sobbed, 'I'm sorry love, so sorry, Sarah's just passed away. Too much for her heart the doctor says it was.'

Tears were streaming down Gwen's cheeks, and Nancy's too. But when Fanny said, 'Taking it badly he is. Poor Tom,' Gwen dried her eyes quickly and made for the kitchen.

Her father was sitting in the wooden armchair by the fire which had gone out, his head in his hands. He looked up as they came into the kitchen, and Nancy went to put her arms about him while Gwen knelt at his side and took his hands in hers.

'She's in the bedroom,' he told them, his voice breaking. 'Doctor Lloyd's just left. I can't believe it, Gwen. She looks as though she's just gone to sleep.'

Gwen went upstairs and that was just how it seemed, she looked so peaceful.

Fanny wrote to Lucy right away, after deciding against sending a telegram. With Danny in the forces, she'd probably have thought it was about him. Anyway she'd get it by the last post. The letter they had back was full of sadness and regret, and a promise to be there in time for the funeral. Gwen wondered how this first meeting with Lucy would go. She was dreading it, for she hadn't seen her since she'd left the house in 1919. Everyone would expect her to forgive but she couldn't forget the misery she had suffered when she'd thought Daniel and Nancy were in love. But when the day of the funeral arrived, Danny, who'd managed to get a forty-eight-hour leave arrived alone.

'Mam woke up with a terrible head. She gets these turns if she's upset. The blinds have to be drawn and she just lies on the bed, but she's usually better next day.'

Gwen wondered if the excuse was genuine or had Lucy been unable to face coming home? Fanny had told her once that Lucy had confided she'd love to come back to Cardiff to live but that it would have to be a district as far as possible from home. 'As though anyone still remembers,' she had added, but Gwen thought they would, especially neighbours like Mabel and Eddie and others who, although elderly now, would have long memories of the street's past.

Now Sarah's name was constantly on Tom's lips. Seeking to give him some fresh interest Fanny took him to Cwm-Mawr to see Lucy for he'd never accompanied them on their jaunts in the past.

Eddie Palmer would try to revive his old interest in politics but even that subject had lost its zest for him now. Fanny cooked his favourite meals and tried to draw him into everything that was going on, but Tom was interested only in the past. The one thing he looked forward to was his Sunday journey to the cemetery.

Chapter Forty

It was the spring of 1944 and still the war was dragging on and on. The long promised D-Day came at last when on the 6th June some 156,000 allied troops crossed the Channel. The new offensive was only six days old when unsuspecting Londoners were attacked by pilotless flying bombs, their true horror unleashed when suddenly the motor would cut out and after an agonising few seconds the bomb nose-dived onto its target.

Iris, Mabel and Eddie's eldest daughter, had been living in London for many years but after a scare when she saw one crash in a neighbouring street, she brought her two-year-old grandson to stay with her mam and dad.

'Awful things those Doodle-bugs,' she told Gwen with a shudder. 'I couldn't believe my eyes when I saw that thing in the sky. Flying low it was. It's not like the usual air-raid, Gwen, there's no warning so you can't take cover. I'll be going back on Monday. Leaving the little one here with Mam, I am.'

It was November before Winston Churchill revealed in a speech on the wireless that a new and even deadlier weapon than the V1 was now being used. The V2 rocket had been causing havoc and terrific explosions since September; now at last he'd given it a name. The forty-five-foot weapon, which carried one-ton warheads, was enough to bring terror to anyone's heart. Being supersonic, it gave no warning of its approach until the devastating explosion brought chaos and horror in its wake.

Mabel and Eddie were now in their late seventies but took looking after young Eddie in their stride. He wanted for nothing, except perhaps his own mam and dad. The trouble was that all the members of the family living near enough spoiled him, and Gwen didn't envy his parents when they finally got him home.

By September the allied forces were racing through the low countries. In December Germany staged a last great offensive in the Ardennes, but just a few months into the new year it became obvious that Hitler's army was on the verge of collapse. By the end of April everyone was saying that the war would soon be over. Union Jacks and bunting were soon on display in the shops while the newspaper headlines charted each new and momentous event. On the 2nd of May they screamed in black headlines that Hitler had committed suicide. On the 5th that the Germans had surrendered in Monty's tent. Then, on the 7th, the headlines announced dramatically: THE LAST HOURS.

As the day wore on hopes mounted. Gwen stayed by the wireless, thankful that the war was ending before Teddy could be called up. At seven-forty her waiting was rewarded at last when an announcement was made that Tuesday the 8th of May was to be a general holiday and was to be known as Victory in Europe Day. Late as it was, people began stringing banners across the streets while Union Jacks flew from windows. When Gwen went to Wilfred Street to discuss the wonderful news she was not unwillingly roped in to help, laughing and joking with the neighbours as they strung flags together and hung them across the street from one bedroom window to another.

At supper Nancy glowed with happiness after an evening discussing plans with her future in-laws.

'I wonder how long it will be before Ray comes home?' she said wistfully.

'Give it a few months, love,' Ted told her. Then, seeing her look of disappointment, hastened to add, 'Well, they're a long way away, and there's an awful lot of them. But Ray may be in one of the first batches, who knows?'

Gwen was remembering her own excitement when the first war ended and she was waiting for Charlie to come home. Remembering too the bitter disappointment and unhappiness she'd known when he'd been forced to marry Lucy instead of herself. Thank God there was no chance of such a thing happening to Nancy. Gwen looked across lovingly at her daughter, thinking what a beautiful bride she was going to make, picturing her in a lovely white gown walking down the aisle of St Margaret's Church on Ted's arm. That was something else she'd dreamt about when she'd been young – having a church wedding and wearing a beautiful dress and there being at least one bridesmaid. Well, the dresses had been ready. She could picture them now as they'd hung side by side in the wardrobe she'd shared with Lucy, her's white satin and Lucy's bridesmaid's dress a pale pink.

At the thought of her own hurried wedding to Ted at the Register Office she felt so glad that Nancy would have a day to remember.

Late next morning she went around to Wilfred Street to join in the fun of the victory party, helping to lay the tables with red, white and blue paper cloths, and arranging chairs from the houses either side of long trestle tables that stood in the middle of the road the whole length of the street.

After the long drab days of war everything looked so

festive: the flags flying in the warm spring breeze, the lamp-posts colourful with streamers, the houses flying Union Jacks. But brightest of all were the children's faces as they waited noisily to take their places at the table.

Iris had come to Cardiff to take young Eddie home, but Mabel insisted she stay overnight, saying, 'You can go back tomorrow, ouer Iris. A day won't make no difference now, and I'm not going to have that little lamb disappointed. Looking forward to the party he is.'

Iris confided to Gwen that ever since she'd arrived that morning she hadn't been able to do a thing with the boy.

'If I say "Don't do that, Eddie", he runs to Mam for sympathy. And he gets it, Gwen!'

'Never mind love,' Gwen told her. 'Mabel won't be there for him to run to when you get back home. He'll soon settle down again.'

Iris sighed, and just then Mabel's little lamb rushed from the house like a small tornado, sliding to an abrupt stop by the table where, thumb in mouth, he gazed in wonder at the red, green and yellow jellies wobbling in the breeze, and the neatly spaced plates of cakes, sandwiches and sausage rolls, and mounds of thinly cut bread and margarine.

'If this party doesn't start soon, he'll be helping himself,' Iris chuckled. But just then the waiting children were shepherded to their seats, laughing and talking excitedly as the jelly and blancmange was ladled out and they put on their home-made paper hats.

'Can't remember having parties like this when we were kids,' Iris said. 'Do you remember, Gwen, when your mam kept the shop in the front room and our mam fell out with her over the noise?'

'I can remember you poking your tongue out at me,

Iris,' Gwen laughed. 'I was glad when the shop was closed and they made friends again. If only my mam had lived to see the end of the war,' she added wistfully, and Iris nodded, suddenly dashing forward as her grandson stretched out to help himself to more jelly.

Gwen was looking around at the happy scene. Neighbours standing talking and laughing in little groups, waiting now the children had been served for the second sitting when they would sit at the tables. Tonight the black-out curtains would remain undrawn and light would stream out from windows and doorways and everyone would be happy. Well, perhaps not those who'd lost loved ones, but they too would be glad the war was over. And there are servicemen still fighting in the Far East, she thought. We mustn't forget them.

It was August before Ray came home, by which time the rooms were decorated, and furnished too. Ted had found Nancy some very good pieces, including a lovely oak dining table and chairs and matching sideboard which he'd restored as new. Nearly all the furniture available in the shops was utility and you had to apply for a permit to buy it. Nancy did purchase a utility bed, for everyone agreed this was one of the few things that should be bought new.

Now that Ray was expected home, Gwen went with her daughter to buy the material for the dress. A dressmaker who lived in Beresford Road was going to make the gown. Fanny was now over eighty and her legs were too stiff with rheumatism to work the treadles of the machine.

They went to David Morgan's where Nancy used to work, and a number of the girls remembered her and came to wish her well. Fanny's generous contribution had been the clothing coupons for, as she said, 'Being a dressmaker all my working life, I've more than enough clothes to last.'

They came home carrying the parcel of white slipper satin, the orange blossom head-dress and veil, and if the latter wasn't as long as she would have liked, Nancy was much too happy to care.

Gwen was wondering how they were to feed the guests at such short notice for even the day couldn't be arranged until Ray actually got back to Britain. But at last a telegram arrived to say he was at a camp in Hampshire and would be home within a few days.

They were married on a Monday early in September, a golden day of lingering summer. Excitement had brought warm colour to Nancy's cheeks, her dark eyes shone and the short chestnut hair curled becomingly about the orange blossom head-dress. Gazing at her, a lump came to Gwen's throat. As the car to take her and Ted to the church arrived, she swallowed hard. Handing her daughter the bouquet of pink carnations and gypsophila, she said softly, 'You look lovely, cariad.' Then she straightened her own wide-brimmed navy straw hat at the mirror and adjusted the carnation on the lapel of her costume. She went down to where Teddy was waiting impatiently at the foot of the stairs, looking very grown-up in a dark grey suit.

The church was full of family and friends, quite a number of whom were coming back to the reception at the flat. Thank goodness everything's ready, she thought. Mabel had insisted, with the help of several younger members of her family, on seeing to things while Gwen was at the church.

'But you're a guest,' she had protested.

'I'll love doing it, Gwen, don't worry. It's Nancy's day, and yours too. So relax and enjoy it.'

Tom and Fanny were already in the pew. After a whispered word with them, Gwen took her place. Dada looks so frail, she thought worriedly. Well, he was over eighty, but had always seemed such a tower of strength until Mama died. He seemed to live now for his visits to the cemetery, cutting and choosing the flowers so carefully from the patch in the garden grown for the purpose.

Once again Lucy was missing from the family gathering but this time her excuse seemed to be genuine. Danny was to be married within a few days at Redruth in Cornwall where his fiancée lived.

The reception went well too, and after Nancy and Ray had left for a honeymoon on the south coast Mabel and her helpers had insisted on staying until every dish was washed and put back in its place. Then Gwen had packed a basket with some of the leftover goodies for Mabel to take home.

'Oh, Gwen! You shouldn't, cariad. You can use those up yourself.'

'I can't, Mabel, really. I'll have more than I need. And to think I was worrying in case we didn't have enough! I was really grateful for those coupons you spared. It's going to make you short for a week or two.'

As Mabel protested that it wouldn't, Gwen thought how wonderful everybody had been. Ray's parents had sent a box of groceries they'd been saving up for the wedding, and both relatives and friends had contributed. Butter could have been short but she'd made a little cornflour into a blancmange and beaten some butter into it to make it go further, as she'd done so often during the war.

By the time the newlyweds arrived back from honeymoon the photographs had been developed. The pair of covered Coalport vases on the sideboard had to be moved to make way for two ornate silver frames. One was a photo of the bride and groom outside the church surrounded by the two families, the other of the happy couple cutting the cake. Gwen wondered hopefully if in due course she would have to move the clock from the centre, should there be a photo of a little grandson or granddaughter to put in its place.

Chapter Forty-one

The 26th of January 1947 was bitterly cold. When the shop was closed Gwen went about the flat with an old woollen dressing gown over her clothes, and despite the shortage of coal Ted lit fires in both the bedroom grates. Earlier in the evening he'd queued at the coal-yard to get a hundred-weight for Tom and Fanny, for neither of them were fit enough to do this for themselves.

The war with Japan was over but the shortages of food and other commodities went on. With some things, it was getting worse; clothing coupons were cut to thirty-six a year, and bread now rationed.

The weather grew steadily colder and soon people were facing the worst freeze since records began. Then came the first flakes of snow, and for the rest of January and all of February it fell relentlessly. Ted, and young Teddy too, were soon exhausted with constantly clearing it from around the shop and yard, then struggling to Wilfred Street to do the same for Tom and Fanny, taking with them some of whatever Gwen had been cooking for the evening meal, be it pasties with more potato than corned beef, or soup with very little meat flavoured with a generous spoonful of Bovril.

Outside a white wilderness would greet them under the

darkening sky, for as fast as shovels flew to clear a path the snow fell silently again, or on some days was whipped into a whirling frenzy by an icy wind.

Gwen worried constantly about her father and Fanny, struggling through the snow to get their groceries, slipping and sliding perilously, her fingers despite warm woollen gloves soon frozen to the handles of the big rush basket she carried.

'They shouldn't be on their own, Ted,' she said after returning from one such shopping trip. 'I asked them again to come and stay here, like you said, but they won't even consider it.'

'If it goes on like this we mightn't be able to get there,' he said worriedly.

'I hope our Nancy won't attempt to go out, Ted.'

'Don't worry, cariad, she won't. Ray's mother will see to that.'

Nancy was pregnant, much to her joy, and the baby was due towards the end of August. With roads and pavements almost impassable and getting worse every day, she was wise to stay at home.

It was a constant battle, clearing the path to the coalhouse. Gwen was thankful they had a toilet in the bathroom upstairs, but there were no such luxuries in Wilfred Street. Teddy now seemed to spend almost as much time there as he did at home, reporting to a worried Gwen that Aunt Fan had taken to wearing a coat around the house, and that Grandad had a shawl about his shoulders, even sitting by the fire.

Throughout February the snow piled up, then at last on St David's Day it began to thaw. But even as people rejoiced, a blizzard worse than any before swept over South Wales, burying roads that had just been cleared, stopping trains, closing factories, shutting many shops, and killing sheep on the exposed hillsides.

It was on the 3rd of March that a knock on the side door just after the shop had closed sent Gwen hurrying to open it. One of the Palmers' grandsons stood there shivering, holding out a note from Fanny. Gwen's face blanched as she read that Tom had fallen while getting a bucket of coal from the shed. Gwen knew Teddy had been round late that morning to clear the paths and sprinkle them with block salt, and he'd told her he'd filled up the coal scuttles. It had snowed since then and frozen hard. The irony of it was that Teddy was already on his way to clear the paths again.

Gwen struggled into her mac and warm boots, her thoughts in turmoil. How serious was the fall? Bobby Palmer hadn't known, only that his father and uncle had had to carry Tom indoors. Ted took her arm and they started off, but impatient as she was to get there it was slow going, the snow frozen like glass in places so that they had to hold on to window ledges or anything they could get a grip on.

When they turned the corner there was an ambulance outside the house, and as they neared it men were carrying Dada out on a stretcher, covered by a red blanket.

Gwen's heart ached for him when she saw the grey face twisted with pain. When they'd put him in the ambulance, Fanny went to climb in but Gwen said hurriedly, 'You stay home, Fan, I'll go.' But her aunt shook her head, saying, 'We'll both go, shall we? I think he's broken his leg.'

When they'd arrived at the Infirmary and Tom had been wheeled into a cubicle, they sat side by side on a bench in the corridor. Fanny said, 'Getting coal he was, Gwen, when he slipped.' And she broke in with, 'But our Teddy said he'd got you enough coal to last.'

'And so he had,' Fanny told her, 'but you know youer dad. Caution must be his middle name. Had to get another bucket in case, he did. "In case of what?" I asked him. The fire was banked up and we weren't halfway through the first bucket.'

It seemed hours before someone came at last to tell them that Tom's leg and hip had been set and the patient was asleep.

'I don't know how long we may have to keep him in,' was the answer to Gwen's question. 'Depends on how he responds. At his age he'll need to be watched.'

By this time Ted and Teddy had joined them, after going back home to put chains on the wheels of the car for only the main roads were kept reasonably clear.

'Why don't you come home with us, Fanny?' Gwen asked as soon as they were settled in the car.

'I can't, Gwen. I've jobs to do, and they've got Tom's address as the place to contact.'

'But we can phone from home and let the hospital know.'

Fanny wouldn't be budged so Ted went first to Wilfred Street. Gwen went in with her aunt, saying, 'We'll pick you up tomorrow. Ted will take us in the car. Oh, Fan, do you think he'll be all right?'

'Well, they said the operation was over and he was sleeping, didn't they?'

But next day when they arrived on the ward the screen was around Tom's bed and Sister came to tell them, 'The doctor's with Mr Llewellyn now. He's got a temperature, I'm afraid, and some difficulty in breathing.'

They sat in the corridor once more, anxious for someone to come and relieve their fears. Then a nurse came and led them back down the corridors to the ward, swishing back the curtain a little so that they could enter. Tom seemed to be in an uneasy sleep, moving his arms restlessly, his face red and glistening with perspiration. Then Sister came, motioning them to step outside, and said, 'I'm afraid it's pneumonia. It sometimes happens in elderly people after an accident.'

'Will he be all right?' Gwen licked dry lips as she waited for the answer.

'Well, he's got a strong constitution for his age. He's obviously looked after himself.'

Hours later they were still waiting in the corridor when a nurse came to tell them Tom was sleeping soundly. 'If you'd like to go home,' she added, 'we'll ring if there's any change.'

They'd been home only a few hours when the call came. Having promised to let Fanny know immediately, Ted got the car out and they started for Wilfred Street, but owing to a further fall of snow it was slow going and Gwen was fretting about the delay. At last they were at the hospital. Her heart beating fast, Gwen led the way to the ward. They were met at the entrance by a sombre-looking Sister who drew them gently into her room, saying, 'I'm very, very sorry but Mr Llewellyn passed away just after we phoned.'

A nurse took them back down the corridor. The wards were quiet now, lights out except for a dim lamp on the duty nurse's desk. Numb with shock, they got back into the car. When they were settled and Ted was getting into the driving seat, Gwen said firmly, 'We won't take no for an answer now, Aunt Fanny. You're coming to live with us.'

'I don't want to be a burden.'

'You, a burden! You've looked after everyone else all your life.'

'I could look for rooms somewhere near, Gwen. I doubt they'd give me the tenancy of the house now Tom's gone.'

'You will not look for rooms! You're going to live with us,' Ted told her. 'Gwen will come to the house and help to sort things out.'

On the day of the funeral the thaw set in in earnest and many who'd endured the ordeal of weeks and weeks of snow had to suffer a new and heartbreaking trauma as pipes burst and homes were flooded. Now it was thawing rapidly, too rapidly as gutters flooded where drains couldn't cope. At the cemetery deep mud sucked at their shoes but a watery sun came out, emphasising the brightness of the hot-house flowers as they were piled high on the grave.

A few days after the funeral Gwen and Fanny were at the house sorting through the rooms to see what could be discarded. It was a heartbreaking task for the accumulation of two lifetimes had to be gone through. Gwen had put aside the cherub clock. It no longer ticked the hours away but her mam had set such store by it. Already there were three packing cases waiting for Ted to pick up. 'Mama would have wanted us to keep this,' she seemed to have said about nearly everything they'd sorted. But there was a limit to what even the spare room above the shop could take, and Fanny was to have Nancy's old room.

Ted would get whatever he could for the furniture which was good but old-fashioned and couldn't yet be called antique, and Lucy must have half of what he managed to raise. She'd been sent a telegram on the day that Tom had died, and when there was no reply Gwen had written a letter telling her the day and time of the funeral. When again there was no reply Fanny suggested she might be in Cornwall with Danny and his wife, but if she was as they didn't have the address Lucy wouldn't know about her father's death until she returned to Cwm-Mawr.

Fanny made a cup of tea and they sat at the table in the familiar kitchen, eating Garibaldi biscuits. Gwen seemed to be surrounded by childhood memories, feeling that if she closed her eyes her mother would be bustling from range to table, tending to the needs of her husband and three little girls. When he'd pushed his plate aside, her father would sit in the wooden armchair and pick up the *Echo*, while she and her sisters, their starched broderie anglaise pinafores rustling, would clear the table and wash and dry the dishes. If she listened carefully she might hear the *Echo* boys running past, shouting the latest headlines, their hob-nailed boots ringing on the flag-stones. She remembered again the January day in 1901 when Queen Victoria had died and Dada gave Mair a halfpenny to run after the boys to get a paper.

Suddenly she became aware that Fanny was staring at her, saying anxiously, 'What is it, Gwen? You haven't heard a word I've been saying.'

They'd left Mair's room until last. It was still exactly as it had been when Mama set it aside as a shrine after Mair's death during the First World War.

First they sorted through the small ornaments on top of the chest of drawers and Gwen found she couldn't part with any of them for remembering her sister's joy as a child in each new item. Next the wardrobe must be cleared and amongst the old-fashioned clothes were the two dresses Mair had asked Fanny to make that summer that Ronald had taken her out in the bath-chair.

When they found the bundle of letters tied with pink ribbon Gwen's eyes became moist: Ronald's letters sent to his dying sweetheart, all of them written during the war. Gwen was remembering how eagerly Mair would wait for them to arrive.

Turning to Fanny, her voice husky with emotion, she said, 'Oh, Fanny! What am I to do with these?'

'Burn them, I would,' Fanny told her. 'I don't think Mair would want anyone reading them, do you?'

The coming of spring and the warm months of summer helped to dim the memory of that awful winter. When, on a hot August evening, Gwen gazed down proudly at her first grandchild in her frilly cot, strange feelings stirred in her. Her own nan had been a shadowy figure who lived in the valleys, and her father's mother had died before she was born. Already she felt a strong bonding with little Bethan.

'How do you feel about being called Nana Lewis?' Ray was asking with a wide grin.

How did she feel? Proud, happy, a little older perhaps, excited at this new phase in her life. She liked being a grandma very much. And Ted? No need to ask, his expression told it all.

Chapter Forty-two

The streets were festive once again with bunting, this time for the Coronation of Queen Elizabeth, and Gwen wished she could be in London to see the procession.

After Ted had been out on a mysterious errand he returned with a twinkle in his eyes.

'Better be here tomorrow morning, Gwen,' he told her. 'There's something being delivered for you.'

'What is it, Ted?' she cried excitedly. 'Oh, come on, tell me, love.' But he only laughed and shook his head.

Gwen knew what she hoped the surprise might be, but feared that it would be too expensive at the moment. But next morning when the delivery man arrived holding a fair-size cardboard box her hopes were rekindled, especially when he said, 'I'll take this upstairs for you, Mrs Lewis. Your husband wants it set up ready for you to use.'

And a little while later, with the nine-inch television standing on a small table near the only electric point, he told her, 'See the Coronation a treat you will on this. Better than if you were in London, I reckon.'

Now the day couldn't come quickly enough. Mabel and Eddie were invited, and of course Nancy and Ray with five-year-old Bethan and baby Thomas, and Teddy and his wife Dorothy and one-year-old twins David and Gareth.

Gwen thought she'd never forget the pageantry of the occasion, wonderful to see even in black and white. The excitement of the jam-packed crowds on the pavements, cheering noisily as the long procession with the fairy-tale coach appeared in the distance, becoming a roar as it drew near. Many had been in their places all night sleeping as best they could, but their excitement never seemed to wane.

When at last the ceremony was over, the procession wound its way under Admiralty Arch and up the Mall to Buckingham Palace. Gwen and Nancy hurried to the kitchen to cut more sandwiches and make a fresh pot of tea, but first Gwen had to force Mabel back into her chair, insisting firmly, 'You stay there and rest.' Even at eighty-seven she was never one to sit still.

Every few minutes one of them would peep into the room to make sure the Queen and Prince Philip and the rest of the royal family hadn't yet come out on to the balcony of the palace to wave.

Thomas and the twins slept peacefully in their prams in a shady part of the garden, while Bethan, who had wheeled an old lace curtain from Gwen, paraded up and down, her chubby little face wreathed in smiles, waving to her subjects just as she'd seen the young queen do.

When everyone had gone home Gwen gave a contented little sigh. Putting her arms about Ted she told him, 'Thank you for a wonderful present. I don't think Mabel and Fanny could believe it, seeing everything as it happened all that way away in London.'

Gwen found that the television was a boon. There was only one channel, the BBC, and that was off the air for interludes throughout the day, and again between six and seven at night, supposedly for the convenience of mothers so that they could get their children to bed, but the programmes seemed to be giving Fanny a new lease of life. Since she had first come to live with them Gwen had felt guilty about serving in the shop while her aunt was alone upstairs, but not any more. Fanny watched everything with interest, even the interlude pictures showing a potter's wheel.

'It's very soothing, Gwen,' she'd say. 'Oh, I'm so glad Ted bought that set for you.'

It was lovely to see Fanny enjoying herself so much. She'd worked hard all her life for other people. To have had all her dreams and hopes shattered when her fiancé had died could have been enough to make anyone bitter, but not Fanny. She'd rejoiced in her sister Sarah's children, making their clothes, giving them little treats, and offering a shoulder to cry on whenever things went wrong. Now it was Nancy and Teddy's children that she spoiled, finding scraps of material for Bethan's dolls from the bag of pieces she'd kept, teaching the clumsy little fingers to sew. And she loved to nurse the babies, singing them the lullabies that Gwen remembered so well.

Now Nancy and Ray came to see their favourite programmes, and Teddy and Dorothy too, and Gwen often said with a laugh that since the arrival of the television she'd used twice as much milk, sugar, tea, and bread and butter, not to mention what went into the sandwiches, than she'd ever used before.

The long hot summer was drawing to an end. When the evenings became chilly and darkness fell earlier, it was lovely to look forward to sitting by the fire and enjoying the entertainment.

Christmas passed with all its festivities. Now, in January, with the sky leaden with snow, Ted and Teddy had gone to an auction sale in town. Tea-time came and the meal was ready. When they hadn't arrived home by six-thirty, Gwen told herself that the sale must have gone on later than expected. It was just after six-thirty that she received the call from Teddy. When he told her that he was phoning from the hospital her heart went cold with fear.

'Dad had a sort of seizure,' he told her. 'He's with the doctors now.'

'How serious is it, Teddy?' Suddenly her mouth was dry and she strained to hear the answer.

'I don't know, Mam. They're still examining him. Shall I come and fetch you?'

'No, Teddy, you stay there. I'll get a taxi.' She knew her voice was calm but her hand shook as she replaced the receiver and dialled for a taxi, while her stomach was churning and her mouth felt parched with fear. He would get better, wouldn't he? They could do such wonderful things today. 'Hold on, Ted,' she whispered. 'Hold on, my love, I'll be with you soon.'

The taxi came almost at once and she went just as she was, flinging a coat over her shop overall. Heart beating fast, she almost ran up the corridor. Teddy, his face pale and strained, was hurrying to meet her.

'How is he?' she asked anxiously. 'Have they told you what's wrong?'

'It was a heart attack, Mam. Dad was in an awful lot of pain, he could hardly get his breath.'

They'd reached the ward now and Teddy was leading her to a bed near the sister's office, a bed around which the curtains were tightly drawn. The doctors had left now and, as she stepped inside her eyes flew to where Ted lay, his face grey, skin beaded with perspiration.

'He's been asking for you, Mam,' Teddy told her, placing a stool beside the bed. She sat down and took Ted's clammy hand in hers, tears coursing slowly down her cheeks, murmuring 'Ted! Oh Ted, my love.'

With dread in her heart she watched his struggle for breath. Then she heard him say her name and, cradling his hand in hers, willed her strength to help him.

The curtains parted and two nurses arrived, one carrying an oxygen mask and the other a cylinder, which she placed beside the bed. As they worked Gwen dried her eyes and, seeing how weary Teddy was looking, whispered, 'Go home and get some rest, son.' But he wouldn't budge.

When the curtain parted once more it was for a tearful Nancy and husband Ray to take their place by the bed, but they could only stay an hour. Ray's parents were with their other son in London and a neighbour had volunteered to stay with the children until Nancy and Ray returned.

It was towards dawn that Gwen felt Ted's hand go limp in hers. Teddy had dozed off from sheer exhaustion but was instantly awakened by her cry. Before they could summon them, the nurses were bending over the bed. Then one rushed away, while the other gently helped Gwen to her feet, whispering, 'I'm sorry, Mrs Lewis.'

Gwen felt numb with grief. Even when they got home and she was telling Fanny what had happened, the strange numbness persisted. Soon Dorothy arrived. Later, going downstairs to let Nancy in, Ray having stayed with the children, Gwen wandered into the shop and picked up a little figurine that Ted had bought from a customer last week. Suddenly she could remember him lifting it up, admiring it, asking if she'd like to have it for the flat. But there'd been nowhere to put it. Tears streamed down her face and Teddy phoned the doctor though she'd refused to have him earlier in the evening.

The doctor gave her something to make her sleep but even so, when everyone had gone and Fanny had reluctantly left her alone, Gwen lay in the darkness wondering how she could possibly go on. There had never been a day since the spring of 1919 that they had been parted, and her love for Ted had grown deep and strong. She whispered his name over and over until at last the pills had their way and she fell into an uneasy sleep. Later, she woke with a start, when, turning to put her arm about Ted, the awful realisation that he was no longer there suddenly hit her.

The following Monday morning friends and relatives gathered in the parlour over the shop for the service. It had been snowing since the evening before and little flurries had whirled into the hall as the mourners arrived. Upstairs the blinds were drawn, the same as in the shop, but the lights were on and a bright fire burned in the grate, drawing the black-clad mourners like a magnet for the day was bitterly cold.

The service was read, the hymns were sung, then although it was usually gentlemen only to the cemetery, Gwen insisted on going. It was as though she couldn't bear to let the coffin out of her sight.

'Best stay here with us, Mam,' Nancy tried to persuade her. 'You'll catch cold.'

'Please, Mam.' Teddy put an arm about her. 'Dada wouldn't have wanted you to go, you know that.'

His arm had still been about her at the cemetery, and when the first clods of earth fell on the coffin she swayed and would have fallen to the ground if he hadn't supported her.

The whirling snow was stinging her face but it didn't matter, nothing seemed to matter. Teddy got her back to the car and sat by her side, wiping the snow from her face.

As the days passed the shop would have remained closed if Dorothy hadn't helped out on the days Teddy was away on business. Even Fanny was shut out. Gwen would close the door and lie on her bed, thinking longingly of happier days. But she had reckoned without her aunt's persistence. Despite being nearly ninety, Fanny was as strong-willed as ever. She soon had Gwen getting dressed again in the mornings instead of hanging about in a dressing gown as she would have done if left alone.

'What am I to do, Fanny?' Gwen asked her in a pitiful voice.

'Ted would have wanted you to carry on, I know that,' had been the reply. 'Why don't you go down to the shop just for a few hours, give Ted and Dorothy a break? He's neglecting his part of the business.'

'I can't, Fanny, there are too many memories.'

'But they're happy memories, Gwen, and you've got a lifetime of them.'

'Oh, Fanny!' Gwen put her hand to her mouth in dismay. 'Oh, I'm sorry. It must have been awful for you, losing your fiancé so young.'

'That's all in the past now, Gwen, though I can plainly remember the heartache it brought. But what are you going to do about the shop? Teddy says lots of the customers are asking for you.'

The shop had been part of her life for so long, and she'd always loved it. Ted had loved it too. She didn't really want to give it up, but she must have time.

As the weeks passed she felt drawn to the shop more and more, but could she face the customers' pity? They would mean well but tears were constantly near the surface these days. One evening Teddy came up to tell her what he'd bought at auction that day. She knew he'd had to close the shop as Dorothy now stayed at home. Her mother found two babies too much to cope with.

'Shall I put tickets on them before I go home, Mam? I have to meet a dealer in the morning,' he asked.

She looked at his tired face and felt ashamed.

'Leave it tonight, Teddy,' she said. 'I'll be down to do it myself in the morning.'

He'd looked so pleased, and she found she was looking forward to the task.

Next morning, to Fanny's joy, Gwen was up and dressed early to unpack and ticket the stuff before she opened the shop. She had made many friends through the shop, especially since the war. People were taking an ever-increasing interest in collecting curios and small antiques. Goss souvenirs were still favourites, together with commemorative china, unusual tea-pots of all shapes and sizes, and Coronation mugs. She'd been asked only this morning to look out for anything to do with Queen Victoria's reign, especially anything made for her Golden or Diamond Jubilee.

Customers loved to chat to her about their hobby, eager to learn anything she could tell them about the things they bought. Sometimes they would want to sell some bargain they'd found at a jumble sale or second-hand shop, proud that amongst the junk they'd recognised it for what it was. Often she'd leave them to browse, turning over plates and cups and dishes to see the maker's mark on the bottom. Now the shop was busier than it had ever been, a place of enjoyment for the small collector. She had taken the precaution of putting the really valuable things away in the glass cabinets and was quite happy for them to pick up and inspect the rest.

At the end of the day when she went upstairs Fanny would have a meal ready, and when they'd cleared the table they'd watch television for the rest of the evening. On Sundays when it was fine she went to the cemetery, but on Wednesday afternoons when the shop was closed the rooms would ring with the laughter and sometimes tears of her grandchildren, leaving her little time to brood.

It was after she closed her bedroom door at night that the memories would come crowding in. They were no longer painful now, but soothing and comforting.

Chapter Forty-three

It was early in March 1963 and almost a decade had passed since Ted had died. Gwen lived alone now for Fanny had passed away three years before at the age of ninety-four. Gwen herself was now seventy-one and long past retirement age, but the shop was her life, its customers her friends, and with the great interest many people were now taking in antiques of all kinds, it had become a thriving little business.

She had just turned her attention to the box of things she'd bought from a customer that morning. She'd ticket them and put them on show, all except the bone china George V Coronation cup and saucer; she knew someone who'd be very interested in that, and the three Pratt pot-lids for another customer who had asked her to look out for 'The Village Wedding' and here it was together with 'Xmas Eve' and 'Our Home'.

She picked up a pretty continental candle-dish with a plump cherub clinging to its flower-encrusted stem. It would have been one of a pair and singly was of little value, but it was a pretty thing. The last item she lifted from the box was a pair of Mason's plates in the Japan pattern and these had the earliest mark used by the brothers: 'Mason's Patent Ironstone China' impressed into the back. Unfortunately the pair had been used for wall decoration and the metal contraption put on to hang them had crumbled away the edges in places.

For some reason, this morning thoughts of Lucy kept coming to mind. Gwen had written to her when Fanny died, putting her own address on the back of the letter. It had come back to her with 'Mrs Roberts has moved, address unknown,' scribbled across it. The few bits of jewellery that Fanny had left to her still waited in a drawer upstairs.

Gwen had just ticketed the last item when the shop bell rang. Looking up, she saw a woman who was not one of her regular customers coming towards her.

'Mrs Lewis, is it?'

'Yes, that's right.'

'I'm a neighbour of youer sister, Lucy. She hasn't asked me to call but I'm worried about her. I remembered her saying that you had a shop in Splott Road so I came to look for the name.'

'Where is my sister living? I don't have her address.'

'In Canton. She came to live next door to me about five or six years ago. She's ill with influenza, Mrs Lewis. Very poorly, I'd say. I called the doctor this morning and put her comfortable, and another neighbour, Mrs James, is staying with her until I get back. She's got no one except her son, and he lives in Cornwall. She wouldn't let me write to him to tell him she was ill.'

'I'll come with you now,' Gwen told her with a calmness she was far from feeling. She was about to come face to face with Lucy after more than forty years. Her hands shook as she packed a few things and took two clean aprons from the sideboard drawer. Turning to the woman who was sitting at the table, drinking a cup of tea, she asked anxiously, 'D'you think I'll need a nightdress? If she's so poorly perhaps it would be better if I stayed a while?'

'I think she'll be needing you for a few days anyway. Mrs James is very good but she's got young children to see to, and I'll do shopping and that but I can't be there all the time.'

Gwen went upstairs to fetch her nightdress and dressing gown, and the jewellery Fanny had left for Lucy though that could wait until she was better. Then she scribbled a note to Teddy explaining what was happening, knowing he'd be surprised when he found she wasn't there. Turning the notice behind the door to CLOSED, she locked it behind them.

The bus to town was almost full and Gwen was glad that they could not sit together for she wanted to collect her thoughts. After all these years to be going to see Lucy again, and she really didn't know how she felt about it. Relief was one of the emotions for she'd often feared that one of them might die before they could meet up again. The old bitterness had all gone, Ted's love had washed that away, but the hurt was still there, that Lucy could have done such an awful thing, especially as she'd known how long Gwen had waited for Charlie to come home.

On the second bus Gwen and her sister's neighbour were able to sit together.

'Very quiet youer sister is, Mrs Lewis. Keeps herself to herself. Pity her son is so far away, and I know none of her other relatives ever visits her.' The woman's voice was puzzled.

'There was a family disagreement years ago,' Gwen felt bound to tell her. 'There's only me left now. I tried to get in touch with her but she'd moved and no one knew where.'

'It may be a blessing in disguise then, her getting the 'flu.'

Soon they were walking down a long terraced street. Stopping outside number thirty-seven, Lucy's neighbour put a key in the lock, saying to Gwen, 'I think I'd better go up and explain about fetching you.' She gave Gwen a rueful look.

Her heart beating fast now that the meeting was near, Gwen looked about her. The narrow passage had a dark oak hall-stand against one wall, on which hung a shabby blue velour coat and a brown mackintosh together with a dark blue felt hat. It was a small house with only two rooms downstairs. The parlour door being open, Gwen peeped inside, surprised to see a sepia photograph of their mam and dad on top of the sideboard, with one of the three of them as children on one side of it and a picture of Danny as a boy on the other. Gwen could remember wondering what had happened to some of the family photos when she and Fanny had been clearing the house in Wilfred Street. Even Fanny hadn't known that Mama had given them to Lucy, and Gwen was touched that she should have wanted them.

The two neighbours were coming downstairs now, and the one who'd fetched her was saying, 'Doctor's been and she's very drowsy. Must be the medicine Sally's daughter fetched.' She nodded towards her companion.

'Thank you very much for all you've done. I'm very grateful to both of you,' Gwen told them.

When the door had closed behind them she hung her coat and hat on the hall-stand, washed her hands and put on an apron, and went upstairs. The first of the two doors led to a spare room containing only a single bed and some packing cases. When she opened the other one and her eyes grew accustomed to the gloom she went across to the bed where Lucy lay with eyes closed and cheeks flushed with fever, silvery hair curling damply about her face. There were beads of perspiration on her forehead. Gwen had to swallow a lump that came to her throat before she could whisper, 'Lucy – are you awake?'

The eyes opened slowly. They were still a deep cornflower blue, and for a moment in the dimly lit room Gwen was reminded again of the young Lucy whom everyone had loved and spoilt.

Lucy was struggling to get up but the effort was too much for her. She sank back, saying in a voice hardly above a whisper, 'Oh, Gwen! It's lovely to see you but I would never have sent for you myself, not after what I did to you. I can't forgive myself, so how can I expect you to forgive me?'

Gwen took the hot hand in hers. It was very rough to the touch, and she remembered the neighbour telling her that Lucy did cleaning for several families.

Her sister appeared to be asleep again and Gwen watched anxiously as the bedclothes rose and fell with her laboured breathing, wishing she'd been here when the doctor called.

The next day when he came in the morning he was very pleased with Lucy's progress though for a few more days Gwen was kept busy bathing the patient and coping with endless mounds of washing, for sheets and nightdresses were soon damp with perspiration. She'd gone out to a box to phone Teddy, asking that Dorothy go round to the flat and pack some more clothes and night things for her, and he had brought them out right away, telling her that he was keeping the shop open as best he could and Nancy had been helping out.

'But it's no use, Mam,' he had added. 'People say they'll call in again when they find you aren't there. Want to chin-wag with you they do, about the things they're interested in.'

'Well, it shouldn't be long now before I come home,' she said thankfully. Apart from the shop, she was missing all the modern conveniences she had at the flat, wishing she had her own washing machine here to tackle the bedding instead of just a zinc tub, a scrubbing board and a boiler without a wringer.

Lucy was looking much better now, sitting up in bed, her hair brushed into a silver halo and a pretty bed jacket about her shoulders. Gwen knew that the one thing her sister wanted most was for them to talk about the past, but no amount of talking could change what had happened, or the repercussions.

Gwen was downstairs in the wash-house. It was filled with steam from the boiler and the tub, but she had little hope of getting the washing on the line. Lucy had asked her to bring up a tray so that they could sip their tea and talk. She sighed deeply, knowing she could put it off no longer. Lucy wouldn't be satisfied until the subject was aired. She obviously wanted to say she was sorry, wanted to beg her sister's forgiveness for all the harm she'd done and Gwen thought she could forgive, for despite all the turmoil at the time she and Ted had shared a happiness that couldn't have been bettered.

She laid the tray with two cups, milk, sugar, tea-pot and a plate of biscuits, and climbing the stairs, pushed open the bedroom door and set it down on top of the chest of drawers, conscious that Lucy's eyes were following her every movement.

'Can we talk now, Gwen?' she asked hopefully as she took the cup from her sister.

'If you want me to forgive you, Lucy, then I do,' Gwen said gently. 'But I don't think I'll ever be able to forget.'

'I'm really sorry for what happened, Gwen. I don't think I've known a moment's peace because of it. I never had Charlie's love. That belonged to you. You know that he left me, don't you? After a while he went to Australia. Made good, I believe, got a ranch or something like that of his own. He got married again to someone out there but she died last year. I had a letter from him the beginning of last week. He's here in Cardiff, staying with his sister. Going back the middle of next month, he says.'

'Well, if Charlie's doing so well, I hope he's looking after his son.'

'That's what I wanted to tell you, Gwen,' Lucy broke in quickly. 'Charlie was never unfaithful to you. Danny *isn't* his son. Oh, I've wanted to tell you this for a long time. What I did to you and to Charlie was so awful, far worse even than it seemed at the time.'

Gwen was staring at her sister dumbfounded. When Lucy stopped, as though finding it too difficult to go on, Gwen said quietly, her eyes on her sister's face, 'Tell me what happened.'

Lucy sighed, saying, 'I hardly know where to start, but do you remember how terrified we were of upsetting Mama because of her heart?'

Gwen nodded, remembering only too well.

'I was desperate by the time Charlie came home from the war,' Lucy went on. 'Vera and I had met two soldiers in the autumn of 1918, and when I was supposed to be at her house we were really out with them. They seemed nice enough but one evening, coming back from a walk, we got separated and I was alone with the one I'd got friendly with. They were expecting to go back to the front within a few days and that night we were going to say goodbye. As we were walking through the park it was almost dark and I remember I was crying because he was going away. I remember him putting his arm about me and pulling me down to sit on the grass, then he began kissing me. No one had told me what might happen, Gwen. I was terrified and began to struggle but it was too late. I was nearly frantic when I found I was going to have a baby. It was Vera who told me that's what was wrong.'

'Why didn't you tell the soldier?' Gwen asked.

'I never saw him again. He didn't forward any address I could write to although he'd promised he would. I'll never forget how I felt – I wanted to kill myself, only that would have killed Mama too. She mustn't know, that's all I could think of. I'd never have done what I did if I could have told her the truth.'

'But that was an awful thing to do, Lucy, forcing Charlie to marry you, knowing all the time that he wasn't responsible. I don't know how he could have fallen for that.'

'That part was easy. He was so drunk. I couldn't have done it otherwise. I waited until you and Aunt Fan went to the tram stop with Charlie's parents, and Mama and Dada were in bed, then I crept downstairs in my nightgown and got under the blanket and lay beside him. Charlie was fast asleep, Gwen, but I put my arms about him and kissed him as the soldier had kissed me. He still seemed to be asleep but suddenly he responded, kissing me hard and moaning, "Oh, Gwen! Oh, Gwen!" I felt awful about it but I had to go on. When he opened his eyes he couldn't believe it was me. Nothing really happened, Gwen, but I had to make him think it had. It was an awful thing to do, I know, but all I could think of was that Mama's life was at stake.'

'But he stayed with you, Lucy, until Danny was eleven or twelve.' Gwen was shaking her head as though she couldn't believe what she'd heard.

'He'd no idea that Danny wasn't his. He adored the boy, they went everywhere together, then we had an awful row. There were always rows but this one was worse than most. I was in a temper and wanted to hurt him so I yelled at him that Danny wasn't his. Charlie left that day but I told everyone he'd gone away to find work. Even Danny thought he was coming back. Charlie sent what he could, and there was always something for the boy.'

Gwen's thoughts were in turmoil. Poor Charlie. In the end it was he who had lost the most for besides his unhappy life with Lucy he'd lost the son who turned out not to be his and the daughter he would never know about. She hoped he'd found some happiness in Australia, but Lucy had said his wife had died. That must have been another bitter blow.

But her sister was talking again and Gwen tried to bring her thoughts back to the present.

' . . . so you see, Gwen, Charlie's here in Cardiff. Asked if you were still living over the shop he did. I wrote back before I was taken ill. He's probably called to see you while you've been here, but he's sure to call again.'

Charlie here in Cardiff. Gwen didn't know how she felt. Her only memories were of him as a young man. He'd be in his seventies now, same as her. Had he grown bald and paunchy as so many men did?

'I'm quite well enough to manage on my own, Gwen,' Lucy was saying. 'But I didn't want you to go home until I'd plucked up the courage to tell you the truth.'

She'd be very glad to get home, Gwen told herself, the shop and her customers were being neglected. She hadn't

373

realised until she'd come to look after Lucy how much she missed it all. She was wondering if she could forget and forgive enough to ask Lucy to come and live with her at the flat. There was plenty of room and there was only the two of them now, but she'd need time to think about it, perhaps have her to stay a few weeks first to see how they got on.

She'd been home only a few hours and had bathed and put on her favourite twin set and a pleated skirt, for being March it was still chilly. When she heard the knock her heart began to pound. If it was Charlie, how would she greet him after all these long years?

She opened the door to a well-built man with wavy silvery hair. When she looked up into the suntanned face a pair of blue eyes met hers, eyes that she would have recognised anywhere as Charlie's. As he followed her up the stairs to the flat, she thought, He's still a very handsome man.

They talked about the past, carefully avoiding the trauma that had parted them.

'You've been happy then, Gwen?'

'Yes, Charlie, I have. I grew to love Ted very much.'

'I'm glad. I always hoped I hadn't ruined your life. We weren't very happy, Lucy and me. I shouldn't have left her to look after the boy but there were special circumstances, Gwen. I had my reasons.'

'It's all right, Charlie, Lucy has told me about Danny not being your son. It must have been an awful blow.'

'It was, Gwen, it was. And both our lives ruined for no reason at all.'

They were sitting at the table and she pushed the tea-things back while he showed her pictures of his station in Australia. After a short silence he said, taking her hand in his, 'I don't suppose you'd consider coming back with me, Gwen, as my wife?'

She nearly dropped the cup in her surprise but managed to steady it enough to set it on the table.

'I'm sorry if it was a shock, love,' he was saying. 'You can think about it and let me know. We loved each other very much once, Gwen.'

She hadn't seen Charlie for well over forty years. The good-looking, self-assured man sitting opposite was almost a stranger. And what would she do in far away Australia, and on a ranch, not even living in a town? She'd always loved the bustle of the city, and the excitement of an occasional auction sale. But wherever she went, she was always glad to get back to the dear familiar shop and the customers who were her friends.

'A lot has happened since then, Charlie,' she told him. 'I've got my family to consider now. My home is here with them. But I'm flattered you asked me.'

'You know, Gwen, my biggest regret is that I've no children of my own.'

He looked so sad that for a moment she was tempted to tell him about Nancy, but only for a moment. It would be madness, she told herself. Nancy had adored Ted. And supposing Charlie wanted the girl and her family to go back to Australia with him? The past had been buried for such a long time and she was the only one who knew the truth. She shivered.

Thinking she must be feeling cold, Charlie took the poker and stirred the fire.

'Well, at least we'll be good friends,' he was saying. 'I feel better now I know you've been all right. I'll write to you, Gwen, and I'll be really looking forward to your replies.'

'Yes, I'd like that, Charlie.'

He had picked up a photograph of Nancy and one of Teddy that stood either side of the clock on the mantelpiece, staring at them until Gwen felt rising panic in case there was anything in Nancy's face that could trigger his suspicions. Her mouth was dry as she waited anxiously for him to speak, but he replaced the photographs carefully, turning to her to say, 'You've two lovely children, Gwen. I wish they could have been mine.'

'I couldn't wish for better,' she told him. 'But those were taken on Nancy's wedding day. They've both got children of their own now.'

She'd been about to reach for the photos which stood on the sideboard behind him, but remembered in time that Nancy's son Thomas had wide blue eyes and a mop of fair curly hair.